VILLAIN
OR VICTIM?

To Donna & George

Bail Lundthene

Oct. 2014

Enjoy

VILLAIN
OR VICTIM?

The untold story
of John Tornow,
"The Wildman of the Wynooche"

A Novel Based on
A True Historical Account

Bill Lindstrom

Library of Congress Control Number:		2014914871
ISBN:	Hardcover	978-1-4990-6156-7
	Softcover	978-1-4990-6157-4
	eBook	978-1-4990-6155-0

Rev. date: 09/15/2014

To order additional copies of this book, contact:
Xlibris LLC
1-888-795-4274
www.Xlibris.com
Orders@Xlibris.com
635961

CONTENTS

ACKNOWLEDGEMENTS

The author would like to thank all those who continually pushed him toward getting this manuscript completed. In the beginning it was the dedication of Rand Iversen, Tom Roberson, John Hughes and Gordon Godfrey and all those who shared their thoughts and opinions on the story of John Tornow. As the project developed, Dana and Faaea Anderson kept my drive going; Ralph Larson is helping with book distribution sales; Susan Larson for valuable assistance with ancestry and census data; Amy Ostwald illustrated the cover and Bob Dick, author of "Skunk Cabbage and Chittum Bark," took the manuscript and made it sing with expert editing. He and his wife, Jan, deserve special consideration for their dedication and hospitality, soldering on despite their own travails. Finally, I would like to thank my significant other, Joyce Hayes, for her patience and understanding under sometimes difficult situations during the final stages of this project.

Cover photo by Bob Dick

Justin Madanifard is shown depicting John Tornow during a re-enactment of the final shootout in which Tornow is killed in the Wynooche Forest. Mark Woytowich videoed the scene in 2013.

FOREWORD

July 2014

Murder. Incest. Sex. Intrigue. Implausible situations. Enigma. Unsolved mystery, a century later. "Villain or Victim?" is a true story of events a century old. It sounds trite, but it's true: you can't make this stuff up.

John Tornow's family follows the early American dream as they emigrate from Germany in the late 1800s and wend their way to the Olympic Peninsula's Satsop Valley. Young John is fascinated with the virgin forest as we follow him through his youth and early adult years. He is a deadly shot and his skill with a knife is practically unmatched. John is big, strong, fit and increasingly reclusive. He is not someone to trifle with in town. In the Satsop Valley wilderness of 1910, John is either a peculiar loner or an apex predator. Or both.

My Godfather, Lem Nethery, was an early Grays Harbor homesteader, timber cruiser and close friend to my father, Malcolm. "Uncle Lem," also was one of the folks detailed to bring out Tornow's body after he was shot and killed in the upper Wynooche Valley. I heard the legend of John Tornow dozens of times as Uncle Lem told me the story every time we visited. John Tornow grew up with me.

As is often the case with a legendary story, many memories are suspect. In John Tornow's case a whole lot is suspect, beginning with his own family. A botched abortion and subsequent trial in which no one seems capable of telling the truth, a questionable trip to an asylum, greed over assets left by deceased parents, set the stage for John. He becomes more reclusive and seemingly unstable as some of his family self-destructs. The deep woods become his refuge from the family's bizarre actions.

Then, it all goes south. John's beloved twin nephews, John and William Bauer, are shot, killed and buried. Circumstantial evidence clearly implicates John. He becomes the chief — no, the only — suspect and from that day forward is hunted by posses and bounty hunters. A novice crime writer could sniff out at least two or three legitimate additional suspects. Two deputies are later murdered, presumably by Tornow, and the manhunt intensifies; yet, John never is charged with a crime. Tornow, meanwhile, shadows the men looking for him and steals food and clothing from settlers, and receives handouts from those who have known him as an odd but decent man.

John survives the next two years by being better at woodcraft than those paid to find him who, themselves, are very good. The odds, however, are not in his favor and he eventually is killed, taking two more deputies with him. Those two sentences cover an incredible story of survival of the fittest, woods skills by the best in the business, good luck, bad luck, and, in the end, tragedy that leads the reader to wonder, "Why? Why did all this have to happen to an unfortunate human being and the brave men who did what they were paid to do?"

Author, Bill Lindstrom, does a masterful job of leading us through the Tornow family's life and times, the daily routines and tragedies that create the story that endures to this day. Bill spent a lifetime researching multiple versions of events, reading century-old court documents, transcriptions, contemporary news articles, interviews, all needed to produce the best account possible of our friend, John.

Bill leaves no stone unturned to tell the story as best it can be told. One of the book's chief characters, *The Aberdeen Daily World* reporter, Dan Cloud, (a real guy) skillfully is used by Lindstrom to leads us through the multiple webs of deceit, crime and tragedy. Lindstrom adds dialogue so we can follow the entire stream of the story, not just the tragic events. It is one of those books that, when you must put it down, makes you want more. When it is done, you want to go back and change it to make a better ending. Alas, we can't do that and the ending is well known to all: John is gunned down in a brutal shootout in which two more decent men are killed, too. Author Lindstrom brings us the facts as best as they can be determined, even if we don't like them.

Bill Lindstrom's thorough research cannot dispel the multiple riddles left behind. Who actually shot the twins? Did Tornow really shoot Deputies Elmer and McKenzie? Did Tornow stay in the upper Satsop and Wynooche drainages or did he venture to one or more of the places where people swear they saw him? Was John sent to an asylum? If so, was it done to access his wealth? Was John responsible for the never-explained disappearance of several folks who ventured into his country never to be seen again?

Lindstrom does his best to answer the questions. He can't answer them all. We are left to form our own opinions of the man. I choose to believe Tornow murdered his nephews in a case of mistaken identity. Further, he likely murdered deputies Elmer and McKenzie. But, I don't know that. Neither does anyone else and there are several plausible alternatives. Remember, Tornow was never charged with, much less convicted, of a crime.

I also believe had Tornow been left alone, he would have become one of those peculiar people at the fringe of society — and civilization in those days — who would have died of natural causes having caused no harm. But, instead of being a footnote in history, John Tornow left a huge footprint and at least seven dead men. Bill Lindstrom tells a great story which I hope you enjoy as much as I did.

Malcolm R. Dick, Jr.
Shelton, Washington

INTRODUCTION

Little did I know when I was assigned in June 1986, to interview Tom Roberson of Elma, Wash., and report on his project to erect a tombstone at the gravesite of John Tornow, the "Wildman of the Wynooche," that it would be a 28-year endeavor.

I had been a city editor at *The Daily World* in Aberdeen, Wash., only a couple of months when the assignment came. I wrote the article on Roberson, who also had composed the "Ballad of John Tornow," covered a public forum in which 284 people were jammed into a bandbox gym at the Mary M. Knight school in the tiny town of Matlock, and talked about Roberson's goal of erecting a tombstone, where only a small stone and a coffee can marked the Tornow grave.

In that forum, many townsfolk shared stories of their parents and grandparents growing up in the area, each with a different view of how the story unfolded.

It wasn't long into the project after I began to conduct interviews, I discovered there was much more to this story. The more I dug, the more convoluted it became.

John Tornow is a man suspected of killing his two nephews on Sept. 3, 1911, touching off one of the longest manhunts in the Northwest at the time before he was gunned down in a shootout on April 16, 1913. Before he was slain, it is documented that Tornow killed three sheriff's deputies and a game warden.

But, what do we really know?

That is what "Villain or Victim" attempts to answer. When finished with the book, the reader will be provided with enough information to formulate guilt or innocence opinions. Was John the villain or victim? Was he friend or foe?

What makes this story so interesting is that it has endured for more than 100 years and there are as many people talking about it today as there were a century ago.

The entire story takes place in the Upper Satsop and Wynooche valleys of what is now Grays Harbor County in Western Washington state. The area lies at the eastern edge of the Olympic Mountains, and at the time was heavily forested old-growth. Montesano is the central hub city in the search for Tornow. It is located about 40 miles west of Olympia, the state capital.

I have attempted through interviews with numerous descendants of relatives, friends, neighbors of Tornow and enthusiasts of the saga, to discern what is truth, or as close as I could get to it.

The account, which starts with John Tornow's parents in Germany and ends with an Epilogue of events that have transpired since the Wildman was buried in 1913, includes exhaustive research of newspaper accounts, books, magazines, census reports and websites.

There is only one fictional character in the book and that is Lindy Fleming, the girlfriend of Dan Cloud, the actual reporter for *The Aberdeen Daily World*. I have used Cloud as the main thread through whom the Tornow story is told. Once he becomes involved in 1911, he conducts interviews, makes treks with the posses, writes his stories (not opinions) and even suffers travails along the way. He's a young reporter, starting as an intern, and he learns the craft as he goes.

All neighbors and friends, sheriffs, deputies and trappers are actual people, who knew Tornow or participated in the lengthy manhunt.

Through census records at the time as well as newspaper accounts, I have attempted to acquaint the reader with the families who knew the boy John Tornow, the young man John Tornow, the outcast John Tornow, the outlaw John Tornow and even the Wildman John Tornow.

The reader will come to "know," and hopefully understand, a far different John Tornow than other books and publications have painted him. Through my years of research, I have come to the conclusion that John is a compassionate conservationist, who likely would have been fine had he been left to live his life alone in the woods, where he was one with the solace of the wilderness.

In one chapter during the manhunt, readers will be acquainted with enough conspiracy theories to leave them shaking their heads in disbelief.

There are several chapters that deal with the Dr. Stapp trial in which he was convicted of criminal abortion in the death of Mary Bauer, the niece of Ed Tornow, brother of John. Talking with folks in the Matlock area, gives us a picture of a rift between the Bauers and Tornows. But that is mostly hearsay — stories and opinion passed down through several generations. Ah, but the truth? That is why there is so much about the trial. A study of the 435-page transcript of this key element reveals in courtroom testimony the chasm that developed between the families and it was never repaired.

Most of the events in the book took place and are based on actual occurrences, but for some events, and of course, the written conversations, the author has exercised literary license. Since there are several newspaper reporters involved, the reader might notice a few inconsistencies.

The name, John Tornow, might not be a household word outside the state of Washington, but most readers will recognize the man in people they know — a boy who had a slight impediment as a result of a childhood illness, a young man who was a loner, perhaps those with inferiority complexes, a man who felt at home in the woods and ultimately a man who was betrayed by society and lashed out to preserve his lifestyle.

Let's look at what we know is true.

The Tornow family emigrated from Germany in 1868, settling briefly in Wisconsin, Nebraska, Iowa and Oregon before arriving in the Upper Satsop and building a homestead in 1882 or 1883. We know John Tornow was born in 1880 in Iowa and nearly died from the black measles as a 10 year old in 1890; he developed a lisp that left him so self-conscious that he became a loner, spending weeks at a time in the woods, even at the age of 12. We know he worked at several logging operations from the Wishkah Valley, west of Montesano, to Mack's Spur, east of the county seat to Simpson Logging in Mason County to the north. We know he had several parcels of property and had more than $3,000 in the bank at Montesano at the time of his death.

We know he became a "dead shot," as one described him, developing superb marksmanship. He loved the woods, and after his brother, Ed, reportedly had shot John's dog, he shot Ed's dog in bitter retaliation,and said he was going to the woods "and nobody better come after me or I'll kill them."

He likely would have been fine, if left alone in the woods, but he wasn't left alone.

And therein lies the rub.

— Bill Lindstrom

1. UPPER SATSOP

1890

Dawn on this gray morning broke much the same as any February day in the Upper Satsop Valley.

The cool drizzle that had been relentless the last four days was falling in heavy sheets now. Yet, the threat of flooding on the nearby Middle Fork of the Satsop was of only minor concern to Louisa Tornow.

In a downstairs bedroom, Minnie, 23, the eldest of the eight children borne by Louisa, comforted her mother, who had broken her right hip on New Year's Day.

This morning the 52-year-old matriarch set aside her obvious pain and focused her undivided attention on the stairs leading to the two second-story bedrooms.

Upstairs in the corner room, 10-year-old Johnny lay near death with fever, the result of a relapse from the black measles.

He had been slipping in and out of consciousness for nearly 20 days.

Louisa couldn't bear another childhood death after losing August and Anna Mary as infants and four others were stillborn. She prayed for a miracle and listened anxiously for any movement, any stirring.

She was told to hold little hope. Dr. French, the family physician and a dear friend, had made that clear a week ago after making the 18-mile buggy trip from Elma.

Louisa and her husband, Frederick Daniel, had summoned the doctor when the boy's condition worsened.

For five days, the kindly doctor had been at the boy's bedside almost constantly, wiping Johnny's brow and chest with cool, damp cloths to relieve the fever.

Edwin French — Louisa often called the family doc by his first name — said he would stay until the end. He was more than a doctor. He was a family friend, and had been for most of the 10 years the Tornows had homesteaded on the Satsop.

Children had come in bunches for the Tornows. Wilhelmine, known by all as Minnie, was just a tot when her parents emigrated from Germany in 1868. The Tornows settled first in Wisconsin, then moved to Nebraska and homesteaded a farm, along with Frederick's brother, August. In 1873, Louisa gave birth to William and the next year Albert was born. Two years later, the family moved to Iowa, where Fred was born in 1877 and Michael John, who went by his middle name, in 1880.

The next year, the Tornows headed west to explore the uncharted Washington Territory, but stopped for a time in Salem, Ore., where their youngest child, Edward, was born in 1882. They arrived in the Upper Satsop the next year.

Minnie had left the homestead when she was 18, marrying another German immigrant, Henry Bauer in 1885. They had two young children, Mary, a charming four-year-old now, and two-year-old Elizabeth, whom they called Lizzie. Louisa was happy when Henry told her they wouldn't be leaving the area. The Bauer homestead was only a few miles west of the Tornows.

Henry, like Fred, was a farmer, but both had started a logging operation on their timber-rich property, clearing it to have their homes built.

Fred had purchased some cutting tools, and with the older boys' help, had cleared a large section, selling much of the marketable spruce and firs to logger Frank Lamb, who lived in the Wynooche Valley, just to the west.

Lamb operated his business out of Hoquiam, a small timber town some 20 miles west of the Satsop. Lamb bought the business from the ailing George Emerson, a man Fred had contracted to help build his home.

The Tornows and the Bauers were both prosperous. Henry's property wasn't as spacious, but he provided an ample living for Minnie and the girls.

All the children from both families attended the Elizabeth School, almost adjacent to the Bauer homestead.

Minnie had become an attractive woman, possessing many of her mother's characteristics — tall, sturdy and independent.

Her stubbornness often clashed with Henry's fiery temper. They had their spats, though nothing serious.

Louisa had cautioned Minnie about having young-uns so early in their marriage, but she desperately wanted to have children, and won that argument.

Minnie was a good mother with natural maternal instincts. She cared well for Mary as a baby. She wasn't a well child, but much of that is behind her. Little Mary is stronger now, still frail, but a pretty little girl.

Lizzie was a quiet youngster, clinging to Minnie, fearful of strangers, particularly shy around men. Minnie worried about that, but Louisa had told Minnie not to fret, she would outgrow it.

———

"Papa's back," Louisa called out to Minnie. "I hear them coming now. I been so worried. It's raining hard for so long. I just knew something had happened."

Yesterday, Fritz — Frederick had picked up that nickname on the Satsop — had taken the three older boys, Bill, Albert, and Fred to Beeville, 10 miles up the road to unload alfalfa. Seven-year-old Eddie would have gone too, but he had a slight fever. Louisa was taking no chances and told Eddie he would have to stay home. Eddie sulked the whole time the boys were gone and refused to do any chores, although his fever had broken.

A sudden storm forced Fritz and the boys to spend the night at the Schaletzkes, something they did often when the road was treacherous.

They had stopped at the Matlock store to pick up a few supplies and were told the narrow road was in danger of washing out. Fritz had run into a neighbor, Charlie Kohlmeier, who had been fishing on the Satsop. He was headed home in a small home-made skiff, and agreed to stop and tell Louisa of their plight.

Fritz and the boys returned to the Schaletzkes for the night.

"Fritz, you know you are welcome to stay another day or so," Ed Schaletzke said the next morning as his visitors prepared to leave. "Thanks Ed, but Louisa'll be worried. We can take the back road. It's longer, but it shouldn't be washed out. We're getting an early start. We'll have to go slow. I should be home by late afternoon."

They took the road through Deckerville, past the colony of lumber camps and down to the homestead. The forest roads, though narrow and a longer route home, were often harder-surfaced and less muddy in such conditions.

Louisa winced. Pain shot up her leg and into the middle of her back, but she raised her aging body up on one elbow and cocked an ear to the door.

There was movement upstairs. She strained to pick up every sound.

"Hear that Min? Hear that? He's coming."

One step creaked, then another, and another.

The weary doctor slowly made his way down the stairs.

With each step, her heart raced, even more than when she took the laudanum, an opiate the doctor had given her to ease the pain.

She feared the worst. Louisa clutched Minnie, grasping for every bit of available strength.

Fritz had bedded the team in the barn, shook off his canvas coat, hung it up on the stoop and slipped off his boots as Louisa had demanded before entering the comfortable home.

Slowly he trudged into the room, gingerly taking a seat beside his ailing wife, so as not to cause her more pain when he sat on the bed. Just then the doctor approached the entrance to the darkened, somber room.

Anxious. They were all anxious, but fearful for the news that could come from his lips.

Dr. French slowly strode toward Louisa. She turned her head away, fearing the worst.

"Louisa …"

"No, doctor. I'm not sure I could last if I lost another child," she said interrupting the doctor before he could finish talking to her.

"Louisa. Look at me, please," the doctor pleaded.

She glanced up and saw a bit of a grin, not the somber look she had dreaded.

It was as if a slight ray of sunshine had slipped through the window coverings and enveloped his countenance.

She had grown to love that pleasant smile, the same one the doctor flashed 10 years ago when Albert and little Fred had recovered from the fever.

She also remembered the day four years ago when he came into the Bauer's living room, offering a blanketed baby Mary for inspection after Minnie had endured a difficult child birth.

Louisa knew its comfort, its warmth. It was a lovely grin, one only Dr. French could possess. It had told her in the past, the worst was over.

This time, however, it didn't reveal the whole story.

"We aren't out of the woods yet," the doctor cautioned. "The fever has broken and Johnny's awake. I feel sure we have saved his life, but by a narrow margin. I'm afraid this relapse will affect him. I'm fearful the boy will never be the same."

The doctor knelt to embrace Louisa and Minnie. Fred, a strong man who rarely showed emotion, placed his powerful arm on Dr. French's shoulder and stroked Louisa's cheek with the other hand.

They all sobbed uncontrollably. Even Fritz. He knew it was acceptable on such an occasion.

He took Louisa's head tenderly and clutched it to his big chest. She felt his heart pounding almost as fast as her own.

Her mind raced with every beat of her heart.

If only …

Johnny had almost recovered from the measles when Louisa fell and broke her hip. Only Louisa and Johnny had remained at home. Fred and the boys had gone to Montesano to sell some crops.

Johnny liked helping the older boys with the cows, but he had not done that chore by himself before. He was proud that on this day, he was going to put the cows to bed by himself.

If only …

If only Johnny hadn't gone out to get the cows when he wasn't well … if only he hadn't slipped into the river and got wet. He is such a good boy, always thinking of others before himself.

Then, as if overcome by her own guilt, Louisa raised her head and turned toward her husband. "If only I hadn't been so clumsy and broken my hip … if only you and the boys were here … if only …"

Fred pressed his index finger to her lips. "Hush now, dear. Don't be thinking such things. It's nobody's fault. It just happened."

She recalled the words of her father when she was a youngster. Growing up in the depressed war-ravaged old country presented one tribulation after another.

His words had been important time and again. She even embroidered a sampler to hang in the bedroom. Her eyes fell on those words now, and she felt a moment of inner triumph.

"What's done is done. We must go on. We dare not dwell on the past, but we must learn from it."

Papa Millenback's wisdom had always been a comfort in the old country and once again she felt that warmth.

Fritz Tornow pressed the doctor for more details about Johnny's condition.

"It's not real good, Fritz," the doctor warned. "No human frame can withstand what he has withstood and be the same. I'm afraid he will be deficient in body or in mind. Only time will tell."

2. HAMBURG

1868

The first thing he noticed was how tall she was. Five-foot, seven or eight, he surmised, a little taller than he.

The young woman was striking, brunette hair flowing in the gentle breeze as she walked with a quick gait toward a well-dressed man at the end of the dock. A young girl, perhaps three or four years old, struggled to keep pace.

He sensed it was not a pleasant encounter. There was a vehement discussion. He was too far away to hear. From their movement and gestures, he knew it was not an amenable situation.

The well-dressed man threw his hands in the air in apparent frustration, turned and stormed down the dock away from the scene of the argument.

He saw the young woman struggling with a cart, loaded with baggage.

Perhaps she could use some help, he thought, striding toward the woman and her child.

The youngster took a seat on the dock next to the rented cart. The young woman continued to load the baggage that the other man had left on the dock.

As the young man with thick, dark hair approached, he could see the young woman was sobbing, obviously distressed over the preceding incident.

She was busy loading the rest of the baggage onto the cart and hadn't noticed the man near her. He moved toward the youngster, patted her on the head, reached into his pocket and handed her a peppermint.

"Let me help," the young man turned to the woman. She stood back, startled to see anyone. Slowly she grabbed the young girl's hand and backed away from the man.

"I want to help," he said again. "I saw you were upset. Are you boarding the steamer to America?"

"Yes," the woman said, wiping her eyes so as not to let the young man know she had been crying.

Without waiting for an answer, the young man began to load the cart. The footlocker would make it difficult for her to handle the dolly. She had three other bags.

She didn't stop him. Child in hand, she backed off and watched.

After loading the cart and taking it to the deckhand, the young man tipped his hat, patted the child on the head and resumed his place on a bench at the end of the dock.

"Thanks. Thank you very much," said the woman, shouting across the dock to where the young man had taken a seat.

Frederick Daniel Tornow was waiting for his brother, August Hanns to return from the depot with their tickets for the steamer.

Fred wondered where August was, but the respite gave him time to relax after the all-night train journey from Fasan near the Poland border.

Boarding time was less than an hour away when August finally arrived with the tickets.

The man who had argued with the young woman earlier, returned, apparently still trying to convince her not to leave. It was another vehement discussion, and she was getting her point across with severe gestures.

"Temperamental," Fred thought to himself. Suddenly she slapped the man, and told him to leave in a voice that could be heard all over Hamburg.

Fred immediately got up and approached the arguing man and woman.

"Having a problem?" he asked her. Looking into his eyes the pretty woman smiled. "No, this rude stranger assumed I was traveling alone and would need his protection and help," she said, although not divulging their relationship.

Turning to the man, she said "as you can see I have help. Now please leave."

At this, August, who wandered off to make sure his and Fred's baggage was ready for the deckhand, spotted Fred and hurried toward him.

"It's almost time. It's time to go," he shouted to his brother.

"Thank you again," the woman said, smiling at Fred. "That's twice today you have helped me. I am Louisa, and this is my daughter, Minnie."

I'm Frederick, Frederick Tornow," he said. "This is my brother, August."

"Have you found us a place to sleep?" Fred asked August. "No, not yet," he answered. "The women and children are not all aboard. Are you going on the steamer?" August asked, turning to Louisa.

"Yes. We must go now," she answered.

"We'll sleep nearby," Fred offered boldly. "Is your husband traveling with you?" he asked, trying to figure out the woman's situation.

"No, I have no husband. That man on the dock — he is not my husband, and he's not a stranger, like I told you. He is the father of my child. He was married and I worked as a maid in his home. I figured it was time for Minnie and me to leave. He was trying to stop us."

"Sorry," Fred said in consolation.

"I'm not," she said.

Grabbing Min by the hand, she hustled toward the plank. "See you on the boat," she said, "and hurry up. I'll try to keep a place nearby."

Louisa shook her head. She couldn't believe she had told a complete stranger of her plight.

The brothers were among the first of the men to line up for boarding, and even then, there was much jostling for the best spots in the crowded steerage compartment.

Louisa stood at the entrance to her compartment and waited for Fred to come by.

The deckhands wouldn't allow her to reserve a compartment, so she was most happy when she saw Fred and August were third in line to obtain a place.

"Right here," she said, pointing to the space directly across. "Here, Fred we'll be pretty close."

The small rooms held two bunk beds, a small closet, a toilet and washbasin. It would be close quarters for the next three weeks or so.

Louisa and Min shared a bunk. Another single woman was assigned the other bunk. Their room too, would be quite crowded, thought Fred, even more than ours.

Fred was glad that the deckhands decided to empty one room to store all the baggage. It would be most uncomfortable in that compartment with the baggage.

All the clothes they would wear for the next three weeks, they carried in a small duffel. Fred knew it would be difficult for August and him, but how much more difficult it must be for Louisa and Minnie.

The boxcar he traveled in overnight from Fasan was confining, but nothing compared to this compartment, he thought.

He only hoped starting over in the new land would be worth being in close quarters for so long.

Fred and Louisa were constant companions throughout the three-week voyage. August assisted by watching Minnie. They seemed inseparable — Fred and Louisa, August and Minnie.

Fred enjoyed watching Louisa play tenderly with the child, and he was surprised when she said Minnie was only two.

She appeared to be a bright child, already talking in complete sentences. Inquisitive and intelligent, and well-behaved too, Fred thought.

"We're gonna go to 'merica, aren't we?" Minnie asked Fred soon after they embarked. "Mama tells me all about the new land. We'll be happy there, won't we?"

Fred thought to himself. "Louisa must know how to read and write English. She has been teaching Min, already."

Standing on the main deck, where he and Louisa spent many hours on clear days, he watched the youngster play with her rag doll. "Does she know the gentleman was her father?" Fred asked.

"No," she answered. "He was a stableman. Only the other servants and his wife knew. I was young and foolish enough to believe he loved me and would leave her. He courted me and slept with me. He said he hadn't slept with his wife for several months and was going to leave her and take me away from life as a maid. I foolishly believed him. After Min was born, he refused to acknowledge her existence. I lied about him, but everyone knew. We drew apart. I knew I had to leave. I don't understand why he put up such a scene at the dock. He agreed to let me go."

"You've had a tough go of it, but relax now and a new life in America awaits you," said Fred. "I've had a bit of a trial to make it here too. I borrowed some money from my father for the journey. I'm just glad I'm here."

And I'm glad you're here too," she thought to herself, smiling at Fred.

"Why did you leave?" she asked. "I know why I had to leave, but why are you and your brother leaving?"

"If we stay, we have no land and August and I are the youngest of six. We have two other brothers and two sisters. My father's land will go to the oldest brother and the next-oldest will help him run it. August and I would be conscripted into the Army. I am not a soldier. I am a farmer by trade."

He told her when he was but 18 in his hometown of Ball, he was drafted to serve three years in the Army, a requirement of all Prussian boys.

"My grandfather wanted me to make the Army a career," Fred said. "None of the other boys wanted that life, and grandpa was hoping I would follow him. I served my time and left because the war was over. He was so disappointed."

Grandpa Turno, as he spelled the name in his country, was a highly-respected general before the German states became divided after the Austro-Prussian War of 1866.

Fred wondered if the woman was genuinely interested in this aspect of his life, or was just being polite and attentive.

"Am I boring you?" he asked Louisa.

"Oh no," she answered. "Please go on."

"When the war was over, I knew I didn't want any more of that kind of life. Father had moved to a homestead in Fasan, and when the two older boys had said they were going to England, Gus and I knew we would be coming in for a parcel of land …

"But what happened?" Louisa interrupted.

"The boys couldn't get the money together to go, so dad deeded them the land."

"Well, you got the money for this trip, didn't you?" she asked.

"We managed to save some money from working on our farm and other farms, and father was considerate enough to help us obtain passage. This is an opportunity to gain our own land. He wanted us to have that."

"Where do you go from New York?" he asked, abruptly changing the subject as thoughts of leaving his homeland left his eyes moist.

"We'll be going to the Oregon Territory," she said. "My mother has some relatives who live in a river valley called Willamette.

"Oregon? That's on the other side of America, isn't it?"

"Yes, it's going to take some time. I'll have to find out how to get out there. When we get to Oregon, we will be met by my mother's cousin. I've been told there is work on the farms and I am no stranger to hard work."

"Yes, you are a strong woman, I can see that. But who will take care of your child?" Fred asked.

"I need no one to watch over me," she snapped. "Where do you and your brother go?"

"We'll be taking a train to the lands they call Wisconsin or maybe Nebraska. That's in the Central part. We've been told there is work for those who wish to farm. Train companies are building a railroad out that way. I learned a bit from talking with Arley. He's the guy I introduced you to the other day. He's going out west soon as we dock."

Spending time with Louisa and Minnie made the time fly by for Fred. He couldn't believe three weeks had passed so quickly.

"A deckhand came by this morning. We'll be in New York tomorrow sometime," Fred said. "One more day and we'll be there. It's going to be hard to leave you," he said, smiling at Louisa.

He awoke early the next morning. He decided he would pose the question to Louisa. She should not be making that long journey by herself.

It was mid-morning when Louisa and Minnie came to the fantail deck to watch. Fred had been there for a couple of hours, patiently, nervously waiting.

"Mornin' Louisa. Mornin' Minnie. Lovely day isn't it?"

"Uh huh," they said in unison.

"Louisa, can we talk, please?"

"Sure, Fred. Let me get Minnie cleaned up and I'll be right with you."

As she washed Minnie's face and tied her long hair in a ponytail, then freshened herself, she couldn't help wonder what was on Fred's mind.

"He's a nice man, isn't he mama?" asked Minnie.

"What? Who? Oh, yeah. Yes, he is, darling. He's a very nice man."

It seemed like hours to Fred before he and Louisa were finally alone on the deck.

Fred had rehearsed and rehearsed how he would approach Louisa. He decided on the lengthy speech, telling her how he felt. His heart raced as she approached.

"I can't let you take off by yourself. I'd worry myself sick," Fred blurted without hesitation. "Please, join August and me on the train," he pleaded. "When we get to Wisconsin, you'll be halfway to Oregon … if you wish to go on. It won't take that long. Maybe only a few weeks."

"Oh, Fred. I don't know. I'll have to think about that. Right now, we better get below. There's a storm coming. We'll talk this afternoon before we dock."

She picked up Min and cradled the youngster to her bosom.

"You like Fred, don't you sweetheart?"

"Oh, yes mama. Yes, I do. And Gus too," she answered.

"Gus? Oh you mean August?"

"Yes. We have so much fun."

Louisa and Minnie had gone to their compartment to take a nap when the steamer's horn woke them. It signaled the approach to New York Harbor.

She had packed everything before lying down. Louisa grabbed Minnie and scurried onto the main deck to see the new land, their new home.

The crossing had taken 23 days, two more than they expected, although it was a smooth trip, and she had slept through the last bit of turbulence that afternoon.

Now, they were almost there.

The vessel entered the harbor and dropped anchor to clear quarantine before continuing on.

With a journey of this magnitude, diseases were quite common with those onboard. Seasickness was usually a particular problem on ships with such tight quarters. Scurvy, a vitamin C deficiency, was also common. But there were no such problems on the steamer that had brought Fred, August, Louisa and Minnie to the new land.

They were anchored less than an hour when the deckhand signaled they were clear to go on.

It was a magnificent view Fred shared with Louisa on the top deck. He reached to put her arm around her. She didn't resist and nestled closer to him. She wondered why he had waited 23 days to do that. He squeezed her closer.

They stood in awe at the wide expanse of the harbor and swift movement of the innumerable ships along its waters.

"Have you ever seen so many ships in all your life?" he asked.

They observed the immense steam vessels called ferry boats. And more double- triple- and four-masted tall ships than they could count.

He wondered how this big ship would get past them all.

Slowly, the vessel pushed into the harbor and past Bedloe's Island, a large block of land that seemed to beckon the visitors to their new home.

"See that island," one of the ship's mates said to the embracing couple. "There's talk of a big monument being erected there one day, a statue for all to see as they enter the harbor."

"It's the perfect spot," said Fred.

"Yes," said Louisa, then without hesitation, repeated it: "Yes, yes, yes. Yes, I'll go with you. We'll go with you."

Fred's eyes lit up. He picked up the slightly taller woman, hugged her ever so tightly. Then reaching down, he included little Minnie in his embrace.

"See that Min. See that," Fred said pointing to the burgeoning harbor of boats. "This is our land, our new home!"

3. A NEW BEGINNING

1870s

C reighton paused to wipe his brow. "Damn this is hard work. Pounding those steel spikes all day. That sledge hammer work gets on my nerves, but the money is good."

Creighton O'Herlihy, Fred and August Tornow had worked together on the rail lines for about six months until Fred decided he had enough money to make the farm self-sufficient.

"I'm glad I'm not working that big hammer anymore," Fred said to Creighton, all the while unloading eggs and vegetables from the back of his wagon for the Irish workers' camp.

Creighton was one of several hundred Irish immigrants who had come to the new land and settled in eastern Nebraska. He started work on the rail line near Lincoln five years ago. Fred and August joined the rail workers when they arrived by train in 1868.

The four had made Wisconsin their first stop, but it wasn't long before Fred had heard that opportunities for homesteading were brighter in the land farther south and west of the Missouri River.

The railroad had been completed from North Platte, Nebraska, to the Iowa border three years ago, and now the workers — mostly Irish and German immigrants — were busy driving the final spikes and rail ties the last few miles to Council Bluffs across the river from Omaha on the Iowa-Nebraska border.

When completed, the railroad would provide overland transportation west from the Mississippi to the Missouri.

Pioneers were rapidly moving west to the land once occupied by seven Indian tribes — Fox, Ioway, Omaha, Oto, Missouri, Sauk and Sioux. Most of the tribes had moved north as the pioneers pushed westward.

More than 200,000 people now made Nebraska their home and Fred felt fortunate to find a fertile piece of land just west of the Missouri.

The modest 80-acre farm he and August owned now provided ample food and vegetables for the railroad workers.

The two Germans found the new land richer than they could ever have imagined — more fertile than anything in the old country — even more so than the rich agricultural land of Westphalia, where Father Tornow had a farm for a time.

Fred and August obtained the plot and a small ranch home from another German immigrant who was moving west. They each purchased 40 acres, but combined their talents to farm it together and they shared the profits. The former owners left it productive with corn, wheat and green vegetables. The Tornows added alfalfa, barley and rye. They also purchased 600 to 700 chickens and a few hogs.

The men initially settled in Bellevue, but found the tiny burg of Papillion on the creek by the same name more to their liking. The settlement of only 200 inhabitants, mostly German and Czech immigrants, was much like Fasan in Germany, where the family spent much of their youth. Papillion, which means butterfly in French, also had a few immigrants from Paris. When the Tornow men arrived, the town was in the process of obtaining a charter. Founders named the city for the abundance of various and colorful butterflies that cruised the banks of the creek.

Papillion Creek flows into the Missouri River, about 30 miles southwest of Omaha, Nebraska, with its stockyards and abundant beef cattle.

Louisa was happy in the small town and on their ranch with a two-story, four-bedroom home.

Soon after they arrived, she and Fred were married. They were in love from the time they left New York. But, also knew their union would likely not be accepted in their new surroundings, with its strong Lutheran background, unless they were married. So, one weekend they secretly dashed off to Lincoln, the state capital, and made it official.

While Fred and August worked tirelessly helping to build the railroad, Louisa used her considerable culinary talents as a cook in the rail camp.

The workers were delighted with the German cuisine she occasionally brought to her meals.

Fred and Louisa decided it was time to expand their family so Minnie could have a sibling or two. They still had their heart set on moving west, but for now, that dream was on hold.

Expanding their family sounded wonderful, but it wasn't going to be that easy. The couple was elated when Louisa became pregnant, but that jubilation was short-lived when the child was stillborn.

The Tornows were sick with grief. Their new doctor — Luther Holmgren — did his best to alleviate the mental anguish for Louisa. He told her it was something that "... just happened. Nobody's fault."

Louisa was beside herself with torment, questioning "Why? Why did this happen? Fred, I did all the right things. I ate good foods, I was in good health, I rested when I got tired. Why, Fred? Why?"

Fred was equally as grief-stricken, but knew he had to be strong for his wife. Doc Holmgren convinced them not to give up and to try again.

The strong husband consoled his wife the best he could.

"Don't torture yourself, dear. "Yes, you did all you could, and what's strange is that you had a pretty easy pregnancy compared to some, like Mattie. She suffered a lot," Fred said of the couple's closest neighbor, who gave birth to a bouncing baby boy a few months ago.

"That's easy for you to say," she snapped at her husband. "You didn't carry this around for nine months. You didn't ... Oh, never mind."

Spending time with Mattie and little Matthew helped Louisa cope and get out of her funk. Mattie relished the help Louisa gave her.

Soon, Louisa was ready to tell Fred she wanted to try again.

They were successful this time and the couple was rewarded with two babies, fraternal twins, one male and one female.

"God has blessed us," Fred told his wife as she held the babies. "I'm so happy."

"Yes, Fred. Now, we have our family."

But, alas, the young couple would be visited with heartbreak when first infant August, then Anna Marie, would be stricken with fever. Scarlet fever the doctor called it.

The babes were just two months old when Louisa and Fred had to bury them.

"Will we ever have any more kids?" Louisa queried her husband. "I was so happy with those babies, then ..."

"Yes, dear. Me too. But you did give birth. We know it can be done and we can try again. Besides, it's fun trying, isn't it?"

"Oh Fred, you devil."

They did try again, and again, then success. In April 1873, Louisa gave birth to a boy they named William.

Then in November of the following year, along came Albert.

The family was getting bigger and now eight-year-old Minnie was big sister to two brothers.

The couple knew if they were going to have more children, it would be prudent to sell their modest home and ranch and find a bigger place.

Fred and August worked hard on the farm to make it prosperous — and it was. They recently made connections with a wholesale market across the border in Harrison County, Iowa. The two made several trips there and Fred started looking for a new home.

"I think I found it," Fred told his wife out of the blue one day after arriving back from Iowa.

"Found what, Fred?" she asked.

"Our new home. It's a little more acreage, but best of all is the house. It's what they call a ranch house. It could be five or six bedrooms and we can easily add on. It's all on one level. No more stairs. I like that. The house is only a couple years old and the farm has many productive crops, just like we have."

"Where is this, Fred?" she asked.

"In Magnolia, In Iowa, about a half-day from here."

"I know we talked about getting a bigger place, but this is so sudden. I love it here, Fred. How did you find out about this?"

"We, Gus and I, know the family that owns it. He produces for Central Market, where we take our crops at Council Bluffs. The farm is just outside of town. The hamlet is like Papillion, a couple hundred people at most. Graham, Graham Schneider, wants to sell and move to Oregon. I told him we were thinking about that too, but not right now."

"Well, Fred. It sounds nice. Can I see it first? Can we take the kids this weekend?"

"Sure, dear. I think we can arrange that. Maybe Mattie can watch the boys and we'll take Minnie with us."

"I'll ask Mattie," Louisa said, her face lighting up with the thought of the new place.

Fred knew once Louisa saw the place she would fall in love with it. He was right.

When word circulated that the Tornows were selling their farm, offers came in droves for the productive land. Their farm sold immediately, and at a far better price than Fred had imagined.

Fred and Gus made several trips to the new homeland to get the crops planted without losing a productive year of harvest. Graham told Fred that much of the farm had returning crops, so only a little manicuring was necessary.

The family moved to Magnolia soon after the first days of spring. Fred, 33, Louisa, 39, nine-year-old Minnie, four-year-old William, three-year-old Albert and a child on the way.

And Gus.

Louisa gave birth to Fred Jr. just before Christmas.

The Magnolia land was even more profitable for the Tornows than it was in Papillion.

Even after purchasing the farm, the two men were able to establish a sizable savings in the bank, which grew with each year's sale of products.

Two years passed and Louisa again became pregnant. But the family would not expand. Another child was stillborn.

Even at her advancing age, 42-year-old Louisa again found herself pregnant once more. On Sept. 4, 1880, Michael John was born in Magnolia, Harrison County, Iowa.

"No more," she told Fred in no uncertain terms. "Our family is big enough."

"I agree," said Fred. "Besides, if we are thinking about heading west, we don't want to do that with a little one in your belly. It'll be a hard enough trip."

Meanwhile, Louisa continued to receive letters from her aunt, who lived near Salem, the capital of Oregon. The letters were always positive, talking about how wonderful it was, urging them to come out west, "to God's Country," the aunt called it.

"It's beautiful here, green all year-round, kind of like the forests back home, only there's not many people here yet," the aunt wrote in a recent letter.

"We are near a town called Salem, about five miles away. It's on the Willamette River. I think I told you about that. The farmland is so fertile.

"There's lots of farming, but also logging near here. What I am saying, is there is plenty of work — an opportunity to start over. You'd like it here. Please think about it. We miss you so much. And say hello to your family. I can't believe it's nearly 20 years since we have seen you. Hope all is well."

Fred tucked the letter in his pocket and headed to the marketplace.

"Carnie, has that stuff we ordered arrived yet?" Fred asked Carnaby Monohan, an Irishman, who worked at the market.

"Oh, yes. I forgot to tell you. That's it over there in the corner — in that crate. I'll help you load it. Came in day before yesterday, I think it was."

"Good news?"

"What?" asked Fred.

"You got good news — in the letter? I see you are teary-eyed, but them's happy tears, aren't they?"

"Oh. Yes. My Louisa has an aunt in Oregon. She wants us to come."

"Well, why don't you? I hear it's called the great land of opportunity. Not a lot of people and lots of prosperity, if you know what you are doing. And you, Fred, you know what you are doing."

"I just might."

The two men lifted the supplies out of the crate and loaded them onto the wagon.

"That's the last of it Fred. Thanks. See ya next time."

Fred reached down, picked up the reins and doffed his cap to Carnaby.

"No, don't think so. I don't think you'll see me for a long, long time. I think I'm going to Oregon. Going soon's I can."

It was a half-day's journey by wagon from Council Bluffs north to Moorhead, where Fred had to deliver the produce to a boarding house he had frequented.

The beautiful trip up the Missouri to the Soldier River gave Frederick Tornow time to ponder the trip west.

"I'll follow the river north and stay in Missouri Valley at Minnie's," Fred planned, referring to Minnie Mether, who operated a boarding house in the summer months, while her father was on the roundup.

"I'll tell Gus soon as I get home," he said to himself. "I know he'll be upset. We've worked hard to get this farm producing like it is. But I've got to think of Louisa, too, and the children."

As his mind wandered to a picture of what the new land might look like, he hardly noticed it was late afternoon and he hadn't eaten.

He pulled into Missouri Valley, the largest city in Harrison County, the one adjacent to Monoma, where Moorhead was located. He was still about 20 miles from his destination.

"I'll grab a sandwich and a beer and get going. I want to make Moorhead before it gets too late. I should be there by 7 or 8."

It was about 8:30 when Fred pulled the wagon into Moorhead. It would have been much earlier, but he broke a wheel, swerving to avoid a flock of sheep that had wandered onto the road. The wagon hit a rut on the side. Broken wheels were common on these roads, full of chuckholes. He had learned some time ago how to repair wagon wheels. Half an hour later, the wheel was repaired and he was on his way again.

Fred tied up the team and walked toward the door. Minnie would be glad to see him, but he decided he wasn't going to say anything about going to Oregon.

He noticed several teams and horses tied up. "The boarding house must be doing well. I hope they have room for me," he thought.

"Hello, can I help you," offered a pleasant, young girl, answering the door. It wasn't Minnie and that surprised him. The young lady appeared to be about 18 and was strikingly beautiful.

"Uhh, yyeah. Is Mmmminie here?" he stammered.

"No, she went down to Magnolia for the weekend. I'm her sister Maryellen. I'm watching the place for her. Can I help you?"

"I need a room for the night. Have you any?"

"Yes, one small one," the girl answered. "That'll be fifty cents."

"That's fine. I'm leaving early for Magnolia myself," Fred replied. I have some vegetables, barley, wheat and some fruit for Minnie. Where shall I put them? By the way, where did Minnie go to in Magnolia?" he asked.

"She's with her boyfriend, August."

Fred's mouth dropped wide open. "What? What did you say?"

"She's at August's. I think he has a farm with his brother up there. Are you a good friend of Minnie's? Did I say something I shouldn't have?" she asked, sheepishly, noticing the startled look in Fred's eyes.

"Oh no," he said. "I haven't known Minnie long, but August is my brother and I didn't even know he had a girl friend."

Suddenly, it dawned on him why Gus had made so many trips recently to Moorhead.

"That's great. Now I won't have to leave him alone," he said loud enough for the girl to hear him.

"Leave him?" she pressed.

"Yes, I have decided I am going to Oregon. It's that I feel so bad to leave August."

Fred woke early after a restful night's sleep. He walked outside and was about to leave when Maryellen came running down the steps.

"Won't you have some breakfast first?" she asked. "It's ready, 'cept for the eggs. How do you like 'em?"

"Up," Fred answered. "I want to get going, but if you have them ready, then I won't have to stop before I get home."

He couldn't help but notice how much the girl looked like her sister. Tall, fair complexion with sparkling eyes, high cheekbones, strong hands that knew a day's work, just like her sis. She was pleasant to talk to. Even this early in the morning she bounced around the room as if she really enjoyed her work. She could cook too. No wonder the boarding house was full and prosperous with those two running things.

Fred gobbled down a big platter of flapjacks, three eggs, patty sausage and some homemade corn fritters. Two cups of coffee later, he bade Maryellen goodbye.

All the way to Magnolia, his mind wandered. He thought about Gus and Minnie. Gus was three years younger than Fred, but even at 34, he was probably 10 years older than Minnie. "Well, Louisa is six years older than me. What difference does that make?" he wondered, saying it aloud as the wagon clomped along the rutted road.

He was deep in thought when a neighbor pulled up behind him and asked to pass him on the narrow road.

Shortly after 4 p.m., Fred guided the team onto the long path that led to the homestead. Gus was plowing in the field, but didn't see his brother.

Minnie Mether saw him approaching and ran out to greet him.

Gus had taken Fred to Minnie's place a couple of times on their runs from Council Bluffs, but he had never noticed that she and Gus were that close.

"Had a good trip, Fred?" she asked with a smile. "Gus's been working hard. A guy came by and wants to buy 200 bales of hay. He's been busy all weekend," she said.

"Yes, I had a good trip, stopped at your place on the way home and met your sister. She's really nice, good cook too."

"Was she busy?"

"Yeah, the place was full. Had to take the small room at the end of the hall."

Gus spotted his brother and Minnie talking near the well and joined them.

"Hey, Freddie. That was a quick trip. Everything go OK? I see ya got the supplies."

"Gus, I gotta talk to you."

"I know. You're upset 'cause Minnie is here, aren't you? Well, Fred, there's something I've got to …"

"No, Gus, I'm not upset. In fact I'm happy for you. It's about time you found somebody."

Reaching in his pocket, Fred pulled out the letter and waved it toward Gus.

"I got a letter from Louisa's aunt yesterday. Gus, I decided we're going to Oregon right after the harvest next month. She says there is great opportunity there. The land is very fertile and grows well for dry crops. But Gus, I hate summers that burn like hell and I can't take these cold winters and biting winds."

"Fred, I have something impor …"

"No, let me finish. I've got a lot on my mind. She talks of a better climate, mild summers and cool, but not frigid winters. She writes of a fertile land, richer even than when papa was in Westphalia. Now that the rail lines have connected the good lands and immigrants are moving west, I'm going to have to go soon. The good lands are going fast. The rush is on, and I must go. I thought about this all the way home from Moorhead.

"And, Louisa repeatedly talked about moving to Oregon for the last few months. I think she wants to get out there too and be with family. It's the only other family she has in this country."

Gus wasn't the least surprised. He had been expecting it for some time. And he had his own news.

"Gus, you know I love you and we have worked hard to get where we are now in this new land. I felt bad most of the way home until I got to Minnie's place and met Maryellen. I feared for leaving you alone. She told me about Minnie being here, and I thought maybe I am not leaving you alone. Maybe now, you have somebody who cares for you as much as I care for Louisa and our children. Is that right?"

"That's right Fred. You didn't know it, but we've been seeing a lot of each other. This weekend, I asked Minnie to marry me. We plan to go to Council Bluffs in a week or two for the ceremony. And you're going to be the best man."

"That makes me so happy, Gus," he said, embracing his older brother with a strong hug.

"Minnie, come here," Fred said motioning to the young woman. "Get in here. You're family too," he said squeezing her and Gus in his embrace.

"I am so happy for you Gus and for you Min. I am also happy for me, for Louisa and my children too."

"What about the land, Fred? Have you thought about that at all?"

"Yes, a little. I know it makes it tough on you, but you are resourceful. Maybe you could find someone to buy it or farm it with you. Or you could buy my share from me and pay me when you can. I know a banker at Council Bluffs. He could probably put together a loan for you to buy it, if that's what you and Minnie want."

"Well, we won't worry about that now, OK, Fred? We've got a lot of work to do before you leave, and me before our wedding."

"Hon, can I say something," Minnie chimed in. "I've got a little money and we want to live here anyway. We've talked about getting our own place, but we could stay right here. I love your place, and you know I've always liked getting my hands dirty. It'd be a lot of work, but with two of us doing it, we could make it a good living."

"I suppose we could," answered Gus. "If we could pay you a little, Fred, until after we get the money back from the harvest. Then we might be able to pay it off. We'll talk about it later, OK?"

"That sounds good, Gus. And, I don't know what you are planning to do with the boarding house, but from what I saw this weekend, I think it's in capable hands."

Now, let's go in the house. We've got lots of news to tell Louisa. She'll be so happy."

4. WESTWARD BOUND

1881

"Come here William. Don't stray near the river," the comely young girl hollered to her little brother. "You know mama doesn't want you near the water by yourself."

"C'mon, Minnie. I wanna play with the froggies. C'mon, let's go," three-year-old Freddie answered.

"Oh, awright. But jus' for a little bit. I'll tell mama. You wait there."

"Mama, me and Freddie are going to the river. We'll be back before dinner," Minnie shouted as she turned to run down the path toward the river. Louisa didn't bother looking up from the churn, but waved one hand in the air, signaling her approval. She was hurriedly trying to finish whipping butter before the weather turned.

"Don't be late," she yelled, without missing a beat. "Min, you kids button up good now. It's getting cold … and stay out of the water. It's too cold to go wadin'."

Louisa was proud of her burgeoning family. Minnie, just a few months away from her 15th birthday and the four boys — William, 8, Albert, 7, Fred, 3 and little John, ready to celebrate his first birthday.

And now a sixth child on the way.

She and Fred had agreed that five children were enough when they were in Iowa, but the 43-year-old Louisa appeared as fertile as the Oregon soil and found herself pregnant once again.

Fred had worked hard to achieve what he had longed for since leaving Germany almost 13 years ago. He had been a tireless, productive worker first in his homeland, Fasan; and in the new country in Nebraska and Iowa.

He thought back to the words of his now-departed father. "You can have whatever you want in life, but you must work hard for it," Krause Tornow told his son. "Go to the new land. Go to America, and make me proud."

While Fred and his brother, August, were always able to be prosperous farming in the Central Plains, Fred strived for more. He was eager to forge new boundaries and explore challenging opportunities.

That's what drove him to leave Nebraska for Iowa and then to head west to Oregon, despite making a comfortable living for his family.

This time, however, it was Louisa more than Fred, who had the wanderlust to explore the newly charted Oregon territory.

The inviting letters from Louisa's aunt were just too much to ignore.

He thought it best to wait until spring before making the cross-country trek. August had married Minnie Mether in August, fortuitously. They made their home on the Moorhead ranch until the Tornows were ready to head west. August made the trek on Sunday and stayed the week working the farm with Fred, then returned to Moorhead on weekends. Occasionally, Minnie would join August and spend the week at the Tornows, particularly in the winter months when the flatland could be frightful.

August obtained a small loan and was able to purchase Fred's share. That enabled Fred to finance the trip west and provide a bankroll when he arrived in Oregon.

The trip west was grueling and took longer than Fred had planned. The money from the farm from August enabled him to purchase the fare for the train, instead of the much-longer wagon ride many pioneers took.

The tracks for the Transcontinental Railroad were completed about a decade ago. Passengers could board at Council Bluffs in Iowa and go all the way to San Francisco on the coast of California.

The Tornows took their brood on the train to Salt Lake City, then after several days layover, boarded a smaller, slower train west to San Francisco. They decided to spend a few days in the Bay Area, then boarded a final train north to Portland, Oregon.

There, Fred purchased a wagon and a team of horses and drove the 35 miles south to Salem, where Louisa's aunt Hilda lived with her family on the banks of the beautiful Willamette River.

It took nearly three weeks to complete the journey and the family was exhausted when they finally pulled into Salem. Within days, Fred was able to find a suitable home with a farm to provide for the family.

He bought a piece of fertile property in nearby Scio, a community of only 20 farmers. But they welcomed the newcomers with open arms.

Oregon, and particularly, the area south of Salem, was everything that Hilda described. The property Fred purchased was rich with fertile soil. But it had more than the Plains' flatlands offered.

Adjacent to the tilled farm, was a serene creek, lined with timber, which Fred could cut for warmth in the stove and fireplace in winter. He didn't have much time for fishing in Iowa, but now with a creek on the property, he figured he would indulge in that recreation much more. They could eat fish anytime they wanted it.

Oregon's mild winters and comfortable spring and summer months were much more to Fred's and Louisa's liking than the harsh winters and searing summer heat in Iowa.

Louisa and Fred enjoyed life in the lush Willamette Valley, but immigrants were moving to the territory in droves. Competition for the farmer's dollar made selling crops more difficult.

Wanderlust ate constantly at Fred. Louisa could feel it too. They had a good life, but Fred believed it could be better. He always did.

He and his main ranch hand, Marshall, talked often about the opportunities for investment in virgin land in the Washington Territory to the north.

"Louisa, Marshall told me about a place he visited last year. It's a couple day's ride. He's looking for a good timber area to log. He wants me to go with him next week and check it out. He says there are lots of timber mills on the coast of the Washington Territory. In a place called Aberdeen, the timber goes right down to the water. There's a whole peninsula of opportunity. He said California lumbermen are buying up a lot of timber, some of it milled on the coast, some of it already processed. Marshall talked about one river — Sheehalis, he called it. A bunch of rivers empty into it. There are rivers everywhere, lots of good fishing."

"But, Fred, we want farmland, don't we? What about farmland?" Louisa asked.

"Marshall said there's good farming land just east of there too," Fred answered. "Rich, fertile land, lots of it. He said if we are going to go up there, we better do it now. Homestead land is available, and real inexpensive."

"I agree, Fred. Go with him. Check it out. We'll be OK. We'll get some of the school kids to help us plant crops. You should be back in a couple of weeks, don't you think?"

"Louisa, I promise, if we go there, we'll build a home and stay there. No more moving. We are getting too old for that, and it's not getting easier to move a whole family. Marshall says the opportunity is now and we have to act quick before the land gets homesteaded. If I find a suitable place, shall I go for it?"

"Yes, Fred. I trust your judgment. You've always made the right decisions. You got a good head on your shoulders. But check around before you go making a big decision like that. You know what people say — if it sounds too good to be true, it probably isn't."

"Yes, dear. I'm just glad I have your blessing."

The men left two days later and headed north to explore their opportunities.

After spending a couple days in Aberdeen, a rough, coastal seaport, Fred left Marshall and found his way east to the area called the Upper Satsop with its acres of virgin territory — fertile farmland, bordered by unspoiled timber.

It was everything he had heard about. He saw a few homesteads, but was told that several logging operations were beginning to move east to the Satsop Valley. Was it too good to be true? Not in the least and he saw it with his own eyes. An agent in Montesano, just east of Aberdeen, directed him to the prime land, best in the valley, about 10 miles north up a one-lane, rutted road.

The agent told him that many German immigrants were flocking to the territory.

He recognized an opportunity indeed. He couldn't pass it up. He knew Louisa would be happy here.

He surveyed the timber about the property and made arrangements with a sawmill owner, who was also a carpenter, to immediately begin construction on a home and outbuildings.

Fred wanted to have a place for his family to move into when they arrived. He knew the home would be crude until it was finished in the summer, but the sawmill owner told him he could have the roof on and walls in place in a month or two.

After viewing the land, plotting where he would build his home and plant his crops, Fred immediately staked his claim in Montesano, the Chehalis County seat. He then made plans to purchase 400 acres of virgin timber in the area known as Upper Satsop. It was far more than he had imagined or much more than he would ever need, but the price for the vast estate was too good to pass up.

Counting the acreage on the farmland where the home would be constructed, its surrounding lots and the 400 acres in the Upper Satsop, it was far less than Fred paid for the 150 acres in Oregon. The best part was that he had to put only $100 down and he gave the carpenter an additional $100.

It was a substantial investment, but one that would serve his family for many years.

Fred decided he would spend the winter in Oregon, prepare the returning crops, then move to the Washington Territory before summer. He knew Louisa would like it there.

Fred was excited with anticipation of the big move. Marshall also found a new opportunity, but he chose to stay on the coast, an area called South Bend on the Willapa River, prime with logging potential.

The two men reunited on the coast and began the three-day trek back to Oregon.

He was glad the next journey would be on the train.

He thought about Louisa, Minnie and the new baby. "Maybe I should go up there until the house is built," Fred told his wife.

She would hear nothing of that. "You aren't going to leave me again."

It was a particularly good yield, and Fred was able to get a substantial price for his crops. Harvest was over early, and he knew he would have no trouble selling the land and house, if he completed the spring planting by mid-April.

Immigrants were moving to the new farming country from the city. One of them, a strong Deutschländer like Fred, offered almost twice what Fred paid for the property. He didn't let that opportunity pass. The new buyer agreed to plant the fall crops for Fred.

The one thing he had no control over was when the baby would arrive. Louisa and the doctor figured it would be mid-April.

They were right on target. Edward arrived on April 17, 1882.

By mid-May, the Tornows were on their way to the Washington Territory.

The route took them from Salem to Portland, where they changed trains for the three-hour ride to Centralia. The train was slow, but more comfortable for Louisa and the kids than the pounding in a wagon.

The Tornows figured it was easier traveling with an infant than with a two or three year old. They weren't accustomed to being cooped up in a tight compartment and Louisa looked forward to the overnight stop in Centralia. They all did. It was going to be a welcome break for everyone.

Thankfully, Fred had made arrangements for Marshall to take their furnishings by wagon as far as Olympia when he left a month ago. Marshall was to leave them with his uncle, who lived by the Deschutes River.

"We're coming into the station, Louisa. We're almost there. Minnie, help the boys get their coats and cases and stay right with us," her dad commanded.

The next morning they boarded the train for a short ride to Olympia.

Marshall's Uncle Roger was there to meet them and had the wagon ready for Fred. He handed the man some money and they started the final leg of their journey.

"It's only about 40 miles now, dear. We've got to go through the Black Hills. It's not bad, though," Fred told his wife. "They call them mountains; they ain't no mountains; no bigger than a molehill. It won't be bad.

"G'dyap, g'dyap," he ordered the team.

"Fred, I love you. I really love you. It's going to be wonderful up there," Louisa said.

Slowly, the two horses plodded along with the heavy load and the Tornows. It was muddy going west over the primitive road after three days of relentless rain, but the skies were clear now.

Louisa found a somewhat comfortable place to lie down. It seemed to her like it had been 20 years since she first laid eyes on Fred on the dock at Hamburg. In truth it had been 14.

As she began to drift off to sleep, she recalled how she readily recognized his good qualities — honesty, strength and sincerity. He had treated her well on the boat, and for the time they were together in Nebraska and Iowa.

She trusted his judgment and relied on his strength. Now they were moving to a new opportunity where she hoped the future held nothing but happiness.

As the loaded wagon reached the Brady Junction and turned north, Fred leaned down toward his resting wife.

"Doing OK back there? It won't be long now, 'bout 10 miles."

Louisa sat up and gave her man a tender squeeze.

"You're a good man, Fred. I love you dearly, and I know we are going to be happy."

———

It had been more than two years since the Tornows moved into their homestead on the Upper Satsop.

Minnie, now 17, wore the characteristics of her mother — tall, shapely, fair-skinned. The winds of the Washington Territory bothered her light complexion, and a few minutes in the stiff breezes brought a deep pink hue to her cheeks. She had long, braided hair, but preferred it rolled up. She was a bright child with a mind of her own, just like her mother. Louisa and Fred often disagreed over discipline of the youngster.

"We've got to keep an eye on her," protective Fred would frequently tell his wife. "She's going to get in trouble."

"What kind of trouble can she get into in the woods, Fred?" Louisa would answer. "Let her be. She's a curious child. She can learn from the woods."

The children loved their new home on the banks of the Satsop's Middle Fork. It was a short walk to the river and Minnie enjoyed its solitude; she often strolled the banks, played for hours and tossed pebbles into the water. She loved how the water rippled when a pebble interrupted its tranquility. The water was cool, but she enjoyed swimming in it, rather than fishing like the boys.

She would walk the boys to the Elizabeth School, which she and the older boys attended. It was a one-room schoolhouse and she liked the teacher, Margaret Carstairs, immensely. It was a long walk, but she savored it, even though she had to chide the boys to keep going, lest they be late.

One day as she was walking home, a good-looking man approached her.

Henry Bauer emigrated from Darmstadt, Germany, in the Southern Rhine area, in 1870. Before coming to the Upper Satsop in 1880, it was believed he spent about 10 years with a Lutheran colony.

He purchased nearly 200 acres of homestead property off the Boundary Road, so named because it was almost on the Chehalis

County line with Mason County. He built a small two-story bungalow amid the towering firs, up a small terraced ridge from the Middle Fork Satsop River.

The ranch was substantial with deep river-bottom soil and he soon grew several varieties of beans, potatoes, peas, onions, cukes, icicle radishes, watermelon, pumpkin and corn. Another parcel of land produced wheat, barley and rye. Still another was full of orchards — apples, pears, cherries and plums. It was a typical turn-of-the-century farm with abundant property.

Henry was equal to the task of the required hard work it took to maintain the farm and keep it abundantly prosperous. He employed neighbor kids to assist him and traded goods for labor with friendly loggers, who supplied him with wood for the fireplace and cook stove.

His life was full — almost.

It would be, if he could find a wife to share the farm and start a family.

He was 27 years old and had a full life ahead of him when he met Minnie Tornow.

As the relationship with Henry Bauer grew, Minnie spent more time away from home when she wasn't needed to watch the boys. And much of it was with Henry.

While it was a long three-mile walk, she found every occasion to go to his ranch.

Occasionally, she would even get to ride one of her dad's horses.

On this day, Henry took the wagon and headed west from the homestead, along a path that would take him to the tiny hamlet of Matlock, the closest place for food and supplies.

It would be the first time he met Minnie, who was escorting the boys home from school.

"Hop in," he said "and I'll take you to the road," he told the young woman.

"Who are you?" she asked before moving the boys near the wagon.

"I'm Henry, Henry Bauer. I live right over there," he said, pointing down the road Minnie and boys had come from.

"OK. I guess it's all right. We've got a long way to go and it's getting chilly," she said. "Boys hop in. This nice man's giving us a ride."

"Are ya sure?" asked William, whispering into his sister's ear. "We don't know him."

"It's all right. I've seen him before. He's just being nice."

The boys jumped into the back of the wagon and Minnie sidled up to Henry.

"Minnie's my name, Minnie Tornow," she said. "You're awful nice to give us a ride. Where ya goin?"

"Matlock. Got to get some stuff for the farm and that's the only place I can get it," he replied.

"Are you going to stay there? It's going to be late when you get there."

"Probably. I've got some family friends I can bunk with and come back in the morning."

She was struck by the young man's confidence and independence, even more when he shared his story of running the farm by himself.

Henry decided he was going to build a new home, a large one with many bedrooms, but that would come later. Right now, he was OK with living in the tiny two-story structure he had built.

It was big enough for him and maybe a wife, but for a family, he would need a bigger place.

"Bye, Henry. Thanks for the ride. Boys, tell Henry thanks."

"Thank you sir," William told him. "Drive carefully."

"See ya again soon Minnie," Henry said as he started to drive the team away.

"I'm sure you will," she replied with a flirtatious wink.

It was her first meaningful contact with a young man and Minnie was indeed smitten.

Tornow family is pictured circa 1892 when John Tornow was 12; From left, back row: Albert, John, Minnie, Fred and William; Front: Louisa, Edward and Frederick Daniel.

5. GROWING UP

1890s

"Eddie, Johnny. C'mon, breakfast is ready. Ya gotta have a good breakfast and get your chores done before school," Mrs. Tornow shouted to her youngest children.

"He's not here. You know that," shot back Edward with sharp insolence. "He's never here. I gotta do everything around here."

Louisa knew Johnny wasn't in his room. He hadn't been home for several days, but she harbored hope he would come sneaking in like a thief in the night, just like he did the other times when he decided to spend a few days out in the woods.

Much had transpired in the nearly decade since the Tornows arrived in the Upper Satsop Valley and built their homestead.

Fred worked hard to support his family. The soil was fertile and supplied all the crops the family needed to eat, and many more to sell in the nearest town, Montesano, 20 miles south. He raised pigs, cattle and chickens to help keep them supplied with meat and also hunted to bring in deer, elk and even an occasional cougar or bear. Fish were also plentiful in the nearby rivers, including the Middle Fork of the Satsop, which came to be known as the Tornow Branch.

Meantime, Minnie and her German immigrant pal, Henry Bauer, were constant companions. When Minnie turned 19, they decided to get married and build the new home that Henry had desired.

Her dad was not in favor of this union as he didn't see much good in the tall, and 10-years-older, Henry.

Louisa saw that Minnie was happy, and the fact they were "just around the corner," helped her get over losing her little girl.

Minnie had four brothers, but, for some reason, she was never close to any of them, except young Johnny. She and Johnny spent time in the woods. Minnie enjoyed the quiet solitude of the nearby woods and often took the youngster with her.

She was 14 years older than John, but, even at age 4, he had an innate ability to communicate with the forest and even the wildlife. This fascinated her.

"Mama, you won't believe this, but Johnny can talk to the animals," she said one day after returning from a long walk in the woods. "We were walking and he turned to me and said 'sssh, sssh, can you hear it? Listen hear she comes.'

"Then this doe walks almost right up to us. I couldn't even see her, I didn't hear her, but he did, then he started talking to her and asked her where her baby was. The mama just looked at him and began nibbling the salal. It was beautiful."

Henry and Minnie were talking marriage, but missing out on the home life, especially with Johnny, caused Minnie to ponder what to do.

But, the dream of having a family of her own was a driving force.

She even shared her decision with 5-year-old Johnny before telling any of the other siblings. "I'm going to marry Henry," she told the youngster, "but I'll still come home often. We can still spend time together. I know we will."

Johnny didn't say much. Just a simple "OK."

They were married in August 1885, in a simple ceremony before a justice in Montesano. Minnie gave birth to Mary the next year on June 14. On October 22, 1888, Minnie and Henry had their second baby, Elizabeth.

She visited her mother often, particularly when Henry traveled to Montesano to sell his crops and get supplies.

Her children were too young to enjoy the woods, but she would bundle them up and make the trek to the Tornow homestead. She longed to spend time with Johnny, but he was rarely there.

Henry, resolved to the fact that Minnie was going to make the trek through the woods to her home, taught her to hitch the team to the wagon. It was much easier than trying to shepherd two little ones through the woods. The girls weren't that strong yet and tired quickly.

When Minnie left the Tornow home for the Bauer homestead, Johnny began spending more and more time in the woods. Often he would tag along with his older brothers, but he had no use for their horseplay and he'd ditch them. More than once the boys returned from school without John.

Louisa didn't worry. He always came home — eventually.

"He's always gone, mama," said Minnie on one visit home when she inquired about young John. She loved her brother, John, and particularly his independent nature. "He's so smart mama. We went to the river, just like me and Willie used to do. He's young, but he knows the trail and he knows where the fish are biting."

Minnie desired to have a little boy, like Johnny. Mary was six and Lizzie four when she got her wish — twice. On July 6, 1892, Minnie gave birth to twins — William and John.

"We named him after our Johnny," Minnie told her mama the day the boys arrived. "Henry named William. I don't know why he chose that name, but I chose John, because I love him and I'm glad he survived those measles. I thought we were going to lose him, mama. It doesn't seem possible that it's been three years since that happened. You hardly know anything happened to him, except for his speech, sometimes."

Louisa worried about John constantly. "Not natural for a boy of 12 to be away from home that much," she'd tell her husband pleading for him to go and find the boy. "Not natural for a boy of 12 to stay by himself in the woods and not tell his folks."

But Johnny had a mind of his own. He loved the woods and he knew them well. Even at this young age, he could handle a gun. He made a lean-to out of fallen timbers, and whittled corner pieces for a perfect fit. He said even when it rained, he was dry and comfortable.

"If he likes it so much out there, let him be," Fred would say when Louisa pleaded for him to go and fetch the kid.

Louisa gained some comfort knowing her troubled little boy seemed perfectly healthy after the measles ordeal, save for this peculiar penchant for solitude with the woods.

She thought about that ominous portent of Dr. French when he told them just three years ago, "he will be deficient in body or in mind."

"That's not so," thought Louisa, flipping a couple of buckwheat cakes she was fixing for Eddie's breakfast.

"He certainly isn't like the other boys, but there is nothing really wrong with him. He's got that lisp in his speech, and he prefers to be alone. That's all. Why look at him. He's even a strapping kid, 5-10, and he's only 12. He's going to be a big boy," she said, now talking aloud with apparent indignation.

"Deficient indeed. The doctor was wrong. He was wrong, terribly wrong. Johnny's fine," she said aloud.

"What you say mama? Johnny's OK, isn't he mama?" asked Eddie, slipping unnoticed into the kitchen.

"Oh, mornin' Edward. Yes, Johnny's fine, just fine. Now eat. There's a lot of work to get done."

"But mama, why do I have to do everything? Johnny's never here to help and the other boys are gone all the time helping Daddy."

"No, Eddie. You can't do everything, but you can do some things. Now, get busy and eat or you'll be late to meet the kids. Then you'll have to walk to the schoolhouse by yourself."

Eddie slowly shoveled in the 'cakes and eggs, snapped up another rasher of bacon and headed for the barn.

He resented having to milk the cows, dump the fodder in the bins for the horses and slop the hogs before school. He had been doing this since he was 7, and almost every day there was a fight to get him out of the house.

"If Johnny was here, he'd have the work all done by now," Louisa said to herself, rinsing the dishes in the warm water.

There was little doubt Johnny had become his mama's favorite since his recovery. She watched over him fervently, fearing the slightest cold would develop into something far more serious.

But try as she might, she couldn't keep John out of the woods. He was so at peace out there. He always finished his chores early, rising well before the chickens. His health was good and she couldn't complain. He retreated to the outside or to the upstairs room when visitors came, but then he always did that even before the illness. He seemed comfortable only around family and some of the neighbors — the Maases, Schaletzkes, Gleasons, Schafers, Mullers, Spaldings, Hollatzes and Kohlmeiers. They all liked him. They said they saw John frequently on his treks through the woods. They marveled how a boy so young was so comfortable in the dense forest.

But then, they were woods people. They understood.

Yet, he was closest to Minnie and he dearly loved her two little babies — William and John.

Henry Bauer never did care for Minnie's brother, John, and tired of his wife's constant visits to her mother's home. As Henry's confrontations with Minnie grew more intense, her visits became more frequent and longer as Louisa's health began to deteriorate.

John would often stop at Minnie's on his way home from school. He played it coy, however, often waiting in a hollow cedar stump until Henry would leave. He didn't understand Henry's attitude, but he learned to avoid him.

"I am going to teach those boys how to fish and hunt," John would tell Minnie. "Soon as they are old enough to hold a pole, I'll take them with me to the river."

Louisa did have one regret: Johnny wouldn't stay in school. He'd start out walking with the other kids, but many days he never arrived at the schoolhouse. She knew the importance of education, and she knew Granny Scott was a good teacher. It didn't seem important to Johnny.

"I know," Louisa thought, "maybe Margaret Carstairs can come over and tutor him when he gets back. He'll learn some reading and writing at least. I heard she did good things with the Maas boy. Couldn't read a word and in a few weeks he was reading catalogs. All Johnny knows about catalogs is the one in the outbuilding."

Fred and the older boys were away frequently this year, especially the boys. They helped on the farm, but were more inclined to work on logging. Clearing acreage that bordered the farmland got the boys interested and they took to it almost naturally. Freddie was only 16, but he seemed to know more than the older boys. Bill and Albert liked working in the woods, but didn't have the aptitude that their younger brother did.

It was hard work, and they were good at their job. They enjoyed it more than farm work. Fred let them run the logging part of the family business and he tended to the farm.

"One day I want to have my own timber-cutting business," Freddie would tell his mom — "just like the Schafers."

The Schafer boys owned the adjacent property to the northeast, just across the main road that connected Brady to Matlock.

John Schafer, like Fred Tornow, had left his native Germany and immigrated to the United States in the 1860s, arriving in the Satsop area in the late '70s. He graduated from college in Bönn before he left Germany, but his schooling as a teacher of language and music was of little use in the Satsop. The elder Schafer sported a white flowing patriarchal beard, and at one glance, one would think the venerable gent had an answer for everything. He didn't, but he did have an imagination, yet lacked ambition.

Fortunately John Schafer found a jewel of a woman in Anna Muller, his second wife. Friends and neighbors called Anna "a pioneer among pioneers."

She was efficient, domineering. She ran her home with a sure hand and good judgment. It was under her direction — not John's — that the fields were cleared. She sowed the oats with her own hands.

"Anna, she get up early and she still work at dark," said Ben Kesterson, a neighbor to the south.

Peter, the eldest of the Schafer boys, was born in 1869 in Wisconsin, where the family initially settled. Hubert was born four years later and Albert in 1879 after the family moved to the Pacific Northwest.

Much the same age as the older Tornow boys, the Schafer lads were chums with their neighbors.

Many of the German immigrants in the Satsop took a stab at logging. After all, while growing up amid the towering firs and hemlocks, the boys saw logging as a natural pursuit.

They saw their neighbors, who had been doing fairly well as farmers, cut trees, buck them, haul or roll them to the river, where they were floated to the mills.

Due to the cyclical nature of the business, many loggers went out of business and became bankrupt. Some even lost their farms and left the valley.

But not the Schafers.

The Schafer boys were determined, and had their parents' consent, but Anna said only under her rules.

Kesterson, who previously lost money in his own logging venture because he lacked a sufficient financial foundation, was hired to work with the boys. Anna knew Kesterson's knowledge and experience would be a bonus for the fledgling operation.

A stipulation from Anna was that farm work was to be carried on as in the past. Logging was extracurricular. Another regulation — and this is where the Schafers succeeded when others had failed — they were not to go in debt for any reason to pursue logging or expand the operation.

"Buy and hire as much as you wish, but borrow nothing, mortgage nothing and pay for what you get," she would chide her children.

When the Schafers drove their first logs from the Satsop down to the Chehalis to tidewater and on to the A.J. West Mill in east Aberdeen, it was a pioneering venture, the first time that logs had been driven from the Satsop River to the Chehalis.

Anna insisted that only the finest logs would be used. That fact soon became known throughout northwest mills, and the tiny Schafer operation was rewarded handsomely for its diligence.

The family had logging in the Upper Satsop much their own way with no other operation even attempting such a venture for several years. They received $2.50 per-thousand board feet, and drove nearly 500,000 board feet to the mills the first year.

Logging Tornow-style, was mostly primitive, much more so than the Schafers. They had neither the manpower, nor the equipment. Only the boys' tenacity kept the business going.

The area they selected to log was only a short distance from the East Fork of the Satsop. They figured six bull oxen would handle the load.

Felling the mammoth firs was relatively easy, though time-consuming. Getting the timber — often 6, 7 or 8-feet in diameter, most of them at least 20 to 30 feet long — through the dense forest and down to the river was yet another matter.

They learned a little about logging when they had to clear the forests for the farm. With only an axe and an adze, the young Tornow boys helped their dad cut and trim the trees to stump size.

Fred would then put a powder charge under the stump and blow it into small pieces. Digging by hand or spade, the boys had to loosen the roots. Once the stubborn roots were freed from the soil, the boys tied a line around the large portion, usually a root wad, with jacks and peaveys, and team of horses; then they pulled them out of the soil and burned them.

The Tornow boys worked well together. Freddie knew how to get the job done, but wasn't as strong as Bill and Albert. Occasionally when Johnny was home, he would tag along.

Once the tall timber had been felled, one of the boys, goad stick in hand, prodded the big bulls, urging them with every excessive grunt, groan and snort to haul the logs on a skid through a prepared clearing or landing. It was Bill's job, as the oldest, to ride majestically on the skid and steady the logs.

Often the bottom of the skid would get hung up on a snag and a "sampson" or long stick would be necessary to loosen the skid. The boys would use a stick to rock the log to and fro until it shook free.

When the logs reached the embankment, the boys branded the end of the logs FTR (for Fred Tornow Ranch), tipped them over the edge and pushed them down toward the river.

When the landing became full of logs, the boys, with some neighborhood assistance, yanked the logs toward the swift-flowing rivers.

It was dangerous work. A misstep at this point on the slippery logs, and one might be washed downriver, or worse, be crushed beneath the onrushing logs.

Every logger had a peavey, a hooked stick tipped with an iron or steel point. With this tool, they would put their entire weight behind the thrust and maneuver the logs into the river until they were headed downstream.

The logs floated down the Satsop to the confluence of the Chehalis and from there west to the mills at Aberdeen, Hoquiam and Cosmopolis.

Thieves, seizing the opportunity in this primitive operation, often pirated the logs, snagging them on their downstream trek, hauling them to the bank, cutting off the branded ends and replacing the brands with their own identification.

Log piracy was common and some operations would often station lookouts in the easy-to-get-to shoals to watch for thieves.

Loggers knew no more efficient nor cost-effective method of getting the logs to the mills. Assessors too found it easier to tax the owners once the logs reached tidewater.

There was legislation afoot to change the taxation method, but the timber barons successfully halted any action as did the unions. They found the present situation much more to their liking.

Alvin Spalding of Elma points to the original Tornow homestead in 1987. It has since been torn down.

This shed is the only original structure remaining on the Tornow homestead. Frederick Tornow used German newspapers to line the interior for insulation.

When the Tornows started to clear the furthermost acreage, Fred saw to it the boys followed the principles established by Anna Schafer.

Fred figured he had the best of both worlds with the knowledge the boys had gathered from palling with the Schafers. Fred was also successful in luring John Minkler away from the Schafer camp.

Minkler had been with the first Schafer operation, but broke with the brothers over procedures in driving logs down the river.

When Minkler joined the Tornow operation, it came with a price. It severed forever, the relationship between the Tornows and Schafers.

Fred tried several times to talk to the Schafers, telling them it wasn't personal, only business. But the neighbors would hear nothing of it, even calling Fred a traitor. "You'll pay for that, Fred Tornow," Anna Schafer vowed.

———

It was another six days before young Johnny came home. The youngster had been by himself in the woods for nearly two weeks, even missing his 13th birthday two days ago.

Yet Louisa had never seen him happier.

"Mama, it's so peaceful up there in the mountains. I like it so much. I got lots of friends."

"Friends Johnny?" asked the perplexed Mrs. Tornow, now fearing for her son's safety. "Who are these friends, Johnny?"

"The animals, mama. The animals. They understand. I lie down to sleep and when I wake, they look at me. They guard me, like a watchdog. They like Cougar too," he said, referring to the spry hunting dog his papa had given him on his 12th birthday.

"Johnny, I worry so when you're gone so long."

"I know mama. I know. This time I went a long way and built a little wickiup. A man helped me. His name is Cy, Cy Blackwell. He's real nice mama. You don't have to worry. I can take care of myself. I followed the Satsop across to the Wynooche. I stayed there in a clearing for a couple of days. They call it the Oxbow. The Wynooche makes a couple of bends, like this," Johnny said, making an up and down motion with his fingers so as to draw a picture of the oxbow in the air. "I found a nice little lake and that's where we built the shack, kind of on a little island. Papa knows where it is. After I built the wickiup, I ran into a couple of loggers who were from the Wishkah. They let me tag along. We found a place to ford the Wynooche and went all the way to the Wishkah.

"Mama, it's pretty there. It's pretty here too, but better there. We gotta go over there. They're starting to build a dam up on the Wishkah. I watched them for a while, then they needed another hand. It was fun mama. They even paid me! See!" the youngster said, flipping a silver coin into the air.

"All the way to the Wishkah," she thought. "Such a big boy," forgetting for the moment she was talking about her 13-year-old son.

"My God, Johnny. That's 20, 30 miles isn't it?"

"They thought I was 16, 17. Couldn't believe I was only 13. I want to go back and work on the dam, mama. Mr. Blackwell said I could help. Splash dam, he called it. They'll be stopping soon for the harvest. I'll help papa with the crops, but when we're done, I want to go back."

"We'll talk about it when papa gets back," Louisa said, hoping her husband would not allow such a venture.

"Now go get washed for dinner and I'll fry up those rabbits you brought."

6. LIFE ON THE WISHKAH

1902

"Cas, whadja think Tornow's bringing us tonight? I got my money on bear."

"Nah, Antone. Gotta go too far to get them, unless he happened to stumble on one. Bet it's elk, or maybe even some cougar. Lot of 'em is running wild up there."

John's ability with a rifle was well-known, not only in the Upper Satsop where he grew up, but also in the Wishkah Valley, west of the Wynooche.

Casimir Mankowski and Antone Malinowski were Polish immigrants, who homesteaded in the Upper Wishkah Valley, and like John Tornow, worked for Cy Blackwell's logging and dam-building operations on the Wishkah River.

The early Indians named the river Wishkah, which literally translates "stinking water." Ironically, some fine-tasting fish come from that river.

Blackwell came to the Northwest in 1883 from Truckee, Calif., where he had a logging operation a few miles north of Lake Tahoe. The site is more well-known for the vicious winter of 1846-47 that wiped out the Donner Party on their trek west from the Central Plains.

Truckee was primarily populated by the tribe for which the city was named. Blackwell learned much from the tribe and it would benefit him on his logging operation on the Wishkah.

Tornow had worked off and on for Blackwell for the last five years and had become one of the hardest workers in the camp. Blackwell often took Tornow with him on sojourns to the Olympics, the rugged mountains to the north. Some were not yet traversed.

John often said he would be the first to cross some of those more primitive peaks, many reaching 7,000 feet.

Blackwell introduced Tornow to several tribal members on their visits into the West Olympics. John became a skilled sturgeon fisherman, in part due to learning techniques from the Hoh tribesmen.

Angling for the 200-to 300-pound lunkers was popular among the tribesmen; John also appreciated the challenge. Blackwell left it to the much-younger Tornow to fight the massive fish.

The West Olympic rivers of the Hoh, Bogachiel and farther south, the Humptulips, yielded the best harvest of these fish.

Sturgeon fishing was an art in itself, and one Hoquiam Indian, Pollocks, was particularly successful. He taught Tornow well, using a large hook fastened to a cedar and spruce pole. The hook has a socket near the eye, which is fitted to a long pole, possibly 20 feet or longer. The fisherman holding the rope and the pole, probes the channel floor for sturgeon. When the hook touches one of the big fish, the line is given a jerk. The pole is then drawn up and the sturgeon plays the line. Big sturgeon often take hours to tire and land.

Tornow also shared his method of catching salmon with vine maples, an art he learned from his teen years. He also taught the tribesmen how to shoot from the hip, another achievement the young man developed early in life.

The first two years he was with Blackwell, John spent only a few weeks in summer and then most of the early winter in the Wishkah camp. Then, after hassling with his older brothers over their smaller logging operation on the Satsop, John left home to work most of the last three years on the Wishkah.

He still returned home to help with the harvest since the older boys left that in their dad's hands. The rest of the year he worked for Blackwell, either on the Wishkah or helping him supply timber for the mills at Aberdeen, Hoquiam and Cosmopolis.

Blackwell was regarded as one of the more successful loggers in Chehalis County, after the Schafers.

While the Wishkah Valley was readily accessible via the Wishkah and East Hoquiam tidewater from the harbor towns of Aberdeen and Hoquiam, it was one of the last areas to be settled in Chehalis County.

Blackwell had built the first splash dam on the river about 16 years prior when he first homesteaded the area. It was a four-gater above a considerable falls. When John first started working on the Wishkah it was his job to maintain the dam.

Initially, he had an easy job, keeping the dam free of debris. Storms, which occurred frequently when ocean winds blew in from the coast, wreaked havoc and kept the big man and his crew busy.

Cy used a bull team to build the dam, but the next year he imported the first steam donkey engine, a Dolbeer, into the area. He used the donkey first in clearing property for the townsite of Carlisle, west of Hoquiam, before moving it onto the Wishkah. Later a second donkey was brought in to log above the falls.

John often lorded the new machine over his brothers and reveled in seeing them green with envy when he talked of how much easier the logging was on the Wishkah.

That certainly didn't endear the big man to his brothers. He was paid three times as much as they were and had bank accounts at both Aberdeen and Montesano State banks.

There was something about Blackwell and the community of Polish immigrants, who settled the Wishkah that appealed to John.

He thought their names strange; seemed as if everyone's moniker was "something ski" — Mankowski, Malinowski, Maslowski, Snarski, Sabanski, Stawski. They were wonderful, good-hearted and hard-working people. Most importantly, they let him be himself. They let him do things his way, and still allotted him time to spend in his beloved woods, which he desired as much as anything.

"I don't care what he does, and when he does it," Blackwell said to Antone. "All I care is that the work is done and on time and he does that."

John's older brothers — Bill, Albert and Fred — never understood him. They couldn't see why he needed to have his space in the woods.

The three older boys were close-knit and John didn't fit in. He was 6-2, weighed 210 pounds and was as strong as a bull — like his daddy. He was never comfortable around them. They thought he was strange.

John was never included in the weekend plans when he was home and he didn't much care. He couldn't see why they had to go to town every weekend, get roaring drunk and raise hell. He called it "the fury of firewater" and had no use for it. They made fun of him for not joining in, called him all manner of degrading names. It was no wonder he preferred working the Wishkah.

The older boys would tell their friends there was "something very wrong" with their brother. They didn't say he was crazy, but they thought it.

There was none of that talk on the Wishkah. It was a big happy family and a hard-working one.

It was a perfect relationship and John responded. Almost without fail, when he left for a day or two once an assigned project was completed, the tall, rugged woodsman returned with enough food for the entire camp for several days.

Big black bear, elk, cougar, fox, squirrel, ducks, frogs, deer, opossum, and of course, fish, particularly steelhead and salmon. John brought them all at one time or another. It became a guessing game. They all looked forward to his return, especially his venison jerky.

Cy had taken some into Aberdeen one week and veteran smokers there said it was the best they had ever eaten.

Tornow's ability with a firearm was unparalleled. He was only 16 when he saved enough money to buy a U.S. Winchester 30-30, a military issue from a friend of Blackwell's who was stationed at Fort Warden at Port Townsend on the northeast tip of the Olympic Peninsula. He was rarely seen without that weapon. Even that firearm was not sufficient for Tornow. He didn't care for the sight on it and fashioned one of melted nickel. His gun was the talk of the Wishkah. And so was his marksmanship.

"Uncanny," the Wishkahans called it.

"I saw him drop an elk from 200 yards with a single shot between the eyes," Cas recalled. "I didn't even have the animal in sight. John and I were out behind Whittier Creek one day and we got into a discussion. You know, the guy doesn't say much, but this day, I guess he felt like talking. He told me how he almost died from the measles when he was a little boy. That's why he has that lisp sometimes, and how it affected his eyesight. After the measles, he had trouble seeing at a distance. You'd never know it to see him shoot that rifle.

"He said he doesn't actually see the animal he is shooting at, but he developed a keen sense of smell and hearing that compensates for that.

"John said he could see the outline of the animal long before I did, and he shoots at the movement. I guess when you spend as much time in the woods as he does, you get pretty good at that.

"It's just the opposite of how you and I hunt, Antone. We wait for the animal to stop its movement, then we sight in on it. He either drops that animal before it stops running or waits for it to move. When it does, Blam! It's all over.

"I saw him stand perfectly still for over an hour one time while a big buck was eating. Finally, that buck up and moved. Hadn't taken three steps and John fired. Dropped that five-pointer right behind the ears.

"You know, Antone, we are lucky to have him here."

"Yeah, I guess Cas, but that kind of shooting is dangerous, makes me skittery. What if what he thought was an animal was a hunter or logger or something? He wouldn't have a chance would he?"

"I guess so, Antone, but that will never happen. I'm just going to make damn sure I'm standing by him when we go hunting."

John didn't come back to camp that night, so the woodsmen settled for some of old Jake Jaklewicz's beef stew. Not bad, but some fresh elk from Tornow would have been tastier.

"Said he was a goin' home for a day, then to Aberdeen for the logging jamboree," Blackwell told the curious campers when they asked about John's absence.

"That's right. That celebration starts day after tomorrow, doesn't it?" Antone asked. "How about giving us a couple of days off. Gotta fix up that old donkey before we can do much work anyway. It's running too sluggish to do anything until we get those bearings replaced."

"Sure, go on, but don't get all drunked up, and stay away from those union s'loons. Heard tell they're finding bodies in the drink every day. Some real mean shit going on down there," Cy said.

———

John Tornow arose early after spending the night in a lean-to not far from Minnie's homestead. He tried to arrive at her place when her husband wasn't there. Henry didn't take too kindly to the time he was spending with the boys.

From a cedar hollow, John watched as Henry hitched the wagon and headed out to work the crops. It was his clue to move in.

"Hey, sis? Min? Anybody here?"

"Oh Johnny, I didn't hear you," she said, rushing to hug her strapping brother. She loved it when he hugged her. His arms were so strong, and she felt comfort in them. She didn't feel that way with her husband.

"Boys. C'mon see who's here," she hollered in the direction of the twins' upstairs bedroom.

The door opened and out popped Lizzie.

"My, how you have grown," John said scooping his niece in his sturdy arms and giving her a squeeze.

"Boys, did you hear me? Johnny, William, come here," Minnie shouted.

"What mama?" said William bolting down the stairs and into the room and seeing the massive visitor.

"Uncle John, Uncle John. We missed you so much. Can we go fishing? Can we, huh? Can we? Mama, can we go fishing?"

"Well, that's up to your uncle. I don't know if he has time for that now."

"Sure, we'll take a couple of hours in the morning, won't hurt none," Uncle John said. "Lizzie, you wanna go too?"

"Nah, that's not for girls," Johnny said, hearing the commotion and racing to hug his uncle."

"Can go if I want to," Lizzie said, snidely. "But I don't, so there. Going to the Maas's anyway."

"Good, let's go Uncle John," the boys said in unison.

"Hold on guys," John told his nephews. "Can't go right now. Gotta wait until morning, got something I got to do tonight. I'll be back by dawn. You boys be up and ready."

"They'll be ready," said Minnie. "Probably be up before that, won't sleep much, I reckon."

John was going to make a quick trip home, but decided to catch a ride from the Spaldings next door and visit the Schaletzkes up toward Matlock.

"They've always been good to me, probably sleep there too," John said after hearing that old man Spalding was heading to Matlock.

"John, I'm not feeling that well today," George Spalding told his neighbor, "but if you want, take the wagon and tell Ed I said hello. I'd like to go, haven't seen him in months."

"Are you sure, Mr. Spalding?" John said, respecting his older friend. "I was thinking about spending the night, but got to get back here before dawn to take the boys fishing."

"You go and bring the wagon back in the morning. Have a good time. You guys always do."

John arrived back at the Upper Satsop Bauer home before the sun was up.

As he expected, the boys were on the front stoop, waiting.

"He's here!" said Johnny, dashing back into the house to tell his mama.

"Don't forget your slickers and galoshes. They're on the back stoop," Minnie hollered as the boys were about to dash out the door. "Could rain any time."

The boys fished a lot, but going with Uncle John was something extra special, something they looked forward to when he came around. It was an activity they participated in frequently since they were little tykes, just old enough to hold a pole and bait a hook.

"Oh Min. Quit your worryin'. I'll take care of the boys. 'Sides, best time for fishin's in the early morning after a storm. And we just had one. Rained pretty good last two nights. Gonna bring ya home some dinner," John said, gathering the two boys on the back stoop.

"Where's your poles?" he asked the boys.

"In the barn, I guess," they answered, in unison.

"Best get 'em and we'll get going."

"Hold on, boys. I'll get them," Minnie interjected. "Henry might be out there," she said in a soft voice so only her brother could hear."

Within a minute, Minnie returned with the poles and the three hustled off together to the Middle Fork of the Satsop River.

"'Member, that spot you showed us last time, Uncle John? Willie and I slaughtered 'em every time we go out," young John said.

"Howdya know that spot is so good?" Willie asked.

"I fished every inch of this river and that's the best. Ain't no spot like it on the entire river or even the main or West forks," the uncle answered. "What makes it so great is the rapids just upriver. It drops off into a deep pool. Sometimes the fish at that spot are so thick ya think ya can walk across water on their backs. I even got a couple of steelies out of that spot."

It didn't take the trio long to light into bite after bite.

"Good goin', guys. Now remember to keep your pole up and you'll land more of them. And 'member our rule, gotta be at least a foot long or we throw 'em back and let 'em grow a little bit. No sense in taking your mama the little ones when we can get the big ones."

"Uncle John? Howscum we don't see ya more often?" young Johnny asked after the boys had filled their creel with trout in about two hours.

"Well, I'd like to be here more often, but I'm working a lot up the Wishkah now and I really like it up there."

"Mama and us miss you lots Uncle John."

"Yeah, I know. Maybe things'll be different soon. We best be getting back, and I gotta get down the road. Going to Aberdeen tomorrow."

John laid the boys' fish on the ground and summoned them closer to him. "Here, let me show you how to clean them and filet them. Your mama will be surprised. She won't have to do that. Got your knives I gave ya last Christmas?"

"You bet, Uncle John. Never go nowhere without it," Willie answered. "We know how to do that. You showed us last time you were here last spring, I think it was."

"I did, huh. Well OK, then, let's get to cuttin'. Gotta git a goin'."

The good fishin' hole on the Middle Satsop wasn't far from the boys' home and the three of them were back within a couple of hours.

"Here you go, sis. All the fish you can eat for a few days. It was good to spend some time with the boys. They are such good kids. Be sure you keep them that way."

"Maybe this winter, we can go elk huntin'. We had fun last year, didn't we?" he asked the boys.

"Oh, yeah we did. I'm gonna get one this time, too," William said.

"We all miss you Johnny," Minnie said, swinging her arms around her big brother. "The boys haven't seen you since last harvest. You see, they're getting big Johnny, almost 11. They ask about you all the time. They are a lot like you, take to the woods, love to hunt and fish. Johnny's inseparable with that knife you gave him, sleeps with it under his pillow. Henry doesn't like it, doesn't like it all. Wants them to stay around the farm and work. You know Henry, he doesn't take kindly to that loggin' and the woods stuff.

"And Mary's getting so big, almost 16. She's been a big help to mama. She's got a lot to do around the place, and you know papa's been poorly. Mary's spending a lot of time over there. The boys are gone for weeks at a time, 'cept for Eddie. He's around home all the time, especially when Mary's there. He never does much. I don't know what's wrong with him.

"You know Johnny, if I didn't know better, I'd say Eddie and Mary were … oh, never you mind now. Get going and take care, and don't be gone so long. We all miss you."

John gave the boys a big hug, then planted a wet kiss on his sis's cheek and waved goodbye.

"Tell mama and papa I said hello and I'll see them in a couple of days. Gotta go to Aberdeen tomorrow. I'm real excited. I'll tell you about it when I get back."

With that, John turned and hustled down the road.

———

It was nearly noon when John arrived in Montesano, having hitched a ride with the Mullers to Brady, then with Emma Kaatz, an old family friend, he ran into at the Brady store.

"Charlie will be at the celebration tonight Johnny," said Emma. "You boys always had a good time together. He understood you better than the other kids. You should look him up and spend some time together. I know he'd enjoy that. He's not made too many friends since we moved to town. I don't like the guys he hangs with, always trying to get him to go in those saloons."

"I'll do that, Mrs. Kaatz. Sounds like fun."

Emma Kaatz and the Tornows had been friends for several years. She had been a neighbor in Brady, but had moved to Aberdeen two years ago. She ran a boarding house and the Tornow boys often stopped for a good night's rest and a hot meal before heading home. However, John had never been there.

Although her boarding house was on Hume Street in the heart of the "red-light district," it was generally regarded by the Tornows and others to be one of the more legitimate establishments on the boulevard. She was also a mid-wife and managed therapeutic baths in her business.

John bade Emma a goodbye and walked down to the depot to purchase a ticket on a paddle boat. It was the quickest way from Montesano to Aberdeen. There were several paddle boats and one sternwheeler daily and John preferred their open air to the dankness of the train which only ran once a day. Locked in a rail car for the half-hour ride to the harbor was not his idea of fun.

The *Harbor Queen* was a little slower than other paddlers, but a more pleasant ride on a warm, summer day.

The clean harbor air with the scent of fresh-cut trees and the whirring of the several mills, dotting the Chehalis River most of the 10 miles to the docks east of the city, was relaxing.

It was a particularly enjoyable journey on such an unusually warm day as this. John picked up *The Daily Bulletin* on the seat next to him and the weather report said the temperature might get into the 90s.

John was quiet and subdued through the boat ride.

He had much on his mind. He had bankrolled a sizeable bit of money and taken some with him when he left Montesano. He had some in the Hayes & Hayes Bank in Aberdeen, but not enough for what he had in mind.

Blackwell, an astute businessman, had convinced him to purchase some property and told him of a good possibility on the banks of the Wishkah, northeast of downtown Aberdeen.

John had seen the property once and immediately liked it. Letting go of the cash was a big step, but he was determined. In his 22 years, he had not purchased anything more than he needed to sustain him — basic food and ammunition — everything else had been provided for him, or he had made it from what he could find in the woods.

This was indeed a big day for the gentle giant.

When the *Harbor Queen* docked, Tornow was one of the first to disembark, hurtling his big body over the side railings and onto the pier.

He ran to the real estate office at the bank and laid down four fifties to purchase not one, but two lots in Aberdeen.

"Lot 4, Lot 3, Stewart Addition, from seller Jean Stewart," Tornow read. Papers tucked under his arm, the big guy bounded out of the claims office like a youngster with a new toy. He was now an official property owner.

He decided to return immediately to the Satsop and share his good fortune with his family.

"Sorry, my friend," said the ticketmaster at the boat docks. "We are having a little boiler problem. She'll not be ready until day after tomorrow. Nothing's running tomorrow 'cause of the holiday. I could sell you a ticket now, but it won't do you any good. There's another boat in about six hours."

Tearing down Wishkah Street with his long stride, John took a left on G Street. Walking the three long blocks, he hurried toward the rail station. It was too late. He saw the train pulling out when he was a block away.

Hurriedly, he approached the window and asked the ticket seller when the next train would be leaving.

He was humiliated and embarrassed when she asked him to repeat his question because she couldn't understand him. Frustration always exacerbated his speech deficiency.

That was one reason Tornow didn't like going anywhere by himself. It embarrassed him not to be understood because of the lisp. It made him self-conscious. It was why he also became withdrawn and often sought solace in the woods when people came to visit the home. Asking him to repeat only frustrated him more.

But the young ticket seller was soft-spoken and had a sweetness about her. He didn't mind repeating.

Finally, she understood. "Sorry sir," she said. "But with tomorrow being the Fourth of July, the train will be laying up in Montesano to bring visitors to town. We are having only one return tomorrow, but that won't be until after the fireworks, after 10 p.m."

Disappointed twice, John hung his head and started to walk away.

"Sir, you should join the celebration. There's big doin's in town tonight. A trolley can get you to Electric Park for all the activities," she said, trying to cheer up the disappointed man. She directed him to the trolley stop.

"How far is Hume Street?" John asked the woman.

"Just up there," she said pointing north. "Only a block."

Tornow thanked the woman, then figured if he could find Emma's son, Charles, the two of them could join in the logging jamboree celebration.

He headed up G Street one block to Hume and over to Emma's boarding house.

"Maybe Charles will be there and I can get some lunch too," he thought to himself.

Young Charlie was home and John wasted little time in downing a plate of fresh eggs, homemade sausage and fried potatoes the young man whipped up for him. His mother had taught him well how to cook.

"C'mon John. Let's go watch the loggers splash down by the lake. There's going to be a shooting contest too. You could win some prizes, John. You're a lot better than most of them."

The teenager's infectious exuberance picked up John's spirits as the two lumbered off for Electric Park on the west edge of town.

It is two miles to the park that sits on the boundary separating Aberdeen from Hoquiam. Both communities, though bitter rivals much of the year, unite for this annual celebration, though several contests, such as the annual tug of war, pit city versus city.

Wide-open Aberdeen is the larger of the two cities, with its main streets of Wishkah and Broadway, Heron and Hume. It is home to the gambling halls that service the loggers and millworkers hungry for brew and the gaming that goes on in such establishments. It's home too, to Hume's rows of bawdyhouses, packed with eager young men starving for attention of a woman after having labored all week in the woods.

Hoquiam is a more conservative community with its illicit activities of alcohol and harlots restricted to the Grays Harbor House, an inn that caters to the more affluent doctors, lawyers and bankers. All other gambling houses, bordellos and dens of iniquity — that's what the clergy called them — had long since been outlawed by a city ordinance.

The two cities are divided by Electric Park, a huge green expanse with a large picnic area, baseball diamonds and an abundant man-made swimming lake.

Each year, on the Fourth of July, the two cities put aside their differences and join in one big bash, usually a three-day affair with merchants selling wares, locals participating in carnival events, a professional baseball game and the ever-popular logging shows and shooting contests.

Charlie led John west of town, then north. The two young men had been walking about a half-hour, but decided to catch the electric trolley to the celebration. John was glad the trolley was there. The events of the day had begun to wear on him. He had covered a lot of ground since leaving Minnie's early this morning before dawn.

Bounding from the trolley, John and Charlie stopped first at the baseball field. John never really understood the apparent pleasure the men seemed to derive from striking the ball while others chased it.

Charles tried to explain that the object was to hit the ball where the other players couldn't get it, then try to run to as many bases as possible before the ball could be retrieved.

Seemed silly to John, but Charlie enjoyed it. John, four years older and a head-and-a-half taller than the Kaatz boy, derived pleasure from seeing Charlie have a good time.

"Let's go watch the logging show and shootin' matches," the young boy said when the game had ended and the Black Cats of Aberdeen had defeated the visiting Mountlake Cougars from Seattle.

"N-nnnnnno," the big man stuttered as he often did when he became overly tired. "It-tttts l-lllate, and I h-hhhave t-ttto l-llleave early."

"Please John. Please. Just a while longer, then I promise, we'll go."

He had always felt comfortable with the Kaatz boy and he knew the youth worshipped his ability as a woodsman and a logger. The boy also paid no attention to his speech impediment.

He relented and the two hustled off to the marksmanship contests that were held against the bluff.

Charles stepped behind John and used the bigger man as a battering ram to forge their way through the elbow-to-elbow crowd. The shooting matches were always popular and drew the largest gatherings, save for the logging shows.

They found a seat on a bench within earshot of the two marksmen vying for the title. The young boy and his giant friend could hear the banter between the two men, chiding each other on their prowess and marksmanship.

"Small one's Colin McKenzie," Charles whispered in his companion's ear. "He's a Teamster, hauls supplies to the logging camp. He runs a company called Union Transfer. Also has a photography studio down on Hume, near mom's. I think he's a deputy sheriff too."

"The big one?" Tornow asked.

The youth leaned over and whispered. "You don't know him? I thought everybody knew Billy Gohl."

Tornow instantly recognized the name and nodded. He heard the name often. Cy Blackwell talked of him frequently and now he was within several feet of the most-feared man on the Harbor.

"Gohl is a notorious tavern owner on the corner of Heron and F, rumored to have mugged and done in drunken loggers and sailors. Some said he killed as many as 100 or so," Charlie said. "His wife runs the Capitol Rooms, across the street.

"We hear things all the time at the boarding house. Nothing could be proven, mind you, but it was heard tell that many loggers, having sold their timber and seeing it loaded on sea-going vessels would frequent the tavern for a few belts before heading back to the woods. After they became sloppy drunk, Gohl had his henchmen relieve the men of their money. Days later their bodies would be found floating in the Chehalis."

Gohl, who also was an agent for the sailors' union, also was said to have a trap door in the back of his saloon. When a card player got out of hand, he was beckoned to Gohl's office, rapped on the head, relieved of his money and had a block of cement tied loosely around his feet. When the trap door opened, the body fell directly into the river. Days later the body would surface when the block of cement would work free of the ropes in the tide. For its bawdy houses and Gohl's reputation, sailors often called Aberdeen, "the Hellhole of the Pacific."

"There were all sorts of allegations, but nothing could be proven," said Charlie. "Only Billy's closest friends and card-playing associates were allowed in the back room. There was never enough evidence on Gohl to search the place, and he kept it well secured, day and night, to be sure."

"He's younger than I thought," Tornow said to himself, "and a lot bigger too."

He watched the tall, stocky man load the lever-action rifle.

Gohl adjusted his bowler and perched himself on one arm on the side of a stump to wait his turn.

"Get 'im Billy. Go get 'im," bellowed one attractive young woman. "Yeah, Billy. He's easy," chimed in another lovely lass.

Gohl winked at both and tapped his back pocket. The ladies knew what that meant.

McKenzie, seeing this gesture, only smirked. "We'll see, won't we Billy," he shot back.

Taking his stance, McKenzie was the first to shoot at the 100-yard targets. He fired rapidly, without hesitation.

The umpire retrieved the targets.

Two bulls-eyes in the first, two hits in the second, nowhere near the center. One bulls-eye in the third and one other hit on the rim.

Not bad, but was it good enough?

Gohl strode to the line, quickly braced the weapon against his shoulder and fired — six shots in rapid succession.

"Tough shit, little man," he sneered at McKenzie.

The umpire retrieved the targets.

One bulls-eye in the first target, two in the second and two in the third.

"Like I said, tough shit, little man. Tough shit."

The umpire asked for silence to present the championship award. The crowd grew quiet.

Gohl's presence demanded that. Not so much out of respect, as fear.

"You could kick his ass, John," Charles blurted through the silence. "You're better than that lily."

"Sh-sh sh-sh-shut up Ch-chchcharlie," the big man turned to his companion. "He'll hear you."

It was too late.

Gohl took two strides, grabbed the youth by the shirt lapel and lifted him a foot off the ground.

"Whadja say smartass," Gohl growled, shaking the already-trembling boy?

"Let go him," said Tornow sternly, but softly, his vice-like grip already clamped on Gohl's forearm.

"Man, don't you screw with me. I'll bust you good," Gohl said. Tornow only tightened his grip.

"Leggo the kid. Leave him be. Now!" bellowed Tornow, his voice commanding attention as a crowd closed in to see the commotion.

Pulling the older, barrel-chested Gohl toward him, Tornow looked deep into the tavern-owner's eyes. "Claim your prize and leave the kid alone."

Gohl loosened his grip on the Kaatz boy and Tornow shoved the tavern owner toward the award stand. He crashed into the podium and sent plaques flying.

Gohl sheepishly got to his feet as the crowd stood in awe. He took a step toward Tornow, then thought better of it as the taller man stood with his arms crossed waiting more confrontation. Nobody had ever stood up to Gohl before and lived to tell about it.

Gohl glared, then without taking his eyes off the giant man snapped, "Well, where the hell is my prize? I'm the champion here, I'll always be."

Tornow put his arm around the young Kaatz boy and guided him safely through the crowd, which was all abuzz at the amazing event. He could hear the whispers all around him.

"We showed 'em, didn't we, John?"

"Yeah, kid. We sure did. We sure showed 'em," the big guy answered.

"Those stories about Gohl are true," he thought to himself as the two hurried off to catch the trolley. He was too tired and beat to walk all the way to Charlie's.

"I've seen that look before — on a coon dog waiting to kill the prey it had treed after a long hunt," Tornow thought to himself. "If we meet again, it'll be on my ground, not in the back room of a saloon in a card game. It'll be in the forest, and I'll be armed."

"C'mon kid. Let's go. Tomorrow we'll grab a pole and go up the Wishkah to do some fishing. The air's cleaner in the mountains."

———

Minnie was glad that Henry was still out in the field when the boys came back. No explanations necessary. It was bad enough that Henry didn't like John coming around, but if he found out he took the boys fishing she'd never hear the end of it, but the hunting, that was another story.

It wasn't bad last year because John came when Henry was gone for a week and never knew the boys were with their uncle. She didn't like to do it, but she chided the boys not to say a word to their father.

The boys knew their papa didn't much care for John, but didn't understand why. They were smart enough to not say anything.

"What a way to live," she thought. Now she'd have to go through that again in the winter. "No," she thought to herself. "I won't worry about him knowing. I'm just going to tell him, then I won't have to worry about the boys or the girls saying anything. I'll just tell him. But not yet, I have a few months. Besides, maybe John won't even come home this winter. He's done that before."

Minnie was playing another one of her mind games, which she had taken to so often in recent months. She didn't like it. It wasn't healthy, but it helped her pass the time and avoid confrontations with Henry.

It occurred more often since Mary had been spending so much time at her grandmother's with her health failing and the boys away so much.

"What am I gonna tell Henry this time?" she thought. What excuse would she use when Henry ranted about Mary being gone again?

"Minnie? You OK?" John asked concerned as his sister stared at nothing in particular.

"I'm fine Johnny. I just miss you so much. And Henry, he's gone all the time. Never see him and I guess that's good. 'Cept that he's not much of a husband, not like I dreamed about. When he's here, he's always yelling about something. He doesn't beat me or anything, but he's always fussin', never happy about anything. I don't know what the kids think. I know the girls aren't happy. That's one reason Mary's gone to the folks so much. She told me she loves me, but doesn't really like to spend time here. I try to spend time at mama's, but Henry, he gets so mad when his dinner isn't ready, and when I go there, I like to spend a day or two, not have to hurry back.

"The boys don't really like going over there. Eddie's the only one home most of the time, and he spends a lot of time with Mary. He's not like you John. The boys don't take to him like they do to you. He's lazy, doesn't do any work he doesn't have to. It's hard on mama and papa too. Oh, now, listen to me going on. I know you gotta go."

"Now, don't you worry. Quit your thinking like that. Ain't doin' you no good to worry. The boys are doing just fine, and looks like the girls are gettin' along all right, too. You're a good mama," said John, cradling his emotional sister.

"Gonna stop a minute over home before I head on. I'll say 'hi' to the folks for you."

It was late afternoon when John crossed out of the low timberland, cut across the pasture and reached his folks' property.

"They'll be surprised, but we can probably have these fish for dinner," the young man said to himself as he climbed the few steps on the back porch.

"Anybody here?" he bellowed into the doorway with a resonance that rattled the wooden building.

"That you Johnny?" Mrs. Tornow called out from the front room.

"Yeah, mama, it's me."

"Oh, Johnny, it's so good to see you! Been so long."

"Not that long, mama. Just last spring, a few months."

"Seems like a year to your old mama. I can't keep track of time anymore and I'm not as spry as I used to be. Been laid up a couple of days with the fever, not myself lately."

"Where's Eddie?"

"Don't know. He and Mary went off somewhere after lunch. 'Spec they'll be here soon."

"Where's papa?"

"I thought he was out by the woodhouse. Didn't you come through the pasture? You should have seen him. Now I'm worried. You know Eddie was supposed to chop that stack of wood out there weeks ago and hasn't done it. I don't know what's come over that boy. He's not like you, son. Can't get him to do a lick of work around here. Oh, he does do the morning chores, but that's about it. Papa said no breakfast until the chores are done, so he's got to do them. Mary's been a help to me, washing dishes, making beds and helping with housework, clothes washing and she's become a pretty good cook too. Just wish I knew where he was, your papa."

"Don't you worry none. I'll go find him," said John, his strong fingers cradling his mama's face.

John hustled out the back door, trying not to let concern show.

"Papa, papa! Where are you?" he called out.

"Johnny, that you?" came the muffled answer from inside the woodhouse as the concern disappeared from the young man.

"You in there?" John asked, pushing the ajar door wide-open. "What are you doin' in here?"

"Well, I'm readin' these old papers and then insulating this shed with them," said the elder Tornow, now nearing 60. "Got a bunch of these papers from the old country the other day. A friend gave them to Charlie Kohlmeier and he brought them to me, knew I had been from Fasan. Course, that was years ago and nothing means much to me over there anymore. One of these papers, that one over there," he said, picking up the German publication. "This one talks about a girl that I knew in school celebratin' her 60th birthday. I'm sure it's the same one. That was interesting, but the main reason I wanted the papers is because they make good insulation, keeps the wood dry in these winter storms. Old Charlie told me that. Never thought I'd learn anything from Ol' Charlie."

"Mama was worried about you. I think she thought you were out here chopping wood and that's not good work for you."

"Now, you don't worry none about your old dad. I'm not as strong as I used to be, but I can still do a good day's work."

"Mama tells me that Eddie was supposed to do that chopping. How come he hasn't done it?

"It's easier to do it myself than to fuss with him, Johnny. I don't know what I am going to do with that boy? He's not like you, Johnny. Hasn't done a day's work in his life, maybe that's my fault for not getting on him more. John, now's as good a time as any to tell you something. Know that land up the Satsop that we logged a few years ago? Well, John. That's all yours. I signed it over to you when I was at Montesano the other day. The other boys all have their own land and their jobs and families. Edward's too young and beside's he wouldn't know what to do with it. I want to make sure you are taken care of … before I die."

"Now, papa. Don't be talking like that. You ain't gonna die. You're strong as an ox. Maybe not quite as fast as an ox, but you're still strong."

"Just the same. I wanted you to have that land, but there's one stipulation. Don't sell it, long's I'm alive. It's to sustain you and besides there's some cruiser been here a couple of times trying to get me to sell. Told him that land, nor this land's not for sale."

John didn't know what to say, but emotional situations often left him speechless. After a few seconds, he gathered his thoughts.

"Thanks papa. Papa, I can't stay long, just for dinner, then I'm gonna meet Ed Schaletzke for a ride to Montesano. Gotta be in Aberdeen tomorrow. But I'm gonna chop that wood for you, 'fore I go. Your axe still in the same place? Gotta work up an appetite for the salmon."

"Salmon? You brought us salmon?" he said smiling, knowing John always brought some fish, elk, venison or other meat with each visit.

It took the big strapping young man only a little over an hour to chop the alder stack down to size and a few more minutes to pile it neatly in the woodshed.

The salmon never tasted better. John gobbled his first helping and then another. Salmon tasted best in the outdoors, grilled with butter on an open flame over cedar shavings, but next to that, his mother's was best.

She had a way of steeping it in corn husks wrapped to retain the flavor for a few minutes before baking it and applying a sauce of mustard greens, chopped garden-grown dill and fresh-churned butter. A dash of homegrown oregano, allspice and a hint of mint were just the perfect touch.

A couple of baked potatoes, sprinkled with parsley leaves and swamped in butter, homegrown banana squash and a couple of pieces of mama's fresh apple pie were all John needed to send him satisfied on his way.

Almost.

"Eddie, come out here. I want to talk to you," the older brother summoned the youngster.

"Now look. All the other boys are away and mama and papa need your help more than ever. They tell me you aren't helping much, spending all your time with Mary."

"Ain't so. You don't know nothin'," Eddie yelled. "You're never here. You don't know what's going on. I do my work every morning. What do you mean I'm not helping much?"

"They told me they asked you weeks ago to chop that wood. How come you haven't done it?"

"Haven't had time, that's all."

"What do you mean, haven't had time. What took up your time?"

"Things. I got things to do every day. Haven't had time. Besides, don't need that wood chopped until before fall. Got plenty."

"I'm jus' asking ya to help a bit more. Papa's getting along in years and mama's not so well either. Just help them out, OK?"

"Why don't you just get out of here. You're never here. You got no right coming around here and telling me what to do. It's not your land, anyway. Gonna be mine someday. I'm the only one here."

"Papa isn't going to leave you a dime, if you don't get off your dead ass and do some work," John retorted.

He knew it would serve no purpose to tell him about the land acquisition — at least not now.

7. THE TEMPTATION OF TIMBER

1906

Watching the lanky figure in front of the mammoth fireplace, W.H. Abel cautiously pretended to sip straight bourbon from the elegantly-cut crystal glass.

He wasn't often invited to the Schafer home, so when the invitation came, he knew it had to be important.

William H. Abel was born in Sussex, England, in 1870, but was raised and educated in Kansas. He had been in Montesano since 1892, when he married Ella Rosmond that same year.

His background had been as a school teacher and newspaper editor before being admitted to law practice in 1894. He rapidly became one of Chehalis County's most respected attorneys.

Returning the glass to the coaster on the mahogany table, Abel leaned back, folded his arms to his chest and listened attentively as Peter and Albert Schafer exchanged sharp words, an uncustomary practice for them.

"That new bill's gonna kill us," said Peter, the elder of the two Schafer brothers. "We already pay more taxes than any of the timber companies around here, and now they want to stick it to us more."

"Oh, it probably won't be that bad, Peter. Besides you always come up with ways to get around paying those high fees. And, Abel here, well that's what we pay him for."

"Yes Al, you're right, but the legislators say this new stuff is going to hit companies like us real hard. Seem's they want to change the way they are going to assess the timber. If that new law passes — and Commissioner Wilson says it's almost a sure bet — the timber cruisers will be all over our land. Hell, it's bad enough now, trying to keep them off the property except when we invite them. With that new law, they'll have open season. They will tax us on the market potential, not the timber we cut for the mills, and that's purely subjective. Hell, we know our timber. Those cruisers will just play guessing games."

"Besides that, what about the younger stands," Peter asked?

"I understand they are trying to get a rider along with that bill to allow for deferred taxation on younger timber," added Albert.

"They're trying, but it doesn't look too good, from what I hear. We've got to go to Olympia and talk to Benn and Minard. Alex Polson should also be able to help us," Peter countered.

K.L. Benn, son of Aberdeen founder Sam Benn, and E.L. Minard were recently elected to the State House. Polson was a timber man who understood the problems of the new taxation and had his eyes on the state Legislature.

As the evening grew on, Abel sat back with his one drink and listened to the brothers' discussion of how many senators and representatives they had in their hip pocket; how many they felt they could manipulate to vote against the upcoming taxation or for the rider. They clearly needed more support.

Abel became intrigued as they bantered back and forth, almost as if he weren't in the room.

It had been a long two hours that Abel watched the two brothers, all the while sipping on the only drink he would allow himself.

The sly attorney once said he got more accomplished by just listening to his clients spill all they knew. Rarely did he interject, unless he was queried.

That was the situation in this room. He was silent, but absorbing everything that was being said.

It was obvious to Abel that Peter was the dominant, controlling brother, as always, even after a few drinks.

Albert continued to smoke the Havanas, downing more alcohol than Peter and listening more, while his older brother babbled on. He knew it was foolhardy to try to calm Peter down once he got a few drinks in him and he got wound up. He just let him ramble on.

Wearing down from the long evening, and the booze, Peter stumbled as he got up from his seat and ambled toward the bar to fetch the pitcher of bourbon. He poured himself a double and refilled Albert's glass, despite his resistance.

"Bill, another?" he asked Abel, acknowledging his presence for the first time in what seemed like hours. He knew Abel would decline the drink and turned away from the attorney almost at the same time he made the offer.

"No, still have some," the Montesano lawyer said, feigning another sip.

Setting down his glass, Albert rose and took a step toward the armoire.

"Are we going to cut that section above the Tornow land this year Peter?" asked Albert leaning down toward his brother's ear. "If we do, we're gonna need that easement and we better get Abel on it right away."

Peter flinched, stiffened and pursed his lips, yet saying not a word. Watching Peter's reaction, Abel could discern a sudden tension about the room.

Clearly, Albert was out of line, and Abel understood that.

"No, Albert, we're not gonna cut that area this year," Peter responded lazily, as if it mattered not a whit. "It's time to call it a night," he said standing.

"You know where the guest room is, W.H., if you want to stay the night. We'll see you for breakfast. If not, I'll have Jacob bring your motor car around."

"This is really unusual," Abel thought. "What's this W.H. stuff? Awfully business-like, and he never asked me to stay the night, not even during the big snow storm last winter. Something interesting is going on. I think I'm going to stick around."

Draining the last drop of bourbon from his glass, Abel slowly rose. "I'll stay the night and leave after breakfast, if that's all right," Abel said, seizing the rare opportunity.

He left the parlor and pulled the door behind him, though not closing it. He knew the brothers weren't through discussing matters. It would last far into the night, and it would probably get a bit boisterous. He thought it best he go to the guest room now.

Waiting for the door to close, Peter Schafer moved quickly toward it and saw the lawyer retreating to the guest room.

"See ya in the morning," Bill, Peter hollered down the hall as Abel opened the door to the guest room on the right wing of the tri-level mansion.

"Yeah, 'night," the attorney answered.

Peter left the door slightly ajar when he returned and approached his brother.

Before he had closed the guest room door, Abel could hear the brothers getting louder and louder.

He strained to hear what they were saying, and decided this was too good to pass up. He crept slowly to just outside the parlor door, where he could hear the brothers.

"Don't you ever goddamn talk about our future plans or cutting or selling timber in front of that son of a bitch," Peter shouted at his brother. Through the crack in the door, Abel could see the veins in Peter's neck about to burst with that furious tongue-lashing.

"But Peter ..."

"Don't 'but Peter' me! The day we begin trusting that son of a bitch is the day we're gonna start losing money and don't you ever forget it!"

Abel gulped. He wanted to leave, but decided to stay. His anger grew. "How dare they ..."

"That jackal's here to serve one purpose and only one purpose. He's here to do what we tell him to do, Albert. He is here to help with paperwork and legal terms. He's the best in the business, but he is not to be included in any of our future plans. I just hope it's not too late."

Abel suddenly felt better about his stature, though he wasn't sure why Peter reviled him so.

Retreating to the chair, Peter relaxed. The brothers sat silently, recovering from the raucous last few minutes.

"I'm sorry, Peter," Albert said finally breaking the silence, then leaning forward to re-light his cigar.

"Don't worry about it. Forget it," the older brother countered. "I do have to admire the asshole. The bastard has the three qualities necessary to be a brilliant lawyer, and don't forget that."

Pride started to well up inside of the eavesdropping attorney.

"He's got a brilliant, creative mind and he has a gift of spell-binding oratory."

Again Abel smiled, his ego swelling, wishing he could share this moment with someone, anyone.

"And what's the third thing?" Albert asked.

"He doesn't have a moral fiber in his body."

They both chortled uproariously, grabbing each other in a brotherly embrace.

"Why, those sons of bitches. I'll fix them. How dare they ..." Abel thought, as the picture of the two brothers cackling at his expense remained vivid in his mind. "I'll remember this. The payback will be hell."

He was about to retreat to the guest room when he heard Peter's voice again.

"You know, Albert, that's an important 600 acres of virgin timber we got up there. That strip of land Tornow's got is all that separates us from a lot of money. If we get that easement, we would be able to build a bridge across the Satsop from our Camp 5. It would be a lot shorter to the Elma-Montesano road."

"No, Albert. We won't cut that timber until after old man Tornow dies, you know that. He's not gonna give us a crossing, but we can get it through the widow when he dies. We'll send old Abel up there to try to get it from him. But I think it's useless. Besides, it's like money in the bank. It's the best 600 acres of pure, virgin timber. It won't cost us anything to transport it. All we have to do is drag it across that strip and haul her down on a skid and dump it in the river. Then we wait for a flood. It sure beats the hell out of transportation costs by rail. We'll just let it sit. It's not going anywhere. We have lots of other timber to cut. That section will make us a lot of money."

"Yeah, if they don't tax us to death on it first," added Albert. "If that new bill goes through, that land could cost us plenty. Virgin timber will be assessed the highest."

"C'mon, it's bedtime. I'm done talking."

———

It was a wonderful opportunity the young, lean boy thought to himself.

After reading all the advertisements in the Seattle newspapers about the burgeoning new territory, the lands of opportunity in the West, O. V. "Ovie" Nelson had been in Montesano only a week when he was hired by W.H. Abel.

Abel was regarded as the most successful lawyer in the county, perhaps the state. After all, he represented the vaunted Schafer Brothers operations.

The young man's head was swimming with the idea of being Abel's law clerk, and this only a week after graduating from Tacoma College and arriving in Montesano with lofty credentials.

By state law, he could be clerk for six months, then be eligible for the bar examination. He could be a lawyer by Christmas.

And that was his goal.

"I know Mr. Abel likes me," Nelson thought to himself. "Imagine, I might even be a partner soon with the most successful lawyer in Western Washington."

"Ovie, c'mon," Abel said to the daydreaming youth. "Ovie, c'mon. We got work to do, and I want you to go with me."

Ovie still didn't hear.

Abel picked up a bulky law tome and dropped it solidly on the floor.

Ovie jumped straight out of his seat and looked Abel in the eyes.

"What was that?" the young man asked.

"Just getting your attention," the attorney said. "C'mon. We've got work to do."

"Sorry, sir, I was just thinking how lucky I am to get this job and work with you."

"Young whippersnapper," Abel thought. "He already knows how to get on my good side. He's going to be good. I gotta keep my eye on him," Abel mused.

They had been traveling by motor car for almost an hour when the vehicle came to rest in front of the white, two-story, flat board farmhouse.

Alighting from the car, the handsome Abel approached the front door of the ranch house. Ovie waited in the car.

As the lawyer stepped on to the porch, next to the kitchen, a young man appeared in the doorway.

"Is your father here?" Abel asked.

"No," the man answered.

"Where can I find him?"

"He's out."

"You must be Edward?" Abel asked of the young man, now 24 years old and the youngest of the Tornow boys.

"Yeah, and you are … ?"

"Abel, W.H. Abel. Where can I find your father?" Abel continued.

"Cross the road, out that way," snapped the young man, pointing in a westerly direction, but offering little information.

Turning and shading his eyes from the sunlight, streaming through the trees, Abel could see the dust of the workhorses in the distance.

"Thank you," he said. I'll find him."

Abel motioned Ovie to accompany him, and the youngster quickly flitted from the vehicle.

"Insolent brat," Abel murmured.

"What's that, Mr. Abel?"

"Oh, nothing. It's just that Tornow boy. You think he could be a little more helpful. He's such a lazy bastard. Everybody says so. The other boys all have their own property and businesses, but not that one. The old man ought to boot his ass out."

As the two set out across the spring-planted front section and approached the man working the draft horses, Abel told the boy to stay behind him and not say a word.

Ovie nodded. "I wouldn't know what to say anyway," he thought to himself, although he was a little disappointed that his boss lacked confidence in him, at least to keep his mouth shut.

"I'll show you a little experience at work," the attorney said, smiling.

Abel couldn't help thinking it odd that Tornow, a not-well man in his early 60s, would be out clearing a field and a young son would be in the house.

"The crusty old bastard's going to be tough enough and I've got to be convincing. This won't be easy," Abel thought to himself.

They walked across the furrows, taking care not to disturb the upcoming crops just now beginning to peek above the soil.

Frederick had heard the motor car before he had seen it approach the farmhouse. He was mystified as he watched the lone figure approach the silo door.

Watching from a distance, Frederick could see Edward obviously point and indicate his whereabouts.

"Edward didn't feel like working again today," the old man muttered to himself. "Only disease that boy has is the disease of laziness."

Turning to his second-youngest son, who was working alongside his papa, the old man said, "Why can't they all have your strength and attitude, Johnny?"

"Papa, this is a stubborn stump. You shouldn't be doing this work. If you give me a hand, we'll get it out. I'll chop out enough from these two roots, then you put the chain around the other root here. We may be able to jerk this stump out."

It had been a long, tiring morning for the old man and his son clearing the far acreage for next spring's planting.

"A couple more days and we'll have this section ready," the old man said to his son. "This is good soil. It will yield good crops. We'll have it ready for next planting."

The old man stopped and rested, but John continued on. Tying the chain to the roots and hooking it to the line, then the workhorse gave it a couple of quick tugs and the roots popped free from the rich soil, where it had been imbedded for some 150 years.

"If they could all be like him," the old man thought, referring not as much to his three older sons, but to his youngest, Edward. He watched his strong son, a giant of a man, take the double-bitted axe and rhythmically bite into the roots, many of them several inches in diameter. "It's so effortless for him," he thought.

Turning his attention to the oncoming men, who were approaching the edge of the section, Frederick could now recognize the slender, handsome lawyer from Montesano.

"What does Schafer's lackey want?" he asked, turning to John.

"Fred Tornow. Good morning," the lawyer shouted as he approached the old man.

"Who's that boy with you?" Tornow asked.

"That's Ovie, Ovie Nelson, my new law clerk. He's learning the ropes, giving him some on-the-job training."

"Mr. Tornow, nice to meet you," the young man said, stepping forward to stretch out his hand, even though the old man didn't cease what he was doing.

"Don't mean to bother you when you are working, but I was on my way to Camp 5 to see Peter — Peter Schafer — and I thought I'd stop for some water."

"Water? Certainly he could have thought of a better excuse than that," the old man thought to himself.

"Well's up near the house," the old man muttered. "Didn't need to come all this way to get river water without a bucket," he snapped, motioning to the Satsop River bank some 200 feet in front of the men.

Caught off balance by the brusque, blunt manner of the old man, Abel silently sized up the challenge. He knew of the bad blood between the Schafers and Tornows, most everybody did. And he saw nothing to indicate that the rift had healed itself. If anything, it had grown, festered.

"He's as tough as leather and he's not stupid either," the lawyer thought, gazing into the dark eyes of the short, stocky immigrant. "I've got to make this believable."

"Well then, I'll get to the point, Mr. Tornow. I've been asked by Peter Schafer to get an easement from you across your land so they can log the area they own next to yours — that land up there with all the hemlock and fir. They hope to log in the next five years and want an easement across your property. We want to make arrangements to float the timber to the mill by spring, and it would be easier if we had access through your land."

Fred Tornow was a shrewd man, even from the day he purchased the property on his first visit to the Upper Satsop. His nearly 400 acres was bought in patchwork fashion, much like a checkerboard. He did that intentionally, so as to have control over the land. He also thought about the day the boys would inherit the land, but now all that had changed.

Tornow smiled and turned away. "He comes right to the point," the old man thought to himself, walking toward the stump that John was cutting. Looking at his son, the old man let out a cackle as Abel and Nelson moved near.

"John, Schafers want to cut that section up on the north end and drop it into the river on our property. Shall we sell them the right to haul it across our land?"

John didn't miss a stroke, continuing to chop up the huge stump, then let loose with a huge chaw of spittle in the direction of the lawyer. It landed at his feet.

"There's your answer Abel. I'll tell you what. The day Peter Schafer cuts that timber is the day it'll rot on the ground before I'll let him cross my land.

"That land there and this here belong to my boy, John," he told the lawyer, realizing at that instant not even John had known of the change he made in his will only a few weeks ago to give him the virgin timberland. "I'll not be letting it be used for cuttin' that timber, strippin' that earth like they've done to their other lands. My boy here, he likes huntin' on that land. He'll not be letting them do that either. So you hike your ass out of here, Abel, and tell Schafer, if he wants to cut that timber, he can build himself a railroad to haul it out. I'm sure that will make it profitable as hell for that son of a bitch. Now I think it best that you get your ass off my land. If you want water, there's a well near the house. And take that young rattlesnake here with ya. Now git," the old man said, chuckling to himself at the apparent victory over the feisty attorney.

"OK, Tornow, have it your way for now. Don't think you have heard the end of this yet."

Red-faced, yet composed, Abel turned on his heels with the young clerk in fast pursuit.

"Bastard. The old bastard can't live forever. And it's going to cost the Schafers plenty to get that easement, but we'll get it."

8. THE HOMECOMING

1909

"John should be here any day, mother," the old man said, turning to his wife. I am going to check the hay in the back property. I feel certain he'll be here today."

"You've said that for weeks now, papa. You keep saying that. And Johnny, he doesn't come."

"I know mother, but I feel differnt today. Sumthin' tells me this is the day. Ya 'member how I jus' knew when he was coming home last month. I jus' knew it. Well, I feel like that now. Put another potato in the pot. You'll see."

Fred and Louisa Tornow knew this conversation well. For the past 11 years, they had to wait for their second-youngest son to return for the harvest. He had done this often since he was 17.

Louisa, a strong, hard-working woman in her early years, had been in failing health for five years now, ever since she fell and broke her hip, the same one that had mended last year. Yet she continued her household chores with the same vigor. She was 71, six years older than Fred, yet appeared at least 10 years younger. An attractive woman in her youth, Louisa still possessed a bright smile and charismatic personality.

Though not deeply religious, she would often utter a prayer to God for Johnny to stay home. She hated to see him leave, but she long since gave up her pleadings.

She did tire of telling busy-bodies where her son was.

"I know it's strange, but he's so content out there in the woods, always has been," was her consistent reply, but she knew he always came home in time for the harvest.

———

"I'll stop and check this section," the old man thought to himself. "From here I can see the river bank. I can see him coming."

A doe and her fawn playfully romped at the river's edge.

The Satsop's Middle Fork was shallow and easily fordable this time of the year, but in winter months, it could be an angry river, roiling from snowmelt in the nearby Olympics.

Salal and any number of wild berries covered the upper bank, but the heat of the last few weeks had dried up much of the fruit and left brushy undercover.

Early September is traditionally hot and dry, but a late afternoon northwesterly wind usually offers a pleasant breeze over this land, where 75 to 100 inches of annual rainfall is not unusual.

There was no wind this day, not a breath of a breeze as the old man surveyed his vast field.

Squinting, he moved both hands to his forehead to shield the searing sun from his eyes. Droplets of perspiration now poured from his brow, burning his eyes.

Fred had begun showing his age the last five years. Now, two months after his 65th birthday, his legs were not as strong, nor was his heart. He was told to slow down, but there was no talking sense to this stubborn old German.

"I'll slow down when I get old," he told Doc French with a slight grin the other day.

He had been in the field for a couple of hours when he thought to himself, "I have to get out of this sun."

Quickly, he walked through the field to the timber-lined edge of the property line.

Finding an old stump, the aging man tenderly tapped it with his foot and looked ahead to a row of stumps. He recalled the day he and John had to fall those once-proud cedars to make way for the back road, and felt sadness wash over him. He sat down, pulled a blue and white-checkered bandana out of his back pocket and slowly mopped his brow. The shade felt good, but even under the cedars and hemlocks, the heat was stifling.

"Must be 85, 90, much too hot for working" he thought. "John'll be here soon, so I won't have to do the hay myself. I'll just sit and wait for a spell."

It had been some years since Fred Tornow had help from the other boys with the farm. He hired a couple of farmhands to help with the crops and haul them to town. The young men were good workers and always got top dollar for the crops. They knew how to work the markets in Montesano, Matlock and sometimes even in Aberdeen. It made it a lot easier for Fred, who just didn't have the strength he once did. He'd still put in a day's work, but near harvest time, he needed extra help.

John would come back in the fall, but the other boys had gone their separate ways. William, the oldest, had moved to Centralia; Albert to Montesano; Fred had a successful logging business in Portland, Oregon; and young Ed, the lazy one, was the only one still at the house. He wasn't counted on to do much of anything.

Fred's thoughts moved quickly to his grandkids, and his wonderful daughter, Minnie.

"I wonder if Mary will ever get married?" he asked himself. "She's 23 now, a pretty girl, responsible. She had that skin problem two years ago, but that seems to be cleared up now. And those twins, William and John. What are they, 16 now? Seems like yesterday that Min had those kids. They're good kids, kind of like John the way they took to the woods life. Lizzie, 21, just stays around the house. She's good the way she helps Min, but she shows little interest in men."

Thinking about his grandkids brought tears of joy to the old man's eyes. He often thought of them when he was in the field.

He was much closer to the riverbank now and could see it clearly. The doe and her fawn scrambled up the bank, and then stopped suddenly as if startled.

"Must be a cougar or bear up there," the old man thought. "Nah, too hot for them. They'd be in the shade on this day." Quickly, the doe spun around, cocked an ear then cautiously backed down the bank nearer her baby. Then she darted, with the fawn in quick pursuit, into the forest and disappeared.

It seemed like hours the old man sat on that stump in the shade and watched for any movement at the top of the riverbank.

"Could it be John who startled the animals?" he pondered. He knew John would often stop dead still in the forest and observe nature at work. It was his way. Continuing to fix his dark, brown eyes upon the area where he first spotted the doe and her fawn, the old man caught a reflection of something in the sun. The glare hurt his eyes, his heart began to pound.

Dr. French had cautioned him about getting too excited. His blood pressure wasn't good. He tried to be careful. Slowly he tapped four fingers across his chest to calm the beating.

"He's back. I know he's back," the old man said aloud, his eyes fixed on that reflection, though the glare made him turn his eyes away. As he looked up, the old man saw a huge shadow slowly, but surely, emerge from the timbers. John was 6 feet, 2 inches tall and weighed 210 pounds. That frame was most imposing, yet magnified immensely through the shadow of the timbers that bordered the property.

Frederick left the stump, stretched his aching back with both hands on his hips. Sitting on the stump had left him stiff and sore. He twisted his body and grimaced as pain shot up his back. He stood straight up to flex his tiring muscles. That helped some.

"It's him. I'd know that figure anywhere," he said.

He wondered where the boy had been this time — "working up the Wishkah? Hunting in the high country or maybe he was at the beach? He talked about going to Pacific Beach or Kalaloch the last time he was home."

He chuckled, knowing full well his giant son was probably in the high country, perhaps even in the West Olympics, the Sol Duc or Bogachiel, or maybe the Hoh, where he wintered two years ago.

"He'll be home for dinner; I knew he'd be here! I better tell mother," he said almost aloud, slowly walking toward the house.

It had been nearly 20 minutes since he left the stump and headed for the homestead. He walked slowly, hardly noticing the heat in all the excitement of the moment.

He knew Louisa had already started dinner. "Had she added a potato and put more meat on to cook?" he wondered. "Elk steaks. I hope she's fixing elk steaks. That's Johnny's favorite," he said.

Louisa heard the familiar clomping of the heavy boots, which Fritz always removed before entering the house. She often called him Fritz as many of his friends did, particularly after young Freddie had become a man.

She heard him shake the boots against the porch, then leave them outside as she requested. The screen door opened, then closed.

Turning her attention away from the stove she watched her husband shuffle to the drain board and peer into the pot of potatoes she was soaking in preparation for dinner.

"There's plenty, mother."

"He's here?" she asked. "He's here?"

"I'm sure. I saw him at the edge of the forest. It'll be a little bit yet, but he'll be here for dinner, always times it right for dinner, doesn't he mother?"

Fred paced nervously across the room that served as living and dining quarters. He decided to wash up and change clothes before dinner. Mother always liked her men washed and clean before sitting down to a meal.

From the upstairs window, Fred could see John coming from afar.

The Tornows were successful farmers and their homestead reflected it. They had perhaps the finest rutabaga patch in the valley and their apple orchard was plentiful.

To the right of the front door was the large family table, a light oak that Fritz and William built. It was originally quite crude with several seams, but the men sealed those with a glue of sap and pine tar. Several layers of lacquer covered the top giving it a lustrous sheen. They were fortunate to obtain three large slabs of oak free of gnarls and even knots.

Mother covered the table with a linen cloth. A visitor would be unable to tell that this fine piece of work was not purchased at a harbor department store.

The chairs, however, were bought — not from a store, but from a house of prostitution in Aberdeen. A fire had destroyed much of the bordello in 1903, including the main room's table. Fred had been told the chairs were slightly damaged and were for sale. He and the boys took a wagon of crops to town, bought the chairs for $29 and hauled them home. He put a finish on them, and they are like new.

He had earlier purchased other household goods from a man named Colin McKenzie. He had been a successful photographer in Aberdeen, but lost his business in the fire that destroyed his lifestyle and most of downtown Aberdeen. McKenzie almost lost his life, suffering a badly injured back when a wall fell on him.

Fred was always finding bargains like that.

Dad Tornow's favorite relaxing spot was an overstuffed Chesterfield he purchased for $18 from McKenzie. Next to the chair was another crude table, a credenza-like piece. On its surface sat Fred's favorite Meerschaum, a tobacco pouch, and wire cleaners. In the compartment below, the Tornows kept old German newspapers sent to them by friends in the old country or purchased on rare trips to Seattle.

They dearly loved their life in Chehalis County, yet they both had a fondness for the old land, though neither had been back since they left more than 40 years ago. Reading newspapers was their way of keeping abreast of news in Prussia and Germany. Fred, the ever-resourceful one, still found old newspapers provided perfect extra insulation in the shed. He would take several papers, press them together and force them into the openings. It helped keep the shed warmer and the moisture out.

Inside the back porch was a large pantry. Mother generally had every one of the six shelves stocked with preserves, canned fruits and vegetables.

There were five bedrooms in the Tornow home, one downstairs and four upstairs. The parents had a large bedroom with a four-poster bed, a four-drawer bureau and two nightstands. A small wood-burner was in one corner and a sewing table in another.

The other second-story rooms were once one room. Fritz and a neighbor, Gus Maas, remodeled it into two, though in fact, all they did was partition it and install a door when the Tornow boys became too old to share a room.

Unlike many homes of this age, there were two bathrooms, a full facility upstairs, and a commode and wash basin downstairs. The Tornows were one of the first homesteaders to install pressurized water.

The building was in the shape of a "T" and included an outbuilding and a large woodshed where John often slept when the house was full of company. A small Franklin stove helped heat the shed in winter.

The family had six horses, three of which Fritz would alternate on the plow. The barn housed a variety of equipment to maintain the farm's immediate 100 acres — two wagons, one large flat cart to carry hay, a baler, thresher, plow and a small tractor.

Many cedars, firs and hemlocks graced the more than 260 acres of fine timberland that Fritz had purchased. Some old-growth spruce and a few alder were also on the property.

The Tornows had done well in the 26 years they had been in the Satsop. Their farm had made them self-sufficient and provided a substantial bank account.

A large potbellied stove in the center of the front room provided ample heat, even in the chilly, damp winters.

Mother Tornow frequently had all burners occupied with boiled potatoes, fresh greens from the garden, the teapot for tea or coffee and fresh meat from the last hunt ready for supper.

Louisa was well-known throughout the Satsop for her hospitality and fine repasts. Hunters and fishermen alike stopped by to visit and partake of the food on their way to, or on the return from, an outing in the Olympics.

They also had periodic boarders, usually timber cruisers who would stay two or three days while on business in the valley. Louisa knew visitors timed their stop to include a meal. She minded not a whit, cherishing the compliments from her guests after a fulfilling meal. Many of the visitors brought meat or vegetables for her to cook. There was something about the way she seasoned her food that was different, so tasty.

"It's the home-grown garlic and shallots," she confided to Mary Muller, a neighbor who pleaded to know her secret.

Wives and children often stayed at the Tornows while their men were on the hunt.

This was disturbing to John. Even as a youngster, the constant swinging door of visitors was upsetting to him. Since he was 10 and was left with a lisp after the bout with the measles, he was self-conscious about his impediment and retreated to the tranquility of the woods.

Now he was coming home, probably only for two or three months, but Fritz and Louisa were happy each time he returned, no matter how long his stay might be.

Louisa quickly moved to the pantry and from its side panel, retrieved the Krupp steel straight razor and strap. Swiftly she stroked the razor along the leather for an even honing.

Fred brought a mug and ceramic bowl from the upstairs bathroom. Louisa filled it with steaming water and set the soap beside her on the table. She retrieved the scissors from her sewing basket. She was ready for her son. She always shaved him and cut his hair first thing when he returned — if he hadn't stopped at Minnie's first.

She glanced out the window and saw her son carrying fresh salmon.

Quickly, Louisa went to the stove, grabbed the chicken she had ready for cooking and placed it in the cooler for another day.

"We're having salmon tonight, father," she said. "Johnny's bringing it. I see it in his hands. He'll want the salmon."

The family was anxious for their son to return, but John didn't like Louisa to make a fuss. They would try to hide their joy.

Clomp, clomp, clomp. He was here! They listened as John gave a sigh of relief. The long trek was over.

They heard him remove his caulked boots and rap them vigorously against the steps to free the mud and debris.

The door opened. John said not a word; first, sobbing Louisa embraced him, then Fred gave his strapping son a strong squeeze.

No words were necessary. The emotions said it all.

John sat down and Louisa began to shave his black hair. It was still wet. He had stopped at the river to bathe before coming home. Even the hot sun had not dried it. His hair wasn't as long as usual, she knew he had it cut sometime during the last spring. Even the beard was not as long, but she continued to shave it. She liked her boys clean-shaven. Fred, however, had a neatly kempt white beard for years.

It was about 40 minutes before John left the parlor and walked upstairs to change for dinner.

Conversation wasn't lacking at dinner. Father talked about the work at hand and mother informed her son what she knew about the other boys, Minnie and the twins.

"Be sure to see the twins and Minnie. They ask about you often," mother chided her son.

John shoveled in the food, eating three big salmon steaks, two helpings of red potatoes, a pile of fresh spinach and a half a loaf of mother's home-made bread with fresh-churned butter. Warm apple-rhubarb pie completed the meal.

He said nary a word, only smiled and kept shoveling.

Slowly, the gentle giant got up from the table, walked into the sitting room and sat down.

Louisa cleared the table and left the two men to visit.

The old man took a seat in the horsehide chair — John already had claimed the Chesterfield — retrieved his pipe and slipped on his mocs.

"Been to the Olympics?" Fred finally asked his son.

The young man raised his eyes from the fire and turned toward his father. "Yes, papa."

Saying no more, the two men sat savoring each other's company without saying a word.

This would be one of the last times the old man and his son would enjoy such a meeting.

John Tornow, second left, worked at the Rogers logging camp in Shelton.

In 1909 and 1910, John worked at the Mack's Spur logging camp, west of Elma. He is believed to be the sixth man from the right, second row.

9. THE CONFRONTATION

1910

The smell of wet wool hung heavy in the room. It was always musty in the Tornow home with the steady spring rains.

"Grandma, can I warm your tea?" pretty 23-year-old Mary Bauer asked.

"Sure," the old woman said, though clearly not as attentive to her niece as she used to be.

"Mr. Abel? May I warm yours?"

"Why yes, dear. That would be nice," the lawyer answered.

Clearing his throat, Abel was about to continue the same conversation he had been carrying on for the last half-hour. He felt he laid sufficient groundwork and now the woman was weakening.

He expected Louisa Tornow to be putty in his hands now that her husband was gone and her health had deteriorated rapidly. Abel hoped the 72-year-old woman's mind had begun to fade.

The attorney reminded his prey of the beauty of her farm and property, commending her for the diligent work she, her husband and the boys had done over the last 20 years.

"It's a fine farm, fine land," he told her, affirming what she already knew.

Then he struck to the heart of his reason for being there.

"We'll leave the land in as good condition as we found it, Louisa. We'll not disturb you or the animals. I promise the cutting and hauling will be done only in the fall and winter after the crops are in, so as not to disturb the fields."

"You'll have to excuse me a minute, Mr. Abel," the increasingly frail woman said to the lawyer.

"Go right ahead. Take your time. Take all the time you need," he told her.

Walking stick in hand, Mrs. Tornow struggled past the flickering fire and into the parlor.

In her advanced years, she vaguely understood that the attorney was offering her $1,000 cash for the right to haul timber across her land. After all, it wasn't even an offer for the land itself, only the right to haul Schafer's timber across her property in the northeast corner of the section and the lower 200-acre parcel near the East Branch of the Satsop River, where virgin old-growth timber abutted the boundary.

Occasionally, she was part of the timber talk when Fritz was alive; she couldn't understand why Abel would be offering so much for what seemed to her an insignificant deal. She had learned early to question such situations and not make any hasty decisions without discussing it with her family.

Now, she was the family decision-maker.

Her beloved husband passed away last August, and now her health was failing rapidly. Until last year, one hardly knew she was six years older than Fritz. Now her age was beginning to show. Her hair, thinning by the day, was almost white; her eyesight was failing; she needed a cane to get around, though she still did the daily cooking. She would sit in the rocking chair on the front porch, knitting for her beloved grandkids, longing and hoping she would still be around to be a great-grandma.

Minnie's kids grew up so fast. Mary is nearly 24, Lizzie 22, and the twins are almost 18.

Mary had scared her a few weeks ago when she had another flare up of her blood disease. Erysipelas, Dr. French called it. She remembered how terrible Mary had looked this time. Reddish inflammation of her arms and eyes particularly. She thought it strange that the doc cut her arm to release the pressure, then coated the sores with iodine. But it worked and now she is fine.

She also worried about Mary's heart, particularly when she became excited, but it hadn't bothered her since she was a child.

"None of them are interested in marrying." Louisa said to herself, concerned for a moment that she might never be a great-grandma. "Oh, I imagine their day will come," she thought, realizing she had been out of the room for several minutes.

Slowly, she moved back to the sitting room where Edward had joined Mary and the attorney.

"You know, I was here four years ago, and discussed this with your husband," Abel said.

"Yes, I remember when you were here, Mr. Abel. Fred …"

"He didn't give me an answer," the lawyer interrupted, lying to the old woman, hoping she wouldn't recall the conversation, if indeed her husband said anything to her. "Now, it's apparent we would like to harvest some timber with no disturbance to your property. That area is prime for harvest."

Abel watched the interested eyes of the young man who had answered the door four years ago.

"He wants to take it," the lawyer thought to himself, "but he's wise enough not to interfere."

"No, Mr. Abel," she said emphatically. "My answer is no. Frederick didn't want the trees hauled across our land. I remember when you were here before. My husband told me you wanted … what do you call it? An easyman?"

"No, it's an easement," the attorney corrected her.

"Well, whatever. Fred didn't want it to happen, and I know John didn't. It's a lot of money you are offering sir, but I can't do it."

Abel sat stunned at the refusal. He figured the old lady would be easy, particularly since only one son remained at the homestead for any period of time.

"But mama," the youngest Tornow boy interrupted. "I'm sure papa didn't know they would pay money for that."

"Edward, you know papa didn't want that section cut and have timber hauled through there. Some of it would have had to have been cleared. You know he said it was not to be," she answered, chiding her son for suggesting such a notion. "Besides, it's not our decision, it's John's."

"John's? What do you mean?"

"It's John's property now, has been for a year or so," she said, revealing to her youngest son for the first time that he had been cut out of a land inheritance. It was four years ago that Fred made the decision, though only officially made so when paperwork was signed early last year.

"I'm sorry you had to come all this way in this weather, Mr. Abel, but you have my answer. Tell Mr. Schafer if he wants to cut his timber, he'll have to find another way to haul it out. I'll follow the wishes of my husband — may he rest in peace.

"Now I'll hear no more discussion. If you wish to talk to John, I expect him here tomorrow or the day after. But I know what his answer will be."

Abel knew only too well what John's answer would be. It wasn't likely to be any different now than it was four years ago. He remembered all too well when the young man nearly spat on him at the mere suggestion. No need to come back tomorrow.

Raising herself from the chair, the aging woman turned to her son. "Edward, see if Mr. Abel wishes something stronger to drink before he leaves. Now, Mr. Abel, you'll have to excuse me," she said shuffling to the door. "I haven't been well. I must lie down."

"Oh, that's quite all right," he said.

It was Louisa's way. Even in the tensest situation, she managed to hold her composure. She was obviously disturbed with the lawyer's presence and requests, yet she calmly turned him down and left him practically apologizing for his intrusion.

"If you wish to stay and visit, please make yourself at home," she said, turning to enter the bedroom.

"What's with this woman?" he thought. "I think I'll have that drink, if you don't mind, Ed. It's a long way to Montesano and it's getting colder. Make it a bourbon. In fact make it a double, straight."

"I've struck out with the old man. I've struck out with John. I've struck out with the old woman," Abel thought. "But I am not out yet. Maybe I can get to her through this stupid, lazy kid."

He took a couple of sips and began to formulate a plan.

"This might be the most important drink I've ever had," he thought, smiling at the notion of trying to maneuver through this difficult situation by attacking the weakest link.

"Thank you Ed. You are most gracious. Your family has been most gracious through all this," Abel said, continuing his connivance.

"Now, you sit down. Let's talk."

———

The sound of the heavy rain on the shake roof was the only noise as the silent figure watched the flames lick at the cedar logs in the fireplace from his chair across the sitting room.

Rising only to stir the coals or place a split block on the dying embers, John watched his aging mother sitting in her rocker, sewing by the light of the fire.

"That quilt will be warmth for Mary," he thought, "If she ever gets it done."

He watched as his mother's willowy frame bent over her work. Slowly, continuously, she moved the quilt closer to her eyes to examine the intricate pattern work to be sure she hadn't slipped a stitch.

He watched her nod approval that each stitch was in its place, then move on to the next square design.

"She's getting old fast," the lumbering giant thought. "Since papa died, she's just fading." He could feel tears welling up inside. He sniffed to feign his watery eyes.

"Cold dear?" the concerned woman asked.

"No, mama, just a draft. I'll throw another log on the fire."

There was something about John Tornow and his mama. They could sit in the room for hours, not say a word, yet there was an aura of communication with them.

The silence of the afternoon was broken only by intermittent patter of rain and the metronome ticking of the large grandfather clock the boys had given their mama two Christmases past.

She could sense his anger from across the room. He didn't come home much, only once since Fritz passed.

She could not forgive the older boys or Edward for not telling John of his father's passing, or at least trying to find him before the funeral.

More than ever, she wanted John here. The other boys had become estranged to her. She missed them, but tired of their fondness for alcohol and womanizing in the bordellos. Fritz told them repeatedly they weren't welcome in the house if they continued that behavior.

The old man tolerated only so long Edward's lackadaisical attitude toward chores and his succession of failures in get-rich quick schemes. She watched and said nothing as each dead-end venture drained more and more from their bank account. Fred had given hundreds of dollars to him until it nearly divided the loving couple.

She knew she couldn't stop his giving in to Ed just as she knew his requests would not cease.

As Fritz became older, he chose the path of least resistance — ignoring the young profligate to preserve harmony in the family.

Then came the day Fred caught Edward and Mary, his granddaughter, in deep embrace.

"He must go. That's the only answer. He must go," the old man told his wife.

"Yes, Fred. He'll never amount to anything unless he learns responsibility on his own," Mrs. Tornow agreed.

That was almost four years ago, shortly after Abel approached Fritz with the offer for the easement.

Edward packed up and moved to Shoalwater Bay, about 50 miles away on the Pacific Coast. Finally, forced to fend for himself, the youngest Tornow managed. It was slow at first as he labored through several jobs. First it was farming, the only job he knew. Then he worked in a drug store. On his infrequent visits to the homestead he talked of going to school and becoming a pharmacist. This pleased Louisa, but each time the discussion for such a career came up, like so many of his intentions, his interest waned.

When Fritz passed away, Edward asked to move back home and Louisa condescended with the admonition that he must rise early and work hard in the fields or they would be in danger of losing the season's crops.

On the other hand, John was her spark.

She knew he was the one the old man had grown to love the most. He was seemingly tireless in his approach to work. The harder the work, the more he enjoyed it. His continuous devotion to his parents only increased with the years. Father and this son had formed a close bond, almost as tight as mother and son. She had grown accustomed to watching the two work hours on end, side-by-side, despite the obvious antagonism of the other boys. Together, they logged, they cleared the land and then plowed it for planting. She knew it was only John's devotion that kept Fritz going as long as he did. Even on his ailing days, he wanted to accompany John to the fields.

Despite the fact he was only at the homestead periodically, John provided a light for his parents.

"He misses papa deeply," she thought, casually glancing and smiling at the tall figure sitting in his father's old chair, Fred's Meerschaum still sitting untouched on the adjacent table. "Fritz was right to leave him this place and that property. John, more than any of the boys, has been responsible for making this home what it is," she continued in her thoughts. "I know Edward will be hurt when he sees the will after I die, but John deserves it."

Fred gave up on them years ago. The other boys only wanted to do the logging and rarely helped with the other chores. "They chose that road and left home early, and they are doing well by it, but they don't need the land or this place," Fred told his wife.

"Only John was there," Louisa thought. "I can always count on him. He wasn't here year-round, but he was always here for the planting and harvesting. And all the neighbors liked John, always asked about him when I went to market. Still, Edward will be hurt. Maybe I'll have that attorney ... what's his name? Nelson? Yeah. He used to work for Abel, but left in a row. Couldn't get along with that shyster. Maybe, I'll leave one of the bank accounts to him. He won't care about the land, anyway, just the cash."

Being alone, sent her mind to racing.

———

She must have been in thought for several minutes when Edward entered the room.

"She's all moved in mama. She's upstairs resting, doesn't feel good today," Edward said just above a whisper.

Mrs. Tornow rose from her chair, her eyes fixed on the steel glare of her son, John.

The big man slowly stood and bent down, his face merely inches from his younger brother's nose.

"If papa was here now, he'd kill you. You know that, don't you Edward. Now that he's gone, maybe I'll have to do it for him."

"Johnny, what are you talking about?"

"You know damn well what I am talking about. Mary."

"It's best for everybody," Ed answered.

"Yeah, best for you," the big man snorted.

"Johnny, you're never here. Mama needs help and this way Mary can help her. She's happy about it, so's mama. I don't know what your problem is."

"That's not why she's here and you know it," John snapped, standing as his mother re-entered the room.

He knelt beside his aging mama, now sitting in her rocker. Louisa placed her hands in John's huge grasp. "It'll be OK. Mary will be a big help to me, and besides, she isn't happy at home. Henry is always griping about her coming here."

"Mama, I can't watch this," he said, leaning forward and kissing her forehead tenderly, while cupping his huge hands around her chin.

He headed toward the door, brushing past his brother and almost knocking him over.

"G-ggggoddddamn, it's cold," John stammered to himself, his stuttering magnified by the intensity of the situation.

He slammed the front door and took off in a brisk trot. Louisa watched her giant son lumber off, Cougar, his trusty, but aging, lab in close pursuit. She knew his anger was building.

When he loped off in such fashion, she was glad he was out there and not in the house. This was one way he quieted down. She knew he would be calmer when he returned.

"I have the mind to kill the bastard," John thought. "Moving her into the house … how could he? How dare he?"

Pacing around the front section, he tried not to think of the situation, hoping to put his anger aside. He was gone nearly a half-hour before returning to the farm house.

He entered from the rear and peered into the room where he knew Mary had stayed since her early years when she came to visit.

The length of her stays had often grown into weeks. She liked it here and was a constant companion for her grandmother. Henry Bauer rarely visited and was jealous that his family spent so much time away.

John had not given it much attention — the confrontation his father and Edward had four years ago — until now, and it was all coming back.

John had wondered incredulously why Edward, seemingly not sick, was in bed that day when he had returned from the spring planting.

Louisa had been strangely silent, and offered only that Edward and "your dad had a bitter argument. He thrashed him seriously."

John knew of his father's stern demeanor and often stubborn resolve, but he had never witnessed the old man losing control.

Edward, likewise, refused to discuss the confrontation or tell what precipitated the beating.

He did show the bruises to his brother and the severity of the beating was a shock to John. He had never known his father to raise a hand to the other brothers or his sister.

When agitated, Fred's calm voice would normally generate intensity. That, and the glare of his ice-blue eyes were usually sufficient to mandate obedience.

Taking a seat on the bunk in the small room, John remembered another frightening incident his father told him.

It was a hot spring day when he and the old man were planting feed corn in the western field bordering the Satsop.

Fritz wandered up to his son, took a deep drink of water and said, "I did it because of her, you know."

John stopped plowing, and looked up quizzically.

"It's not natural, John. She's too young and too innocent. Edward knows better. It's not natural for an uncle to lust for a niece. It's not right," the old man continued as disbelief gripped his son.

"It would kill your mother if I made him leave, but I'll have no more of it. You best tell him. It'll be worse next time, if I catch him alone with her again."

Edward and Mary weren't together much for the next few months, until late fall when John had left.

John had wondered how it happened that Edward finally left home. Then one day as he was working in the field just before Fred died, his father told him the incidents of that fateful day.

"Mama and I were going to go to Matlock for a potluck with some logging families. Edward said he was going fishing and we left Mary alone in the house. We asked if she wanted to go, but she said she was tired and would rather rest. She helped us load the wagon and bade us goodbye. We were leaving early to enjoy a leisurely drive. Edward left just before we did. About five minutes up the road, I remembered I forgot my pipe. Mama said to forget it for one day, but I said we left early and it would only take a minute. How wrong I was.

"I turned the team around and headed back. When I got to the house, I noticed that the barn door was open, so I walked over to shut it. When I got there, I heard Ed's voice and then I saw them. He was on top of her. I was overcome with anger. I reached over and grabbed a shovel and lit out after him. She ran buck-naked screaming into the corner. Edward just laid there. I raised that shovel and let him have it in the back. I didn't hit him real hard, but hard enough to crack his ribs. He got up and tried to get away, but I tripped him and was going to bust him in the face with my fist."

"No grandpa. Stop, stop," she screamed.

"I thought better of it. I was on top of Edward, and John, I could have killed him! I don't to this day know why I didn't hit him again? Mary, I guess. I suddenly came to my senses. 'If I ever catch you with her again, I'll kill you,' I told him … and John, I really meant it. I told him I wanted him out of the house by nightfall and I let him up. He ran out of the barn. I don't know how mama didn't hear the commotion, but she didn't. Mary was trembling so. I approached her and I cradled her shaking body. 'Let's get your clothes back on dear,' I told her. I just sat there for a minute and turned my back as she dressed.

"Did he, did Edward …"

'No, grandpa,' she interrupted before I finished the obvious question. I think it best that you go home now. I can drive you if you like."

Fred continued with his description of the event: "I just told mama, 'Edward is leaving and I am taking Mary home. We'll be late for the potluck, probably spend the night at the Schaletzkes.' She never said another word about it."

Until then, John hadn't realized how deceitful his younger brother had been.

"Mary was like a sister to us," he remembered, what with her fair complexion, light hair and slender willowy figure, she so resembled her mother. "How lucky a man would be to wed such a pretty young girl."

He was dumbstruck by his own ignorance, recalling how over the years his younger brother and niece had grown so close. He never thought it strange that they were always together, or that Edward was the one to offer to drive her home in the wagon after she had spent the day or the night.

"Sometimes he would even walk her home. I should have thought that strange behavior for Ed," John surmised.

That day he understood why she was still single and remained without suitors.

The next time John saw Edward, he challenged him with his father's accusations.

He didn't believe for a minute when his younger brother said his father was wrong and had merely happened upon an innocent peck on the cheek, and his father would not listen to any explanation.

He had heard the words of his brother that day, yet in his heart, he knew there was a lie in those eyes and on those lips.

Seeking reconciliation between Edward and his father, John cautioned against him ever being alone with her again.

John knew in his heart he was right and the old man's actions seemed vindicated when Mary failed to spend any nights at the homestead that summer with Edward gone.

But when the old man died, Edward jumped at the opportunity to move back in, planning all along to move Mary in as a "permanent housekeeper."

This didn't set well with Mary's father either. Minnie seemed to be shielded from the situation, but not Henry.

He felt there was something strange about the goings on from the beginning. If he had his way, Mary would not frequent the Tornows, except at family gatherings.

But Minnie condescended to her helping at the family home as often as possible.

"Mama needs help with the chores," she would say, trying to appease her husband.

"With all those strong boys in the family, she shouldn't need any help at all. One of them should be there helping. And, Edward? They don't make him do anything." Henry would say. "It's not good for Mary to be around there that often."

Once, when Mary stayed at the Tornow home for several days at a time, Henry told Minnie "I am going to go get her and she's not going back there."

He wasn't successful. Mary enjoyed the Tornows' company and simply told her father, "I'm old enough. I'll come home when I am ready."

And now she's living here," John thought as his mind vividly returned to the present. "He's moved her right in.

"I'm leaving in the morning. I'm going to take that job in Elma at Mack's Spur. I'll be gone before they get up."

10. LIFE ON THE WYNOOCHE

1910

"Willie, Johnny. C'mon in. I am glad you boys are here. You are getting so big. I don't see you very often, anymore."

"Mom sent us here to see how you were doing, and check on Mary. She worries about you two so much. Actually, dad wanted us to try to bring Mary home with us, but we doubt she will come. She and dad had that big row and we rarely see her."

"Well, she's getting fat and sassy, my cooking you know," the old woman told her grandkids, without letting on she thought the girl might be pregnant.

"Would you help grandma with the milking? My legs are bothering me so. John hasn't been here for a couple of weeks and Lord only knows where Edward is.

"Sure, grandma, we'll do that, I already noticed she was ready for milking."

"Take Mary with you. It will do her good to get out with you kids. I think she's in her room."

"Mary, you in there?" William shouted at the door after getting no response from his knock.

"No, I'm over here," she said, the voice coming from the bathroom at the other end of the narrow upstairs hall. "I'm not feeling well. I'll be out in a minute."

"We'll wait downstairs for you," he answered.

It was several minutes, perhaps twenty before Mary slowly walked downstairs, hair disheveled, dressed in a loose-fitting gown to hide her condition. Hands clasped around her tummy, Mary looked nothing like the attractive sister the boys had known so well.

"Mary, what happened?" Johnny asked, rising to help his sister down the final two steps.

"Like I said, I'm not feeling well. Spent all morning in the toilet, first one end, then the other. I hope I get over this soon. I'm not much help to grandma this way."

"Where's Edward?" William asked.

"Haven't seen him today, but I haven't been anywhere except my bedroom and the pot.

"We were waiting for you to help us with the milking, but I can see you are not up to anything like that."

"How's mama?" she asked.

"Fine, but she misses you so much," Johnny answered.

"She doesn't come around much anymore. I miss her too."

"It's because of him, you know."

"Who? What?"

"Mary, you know what I'm talking about. Papa gets so mad. Rather than fight, mama just stays home, unless he's gonna be gone a while," William answered. "Yeah, and since we finished clearing that north section, he's home all the time now."

"Don't tell mama I've been sick. She'll just worry. It's not bad, just uncomfortable. I'm sure I'll be fine in a couple of days. Now best you boys get out there and squeeze some teats before she explodes."

"Yeah, and while you're doing that I'll put on a mess of chicken for us," Louisa said as they left.

"None for me, grandma., don't feel like eating. I'm going back to bed."

The old woman watched Mary slowly trudge up the stairs and the boys amble down the path toward the barn to pick up the milking stools and pails.

Louisa picked up her knitting bag and retreated to her favorite rocker, dragging it to the front porch to take in some of the early morning, late-summer sunshine.

"She's spending a lot of time in the bathroom, particularly in the morning. I think it's more than just an upset stomach," Louisa thought. "Her tummy's starting to show and those breasts … she is starting to look like her mama. Never had much 'til now. If she is not pregnant, I'm not Grandma Tornow," she said chuckling to herself and managing a slight smile. "Great-grandma. I'm going to be a great-grandma, finally."

A tear began to form at that thought. "I'll just nod off a bit while the boys are gone before I have to go stoke the fire and get the chicken frying." she drifted off in her rocker.

"Mary didn't look well, did she Willie?" Johnny asked his twin. "Did you see her tits? They were huge! Even in that gown, they stuck out."

"Johnny, shame on you, talking about our sister that way; yeah, mama was right; she's got to be pregnant, but she doesn't look happy about it. 'Cept those boobs. I remember her crying to mama because she didn't have any. She was so self-conscious about that. Well, man she's got some now."

"Willie? Ya think it's Uncle Eddie's?"

"Who else?"

"It's just that they've always denied there was anything going on."

"Yeah, I know, but ever since that day when grandpa brought her home and Uncle Eddie left home I sure wondered. She didn't go back there 'cept with mama and us that summer."

"That's right. Then when grandpa died, he moved back in, and I know they spent a lot of time together in Aberdeen. I don't think grandma knew much about that. Uncle John sure did, though. He knew there was something happening, but said Uncle Eddie denied it to him, too.

"Yeah, Uncle John told me about the thrashing grandpa gave him one time when he caught them. Always denied that ever happened, but Uncle John said he saw the bruises."

"I guess what makes me think it's his is what happened this spring. She had always taken the small room on the first floor, but when she moved in there to take care of grandma this time, she took an upstairs bedroom, right next to Uncle Eddie's."

"Yeah, you're right, Willie. But remember, too, that grandma couldn't go up and down the stairs no more with that hip. She had to move to the downstairs bedroom."

"That's right, I forgot that. Your pail full, Johnny?"

"Yeah, yours?"

"No, but she's done."

"Good, I'm getting hungry. Can already taste that chicken."

The boys headed toward the house and saw smoke coming from the cook stove. It meant grandma was getting the food ready. Mrs. Tornow was never one to prepare chicken or other meat just for supper. It was often a breakfast staple, as it was this day.

When the morning chores were done, it was time for breakfast, and for the Tornow family that often meant the biggest meal of the day.

It could be chicken, biscuits and gravy, rabbit, or even elk. Of course, bacon or a side of pork — chops, steak or ham — along with eggs, were also served. Whatever was on the table was at the whim of Louisa.

"Why don't we go and see if we can find Uncle John? Haven't seen him in a while. We can spend a couple of days with him up there. He'll probably have some elk, always does."

"Sounds like a plan … after we eat. Can't miss grandma's chicken."

———

The milking done and their bellies full of pan-fried chicken, biscuits and gravy, like only Grandma Tornow could make, the boys arrived home before noon.

"Think he's at his usual lean-to up the Wynooche by the Oxbow?" Mrs. Bauer asked her boys when they told her they were going to look for Uncle John.

"Probably," Johnny answered. "Grandma said he came back from Elma the other day and then left, saying only he was going into the woods."

"That's likely where he is," Minnie said. "Talked to Mrs. Oien yesterday and she said she saw him go by their place. That's on the way, didn't stop though. She hollered at him and waved, but John didn't respond. Probably didn't hear her."

"We best get going, mama. Likely take us best part of the afternoon to get there. Don't worry, it's a warm day," William said.

"Yeah, it'll be fun. Maybe shoot us an elk, or maybe even a bear," Johnny added.

"Oh, don't be silly Johnny," his mother said. "Now you boys better git, and take care. Best be back by Monday. I think your father has some clearing he wants you to help with. Tell John to come by here on his next trip home. Probably time to cut his hair."

"OK, bye," the boys said in unison.

"Oh, mama, by the way, I think you're right about Mary," William said, grabbing Johnny by the shirt and hustling out the door. They took off in a trot around the back of the house and started across the field before Minnie had realized what the boys meant.

"Willie, Johnny. Get back here," she shouted.

It was too late. They were out of sight.

"That was mean, Willie, telling mama like that. She's gonna be worried the whole time we're gone."

"Yeah, it probably was, but I didn't want to talk about it then. We'd like to never got out of there."

"We'll have to face her when we get back, but let's have a good time now."

———

"Any of you guys seen John Tornow?" William asked a group of men who were logging off the West Boundary Road.

"Couple of days ago he bounded through here," answered one of the Brehmeier boys.

"It wasn't couple of days ago," another shot back. "Jus' yesterday."

"Good," Johnny replied. "Say where he was going?"

"Nah, but it's probably a good bet he's up at the Oxbow. Spends a lot of time up there. You know, he's sure got the good life. Doesn't have to work unless he wants to, and if you like to be alone with nature, he's got it made."

"Yeah, I know what you mean," said William. "We're trying to find him. Gonna spend a day or two out there with him. We used to do that a lot in summer times, but we've been working more on dad's place lately, or log camps."

"Well, Willie we better get going if we are going to make it by dinner time."

"Johnny, you're always thinking about eatin'. That's all you do."

"Don't either, but you know how good Uncle John's elk is. He sure knows how to fix it, says something about using cedar chips to give it that good taste; nobody smokes it like he can; best jerky around. I saw Cy Blackwell the other day, and he was trying to find Uncle John just to get some jerky from him. When a guy comes all the way from the Wishkah just to get jerky, it's gotta be good stuff."

John Tornow was well known throughout the Upper Satsop. Everybody knew the gentle giant, as he was called for his smooth, even disposition and mammoth stature — unless you got him riled.

"He'd give you the shirt off his back, if you needed it or take yours from you, if you crossed him," Ed Schaletzke, a Tornow neighbor, once said when asked what he thought of the big man.

"Let's pick some salmonberries," Johnny said. "Or huckleberries," the other twin answered. "That big patch is just around the bend."

"They sure are flavorful this time of year, aren't they Willie?"

"Yeah, but we best not waste any more time. You know Uncle John. He waits for nobody when it's dinner time."

The boys turned up the last stretch of trail and past the final logging camp.

"Just a little bit more now. It's kind of like a hideout. You gotta know where you are going, or you'd never find this place, but that's the way Uncle John wants it."

"Uncle John! Uncle John! It's us, Willie and Johnny. Are you here?"

There was no answer.

"Uncle John? It's the twins. Are you here?" they called out again, sloshing through the last bit of marsh before approaching the long log they needed to cross to get to the wickiup.

The log was suspended in the pond that this time of year had only a trickle of water, but in winter and spring months was full.

Still no answer.

"I don't think he's here."

"Maybe not, Johnny, but let's go on across and see if we can tell if he's been here recently."

With caulked boots, the walk across the log was a snap, but neither boy wore them on this day. John Tornow was never without them.

"It's very slick. Watch yourself," William called out.

"It's probably just as easy this time of year to walk through the marsh."

"Yeah, if you want to get all muddy," Johnny answered. "Nobody here."

"Nope," William said, "but I don't think he's gone far. He'd never leave without putting the fire all the way out, and these embers are still warm. Probably went to the Wynooche to catch a fish. Let's just lie down here and relax. I'm worn out after that long hike."

"Me too," said Johnny. "We made pretty good time though, even stopping to talk to those guys and picking them berries. Glad we got some berries. It might be a while before we eat."

"There you go again, always thinking about eating."

The boys pulled out the light canvas groundcovers they had packed and laid them on the dirt. Within seconds of lying down, they both fell sound asleep.

It had been a couple of hours when William woke up hearing a rustling outside and nudged Johnny.

"What? Why did you wake me up?" the other twin said, not noticing that Johnny's finger was across his lips, urging him not to make a sound.

"Someone's coming," he said in a whisper.

Just then, the big man bounded around the corner of the wickiup, his rifle drawn as he approached the entrance.

"What are you?" … he started to say to the intruders when he noticed it was the twins.

"Geez, Uncle John ya scared the shit out of me." Johnny said.

"Yeah," added William.

"Well, you scared the shit out of me too. I saw the footprints, and you know I don't like just anybody being here. I'm glad it's you guys. Sorry if I frightened ya. Can't be too careful up here, you know."

"What's for dinner?" Johnny chimed in, changing the subject to his favorite.

"You know, Uncle John. That's all that kid has talked about since we left. Food."

"Elk OK with you guys?"

"OK? We were hoping you were preparing that."

"Me, preparing? I think I'll let you guys do it. You just had a nap and I'm tired. Got this mess of fish we'll have to eat up for breakfast. How long you guys up here, anyway?"

"Gotta be back Monday morning, so we'll leave Sunday sometime, if you don't mind us tagging along with you for a couple of days," William answered.

"Johnny, go out and get the steaks. The meat is hanging on the line in that burlap sack about 50 yards to your left. Remember, up here ya gotta hang everything up, out of the bears' reach. Had one here day before yesterday, and it damn near was big enough to reach it. I sat right here and watched the old sow. Boy, was she mad. She wanted that meat — bad. She swatted at it and swatted at it, then stomped her feet and stormed off, just like a kid when he didn't get his way."

———

"Those cedar chips make a difference, don't they Willie?" said the uncle after they had chowed down several strips of elk, wild chard and some little wild blackberries, plentiful throughout the Wynooche Valley.

"Yeah, brother. You did a good job," Willie said.

"You guys seen your grandma lately?" the big man asked.

"Today. We were over there today, helped with the milkin' this morning before we came up here," William answered.

"How is she?"

"Didn't look too good. Been hobbled with that hip. Couldn't get out to do the milking."

"How about Mary? Or Edward? Couldn't they help?"

"Mary was awful sick and I don't know where Edward was. Wasn't home though."

"Uncle John? When's the last time you saw Mary?"

"Just a few days ago. She didn't look too good, been throwing up a lot."

"Notice anything else about her?"

"Whadya mean?" the uncle asked.

"I mean how did she look to you? Did she look fat?"

"What you trying to say Willie?" Are you saying she's ... ?"

"Can't say for sure, but I wouldn't bet against it. Got all the signs."

"Ya think she's been with Edward again? I knew that would happen if she moved in there. I told mama I didn't think it was a good idea. She said Mary would be such a help. She thinks so much of that girl, and I do too."

The big man sat in silence reflecting on the previous conversation for several minutes.

"Hey, Uncle John, what we gonna do tomorrow?" Johnny asked.

"I don't know. We'll decide that tomorrow. That's one thing about being out here by myself. I answer to no one, and I have no time schedule. I do what I want, when I want. One thing I gotta do pretty soon is find myself an older elk. Gotta go up a bit for them. The older ones have a thicker skin and I don't have to tan it as long for a good winter coat. Course all I do is skin it, hang it out to dry, put some gun oil on it, dry it some more and then tie a rope around it. Can't beat it for warmth. Ya learn these things being out here after a while. Ya gotta to survive."

"Uncle John, you're pretty smart, aren't you?" asked Johnny. "I told those guys that make fun of you that you are smarter than they are. Just because you don't have the book learnin' that some of them have, doesn't mean you're not smart. Bet none of them know the things you do about woods livin'."

"Oh, pay them no never mind. Don't matter to me what they say, as long as they leave me alone," Uncle John said. "Hey, wait until morning and I'll show you my watchdogs."

"Watchdog? I thought Cougar was your watchdog? asked Johnny. "And he's still at grandma's, isn't he?"

"Yeah, Cougar is at grandma's, getting too old to travel up here with me. But that's not what I'm talking about. You'll see tomorrow. I've got a little bit of blackberry brandy here. Cy Blackwell gave it to me. Gotta learn how to make this stuff. It's the only liquor I touch, and just a bit at that. Only need a short snort and it'll warm you up. Take a little nip and let's hit the sack."

The boys each took a swig from the flask, then laid down and were out immediately.

"Good kids," the uncle said to himself. "God, they're good kids."

———

The smell of fresh fish frying in the pan and the crackling of the fire woke the boys. The warm sun peaked through the dense forest, striking William square in the eyes.

"'About time you got up. Been up for hours," the big man said, his frame blocking out the heat of the fire.

"Boy, I slept good," said William, now huddled about the fire. "Must have been that brandy."

"Johnny, get out of the sack. Time to get up," the uncle called.

"What time you think it is, Uncle John?"

"Well, you oughta be able to figure it out. See where the sun is?"

"Oh, yeah, I remember that from school," said William. "Let's see, if it's straight overhead, then it's high noon. Right?"

"Yeah. That's right. So what time do you think it is?"

"Well, can't be much more than 7 or 8, don't you think?"

"I'd say that's close enough."

"That fish 'bout ready?"

"Yes, it is. Get your brother out of there."

The boy reached over and picked up a stick and lofted it in the direction of Johnny, still sacked out.

It struck him on the side of the head and he bounded to his feet immediately.

"What the hell?"

"Oops, sorry. Didn't mean to hit you on the head," William said with a snicker. "Time to eat."

"Yeah, well, I'll get you back, just wait. Did you say time to eat? What's cookin'?"

"Uncle's frying fish and I don't know what else."

"Potatoes and onions. Can't have fish without potatoes and onions. Stopped by Kuhnles and they gave me a big sack. Had some roastin' ears in it too, but I ate them the last two days."

"Trout? Uncle John."

"Yeah. Wanted to get some steelhead, but lost the only one I had on. It's a little early for them, but we may get lucky later on, if you guys want to go to the Wynooche."

"Sounds great," the boys answered.

"Gonna have to eat out of this pan, though. I don't have anything else. Got a pretty good mess of these little guys, but there's one big one, can't even fit him in the pan."

"We got some flat pans in our sack that we used at the logging site last month," said Johnny. "That'll work."

"Better chow down good. Never know when your next meal will be up here," the big man chided the boys.

When they finished eating all the fish and potatoes, not a scrap left, Johnny picked up pans and utensils and walked to the pond to wash them. Meanwhile William straightened up the camp and put the groundcovers away.

Uncle John always liked to have a neat camp. Told the boys he wanted it kept that way. They knew he meant business and complied with his wishes.

"How about the watchdog, Uncle John?" William asked.

"Yeah, you were going to show us your watchdog," Johnny reminded him.

"Sure, I'll do that, and then we'll go see if we can find some steelies.

"See those elk hairs hanging over there on the side of the lean-to. Well, pick up a couple of the strands and follow me."

The boys walked out, following their uncle to the big log across the pond.

"What's this all about Johnny?" asked Willie.

"Beats me," the other brother said.

"You'll see in a minute," the uncle answered.

"Hear those frogs. They're everywhere. Now reach down and grab me a couple of them. Big ones are better."

"How's this, Uncle John?"

"That's a fine one. Now you grab one Johnny. Willie take these elk hairs and tie several of them together so they're about three feet long. Make a loop on one end and hook it around the frog's back legs. Johnny, you got yours ready?"

"Yeah just about. Now what do we do?"

"You take the other end of the hairs, tie them around this log, so the frog can move about on the top, but not get in the water. It's pretty easy now because there isn't much water in the pond. It's a little trickier in the winter and spring when there's a lot of water. Now, before you tie it, Johnny you walk across the log to the other side and stay there until I tell you to come back. OK, Willie got yours tied around the log? Go on tie both of them."

"Johnny? Hear that. It's real quiet. The frogs stopped croaking. Now start across the log and see what happens."

"My God. Such a racket," the twin said. Soon as he stepped on the log and sent it moving with the water, the frogs went crazy with unceasing croaking.

"Pretty clever huh? Them's my watchdogs. Ain't nobody gonna sneak up on me. Course there's only one way in to the wickiup too. Always built them that way, can't be too careful."

"That's the cleverest thing I've ever heard of," the boys said almost in unison. "That doesn't hurt 'em does it?" Johnny asked with obvious concern.

"Nah. They just can't go too far that's all. C'mon let's get outta here and find some fish."

11. THE FUNERAL

November 1910

Entering the warm, but cozy front room, Minnie Bauer approached her daughter.

"Won't you come home? Please Mary? Your father and I want you to come home."

"You know that's not true mama. You may want me to come, but papa? He told me to rot in hell last time he was here. You heard him. It wouldn't work, wouldn't work at all. Besides, grandma needs me here."

"Honey, he's mellowed a bit now. Even said he missed you the other day. Yeah, he was pretty mad the last time, but can you blame him? What a way to find out his daughter's pregnant, and by your own uncle! The least you could do was tell us first. But to hear it from a neighbor, that really hurt him, dear."

"Sorry, mama. But it wasn't my fault."

"Not your fault? Of course, it was your fault to get in that situation."

"No, that's not what I meant. I meant it wasn't my fault that papa found out the way he did. I didn't know for sure, and I wasn't going to say anything. I was ashamed anyway. Then Mr. Maas saw me at Dr. French's. The doctor didn't know I didn't want to say anything right away. He proudly put his arm around me and said 'this little girl's going to have a baby.' It was too late to do anything. What's said is said. But they don't know who the father is, and I am going to keep it that way. Besides, I'm not sure."

"What? Mary? But I thought …"

"I know what you thought and that's what everybody thinks. But I'm not so sure. Edward doesn't even know I'm pregnant and I'm not saying anything until I start to show."

"You mean there were others?"

"Well, yeah. Eddie and I went to Aberdeen for a dance in June or July. I don't remember. We were drinking and he got mad at me for something. I think another guy asked me to dance. You know how possessive Edward can be. Well, he said he was going to leave and go somewhere else. He'd pick me up later. I was really upset, and I told him to get lost. I'd find another way home, somehow. We were with some friends and I felt I'd be fine. I was drinking a lot, and hadn't drunk much lately. It really affected me and one thing led to another.

"This guy was real nice and said he would be glad to give me a ride home, but couldn't do it until the next day. I really fell for it, and the next thing I knew we were in bed. I woke up early in the morning and felt terrible. Got dressed and went down to Emma's — Emma Kaatz, you remember her, don't you?"

"Sure, nice woman," said Mrs. Bauer.

"She understood and arranged for a friend to give me a ride home. On the way home, he told me about me a doctor in Aberdeen who could take care of me, if I was pregnant and if that's what I wanted. I never told Edward about it, and I won't."

"Was that the only other time?" Minnie continued to probe.

"No. One other time, but I don't want to talk about it because you know him."

"What?" Minnie said of the stunning revelation of her promiscuous daughter.

"He's a timber cruiser, stayed here for a week. I really thought he loved me. We wrote letters for a month or so, and then I didn't hear anything from him. I wrote again and his letter was returned."

"Is that all. Have you told me everything?"

"Yes, mama. That's all. Oh, mama, I'm so sorry. I just don't know what to do."

"What's Edward going to do?" Minnie asked.

"He said he would take care of me, but I don't know what I want to do. I won't marry him, of course. He said we could get married and move away so nobody would know. That's not the type of life I want mama. I just don't think I want to have a baby right now, not here. Grandma's getting worse. I really don't think she's going to be with us much longer. Doc's got her all doped up for that hip, and now she's got pneumonia. He's real worried. He told me he finally got word to the boys and they're all coming. Just hope they get here in time. It will be good to see them all again. Haven't seen them since grandpa's funeral, and then they weren't here very long. Seems we only get together at funerals, not much of a family anymore."

"She's asking for you John," the good doctor said, motioning the big man to come to the back bedroom.

"She's getting weaker. I don't think it will be much longer, perhaps tonight."

John arrived the day before after spending the past three months in Elma on a logging operation near Happy Hollow. He hadn't received word of his mother's ailing health, but something told him to head home right away.

"Can't explain it," he told Minnie upon his timely arrival. "It was a feeling, I just knew I had to get home and do it quickly. They were nice to let me go, but I woulda come anyway."

Gathered in the front room were the somber family — Minnie, her daughters, Mary and Elizabeth, her twin sons, William and John, and John Tornow's youngest brother Edward. Two other brothers, Bill and Albert were en route, Bill, from Centralia, and Albert from Montesano.

They were still awaiting word from Fred, who was expected to leave Portland any day. John doubted he would be here in time.

"Mama," the big man said, gently clasping his huge hands around hers. "Are you in pain?"

"No, son. Doc French has seen to that. I told him I didn't want to suffer, just ease the pain. Are the other boys here yet?"

"Not yet, but we expect Albert and Bill any minute. Don't know about Fred. You rest now, mama. I'll be right here, if you need anything."

"Johnny, it's all yours now, you know. You take good care of it. I know you will."

"What mama?"

"That land up yonder, it's all going to you. That land is all yours, but this homestead you'll split up equally. The older boys, they have their own places, their own lives. Never see much of them, anyway. You and papa worked hard to get this place looking nice. You always came back for harvest, and when a clearing was needed, you always helped. You deserve it."

"But mama, what will the other boys say? How about Edward?"

"Edward, well, you know Edward. I know he wouldn't take care of it like you would. I left him some money in an account at Montesano. There's some for all you boys, and I already gave Minnie her share. She has been so helpful, and Mary too."

"Edward was supposed to have logged that parcel and we were to split that money," said John. "Never saw any of it, though mama. I'll talk to him about it."

"Best you rest now. I'll send doc back in. I hope the boys get here soon."

"Johnny, you're a good boy, a fine young man. You live a different life than others, but that's OK. You're happy, aren't you?"

"Oh, yes, mama. I like the time I spend here with you. Now don't take this wrong, but it's nothing like being in the woods. If I had my way, I'd build a little cabin out there and just stay there. I'm close to nature. Maybe I can do that more now. Course I'll still have to come to Min's and get my hair cut, needs it now."

John could see his mama drifting off and he stood to leave, unclasping his hands from hers.

But she wouldn't let him go, tightening her hand around his with a squeeze that must have taken every bit of energy she had left.

"John, my big John. I love you. I'm going to sleep now."

"Love you too, mama, so very much."

Those were the last words the two spoke to each other. She never woke from her sleep.

———

"Did she suffer?" the young man asked his brother. "No Albert. Not much over the last couple of months. After she fell and broke her hip again last summer, she was in a lot of pain, but Doc French gave her some medication to ease that. When she got pneumonia two weeks ago, she didn't have any fight left in her. Just wish you guys had gotten here a little earlier to say goodbye. She was hoping for that too, but she couldn't hold out any longer. Her old body just surrendered."

"Tell me how it was," Bill asked.

"We were just talking. I was telling her how much I love to be in the woods. One of the last things I said to her was that I needed to have Min give me a haircut like she always does. She grabbed my hand, gave it a squeeze and said she loved me. That was it. She went to sleep and never woke up."

"Wonderful, I'm just glad she died peacefully. Wish we could have spent more time here, but couldn't get away last year," Bill said.

"Yeah, me too," added Albert. "Hey, I hear a wagon. Bet it's Fred. Been a year since I've seen him. The last time was at papa's funeral."

"Am I in time? Is she still here?" the eldest of the Tornow boys asked when greeted at the stoop.

"No, Fred. She left us this morning. Went to sleep and never woke up," said John. "Doc French said she was gone when he checked on her about 6. He stayed here last night and has stayed several nights. Not any docs like him around anymore."

"I loved her. I really did," Fred said, sobbing uncontrollably. "I'll miss her. If I had only been around to get the message when it first arrived from the courier, I might have gotten here in time, but I was out in the woods. Didn't get back 'til the next day."

"That's OK. Albert and Bill didn't get here until just a couple hours ago."

"I would have been here earlier, but the message I got didn't indicate that much urgency. Mama's been sick before and gotten over it," said Albert.

"The thing is we are all together now," said John. "Seems like only funerals can get us together like this. We should be more of a family."

"Where's Eddie?" Fred asked.

"Up with Mary, I suspect," John answered.

"Mary?" queried Fred. "Who's Mary? Don't tell me my little brother went and got himself hitched."

"Not exactly," said John. "It's Mary, Min's oldest."

"What are you trying to tell us?" he asked.

"What I am trying to say is that Edward went and got himself in a whole lot of trouble, and ain't nobody gonna bail him out of this one."

"Are you saying what I think you're saying?" asked Bill almost in unison with Fred.

"Yep, he went and done it to her. She's probably four months along now," said John. "He still denies it and Mary won't say, but everybody believes it's his."

"How did mama ever put up with that? Papa kicked him out when he caught them. What was that, four years ago? She was just a kid then, 17, 18?"

"No. 20," answered John.

"Really, Mary's that old?" asked Bill, disbelieving that his little niece, the little girl he used to bounce on his knee and to whom he sang nursery rhymes, could possibly be that old.

"Well, I guess she's old enough to know better then," said Fred.

"What I heard, is that he took advantage of her," said Albert. "Moved her in as a house maid after papa died to help mama. Moved her right upstairs next to his room. With mama's bad hip she couldn't get up the stairs and keep an eye on them."

"Ya got it right Al," said John. "And I can't forgive him for that. He's never done a lick of work around this place, owes us all some money for the logged-off section that papa gave us. Never saw a penny of it."

"How about Min? Couldn't she keep Mary at home?" Fred asked.

"She tried, but Mary preferred it here," John answered. "Can't blame her too much for that after the row Henry and Edward had earlier. Henry tried to get her to come home a couple of times, but was always likkered up and she wouldn't go. He and Edward had it out one day, and he just told her to rot in hell. Never saw him after that. Not much of Min either."

"Where is Min?" Albert asked.

"She's talking with the preacher now. Should be here any minute. I think the funeral's gonna be on Saturday. Mama hasn't been well enough to go to church in quite a while, but she asked us to have the funeral in the little Lutheran church in Matlock. She liked it when she could go."

"I think I hear Min coming now," the boys said. "It'll be good to see her."

"God, I'm glad you all finally got here. Wish it could have been earlier. Geez, you guys look great — for old men," Minnie said after arriving back home from Matlock, where she completed funeral arrangements.

"Old men? You should talk, sis. For someone pushing 50," kidded Bill, who loved giving his older sister a bad time about her age.

"Fifty? C'mon now. That's old, and I won't be there for another seven years."

"Seems like nothing's changed around here. You two always talking about your age," said Albert.

"C'mon let's see what's here to eat and then we'll talk about the funeral arrangements," she said.

"It's gonna be at noon Saturday. That's three days and it will give us time to get the word out and make arrangements. It will be at that little Lutheran church at Matlock, like mama wanted," Minnie said. "It's going to be simple, but there will probably be a lot of valley folks there. Mama was well known all over this area. Got a notice in the paper tomorrow."

"What kind of service do they have?" asked Bill.

"What do you mean? It's a simple service, minister says a few words, there's an organist and I might see if Greta Kohlmeier can sing "Nearer My God To Thee." Mama asked if that was possible. Greta wasn't home when I went by there today, but the pastor said he likely would see her tonight. He said he was sure she would."

"I don't want an open casket," said Fred. "I didn't get to see her when she was in failing health, and I'd just as soon remember her the way I saw her last."

"It's a closed casket. I already talked about that with the man from Whiteside's, the mortuary in Montesano," said Min. "I think we got everything arranged. They were really nice. A representative was in Matlock already, and he met me at the church. Had everything all laid out. All I had to do was answer some questions and write a check."

"Well, I don't handle these things very well," said John. "I'm going for a walk. See you after awhile."

The big man had been walking over the property for some time when his thoughts drifted back to Edward and the money he was supposed to pay the brothers when he had the property logged. He became enraged at the thought.

He decided he was going to confront him right now. "He's not going to get away with this," he thought, heading in a trot back toward the house.

He was just past the barn when he noticed Edward and Mary arm-in-arm coming around the corner.

"John, hi. Brothers here yet?" Edward called out.

"Yeah, been here awhile. Where you been?" snapped the big man.

"Went for walk to the pasture, such a nice day for November. Don't get many like this," he answered.

"Mary. Good to see you too," he said, finally acknowledging her presence.

"Would you excuse us a minute. I have something I want to discuss with Edward."

"Sure. Eddie, see ya at the house. I'll go visit with your brothers. It'll be good to see them."

"What's up, big brother?"

"I want to talk to you about that property that papa left us in the northeast section."

"Yeah. What about it?"

"Well, you were supposed to have it logged and branded, then take the logs to the river, dump them over the embankment and float 'em down to the A.J. West mill on the Chehalis. You said you had a couple of guys who were going to help you."

"Yeah, we did that several months ago."

"You were supposed to split the money you got from the mill with the five of us. That's why papa gave us that property. Whatever happened to the money? None of us saw a penny of it."

"Spent it."

"Spent it? On what? Another of your foolish, hair-brained, get-rich-quick schemes?"

"Yeah, it was supposed to be a sure thing. Didn't turn out that way."

"Damn it, Edward! I don't want to hear about it. You've blown everything you got your hands on. Well, you won't have anything more to blow, and now you won't have mama to come crying to either."

"What are you talking about? Mama left me some property in her will and some money too, didn't she?"

"Nope. A little money in Montesano, but that's all. You burned too many bridges around here, and I am glad she saw through you. You won't screw around with any of us anymore. I'm getting out of here. I can't stand it. Going to the woods, and I want to be left alone. It's all up to you. You are on your own now. You have nothing here. I want you gone, now."

———

John crouched beside the stump a few yards from the edge of the family cemetery just a few miles north of the homestead. From here, he could see all he wanted, and he could hear most of the ceremony.

A last-minute change by the family moved the ceremony from the little Matlock church to the family cemetery where the patriarch was buried. Having it out in the open allowed more people to attend. It was the right decision. The little church wouldn't have held near this many people. And the weather, while crisp, co-operated with some sun-breaks.

The big man watched as Albert, Fred, Bill and Edward, and the twins, William and John, carried the fir casket that held his mother to her final rest.

"I can't understand why John isn't here," Fred said to the other pallbearers. "He was here, we were talking, and then he was gone. But I certainly believed he would be here for the funeral. He knew where it was, when it was. He knew we moved it, didn't he?"

Edward didn't utter a word.

"He can be real strange sometimes," said Albert. "I don't think I've ever really understood him. Not sure anybody does."

The big man wanted to jump right out and say something, but he couldn't. It was something he knew he could best handle from afar.

"Well, I think he's here. He's with us," said John, the Bauer twin. "He said he didn't want to carry the casket, couldn't bring himself to do that. I know he doesn't like crowds, but I bet you anything he's here, just kind of hiding, but he's here. I know it."

He could see all the neighboring families who had turned out to pay their last respects.

There were the Schaletzkes, Kohlmeiers, Maas's, Spaldings, Hollatzes, Brehmeiers, Kuhnles, Gleasons, even the Schafers and W.H. Abel. John spotted old Cy Blackwell and Joe Malinowski, who had come over from the Wishkah.

Oh, how he wanted to step out and see them, thank them for their help and support when he needed it most. He was about to take a step when he saw many folks he didn't know. He was sure he was in the right place this time. Out of sight. He didn't want to see anybody he didn't know. Yes. He was sure he had made the right decision.

"Let us pray," John could hear the good pastor say. He wasn't able to hear all the words of the prayer, nor could he hear all of the eulogy.

But his eyes began to water when he heard "Louisa was a woman who loved life and all there was in it. She was loved by everyone, and respected by all. She was a survivor who came from the old country, and with her husband, Fred, lived a good life in our beloved valley, and raised five boys and a girl. She loved her family and her family loved her. And she was loved by all. I knew not one person who didn't think the world of Louisa.

"She was a hard worker and she will be most remembered for her wonderful hospitality and those great meals. No doubt many of you, if not all of you here, have had an occasion to dine at Mrs. Tornow's table. You know what I mean, the woman could cook.

"She was a fighter through physical adversity in her later years and she fought a good fight until the very end. Today, she has been reunited with her beloved husband, Fred, with whom she had more than 40 years of holy wedlock.

"We come today to remember Louisa, a woman we all loved and cherished. May God be with you, and bless your family in these days of celebration, not mourning."

That was all John could take. He felt tears coming uncontrollably. "Oh, mama," he said, sneaking one last peek at the casket. He left in a hurry, lumbering through the dense forest and along the river until he reached the logging road that led to the Wynooche.

At last he was comfortable again. At home in his beloved woods.

The Bauers' homestead in 1900, above. Right, Henry built his first home in about 1885. He and Minnie lived there until the larger home was erected shortly after their marriage in 1885. This photo was taken in 2014.

This is the Bauer homestead as it looked in 2014. Many revisions have been made and it needs a new roof.

12. MARY'S DECISION

November 1910

"**D**oesn't feel much like Thanksgiving with her gone, does it Edward?"

"No, it's not the same without mama, Mary. I miss her, she was a good person. Doesn't seem like she's been gone for — what is it, 11 days now?"

"And we can't go to Min's place," said Mary, obviously now showing some disdain for her mother, whom she always called mama before. I wish Bill and the boys could have stayed at least until after today, been nice to have some family here for Thanksgiving. Just doesn't feel like Thanksgiving to me."

"Well, we do have each other, don't we Mary?" asked Edward, moving nearer his niece.

"Yeah, we do. By the way I'd like to go to Aberdeen with you Saturday. Ya still going aren't ya?" she asked, changing the subject.

"Sure, gotta. Gotta get some money. Mama didn't leave much at the bank, but I got a few logs to collect on. Also got a mess of apples I can take too. Yeah, that'd be fun. Just the two of us. Maybe we'll take in a movie and stay the night at Emma's. I gotta pay you for two months of work. We'll stop at the bank; I gotta cash this check from the creamery."

"OK, but I'd like to see a doctor while you're doing your peddling. Mrs. Kaatz said she was going to talk to a Dr. Stapp. He's been around a long time. I talked to her at grandma's funeral and she said I oughta have this blood condition looked at," Mary said, referring to her erysipelas which started to break out again."

"Mary, are you OK?"

"Oh, yeah, I'm just a little nervous. You know I have this heart problem, and now this is acting up," she said, pointing to the swelling in her arms and face. "Started up again right before grandma passed.

Seems like when I get nervous or excited it acts up. I just want to have this checked by another doc."

"What's wrong with Doc French?"

"Well, nothing, but he said he was going to be away for awhile. Saw him just last week and he said I was doing OK. Told me I best start eating better. 'Got to keep up your strength, child' he told me. "Always called me child."

"I gotta keep up my strength too," Edward interjected. "What's for dinner?"

"My God, man. You just finished a big turkey dinner couple of hours ago. You can't be hungry again. I'm worn out. Gonna go take a nap. You want something more to eat, fix a sandwich. Mama sent over some bread with the twins yesterday."

Mary retreated to the upstairs and the comfort of her bed, where she had been spending a good portion of her time lately. It was her time to be alone and just think. Think about the next few months, the next few years, her future, her baby.

The baby occupied her mind constantly now that she could begin to feel its presence in her womb.

"How can I possibly have this baby?" she thought. "What kind of home can I give it? I can't possibly marry Edward. I don't love him. I don't even know if the baby's his. I can't move back in with mama with a baby. Papa'd never allow it. What's the answer? What can I do? What can I possibly … ?" she sobbed loudly, muffling her mouth before finishing the sentence. I'll take a bath before I nap. Maybe that will help."

Mary slowly removed her shirt and looked down at her protruding breasts, now starting to develop sizeable cleavage. "Finally," she said cupping her hands on her bosom. "Finally I got some boobs." She unhooked her brassiere and let it drop to the floor.

She sat on the edge of the bed and thought about nothing in particular for several minutes, all the while her hands cupped her breasts as if she were surprised by a gentleman intruder. But there was no one in the room.

She lay back on the bed, threw a leg up in the air in a somewhat playful manner. Then in a sultry, sensual change of attitude, Mary slowly removed one leg from her pants, then the other one using her toes, she pushed the wool socks off her feet. Rising to her feet, she slithered out of her panties, picked them off the floor with her toes and kicked them near the door. For a few minutes she writhed and wriggled at the pleasure of her new-found figure. She tweaked each nipple and marveled how hard, how quick they protruded. "Hmmmm. I like this," she said a bit above a whisper.

This was not Mary's usual demeanor, a sedate, reserved young lady, though easily prodded into submission by the emotion of the moment. Then she plopped on the bed. She lay there several minutes, totally naked, and then burst into tears, then loud sobs. She cried and cried and cried.

Finally, after what seemed like many minutes, she rolled over, wiped her reddening eyes on the sheets and stood up. Slowly she walked down the hall to the bathroom. Mary, always a modest young lady around the house, showed no concern for modesty, even with a belly starting to show.

She ran the water a bit hotter than usual and sat on the toilet almost in a daze as the room began to steam.

The Tornows had one of the first homes in the Upper Satsop with full running water, hot and cold. Baths were a luxury in the Tornow household. Louisa enjoyed it so, even though after she broke her hip, she needed help to get upstairs, then in and out of the tub.

When the tub was about half full, Mary stepped in, steadying herself against the wall, her head becoming light, her strength sapped by the heat enveloping the room.

She laid down to immerse her body in as much of the water as possible. As the water rushed over her neck and down her breasts, it sent a chill through her body.

She placed her hands on her belly and thought about the little life beginning to form in there. And the world she would be bringing it into. How would she care for a little one?

Suddenly, it became very clear what she needed to do, the only answer. Again the tears flowed.

Mary had been dozing for nearly a half-hour in the now tepid water when a knock at the slightly open door startled her.

"What? Who's there?" she screamed, sitting bolt upright. "Who's there?"

"Who'd ya think it was?" Edward snapped.

"Oh sorry Eddie. I fell asleep. I better get outta here before I catch a cold. Hand me a towel, wouldya?"

"Edward. No," she scolded, pushing his hand away from her breasts. "Now git downstairs. I'll be there in a few minutes."

———

Saturday morning was crisp in the valley as Edward rose early to gather another burlap bag full of apples before heading to Aberdeen. He was proud to have everything ready to go before 8 a.m.

"Mary, c'mon let's get going. I wanna catch that noon train. Bundle up, it's a chilly morning, must have been below freezing last night. Frost's still on the ground."

They were several miles down the road before Mary said a word to Edward. He contemplated his impending sales at the market and she was in deep thought about the big decision she must make.

"What? What did you say Edward?"

"Where were you, Mary?" he snapped, obviously referring to her mental state. "You haven't heard a word I said. It wasn't important anyway. What are you thinking about?"

"Nothing, just thinking."

"We're making pretty good time. Should be able to get some lunch at the Montesano House before we board. Hungry Mary?"

"I'm OK, had an apple before we left. Might have another one too, they're pretty good. Should get a good price for them."

Edward knew he had to leave the homestead where he was raised, but with John off into the Olympics or somewhere away from home, he knew he would have a few months to make that decision. But, what about Mary?

It was nearly 11 a.m. when Edward pulled the wagon into the lot at the train station. They walked a couple of blocks north to the center of town.

"You go and sit down up there and have a cup of tea," he said pointing up the steps of the Montesano House, the town's finest eating establishment. "I'll be there in a minute soon's I cash this check. Order me a cup of chicken soup and a beef sandwich, and some hot cider. Cider sounds good on a cold day. Maybe some fried taters too. Get what you want, better eat well. Don't know when we'll eat supper."

I will, but I need to pop into Valentine's for a minute. George Valentine owned Owl Rexall Drug on the corner of Main and Pioneer and Mary was in need of the miracle drug, she called it. "This stuff's good for what ails you," said Valentine, handing Mary the tall bottle of Foley's Pain Relief. While it was an external lubrication, it seemed to take care of her occasional diarrhea. Even the pharmacists were baffled by the stuff.

"Don't know why it works, but it sure does," said the druggist, a Monte pioneer.

"Yes, it does. And I need it now. Can I use your bathroom?"

Sure, Mary. It's right back there."

"Oh God, that's better. Really soothing," said the young woman after rubbing the liniment on her belly.

Edward cashed his check at the Montesano State Bank and entered the Montesano House.

"Hey, Tornow. What's up?" asked the young man, sitting at an adjacent table.

Edward had made acquaintance with young Dan Cloud, the Montesano *Vidette* reporter and a correspondent for *The Aberdeen Daily World* when the reporter was investigating a fraud charge involving a timber cruiser a few months ago up the Satsop. Since then, he read all the young journalist had written every week in the paper.

He had watched the young reporter, a Nisqually Indian, grill the cruiser with some probing questions that ultimately resulted in the suspect being jailed. "Kid's got balls. He's going somewhere," Tornow thought to himself, while watching the investigation unfold.

"Going to town, peddle some apples and collect for some logs," Tornow answered. "Got my niece, Mary Bauer with me. Say hi to Dan Cloud, best young reporter in the world."

"Nice to meet you Mr. Cloud," Mary replied.

He couldn't help but notice that the young woman was attractive, yet appeared overly nervous, fidgeting with her tea cup, then her hair.

"Why, Ed you ol' devil. Where you been hiding this pretty young lady?" Cloud said.

"Just up on the ranch. She did housework for my mama until she died two weeks ago. She's a good girl, works hard too."

"Go on. You're embarrassing me," said Mary, sliding her chair closer to the table to hide her condition. She found the young, dark handsome reporter to her liking, but was obviously uncomfortable meeting him at this time.

"Now, Mary. Boyer was it?"

"No, sir. It's Bauer, B-A-U-E-R," she corrected him.

"Sorry, Mary. You tell your uncle to bring you to town more often," the reporter said, smiling at the young woman, who, now more relaxed, returned the grin.

"Bank's open today isn't it?" Cloud asked.

"Yeah. Just came from there. Working on anything interesting?" Edward probed.

"Nothing really. I'm trying to get to the bottom of this new timber legislation. Probably affects you guys. They been working on it a few years now. Heard some of the timber barons tried to get the politicians in their back pocket at that fundraiser last week. Looks like it backfired on them. The guys at Olympia got together and won't budge, seems their price went up, and unless the foresters come up with some more money — big money — it could pass this session."

"You mean the one that allows timber cruisers to assess taxes on marketable property, not just cut timber?" Ed asked.

"Yeah. That could change a lot of things up your way, Ed. Crime of it is that you smaller woodlot owners really get hurt. You feel it the most."

"We sure do," Tornow said, glad that the conversation switched away from Mary, but still not liking what he was hearing. "Hey, ya seen Abel lately?" he asked.

"No, he's down in Centralia on some case. Won't be back for a week or so."

"Cloud, good to see you. Gotta go. Maybe I'll look ya up when I get back in a day or two. I'd like to know about that bill. Could tell ya thing or two."

"Sure, Ed. Have a good trip," the reporter said. "Mary, nice to meet you. Take care of your uncle," the reporter said as the two left the table.

13. THE TRAGEDY

December 1910

"What a shame. That young girl. Her whole world ahead of her and now she's gone," the young reporter said to himself as he drove the newspaper's motorcar past the middle fork of the Satsop River. Homesteaders knew it as the Tornow branch.

He was en route to see Ed Tornow and what he hoped would be an exclusive interview and a scoop for *The Aberdeen Daily World* since it would be several days before the weekly *Vidette* would appear.

Cloud had just left the Chehalis County Courthouse, where a note on the sheriff's report from December 2 read simply: "Girl found dead in boarding house in Aberdeen. Suspicious circumstances. Name of deceased: Mary Bauer, Upper Satsop."

The reporter's mouth dropped when he saw the item. "Wasn't that Tornow's niece's name? Sure it was. What happened?" he wondered.

"Know anything about this suspicious death in Aberdeen?" he asked Sheriff Ed Payette.

"Only what's there," the sheriff answered without looking up from the memo sheet. "Call Dean or Smits. They sent the memo," he said, referring to Aberdeen Police Chief George Dean and County Coroner Paul Smits.

"Right," the reporter said, pushing the file aside. "See ya later sheriff."

Cloud thought about calling to get more information, but he knew he wouldn't be able to get much. He'd just go talk to Tornow. Maybe the authorities don't even know of his connection. "I hope he's not involved in anything," the reporter thought as he pulled the motor car in front of the Tornow ranch house, the adrenalin now flowing with this impending story. "But if he is, I'm going to get that story. Gotta get this road fixed. Too many holes," he thought before pulling the motorcar into the Tornow's drive, about 12 miles from the sheriff's office.

"Tornow? It's Cloud, Dan Cloud! Anybody here? Tornow? Ed? Ya here?" he called out, noticing that the front door was wide open. "He's got to be somewhere. Door's open."

He walked around the house and toward the barn. "Tornow? Where are you?"

Just then a young man walked out from the barn.

"Who are you? I'm looking for Ed Tornow. Seen him?" asked the reporter. "Who are you, anyway?"

"I'm Charles. Who are you? What do you want Ed for?" the brash kid replied.

"Is Edward here?" the reporter asked again.

Mary Bauer's tombstone in the Grove Cemetery. She died December 1, 1910, following a criminal abortion.

"He'll be back in a minute. Now, who are you?"

"I'm Dan Cloud, reporter with *The World*. He knows me."

"Who are you?"

"I'm Charles, Charles Kaatz. We got to go to Aberdeen. Got some bad news, his niece died. We was going back Saturday to pick her up."

"I'm so sorry. That's why I am here. Want to talk to him about it. Ya knew her too?"

Sure, she was at my mama's yesterday. She been up to see the doctor. That's the last I saw of her. We came up here last night."

"How long's Ed gonna be?" the reporter asked.

Just then Tornow came on a trot around the back of the barn to see the two talking.

"What the … what the hell does he want? No time to chat now. Gotta get rid of him. Gotta get to Aberdeen," Tornow thought to himself. "Cloud. What the hell you doing here?" he asked.

"Waitin' for you. Got a minute? Want to talk to you."

"Not really, I got to go to Aberdeen. Want to catch that noon train."

"I'll only take a few minutes. First, let me say how sorry I am about your niece. She seemed like a lovely girl."

"Thanks Cloud, but I really got to get going," said Edward. "I see you met Charlie. We got to get going."

"Wait, Ed. Just a couple of questions, please."

"OK. You got five minutes," Tornow answered, wondering how the reporter could have found out about her death so quickly. "God, this kid's good," he said to himself.

"How did you find out about it, anyway? I just heard a couple of hours ago, myself."

"Saw a memo in the sheriff's department, recognized the name and I hightailed it up here. Nobody knows I'm here."

"Well, Cloud you're my friend, I'll tell you what I know."

"What happened? What do you know?"

"I don't know much of anything yet. Charlie Muller rode up about 8 a.m. and told me that they found Mary dead this morning at Emma Kaatz's place. He's the only one with a phone. Said the Coroner called him this morning and asked if he could get in touch with me and Min. That's her mama, my sister. He knows Emma Kaatz. She must have asked him to reach me. Charlie said they don't know how she died, but the doctor said it was heart failure."

"When did you last see her?" Cloud queried.

"She was fine when Charlie and I left there last night to catch the train. Wasn't she Charlie?"

"Yeah, fine. She was in bed, but I don't think anything was wrong. Mama would have said so if there was."

"That's right, Cloud."

"Ed, let's start with what happened after you left me at the Montesano House and got the train last Saturday, and don't leave out anything."

"What's all this about? You don't think I had anything to do with her death, do you? She was my niece. She lived in my home for a long time. I loved this girl. I don't mean that I loved her like that, she was family, we all loved her."

"Yes, Ed, I know that, and no, I don't think you had anything to do with her death. I'm just trying to find out as much as possible about what happened. The easiest way to do that is to retrace your steps over the last few days."

"All right. We took the train and arrived in Aberdeen about 1. We went right to Emma's. It was only a few blocks from the station."

"What's Emma's address?" the reporter asked, turning to the youngster.

"106 West Hume, near the corner of Broadway," Charles answered.

"What did you do then?"

"I went to the boom office to look over the records."

"To where?" the reporter interrupted.

"The boom office. Chehalis Boom Co. on Wishkah to see how many logs we had there. I hadn't been paid for them. A bunch floated down after that big storm we had in October.

"Was Mary with you?"

"Yes, she went with me. We only stayed at Emma's about 10 minutes. After I got through with the log records, we went to try and sell my apples at some little fruit stands in Aberdeen, then we caught the trolley to Hoquiam.

"We got back to Emma's about 6 or so. We ate supper about 8 or so, then went to the show at the Grand. Saw 'Prince of Pilsen,' and got back home about 10. We stayed the night at Emma's."

"That was Saturday, right?"

"Yes."

"What happened Sunday?"

"I spent much of the day at Smith's Electrician's office, looking at some of their engines. I figured to take some $200 in stock in the company, pay some down and the rest over time. We talked for a while and then worked out a deal."

"He was working on Sunday?"

"Not usually, but he knew I was coming. Mary came in later, about 3 or so, and asked me to go uptown with her. We went back and got our overcoats, it was freezing out. When we got out in the alley, she stopped and said she wanted to tell me something. She says 'this is going to be a secret. I don't want you to tell anybody.' So I said all right. It was then she told me she was pregnant. I was shocked. I couldn't believe it. Figured the added weight was just mama's good cookin'."

"Pregnant?" Cloud asked, trying to think back to seeing the girl in the restaurant just a few days ago. "She didn't look pregnant to me," he thought to himself.

"Well, that's what she said, and I was just as surprised."

"What did you do after that?"

"I wanted her to go home with me right then, but she refused, said she was going to stay about a week at Emma's. She wanted the doctor to look at her erysipelas."

"Her what?"

"Erysipelas. She had this blood disease. Caused her hands to swell sometimes and she'd break out in a rash over her face, arms and legs."

"That's strange. Didn't see anything like that last week," the reporter thought to himself, then recalled that Mary had much of her skin covered with a heavy sweater during their meeting.

"So what happened next, Ed?"

"Mary said she had decided what she was going to do and asked me to go to the doctor with her. She wanted to see Dr. Stapp."

"Dr. Robert Stapp? In the Finch Building?"

"Yes. That's him. Emma had mentioned that she knew a doctor who could look at her disease. That was one reason why she went to Aberdeen with me. I didn't know where his office was and Mary said she didn't know either. She said she was going to ask Emma for a doctor. We got his name, but didn't ask Emma where his office was. We were walking around awhile and she spotted his sign. Said she wanted me to go up and talk to him."

"What did she want to know?" the reporter queried.

"How much it would cost for an abortion? How long it would take? How long she would be out of work?"

"Stapp gave you these answers?"

"Yeah. He said he could do it. It would cost $50. I asked him about her health, the erysipelas. I wanted to know if it would affect her in her condition. He said 'I'll guarantee a safe cure, without injuring her health — for $50.' He said she would be out from the effects for about 24 hours, and possibly be back to normal in about three days, not any longer than that."

"Then what did you do?" Cloud asked.

"I asked him if she had to go to the hospital, and he said it wasn't necessary, he'd do it right in the office. He asked me where she was staying, at what hotel, and I told him we were staying at Emma Kaatz. He didn't like that. Said she was against any work like that. He wanted me to bring her back about 8. I didn't know if she had the money or what her plans were, but I told him Mary would be there. He said bring the money. Then I went back to Emma's."

"And was Mary there? Did you tell her what you found out at Stapp's?"

"She was talking with Emma when I got there. I motioned to her and we went upstairs. I told her what the doctor told me. I told her she didn't have to go back there, if she didn't want to."

"She said she wanted to go through with it, right?" the reporter pried.

"She was frightened, but said she didn't see any other answer. I told her earlier that the best thing for her to do was to go to Seattle and stay until her time came, then go to an Orphan's Home and leave the child there when it was born. She said she didn't want to do that, didn't have money for that."

"How about the money for the abortion?" Cloud asked. "You told her how much it would cost? She paid for it?"

"Yes. She said she could handle it. She said she had some money and I also paid her for housework that I owed her."

"You went back to Stapp's then?" Cloud asked.

"No. I went over to Smith's and wrote a check for $50 on the stock and then I went home."

"Did Mary go back to Stapp's that night after you left?"

"I guess so. But I don't know that for sure until I get back to Aberdeen or to a phone to talk to Emma. I had told Mary before I left to have Mrs. Kaatz or Mrs. Prouty — that's Emma's daughter — take her, if she needed to go out."

"Did Mrs. Kaatz know anything about your visit to Stapp?" the reporter asked.

"No. All I said to Emma before I left was that if Mary needed to see the doctor, would she or her daughter please take her. That's all I said and she said she would."

"Then you left for the train?"

"Right. Charlie and me. We got the 6 o'clock train."

"That was last night, right?"

"Yes. OK, Cloud you've taken all the time I can spare. We got to get to Aberdeen and find out what happened. I'm just sick."

"Ed, you've been most helpful. I know it hasn't been easy for you, but I appreciate it. Do you think Mrs. Kaatz or Dr. Stapp will talk to me?"

"I imagine Emma will, but I doubt Stapp will say much. I imagine they'll try to nail him. If she had that abortion and died because of it, he's in a lot of trouble."

"Ed. Just one more question and I'll let you go. How about her parents? Where are they?"

"Charlie Muller said he was going over to tell them. That's Henry and Minnie Bauer. Minnie's, my sister and Mary's mother. They live about three miles from here, up to the West Boundary, then west about half-mile, off to the left, down in a little valley. Got a nice place up there. Little bigger than our place."

"They home?"

"Don't know. Imagine they're fixin' to go to town too. At least Henry."

"When did you see them last?"

"Henry and I don't get along. Used to, but since Mary's been with us, he's been distant. Min hasn't been here in a couple of weeks, not since mama's funeral."

"You say they are right off the West Boundary? I think I'll drive up there and see what they know before I head to Aberdeen."

"I don't care. I got to get going. Probably won't catch the train until 2:45 now," Tornow said. "C'mon kid, finished hitching the team yet?"

"Yeah, Ed, I'm ready. Mr. Cloud, nice to meet ya. See ya again."

———

"I'm looking for the Bauer place," Cloud said, approaching a young boy and his German shepherd walking along the West Boundary Road.

"Just down there," the youngster pointed. "Second drive on the left, go to the end."

"Thanks kid," Cloud said, flipping a nickel in the boy's direction.

"Gee thanks, mister!"

Cloud found the drive and pulled in, parked his motor car and walked on to the porch. He was met at the door by a monster of a man, wiping a tear from his eye.

"Help ya?" the big man asked.

"Uh, yes. I'm looking for Henry Bauer."

"Ain't here," the man snapped.

"John. Who's there?" Minnie asked, peering at the door.

"Don't know. Never saw him before."

"'Scuse me. Mrs. Bauer?" the reporter asked.

"Yes. What can I help you with?"

"Name's Cloud, Dan Cloud. I'm with the *World* and I wanted to ask you about your daughter, Mary. Let me first say how sorry I am about what happened. I met her and Ed last week at Montesano. Such a nice girl. What a tragedy."

"I don't think my sister feels like talking now," John said, moving to escort the young reporter off the porch. "Maybe later."

"That's all right. Maybe talking will help me," Minnie said, motioning to John and the reporter to have a seat. "This is my brother, John Tornow," Minnie said.

"Thank you, John, nice to meet you. You're Ed's brother? I know this isn't easy for you, either of you. I just left Ed. He's preparing to go to town," said the reporter, still shaking the big man's massive hands.

"Ed? You saw Ed? How's he doing?" asked Minnie. "He must be broken-hearted."

"Yes he is, but he's holding up pretty well. He took her to Aberdeen, you know."

"I didn't know that. Charlie … Charlie Muller, he told us about it this morning. Didn't have much information. Just said she had died at Emma Kaatz, he didn't know how. Just found her this morning. Henry, he's my husband, he's already left. I'da gone with him, but my boys — the twins William and John — are supposed to be here tomorrow. They've been logging with their Uncle John up by Shelton. John came down a day early to go to town. When he does, he usually stops here. He was here when Charlie came by this morning."

"Minnie. I just knew it was going to come to no good. Mary in there with Ed. I tried to talk to him, you know that Min. Tho bullheaded that boy. Wouldn't lithen to nuthin' anybody thaid!" John yelled, the lisp from a childhood illness clearly audible when he became upset. John buried his face in his hands as emotion overcame him.

"Did you folks know that Mary was pregnant? That she went to Aberdeen to get an abortion?"

"What? An abortion? She never said anything at the funeral," said Minnie. "That's the last time I saw her. Two weeks ago at my mama's funeral. She wasn't feeling that well, but she didn't say anything about an abortion."

"How do you know that?" John asked.

"Ed told me. Just a while ago."

"Why that no good thon of a bitch. I'll kill him. He went and got her pregnant and now thith," John snapped, leaping out of his chair and stomping his foot on the wooden slats with such vigor that the whole building shook.

Cloud was frightened at this outrage, but Minnie calmed the waters.

"Now, Johnny. Don't go jumping to conclusions. We don't know that happened," said Minnie, trying to quiet her ranting brother.

"How the hell elthe do you think it happened?" he shouted.

"Uh, 'scuse me. Uh, you all think the baby was Ed's?" Cloud asked, feeling the adrenalin building again with all the interesting information he was able to glean from this interview.

"Yeah. That's what I think. He moved her in there, to our house after papa died, right upstairs next to his room. He said she was going to be a housemaid for mama. Papa told me about catching them a couple of times, once in the barn. Whaled the devil out of Ed, papa did."

"Now, John, let's not air our dirty laundry in front of a stranger," Minnie pleaded.

"What did you and your husband think of this arrangement?" Cloud pressed for more.

"We didn't like it. Henry was real upset. Went down there a couple of times to bring her back, but she wouldn't come. Edward said mama needed her to help around the house when she was so sick in her late days. Edward paid her well to do the house chores. Henry made quite a scene the last time he went there.

"Mary was very upset. It wasn't like her. She even cursed at her papa. He never went back, hasn't even talked to her," she said, forgetting for the moment that Mary was gone before bursting into tears ... "And now, they'll never get the chance ..."

"Mrs. Bauer. I'm sorry. I didn't mean to upset you. I just wanted to get some facts from the family," Cloud said.

"Oh, I'll be all right. It's just that she was so young and had her whole life ahead of her."

"I'll just take a couple more minutes of your time, if I may. Do you know Emma Kaatz?"

"Yes, but not well. She was a friend of mama's. Been up to the house a few times when mama was alive. She also knew Ed, and John, you knew her too didn't you, John?"

"Yeah. Been there a couple of times. Spent some time with her boy, Charlie," said John, now much calmer and speaking clearly. "My brothers, Will and Albert, also knew her. She runs a boarding house, one of the better ones, but her place was on Hume in the bad district. I think she also did some of them mineral baths, but it wasn't one of those whoring places like a lot of them," said Tornow.

"I saw her briefly at mama's funeral. She, Mary and Ed were talking a lot," Minnie said.

"Did you know she — I mean Mary — was going to Aberdeen?" the reporter asked.

"Not until a day or two ago. Got a letter that said she was going to be in Aberdeen for a week or so, staying at the Kaatz place. I hadn't talked to her in two weeks, then she writes this letter, but it didn't say anything other than she was staying in Aberdeen. It was strange," Minnie said, shaking her head.

"Do you know Dr. Robert Stapp?" the reporter continued.

"Stapp? No. Can't say I do. You, John?"

"Never heard of him. Why?"

"Ed said he had taken her there for the blood disease."

"Erysipelas," Minnie said.

"Yes. That's it. But when he got there, she told him she wanted to get an abortion. It was the only answer, she told him. Ed told me that he tried to talk her out of it. Wanted to take her to Seattle and have the baby, then go to an Orphan's Home and leave the baby there. But she was determined to go through with it. That's all I know. Just between you and me I think there's a lot more to this that we don't know. I'll keep you informed as I can. Now I better get going to town and get this in the paper. You have been so kind, so gracious. I'll be in touch."

"The paper! You going to write that stuff in the paper?" John blurted at the young scribe.

"Got to. This is news. Not all of it, of course. It's a tragic story. What you and Ed have told me is important to solving what really happened in that doctor's office."

"I guess so," answered Minnie. "But, John, the paper? Now everybody's going to know about our situation."

"From what I hear, Min, everybody knows about it already, and if getting this out in the open will help find out what happened in Aberdeen, then I guess it's all right," John said.

It wasn't often that Min acknowledged her brother was right about things like this.

"You're right. I know, but Henry ..."

14. THE PLOT THICKENS

December 1910

It was nearly 7 p.m. when the train pulled into the Aberdeen Station and Dan Cloud climbed off.

"Hmm, 106 Hume. Can't be but a couple of blocks from here," he said to himself as he began walking up K Street toward the red-light district to Emma Kaatz's boarding house.

"Hey Smits" Cloud called to the County Coroner who was just leaving the Kaatz place. "Just the guy I want to see."

"Not now Cloud, got to go back to the office, been a busy day."

"Done the autopsy yet on the Bauer woman?"

"Tomorrow morning."

"Good, I'm staying over. I'll want to talk to you. Mrs. Kaatz home?"

"Yeah, I just left her. Interesting case, I'll know more tomorrow. Looks like heart failure, but don't write that yet."

"See ya tomorrow," the reporter said.

"Rooms for Rent By Day or Week" was the sign in the window, below that, "Medicinal Baths."

Cloud walked up the stairs and knocked lightly on the door.

No answer, so he knocked again, harder this time.

The door opened and a stocky woman answered.

"I was in back of house, didn't hear knock," Mrs. Kaatz said in a chopped German accent. "Can I help you?"

"I am Dan Cloud, reporter for *The World*. I'd like to talk to you about Mary Bauer."

"What 'bout her?" she asked, not willing to volunteer information to the reporter. "What you know?"

"I know she was found dead this morning in your house and I know Ed Tornow brought her to your place. I know he took her to Dr. Stapp, then returned to his home. I know there was an abortion performed and she died."

"You know all that, huh? Not much else to say."

"Well, is that true? Like I said?"

"Ya. Dis is true," the woman answered. So, how can I help you?"

"I'd like you to fill in the gaps."

"Fill in ze gaps?" she asked, clearly not familiar with that term. "What you mean?"

"Tell me what you can about what happened. What is your story? After Ed Tornow went home Sunday night, did you leave the house?" the reporter questioned.

"Ya zir. Ve go to doctor. She asked me to go along, Ed told her that I go with her if she need."

"What time was that?"

"'Bout 7, 7:30."

"And the doctor?"

"Stapp."

"He kept night hours?"

"Ya. By appointment I guess."

"Did you know why she wanted to go to the doctor?"

"Na, she didn't zay."

"She didn't say she was pregnant?"

"Na, I not know that until ve got to doctor."

"Ed Tornow didn't tell you either?"

"Na, he no zay word about it."

"You didn't think it strange when Ed asked you to take her to the doctor?"

"Na. I knew she had blood disease. Talked to her at her mum's funeral couple weeks ago. I told her I knew doctor that might help."

"That was Stapp?"

"Na, Watkins."

"But you went to Stapp?"

"Ya. Mary said she wanted to go zee Stapp. Said her uncle had talked to him early that day. So ve go."

"What did you do there? Did you go inside?"

"Ve ver in the vaiting office about 20 minutes. Dr. Stapp come in, told Mary to go inside. She wouldn't go alone, so I go vith her. To private office."

"Go on."

"After a couple of minutes he come in, tell Mary to zit on operating table. I knew den she vas going to be operated on for pregnancy."

"Then you saw her get on the operating table?"

"I don't know how I shall express myself? If you don't vant to get on such table, you have no business to go der. He had a pan full of zings. After I see zings, I vanted to get up and go. I know vhy ve ver der zen. I no like doctors who do zat operation."

"But you didn't leave? Why?"

"I no vant to go. I vanted to see vat vas going on. She needed me."

"You stayed there and saw what was going on?"

"Ya. He took sheet and covered her. He took some zings and performed the abortion. She hollered and took my hand. Took 10 minutes."

"How did you know that was what he was doing?"

"I'm midwife. I know zis."

"Then what did you do?"

"I read a magazine until she vas ready to go. She opened her pocket book and took out two twenty dollar gold pieces and a ten and gave zem to him, then ve go home and she vent right to bed."

"You didn't talk about it?"

"Na. I didn't vant to talk about it. I vas deceived by friend, I vas badly hurt."

"You didn't ask her anything about her condition, why she did that?"

"Nussing. I just told her go to bed. I felt like telling her to get out of house. I have four boys home, the youngest is 15 ..."

"You found her dead the next morning?"

"Na sir. Not zat day. Ze next."

"What did you do the next day, the day after the abortion?"

"I go to her room mid-morning. She vas still sleeping. I vent in and der ver some soiled sheets ... awful ... like from childbirth. I told her she better go to doctor. I vanted to telephone her folks, but dey don't have phone. She said 'Don't tell dem. I vould rather die before I vould disgrace my mama.' She vould not let me and I vanted to telephone for Dr. Watkins and she vouldn't let me. I took soiled cloths and soaked them. Gave her clean ones."

"When did you next see her?"

"Later zat day. I vent to door to check on her. Her eyes ver almost svollen shut. She could hardly zee and I ask her vat vas wrong with eyes. She said 'I can hardly zee from my eyes.' I tell her to come down and

I bathe them in warm water. Her eyes ver svollen with big rings black on both eyes."

"Is that from erysipelas?"

"Ya. Zee eyes zey svollen, zee hands and feet too. Zey also call it 'St. Elmo's' or zomzing like dat."

"I think it's 'St. Anthony's Fire,' Cloud corrected her. "I did some research on it before I came here. Then what happened?"

"Zee bathing helped svelling go down zom. She had fever from zee svelling too. I vanted to call Dr. Watkins, but she still vouldn't let me. I tell her I'd vait until morning, and if she vasn't better, I'm calling him. She said OK and vent back to bed."

"Then you didn't see her again until you found her dead?"

"Na. She said she vas feeling better after supper. She didn't eat, but she come downstairs. I vas vatching my daughter's baby. Mary seemed to do better. The svelling was down. She looked like she cried a lot. Ve ver talking. She told me about 'sveetheart' dat come to Tornow home, den deserted her. She started crying, said she didn't know vat to do. I told her it vas time to start over, make new life, and she zeemed happy. I told her I vould help, if she like. I told her I didn't like it dat she deceived me, but I understood."

"Then what happened?"

"I did zee zupper dishes and she zat on chair and played with my granddaughter. Zuddenly she started breathing hard, and had both hands on breast and on heart. I tell her she ought to go to zee hospital. I tell her I vish I could get in touch with her folks. She begged me not to try. "Don't do it. I von't go home. I von't," she screamed at me.

"Did you ... ?"

"Let me finish. You ask me vat happened. It vas nearly 9 o'clock and I say 'you have to go to hospital. I don't have house to keep sick people.' Zen Mary zay she velt bad, turned very red in face and became pale. I vas vorried and I ask her vare her pains ver. She said 'It hurts me very bad in back of my eyes ... and my neck. It seems like it break in two, my arm is heavy as thousand pounds. I can hardly breathe sometimes.'

"I said I vas going to see Dr. Stapp and get zom medication. I hurried up zee street. He vas der. I tell him vat vas happening and he give me pills to give her and call him in zee morning. I give her two pills and she vent to bed. I tell her to sleep as long as she vanted and

I vouldn't vake her. I didn't vake her. I had vaked up in the night and listened and I didn't hear a sound of Mary.

"It vas about 11 in zee morning, and I still didn't hear a zound of Mary. I said to my daughter 'I just vonder vat is the matter. She don't vake up,' and my daughter say 'mamma why don't you play a couple of pieces on the Graphapone and vake her up?' I did. I play loud, three pieces and I didn't hear a sound. I tell my daughter zomzing not right.

"I vent to her door and no answer. I hammered vith my fist and no answer. I looked in zee keyhole and saw key in zee lock from inside. I hollered to Hattie, my daughter, to bring me zee ax. I give it big vack with zee axe and lock broke. Zee door fell open. I run right to zee bed and it vas in zee very best condition. She vas on top of quilt. She lie her face on her left hand and her face vas to zee end of pillow and her hair vas laying on the bedstead. She had beautiful hair and I grabbed shoulder and shook her."

Cloud sat rapt in the room, scribbling as fast as the midwife could talk, explaining exactly what she saw.

"She vas laying zat way and fist was shut. I grabbed shoulder again and hollered 'Mary, Mary, me God.' I pound hard to bring her to. I tot first she fainted. I couldn't bring her to. I holler to daughter, tell her to phone quick to doctor. She call five or zix of dem. I don't know. Dey vere all busy. Finally Dr. Chamberlain came and I said 'Is she dead?' and he said 'Yes, maybe two hours.' I felt zo bad about it. Zee doctor called coroner and Mr. Smits come over. He look at everything in room. Took tablets in small yellow sack, poured zem in his hand and lifted zem up and looked at zem. Den he put zem back in zee zack and said 'Don't let anyone else in zis room.'"

"Is that it?" the reporter asked, noting that he had spent nearly an hour with the woman and hadn't asked a question for quite some time.

"Almost, let me finish. Smits said he would zend undertaker over, but Stapp arrive first, 15 minutes after zee coroner left. He asked vare she vas and said he vanted to zee her. I said she vas upstairs, but zee coroner said to 'shut door, not let anyone in.' He said he just 'vanted to look,' zo I let him go. I vas vith him, but I didn't vant to be. He said 'Looks to me like she die of heart failure or heart trouble.' He looked around and zeen zee little sack with zem tablets and he took zem and put zem in his pocket. I said 'Doc, you let zem lay. Zee coroner saw zem and will ask vare zey vent.' He said 'Never mind. Shut up. Come to my office. I vant to see you.' He left, but I never vent near Dr. Stapp. It hurt me. I felt zorry for her mother, very zorry."

"Did you tell the coroner about the pills?"

"Ya. He come back and saw zey veren't zer and asked me about them, so I tell him. The Police Chief vas here too. He just talked to Ed Tornow. I think zey are going to arrest zee doctor."

———

Cloud left the Kaatz house and headed over to the Finch Building, hoping to get an interview with Dr. Stapp before walking to the World Building to finish up his story.

The Finch was only a few blocks east from Kaatz's house at the corner of H and Heron streets. At seven floors, it was the tallest building in the city and constructed on pilings over wetlands. It was regarded as one of the best-engineered buildings in the Northwest. The county's top doctors and lawyers had offices there.

Cloud looked up and saw a light on the second floor.

"Must be him," he thought. "I hope so."

The main door was still open. He entered and climbed to the second story and down the hall to where the light was on. He rapped lightly, so not to frighten the doctor.

"Dr. Stapp?" asked the reporter of the man in his late 40s, who opened the door.

"Yes, can I help you? I am closed, except for appointments."

"I'm Dan Cloud, reporter for *The World*. Like to ask you about a Mary Bauer."

"Who?"

"Mary Bauer. You treated her this week and she died this morning."

"I'm sorry. You must be mistaken. Never heard of her."

"Emma Kaatz. You saw Emma Kaatz last night?"

"I know Kaatz. Runs a boarding house, doesn't she? Haven't seen her for weeks, months maybe. Now git out of here. I've got a lot of work to do."

"One more thing. You perform any abortions this week?"

"No. Now get the hell out of here before I call the police."

It wasn't the desired end to a perfect day that Cloud was hoping for, but he still had a solid story for the afternoon's *World*. He walked a few blocks to the news building and went inside. He was the only one there as it was nearing 10. He figured he'd get most of the story done that night and finish it up in the morning after the results of the autopsy.

The adrenalin was building. Easily, this was the young reporter's top story in the few months he had been at Aberdeen. He dialed Werner Rupp, the *World's* editor, at his home and told him what he had found.

"Write it for all it's worth kid. I'll talk to you in the morning," the veteran editor told the youngster.

The words flowed easily as he sat at the Underwood and pounded vigorously.

He decided he was going to allege Stapp's involvement, even though the doctor flatly denied it. Kaatz and Tornow both implicated him. He wanted to get an official on record, but that would have to wait until morning. At this point, they hadn't even talked to Stapp. But after the autopsy …

It was about midnight when he wrapped up as much of the story as he could write.

"I deserve a treat tonight," he said to himself. "I'm going to stay at the Washington."

He proudly walked a few blocks down Heron Street to K and the stately Washington Hotel, the city's finest. He was hungry, but meals were not served after 8, so he ordered a take-out sandwich and went to his room, stopping to ask the clerk to call him at 6.

"Wow. They'll be proud of me," he thought to himself, collapsing on the solid mattress and falling into a deep sleep.

The ring of the phone jolted him out of bed.

"Couldn't be 6 already," he said, reaching the phone. But it was.

He took a quick bath, dressed and headed to the *World* office.

"Kid, I think ya got a good, solid story here," Rupp said after reading Cloud's draft. "Got a few problems we have to take care of though."

"Yes sir. I think a lot will clear up after the autopsy. Should be done by 8 or so. I expect there may be a new cause of death. I expect abortion and I suspect that Dr. Stapp will be arrested for questioning."

"Can you get that information this morning? I'll hold this a couple of hours."

"Yes, I hope so. First, I want to try to get Chief Dean or some official to make some kind of statement regarding the investigation of this case."

"But, if they only know that the cause of death is heart failure at this point, why do you believe they are going to say anything different?"

"I know Dean has questioned Kaatz and had Tornow at the station last night. We're not alleging anything, just quoting those two as having been at Stapp's."

"Yeah, kid, I know, but I'd be more comfortable having Dean or Smits on the record. Go and get it, if you can."

Cloud arrived at the police station and walked in. "Chief here?" he asked the clerk.

"Yeah, Dan, but he's with the coroner right now," the attractive brunette clerk said. Lindy Fleming had taken a liking to the reporter almost from the first day she met him. He never had a problem getting information from this clerk.

"What's that about?" he asked her.

"I'm not sure. A girl died at a boarding house and they thought it was a routine heart failure, but he and Smits have been in there a long time."

"He must have done that autopsy early. He told me he wouldn't be done until about 8."

"So, you know about this?"

"Yeah, and I gotta talk to them, now. Got a deadline to meet."

"I can't let you go in there."

"C'mon, Lindy. All they can do is tell me to get out. Let me try, anyway."

"It's your butt," she said opening the door, then kicking him playfully in the rear.

"Chief. Coroner. I know you're busy, but I've got a couple of questions I need to ask you about the autopsy."

"Cloud, you know about this? What do you know?" Chief George Dean asked.

"I won't tell you what I know yet. Just answer me some questions first."

"Ya got spunk kid. That's all I can say," Coroner Paul Smits said, shaking his head.

"What is your conclusion as to the cause of death after the autopsy?"

"Can't tell you," the Coroner said.

"Why is that. It's not heart failure was it? What do you think?"

"If you can't tell me, can you answer me yes or no? Did an autopsy show that an abortion was performed?"

"Yes, I'll say that much since you seem to have done your homework. How did you know that?"

"Emma Kaatz and Ed Tornow both said that."

"You talked to them already? Good God kid, don't you ever sleep? When did you see Tornow? He was at the station all night."

"Saw him yesterday before I headed here. He and Kaatz's stories jive pretty much, but I haven't had time to check out the details. By the way, have you talked to Dr. Robert Stapp at the Finch Building yet?"

"No," answered the Chief. "But we're going to."

"Gonna arrest him?"

"Let's just say we want to ask him some pertinent questions," the Chief, said, smiling.

"Prosecutor Campbell been alerted to this yet?" Cloud asked.

"Yes, he's aware, and I expect Bill will be here this morning," answered the Chief, referring to Attorney William Campbell, the county's veteran prosecutor.

"One more question I am dying to ask you, Mr. Smits," Cloud said chuckling at his pun with the Coroner.

"Yeah. What's that?"

"Was the abortion clean?"

"Cloud. I can't tell you that," the coroner said looking for affirmation from the chief.

"It wasn't was it? That bastard doctor botched that abortion didn't he? He killed that poor girl."

"You didn't hear that from me," the coroner said.

"Nor me," the chief answered.

"Thanks guys. Gotta write this thing now."

"Cloud. Be careful. Be careful what you write."

"Sure chief. See ya later. Call me if you arrest Stapp before deadline, no later than 10. I'm probably going back to Montesano tonight."

Cloud knew what he had to do. He had to make one more run at Stapp before putting this story to bed, and before the authorities got there to arrest him. The reporter knew what the coroner's comment "you didn't hear that from me" meant. It usually meant the answer to his question was "yes," but confirmation would have to come from another source.

Cloud had most of the story written when a call came from Chief Dean. It was the confirmation he had been waiting for.

WELL KNOWN MAN
HELD IN JAIL
ON UGLY CHARGE

The headline screamed across the December 5, 1910, evening edition of *The Aberdeen Daily World*.

Dr. Robert M. Stapp Taken by
Authorities on Charge of
Manslaughter

was directly under the main headline

"Robert M. Stapp, one of the best-known physicians in Gray's Harbor, was arrested this morning on information filed this morning in Superior Court by Prosecuting Attorney William E. Campbell, charging him with manslaughter.

"The information alleges that Dr. Stapp performed a criminal operation, which caused the death of Mary Bauer, a resident of Satsop, the woman dying at the apartments of Mrs. Kaatz, a midwife, who resides on Hume Street between Broadway and K streets. Stapp was immediately taken to Montesano following his arrest, where he is held until $5,000 bonds can be secured.

"Mary Bauer, who resided with her parents in the Upper Satsop Valley, came to Aberdeen November 27 and was taken suddenly ill two days later, death resulting December 1. Following the sudden death, County Coroner Paul Smits was notified and an autopsy was performed by a number of Harbor physicians.

"Following the report of the physicians as to the cause of death, Prosecuting Attorney Campbell and Chief of Police George Dean began working on the case. Stapp's arrest followed."

———

Cloud was right when he told Minnie Bauer there was more to the story — a lot more.

And even more was unveiled in the next day's issue when Stapp flatly denied all charges.

"I don't know a thing about it," the doctor declared most emphatically. "Furthermore, I never heard of the woman ... I don't know that she was ever in my office. I never heard of the name and know absolutely nothing about this case, except what I have read in the newspapers.

"It was a surprise to me when they told me I was wanted in Montesano," Dr. Stapp told *The World*. "I went gladly because I have no fears. I have never heard of the girl mentioned in the case, and cannot figure out just how I have been connected with it."

Stapp was released on bonds and promptly retained Elmer E. Boner and Walter I. Agnew as his chief counsel.

15. THE TRIAL BEGINS

February 1911

"Cloud, come in here," the gruff-voiced editor bellowed across the city room as the young reporter was about to head off to check the police beat.

"Shut the door."

This was the first time that the young scribe had been summoned to the big man's office alone with the door shut. Young reporters were called cubs until they got the "BIG STORY." It was something the kids strived for, all reporters did. Some never shed it and would be cubs their entire career.

Dan Cloud was no longer a cub. He had been working only a few months with the *World* as a freelancer after interning at the weekly *Chehalis County Vidette* at Montesano during the summers following his junior and senior years in high school. He had done some reporting as an intern at the *Bellingham Herald* when his father was publisher at the Lynden *Tribune* before coming to the Harbor.

It was a dream come true for a young Nisqually Indian, who became one of the first from his tribe near Olympia, the state capital, to go on to college. His mother was one-quarter Nisqually. When Dan was a grade-schooler, his father worked for the *Tacoma Ledger* and later the *Tacoma News*, which he owned.

When he was a junior in high school, his family permitted him to move in with good friends in Satsop, if he would work after school and on weekends. The house was adjacent to a mercantile and soon he was able to obtain work there. He loved the Harbor's slower-paced lifestyle, but his goal was to work to get enough money to attend the university and become a journalist, like his father.

Dan was ambitious, a good-looking youngster, with a dark complexion. He worked afternoons and weekends helping out County

Commissioner Wilson, who owned the mercantile at Satsop. The commissioner liked young Cloud from the first time he had met him.

The young man enjoyed spending time at the store. It was not only where many of the Brady and Satsop folks came to get supplies, but also was a gathering spot for those heading east from the county seat at Montesano, or traveling west from Olympia to Montesano, Aberdeen and the Olympic Mountains.

"I've got the storeroom cleaned up and the floors swept," the youngster told the commissioner. "Could I wait on customers? I can count money," he asked one day.

Cloud showed great aggressiveness in learning the business, and was soon a favorite with the locals. Wilson was also becoming more active in local politics and spending more time away from the store.

"Ya know, Mr. Wilson, if you had a little cafe here, you could do even more business. Everybody stops on their way through," the brash kid suggested one day.

"You're right kid, but how are we going to pay for the additions?" the commissioner asked.

"Easy," said the kid, now a high school senior. "Let's expand our fishing supplies. You give people the best stuff to go fishing and sales increase. You take that idea to the bank and get a loan and build a small room for a cafe. You'll have the loan paid in no time. And I can run the cafe and the store for you."

"Where did you ever learn that stuff?" the commissioner asked.

"I heard a friend talking about expanding his logging business. He didn't have to have the extra logs, just a good plan to get them and then the bank would loan him the money. "I thought if it worked for them, why not here?"

In no time, Wilson was at the bank, talking about the plan to the loan department. The bank was supportive and gave him the money. He was able to expand his fishing and hunting supplies until he had the best offerings available on the Olympic Peninsula. People came from all over, not only to get basic supplies, but also for top-of-the-line fishing and hunting gear.

By summer, Wilson had the cafe opened and every lunch hour it was full. In bad weather, the place was often packed all day long.

The kid was right, and Wilson rewarded him with a big raise to $2 a week. That was a lot of money for any young laborer, let alone a high-schooler. It was enough to pay the bills. That year also he talked his way into an unpaid internship at the *Vidette*. The next year, his senior year, he did some correspondence work for *The Aberdeen Daily World* and received a small stipend.

Cloud continued to work at the store through his senior year. He also was cultivating a nose for news that would stand him in good stead later and help him get a full-time job at the *World*.

"Mr. Wilson, I've worked here for four years, but it's time to leave," the young man told the longtime commissioner one day. "I'm going to school, to the University of Washington in Seattle. I want to be a journalist."

"That's an admirable goal," the commissioner said, "but college costs a lot of money."

"I know, but I've been saving. I've got about $75, and they told me I can work for the college daily newspaper and make some more. Mr. Wilson, you know that's what I always wanted to do. It's been fun working for you. I've learned a lot and I'll never forget it, but it's time to move on."

Cloud spent much of his early college days writing sports stories, but was sent out on an occasional news story. It was an interview with the school's finance administrator that led him to believe there was some misuse of funds.

The resourceful, young reporter, continued to ply his sources for this story.

"That kid's been in there for hours," said one secretary in the records office. "Wonder what he's up to?"

Two days later, Cloud marched in, evidence in hand, to the school president's office. After scrutinizing the reams of material the kid had uncovered, the university president and the Board of Regents, then summoned the university's attorney. After examining the evidence, the attorney suggested they approach the administrator in question. Under pressure, the man buckled at the overwhelming case against him and resigned.

It was Cloud's banner story atop the school's *Daily*, which was picked up by the *Seattle Post-Intelligencer*. It later resulted in the charge of embezzlement and subsequent conviction of the finance administrator.

After that story, Cloud knew his calling. He wanted to be a journalist, an investigative reporter. By his senior year, he was the paper's editor.

When he graduated, he was dogged by the Seattle paper, whose editor desperately wanted the young man to work for him, but Cloud desired to work closer to the Harbor, which had become his home, and turned down an attractive offer.

"Thank you, sir. Your offer of $5 a week is most generous, but my family needs me closer to home and I can get a job at the weekly in Montesano and learn a lot there. Maybe, after I get a few stories and a year or two of experience, I can come back here," he told the editor.

He had worked at the *Vidette* in Montesano during the summer of his junior year in college, and was offered a full-time job after he graduated.

While covering a routine accident in which a man, who had been drinking alcohol, ran his truck into the East Fork of the Satsop, the reporter felt there was much more to the story. Cloud was on the scene, and while the man appeared particularly evasive, the authorities dismissed the case as a man drinking too much, fined him and closed the case.

The young reporter's nose sniffed out much more. He dug into the background of the driver, then conducted his own surveillance for several weekends, eventually taking the paper's photographer with him to snap photos, exposing a large still and bootleg operation near Deckerville. The man had six others working for him, and with Cloud's persistence, officials were able to bring charges and subsequent convictions against all but one of them.

It was this aggressive drive that led the *World*'s City Editor, Bill Irvine, to contract Cloud to be a part-timer for the daily newspaper as well as the weekly *Vidette*.

It was an amicable arrangement the two papers had struck with another reporter years before, so there was precedence. Much of what Cloud had done so far for the *World* was to phone in daily reports to the rewrite desk from the county. But lately, he had taken to making the trip into Aberdeen in the afternoon or early evenings, filing a story and calling in updated information for the next afternoon's paper. He had become well known at the courthouse to most of the attorneys and was never lacking for a ride between Montesano and Aberdeen.

Now, after only a few months he had surged ahead of veteran reporters at the *World*, and he was no longer a cub. The Stapp story removed all doubt.

He took a chair in front of the desk as the editor lit up a cigar. "Smoke, kid?" he asked, knowing the youngster didn't smoke or drink.

"No thanks, sir. I don't smoke."

"Good. Don't start," the editor proclaimed.

Cloud still wasn't sure if he was in the boss's office — to be reprimanded or what.

He let his mind race, thinking back and trying to recall something he might have done wrong with the Stapp story, or anything he may have said or done. He couldn't think of a thing, but the reaction was normal for a young reporter.

"Sir, did I do … ?" he stammered.

"No," the editor interrupted. "In fact, the contrary. You did a splendid job on the Stapp story and I want it to be your story. Kid, you're going to cover the trial. You deserve it, and I know you can do it."

"Sir, thank you, sir. I can do this! I've got all the background." the reporter said, already formulating in his mind the many stories he wanted to do on Stapp's background, the Bauer girl's background, and Ed Tornow. The family had already told him much about this unusual relationship.

———

The trial opened in Montesano on February 15, 1911, before Superior Court Judge Ben Sheeks, the first major event for the new courthouse.

Sheeks had been appointed by Gov. M.E. Hay to the Superior Court of Chehalis County when a second justice position was opened a year ago. His appointment came as a shock to many as the venerable gentleman was 68 years old.

Sheeks was in Aberdeen only a short while when the appointment came. The governor was well aware of Sheeks' ability. He graduated from the University of Miami in Florida, then moved to the central United States. During that time, Sheeks was legal counsel for the Mormon Church, representing the church on several occasions before the U. S. Supreme Court, though he was not a Mormon.

He had become the personal attorney for Brigham Young.

In the early 1900s, he moved to Tacoma and in 1908, started a private practice in Aberdeen. He was eager to locate his office at the sparkling new courthouse in Montesano, a beautiful domed sandstone structure that opened just a month before the Stapp trial was to begin. Some thought the structure was too lavish and too large for a county the size of Chehalis, but this was a boom time for the area with shipbuilding and logging bringing in huge caches of money. The government folks in the know also figured the county would soon be taking on a new look.

In March 1907, the State Legislature enacted a law dividing the county. The Weyerhaeuser Timber Co., a lumber giant and one of the largest land-holders in the Northwest, and local Montesanans took the matter to court. The issue bounced around the legal system for two years. They knew it would be only a short while before there would be a Grays Harbor County, the name they sought to distinguish the area from the city of Chehalis in Lewis County to the south.

Debates and wrangling were nothing new to Montesanans. In fact, the town's name was founded in debate. In 1860, the county seat was located in the house of J. L. Scammons on the south side of the Chehalis River. His wife, Lorinda, a most religious woman, wanted to call the new city "Mount Zion."

But the fireside council, led by Samuel James, opted to call it "Montesano," which had a more pleasant sound and its Spanish meaning "Beautiful Mountain," was similar.

There would be more wrangling between Scammons and S.H. Williams who had purchased about 16 acres on the north side of the Chehalis River, a mile and a half from Scammons. He called his plat "Montesano." A townsite struggle ensued, but the county seat remained at the Scammons' place, while the Williams' plat became more populous.

In 1886, voters decided to move the county seat to the platted town at Montesano, while the Scammons site became known as South Montesano. A school teacher, Charles M. Byles, was instrumental in helping to build the platted city.

———

Aberdeen doctor Robert Stapp was being tried on a charge of criminal abortion, amended from an initial charge of murder in the first degree and amended after that from manslaughter, although the latter could still stand.

County Prosecutor William Campbell, lead counsel for the prosecution, argued in his opening statements that evidence would show that Dr. Robert Stapp was a callous physician, who on Thursday, December 1, 1910, did perform an abortion on Mary Bauer, age 24, and as a tragic result of that illegal action, the young woman suffered heart failure and died the next day.

The doctor's defense was in the hands of crafty Aberdeen attorney Elmer Boner, who argued that witnesses would testify that Mary Bauer suffered from a blood disease and a bad heart. All of that was aggravated by an application of iodine that contributed to her death.

Boner would argue that Stapp declared the matter a mistake; that he not only did not perform the operation, but had never seen the girl and did not know of her condition.

First witness for the prosecution was Henry Bauer, father of the deceased girl.

Cloud had yet to meet this man, and had been rebuffed on every attempt he had made over the past two months to talk to him. He knew Bauer had an intense dislike toward Ed Tornow, his wife Minnie's brother. Minnie and her brother, John, felt the same way.

He listened intently to every word as Bauer, under questioning from Campbell, said he wasn't aware of any heart condition that his daughter, Mary, suffered. At first, Bauer said he wasn't aware of Mary's skin condition (erysipelas); then later testified that she did receive some medication in the spring of 1910 from Dr. French, the family physician in Elma.

Defense attorney Boner was far less gentle with the grieving father, who testified that in September, Mary first complained of a stomach ailment. Cloud had been told by the coroner that conception was likely in early August. Boner, noticing anger in Bauer's voice, decided to pursue an earlier line of questioning regarding the housing arrangement that Mary had in the Tornow home. Ed Tornow moved Mary into the Tornow home to care for his aging mother, Mary Bauer's grandmother.

The exact transcript from the court reporter:

Boner: How many was in the grandmother's family then?
Bauer: There is six — six grown children: Minnie, Fred, Albert, William, John and Ed."

Boner: Living there at the time, besides Mrs. Tornow?

Bauer: Only one.

Boner: Who was that?

Bauer: Ed Tornow, the youngest.

Boner: And they lived there in the Tornow home, the grandmother and her son? Is he a brother of your wife, Minnie?

Bauer: Yes.

Boner: And uncle of your daughter?

Bauer: Yes.

Then, after Boner switched his questioning back to Mary's precondition, he returned to hammer at the Bauer-Tornow rift that he perceived was growing at the time.

Boner: Were you ever at the Tornow home when your daughter lived there?

Bauer: I was a few times.

Boner: Do you know where she slept when she was there?

Bauer: No, sir. I do not.

Boner: You don't know in what room?

Bauer: Yes, she slept upstairs, in the southeast corner of the house.

Boner: Do you know where Ed Tornow slept?

Bauer: I don't know.

Boner: Did he sleep upstairs?

Bauer: I could not tell you. I guess he did.

Boner: Do you know where Mrs. Tornow, the grandmother, slept?

Bauer: She slept downstairs. I guess Ed slept upstairs. There was only one downstairs bedroom.

Cloud quickly made a note. "Grandmother had to sleep downstairs. She had a broken hip and was bed-ridden much of the last several months."

Boner: Where was it that Mary stayed after November 13, 1910, after the death of her grandmother?

Bauer: She stayed at the Tornow house.

Boner: She and Ed Tornow lived there?

Bauer: Yes, sir.

Boner: Was that agreeable with you?

Bauer: It was not.

Boner: It was not?

Bauer: No, sir.

Boner: You desired her to come home, didn't you?

Bauer: I did. I asked her to come.

Boner: You expected her condition, didn't you, Mr. Bauer?

Bauer: You mean her being pregnant?

Boner: I do.

Bauer: No, I didn't expect it. But I didn't think it looked right for her to stay there.

Boner: Didn't you suppose that all wasn't right with the girl?

Prosecutor Campbell: I object your honor. This line of questioning is wholly immaterial. This is not cross examination. It is an attack on the credibility of Ed Tornow, rather than that of the witness who is testifying."

Boner: In this kind of case it is, your honor.

Judge Sheeks: I think it is cross examination, counsel. You may ask the question.

Boner: Didn't you suspect that all wasn't right with your daughter?

Bauer: No, I didn't because I could not tell, although I didn't want to have her living there.

Boner: Wasn't it because you suspected that there was too much intimacy between your daughter and the young Tornow?

Bauer: I didn't, on account of him being my wife's brother.

Boner: Didn't you talk this matter over with your wife? And didn't you object very strenuously to her staying there at all?

Bauer: I told her it wasn't a good place for her to stay.

Boner: And this was more than talk, it was a very heated argument, was it not?

Bauer: Yes, we had an argument about it.

Boner: And you had considerable trouble about it? You contended that she ought not to stay at Tornow's and you wanted her to come home?

Bauer: Yes, sir.

Boner: Didn't this happen before the grandmother died? Didn't you object to it strenuously before she died?

Bauer: Yes, that was about in May.

Boner: You didn't want her to stay there?

Bauer: I didn't want her to go there at all in the first place.

Boner: It didn't look right to you, did it?

Bauer: It did not.

Boner then left that line of questioning and switched to the night at Aberdeen and the relationship between the family and Emma Kaatz, the woman to whom Ed Tornow had taken Mary when he arrived in Aberdeen before going to the doctor.

The girl's father went on to testify that he had known Emma Kaatz only briefly, saying she had been a friend of his wife's and Mrs. Tornow, who came to his house three or four times when he had been there. Bauer said he had seen Mrs. Kaatz last at his mother-in-law's funeral in November.

Bauer testified that he attempted again to bring Mary home a final time after the funeral, but again was unsuccessful. He had testified that he was going to take Mrs. Kaatz to Montesano to catch the train to Aberdeen following the funeral.

Boner: When you brought Mrs. Kaatz to the station here at Montesano, you told Mary to be ready to go home with you when you got back, did you not?

Bauer: I did.

Boner: And did she? Did Mary, go?

Bauer: She didn't.

Boner: Why didn't she go?

Bauer: She said that Ed wanted her to stay, and Will wanted her to stay for a couple of days. Will is Ed's brother.

Boner: That was about the 14th of November?

Bauer: No that was about the 16th.

Boner: Was Will Tornow there at that time?

Bauer: Yes, sir.

Boner: How long did he — Will Tornow — stay there?

Bauer: I don't know. I never went to the Tornow house after that day.

Boner: You never went to the Tornow house after that day?

Bauer: No, sir.

Boner: You were very much angered by the situation, the turn of affairs at that time, were you not?

Bauer: Yes, sir, I was.

Boner: You had made up your mind that you would not have anything more to do with the situation and went home?

Bauer: I came to Montesano that day and when I went back, I stopped to pick up Mary. When she wouldn't come, I left and I never returned.

Boner: It was then you made up your mind to have nothing more to do with the affairs of Ed Tornow and your daughter, if she intended to stay there? You washed your hands of it?

Bauer: Yes, sir. I was ready to quit.

Boner: Did you ever go so far that you said you would disown her and she could not come home, if she continued to stay there?

Bauer: No sir, I didn't.

Boner: Didn't you say at that time that unless she came now, that she must not come at all?

Bauer: I did not.

Boner: Didn't you tell your wife that?

Bauer: I told my wife to go after her. Mary refused to come with her. Later, I asked my wife to take Mary's clothes to her and tell her that I didn't want to see her anymore.

Boner: And when was the next time you saw your daughter?

Bauer: Not until …

At this point, Bauer finally showed emotional grief, breaking into a sob and the attorney told him to take a minute that everyone understood.

Bauer finally continued, though sobbing, his voice broken. He said he hadn't seen his daughter next until December 2 when he went to the coroner's office.

Boner, for some reason, seemed bent on hammering at the rift that was becoming evident to all in the courtroom between the Tornows and the Bauers, or at least Henry Bauer.

Mrs. Bauer, Minnie Tornow Bauer, however, presented an entirely different demeanor under questioning. She was on the stand only a few minutes, but in that brief period, left no doubt that she cared deeply for her daughter and made repeated attempts to bring her home, knew more about her condition than her husband, and wasn't as well acquainted with Mrs. Kaatz as Ed Tornow had earlier alleged.

After the first day, Boner had already implanted in the jury's mind a credibility gap in advance of testimony by Ed Tornow and Emma Kaatz.

Judge Sheeks called a recess at this point, adjourning until the next morning.

Cloud went into the clerk's office to gather his thoughts and have a cup of coffee.

Under testimony, Minnie Bauer related Mary's past health history, which was extremely crucial in this case.

Cloud asked for, and received, an exact copy of Mary Bauer's health history as reported by her mother.

The data sheet read: "Initial illness: 1903-04 during the school year at St. Rose Academy in Aberdeen. Patient "catched cold" had temporary amenorrhea (cessation of menstruation);

Spring, 1907: Again disturbance of menses.

Spring, 1909: patient had first symptoms of sepsis and septicemia, (a local infection and blood poisoning). After an interval, patient developed erysipelas."

Cloud saw this notation: Note on erysipelas. Also "St. Anthony's Fire," an acute febrile associated with a local, intense reddish inflammation of the skin and subcutaneous tissues, frequently of the face, caused by a streptococcus. Also a fatal disease of swine." — *Source: Webster's Unabridged.*

The data sheet continued: After initial diagnosis, went to a different physician, told her mother the doctor diagnosed indigestion. Physician note: Pregnancy suspected.

"Patient responses: After 1907-08 illness, patient had a few dizzy spells, responded to medication (digitalis); patient edema at time of erysipelas.

Patient's previous health: tall, strong, active, inclined to drive self, farm girl, home girl."

Cloud jotted a few notes to pursue for his story. Boner skillfully elicited facts that Mrs. Bauer cared for her daughter, that Ed Tornow was playing on the emotions of Mary's parents to prevent Mary from coming home and that Mrs. Kaatz was not exactly the longtime family friend of the Tornows, though apparently she was known for some time by the Tornow boys.

"Yes, that's right, Cloud. I'm trying to impugn the testimony of Ed Tornow and Emma Kaatz before they take the stand. Campbell needs them, but how credible are they going to be in the eyes of the jury?" Boner replied when asked by Cloud about his strategy.

"But, you know, you can't write any of that I just told you. You know that, don't you?" Boner emphasized. "It's off the record."

"Of course, Mr. Boner," the reporter said, nodding in agreement.

"But, it was evident in your line of questioning and I am going to report the facts. How about tomorrow and Friday? What can I print tonight about that strategy?"

"Let's just say today's questioning set the stage for a couple of interesting days when we get Tornow and Kaatz on the stand," the sly attorney said. "I think Prosecutor Campbell's going to have a difficult time."

"I want to talk to the Bauers before they head home," Cloud thought to himself.

"Seen the Bauers since court? he asked the attorney.

"They were talking with Campbell a while ago in the room by the chambers. Don't know if they are still there."

"I'll check it out. See you tomorrow Mr. Boner."

Cloud hustled down the corridor and saw Mrs. Bauer, alone, wiping tears from her eyes.

"Here, Mrs. Bauer, take this," said the reporter handing the distraught woman a tissue.

"Thanks young man. This is hard on me. Henry went home to tend to the farm and I'm going to stay at the Montesano tonight. It's easier than making the ride home."

"How about your brother?"

"Ed, oh I guess he went home, too."

"No, the other one, John. Isn't that his name? Why isn't he here to help support you? Testifying in court about the death of your daughter is not easy. You could use his help, couldn't you?"

"Sure, it would help, but John is helping me. He's taking my boys to work with him at a logging camp after the trial. He's so good with the boys, taught them everything they know. It's good for them to be away from home. They loved their sister, even after she left home."

"Did they ever confront Ed about Mary living at his house?" Cloud inserted, seeing an opportunity to pursue this subject.

"A couple of times, but they never got along with Ed. Henry was so jealous of John and his relationship with the boys. Ed wasn't like that. Oh, he did some work, but not like John, and he doesn't know the woods like John does.

"The boys worship their Uncle John. They were just about 10 when John started taking them into the woods on overnighters, then it was a week a time. They knew the woods as well as John did before they were teenagers. He taught them how to shoot, hunt, whittle with knives and to survive.

"Once, Will and John — that's the boys — took me into the Upper Wynooche area, up by that Simpson Camp where the log train starts. I wasn't feeling too well and they decided I needed to get out and away from the house. They loaded me on the wagon and off we went. It wasn't far off the main road where they had built this comfortable little lean-to, and lined it with elk hide. They had a fire pit and had made shoes out of tanned hide. I couldn't believe what I saw. My boys had as much up there as I had in my house, and they made it themselves. They said John helped them. My goodness, I am rambling aren't I? But I love to talk about my boys and my brother. He's so good to them, not like the others in the family."

Without even asking, Cloud was able to glean the information he was after. Indeed, not all Bauers had a rift with the Tornows.

"Mrs. Bauer. You're not rambling at all. I appreciate it and besides, it got you off the trial for a few minutes, didn't it? Now, you have a good night. Get some food, some rest and I'll see you tomorrow."

Cloud's next move was to seek out Campbell, whom he found at the Montesano House grabbing a quick bite before heading back to Aberdeen.

"Catch a ride with you back to the office, counselor?" he asked of the prosecutor, who was finishing up his smoked turkey and bacon sandwich.

"Sure, Cloud. Howdja like it today?"

"Interesting, but I wish I knew where you were going with your questioning."

"Ah, my good lad, that's what makes these trials so compelling, so much fun every day. Ya gotta keep 'em guessing. C'mon let's get outta here. I'm tired."

"Let me grab a sandwich to eat on the way. I'm not going to get a chance to eat when I get back."

Cloud ordered his favorite — roast beef, tomato, cheddar and avocado on rye — bagged it up and headed to Campbell's motor car.

"I gotta ask you one thing about this trial," probed Cloud when the car had covered about half of the 12 miles to town. "What's your trump card? Don't you think Boner got the best of you today?"

"Sure he did. I know what he's doing, but Tornow and Kaatz are not that important to me. I got better stuff on the doc. Don't write a word of this. I'll deny it if you do, but that doc's scum. I found some dirt on him. You can too. That's all I'm going to say. You watch. I'm going to hand Boner Stapp's head on a platter. He's good as up the river."

"Up the river? I don't know what you mean."

"Oh, that means he's heading to prison."

The ride to Aberdeen went particularly fast this day. It always did when Cloud could get someone engaged in conversation.

"Thanks counselor, he nodded to Campbell, referring not only to the ride home, but also for the tip on Stapp.

"Oh, they are clever," the reporter thought of the two longtime friends, who became adversaries for justice, and whom he must now study intently to get his story.

"Gosh, Mr. Rupp. Ya going to spend the night?" Cloud asked the editor, the only other person in the newsroom.

"How's the trial today?" he asked, ignoring the reporter's question.

"Well, I got lots of stuff, but I don't think it's much to write about yet. I could rap out a piece, but I think it will be better tomorrow. We published the opening arguments for today's paper, and I did call in a new lead, so, if you agree, I think we can hold until after tomorrow morning's testimony for the next story.

"Let's hear what you got today, and we'll decide," said the editor.

Cloud related the essence of the testimony from Henry and Minnie Bauer, and the editor agreed that a "brief" in Thursday's paper would tell the reader that the trial was continuing. It was agreed that he should call in a fresh lead before deadline, featuring the morning testimony, then file a comprehensive story for Friday afternoon, based on what was expected to be a hectic day at the trial.

He bade the editor a good night and then headed to the police station.

"Gotta find something on Stapp," he thought to himself, "then I'm going home."

"Hey, Lindy. How ya doing?" he asked the shapely clerk at the police department.

"Just great," she answered. "What ya want me to do for you now?"

She knew this young buck was after something the way he romped into the office and plopped down on the edge of her desk.

"Lindy, how can you say that? I just came by to see you … and …"

"See, I knew it. You didn't come just to see me," she said, tugging at her skirt that had climbed above her knees.

"Well, I did, but I also need some information."

"Okay, smartie. What kind of information?"

"Well, are we alone?"

"Yeah, but what's this all about?"

"C'mere," he said, motioning her closer, then seizing the moment he had often hoped for, started to whisper into her ear, but instead nibbled it.

"Danny," she said, flushed to embarrassment by the impulsive reporter.

"Yessss?" he answered, still within a breath of the young, attractive woman.

"Now, what was it you wanted?"

"What time you get off?"

"Ten or 15 minutes when the deputy returns, and you best not be sitting on my desk then," she said, without even thinking that she had virtually accepted a date with the persistent reporter.

"Great. Gives us just enough time."

"Enough time? Time for what?" she asked, pushing Cloud away.

"Enough time for you to get me the file on Dr. Robert Stapp."

"But Danny, I can't do that. That's private, police information."

"Oh, I know that, but you can excuse yourself to go to the washroom and I'll get it. Just tell me where it is."

"Oh, I don't know."

"Sure, you can, but we better hurry, if the deputy is due back."

"He won't be here before 8, never is."

"OK. You go powder your nose, or whatever it is you women powder, I'll get what I need, then I'll take you to the Washington for dinner."

"Oh, Danny, you rascal. You know how to charm me, don't you?"

It took him just a minute to find what he was looking for, and hastily copied the information from the police reports.

"Stapp, Robert M. Aberdeen physician.

Arrested: Dec. 2, 1910. Manslaughter, abortion.

Previous arrests:

July, 1904: Illegal dispensation of drugs. No charges filed, case dismissed, insufficient evidence;

July, 1905: Alleged conspiracy in abortion, charges dismissed. No evidence. Co-conspirator admitted guilt in plea bargain, absolved Stapp;

April, 1907, alleged abortion. Case dismissed, insufficient evidence;

May, 1908, alleged abortion. Case settled out of court, no charges."

Until 1904, the record on Stapp was clean, and he had been practicing in Aberdeen for some 15 years before that.

Then, the problems started, subsequently shortly before a divorce.

"This is hot stuff," he shouted as Lindy Fleming came from the washroom into the file section.

"Shh. Got what you need?"

"You bet, sweetie, and I owe it all to you."

"Now get out of here before you get caught and we both lose our jobs."

The two enjoyed a delectable salmon dinner, baked potato, green salad and vegetables. It was sixty cents, expensive at Aberdeen's best restaurant, but to Dan, it was worth it.

"How about some dessert?" Lindy asked with a twinkle in her eye.

He'd got lucky once this night and thought to himself. Gee, it's late. It's a long way to Montesano, and I still don't have a ride.

"Just exactly what did you have in mind?" he asked, clasping his hand in hers.

16. ED TORNOW TALKS

February 1911

As the train rounded the bend and roared toward Montesano, Cloud allowed himself to reflect on the previous night, a situation he knew he couldn't afford to pursue either financially or emotionally — at least not now that his career has forged into high gear.

"Nice girl, but I just don't have time with the trial and all to get involved. What am I saying? I am involved, and so is she, like it or not after the help she gave me at the station. And she did say, 'see ya soon' when I left and that long kiss we shared meant something. Oh, God. I gotta get my mind back on my work."

He carefully tucked the folded piece of paper on which he had quickly copied the information about Stapp into his shirt pocket, pulled out a pad of paper and began to jot some notes about Ed Tornow.

"Tornow, 28; Mary Bauer 24. She lived in Tornow home alone with Ed since Nov., 1910, when Mrs. Tornow died. Bauer, blood disease, pregnant August. Tornow took Bauer to Aberdeen, Nov. 26, then to Stapp. Dec. 1. Died. abortion Dec. 2. Stapp arrested Dec. 5. stayed at Emma Kaatz. Something not right. Incest? Abortion Nov. 27, botched, butcher, butcher. Which one?"

The pencil fell from his hand to the coach floor as Cloud nodded off.

The shrill whistle as the train pulled into the Montesano station awakened him with a start, his head bobbing against the seat back. He walked the few blocks up to Pioneer, then up Main to the courthouse. "That new clock and dome is going to be beautiful when it gets done," he thought to himself. "It's going to be the finest clock of any county seat around and it's right here in my hometown."

He was about ready to step across Broadway when Ed Tornow grabbed his arm.

"Hey, hey. How's the big time reporter?"

"Tornow. You startled me. I didn't see you. Ya ready for today?"

"No, I'm not. I'd rather do anything than go on that stand today. Cloud, you have no idea how difficult it is to sit up there and have them fire bullets at you. I'll probably crack."

"Ed, calm down. You'll do just fine," said the reporter, wise beyond his years. Suddenly he became a settling influence on the much-older Tornow.

A strapping young man in pinstriped-suit sauntered up to the men. "Tornow. Just the guy I wanted to see," said Ovie Nelson, the young protégé of attorney W. H. Abel.

"Nelson, not today. Got a lot on my mind," said Tornow. "Ya met Cloud?"

"Can't say that I have. Cloud, eh? Not Dan Cloud, the reporter?"

"In the flesh," said the journalist, flattered that he was recognized, if only by name.

"Been reading your stuff, not bad, not bad at all. Ovie Nelson," he said extending his hand.

"Tornow, we gotta talk," Nelson said, grabbing him by the arm. That timber deal we talked about. Got a proposition for you."

"Nelson," said Tornow gritting his teeth and glaring at the young lawyer. "Not here, not now. Cloud. See ya in court. I'll be right there," Tornow said, almost shoving the young attorney up the steps to the lobby.

"Nelson, nice to meet ya."

"Yeah, same here."

"What the hell you mean bringing up that stuff now? Don't you think I got enough on my mind?"

"I just thought you might want to hear the deal Abel has to offer you," the attorney said.

"Well, I do, of course, but now I got to get to the courtroom. I'm first up on the witness stand and that's going to be more than I can handle right now. I promise we'll get together soon's this thing's over."

Cloud took his seat in the courtroom, opened his note pad to the page that he began on the train.

"Timber deal?" he penciled next to the notes on Ed Tornow. Then he circled it to be sure not to forget it.

———

   "Now, Mr. Tornow, you testified to Prosecutor Campbell that Mary was living with you and your mother, and that you paid her a salary of $20 a month to start, then later raised it to $25?" stated Walter I. Agnew, assistant defense attorney, to whom Defense Attorney Boner handed the task of cross-examination.

   Ed Tornow: Yes, that's right.
   Agnew: When did Mary come to work for you?
   Tornow: I don't remember the exact date, but it was along in October 1909 some time. It was a couple months after my papa died.
   Agnew: Who was at the place then? Who was living there?
   Tornow: Myself, my brother Albert, and my mother.
   Agnew: Your brother stayed with you about how long after that?
   Tornow: About six weeks, I guess.
   Agnew: Mary worked at the place, then, up until she went to Aberdeen on November 26, 1910?
   Tornow: Yes, sir.
   Agnew: And all that time, she did housework?
   Tornow: Yes, sir. Housework and cooking.
   Agnew: How many rooms are in the house?
   Tornow: Eight.
   Agnew: How many sleeping rooms?
   Tornow: Four
   Agnew: Three upstairs and one downstairs?
   Tornow: Yes, sir.
   Agnew: Where did your mother sleep?
   Tornow: Downstairs.
   Agnew: Where did you and Mary sleep?
   Tornow: I slept in one end of the building as a rule, and Mary slept on the south end.
   Agnew: Upstairs?
   Tornow: Upstairs right over my mother's room.
   Agnew: After she had been working at the place, did you have any company at all? Did you keep any boarders or anything like that?
   Tornow: There were boarders there occasionally.
   Agnew: What kind of boarders were they?

Tornow: Different kinds that came along and stopped.

Agnew: How long would they stay?

Tornow: Some cruisers have been there sometimes and stayed two or three days, sometimes a week, but none until after Albert left.

Agnew: Sometimes a week; what one stayed there a week?

Tornow: Why, a timber cruiser from down south, I guess, stayed that long.

Agnew: What was his name?

Tornow: I don't remember his name.

Agnew: Did Mary keep company with any of these cruisers?

Tornow: She didn't really keep company with them, although she talked to them.

Agnew: She had talked to them?

Tornow: Yes, sir.

Agnew: Did Mary ever have any steady company, at all?

Tornow: No, sir.

Agnew: She didn't go with anybody?

Tornow: No, sir.

Agnew: These cruisers or boarders that happened to be there for a day or two — did she talk to them?

Tornow: Yes, sir, certainly.

Agnew: Now, all the time that she lived at your place, there was no one person that she kept regular company with at all?

Tornow: No, sir. Not that I know of.

Agnew: You would have known it if she had?

Tornow: If she had any steady company, I would have known.

Agnew: She was there every day and cooked your meals, did she not?

Tornow: Yes, sir.

Agnew: Morning and noon and night?

Tornow: Yes, sir.

Agnew: And she slept here at your home?

Tornow: Yes sir, I said that already.

Agnew: And was she away overnight from home any night during that time?

Tornow: No, sir. I don't think she was.

Agnew: She was there all the time?

Tornow: Yes, sir.

Having established testimony that Tornow was the only likely male company that Mary Bauer had for any period of time, Agnew immediately switched his questioning to the many times that Henry Bauer had attempted to get Mary to come home.

Cloud and the jury listened intently as Tornow repeatedly denied that he objected to Henry Bauer's request for Mary to return home, then after continued grilling, reversed his course to say that there was one request, but not until after his mother died.

Agnew continued to hammer at the credibility of this witness, now in regard to his relationship with Emma Kaatz.

Agnew: Did you know what her business was?

Tornow: No, sir.

Agnew: You never knew what her business was?

Tornow: I knew she was running a rooming house down there.

Agnew: Didn't you know she was practicing medicine to a certain extent? Didn't you know that for a fact?

Tornow: No, I never knew she was practicing medicine.

Agnew: I am not talking of your own knowledge: I will ask you what you knew of her occupation, what you learned from others.

Campbell: Objection, Your Honor. Relevance. Hearsay.

Judge Sheeks: Relevance goes to character, knowledge of witness, whether he knew beforehand or what he found out later. I'll allow. Witness, you may answer.

Tornow: Why, I didn't really know what her occupation was at the time.

Agnew: Did you know what her reputation was in regard to that, to her occupation?

Tornow: No, sir.

Agnew: You didn't see that she advertised as being a midwife?

Tornow: No sir, I did not.

Agnew: And that she advertised steam baths and gave medical treatment?

Tornow: No, sir.

Agnew: And you have known her for 10 years?

Tornow: Yes, I first met her 10 years ago.

Agnew: And how many times during those 10 years had you seen her?

Tornow: I don't really know, because for three or four years afterward I hadn't seen her at all.

Agnew: For three or four years afterward you never saw her at all?

Tornow: No, sir. I never saw her, outside of when she would be up to the ranch visiting my parents.

Agnew: How did you come to see her in Aberdeen?

Tornow: My brothers, John and Albert, had been stopping at her place and got acquainted with her and with her son. When we were in Aberdeen we went to her house one evening and stayed there a little while. That was about three years ago.

Agnew: Did you ever go and visit her again?

Tornow: Yes, I have been there.

Agnew: A number of times, then? How many times?

Tornow: Well, I don't remember.

Agnew: You don't remember?

Tornow: No, sir.

Agnew: You used to go there quite frequently, didn't you?

Tornow: I'd generally go and stop in a few minutes whenever I was in town, but would not stay very long.

Agnew: You stayed for a few minutes?

Tornow: Yes, sir.

Agnew: And you just visited? Did you room there or anything of that kind while you were in town?

Tornow: No, sir. I stopped one night before.

Agnew: Did you eat any meals there?

Tornow: Yes, I got a meal or two there.

Agnew: And conversed with her about business and all that sort of thing, didn't you?

Tornow: No, sir.

Sheeks: Counselor. Get to the point.

Agnew: I am your honor. Did you see any patients around there when you were there?

Tornow: No, sir.

Agnew: Did you see any roomers there?

Tornow: Yes, I saw roomers pass by and go upstairs.

Agnew: Men or women?

Tornow: Both.

Agnew: You say you were there frequently during the last three years, eating at her house, called to visit her at frequent intervals, and still you say you don't know what her occupation was?

Tornow: No, sir.

Agnew: Your honor. I'd like to request a brief recess to discuss an important item with my lead counsel.

Sheeks: We'll recess for 15 minutes. Members of the jury, counselors, be back in your seats by 10:30.

Seeing this brief opportunity, Cloud raced into the commissioners'
office to phone in a lead for the afternoon paper.

MONTESANO — *After two days of opening statements and general
background from the family of deceased Mary Bauer, the trial of alleged abortionist
Dr. Robert M. Stapp resumed this morning as the defense sought to discredit one
of the prosecution's key witnesses.*

*Ed Tornow, a resident of the Upper Satsop Valley, is the man who brought
his niece, 24-year-old Mary Bauer, a resident of the same house, to Aberdeen on
November 26, 1910.*

*It was on this fateful trip, December 1, on which Bauer, who was four months
pregnant, became ill and was found dead the next morning at the Aberdeen
apartments of Mrs. Emma Kaatz, 106 West Hume St.*

*The prosecution alleges that Tornow, 28, took the young woman to Stapp, who
then performed an abortion on her, and sent her to the Kaatz house to recover. The
prosecution further alleges that the abortion was not done correctly and resulted in
Bauer's death.*

*Tornow was on the stand only a short while under direct questioning from
Prosecutor William Campbell, who seemed intent only on showing that the witness
did indeed bring Miss Bauer to Aberdeen, then to Stapp's office, later to Mrs. Kaatz
boarding house, then took the train home with Kaatz's son Charles.*

*But William I. Agnew, assistant attorney for the defense, probed into Tornow's
relationship with the unfortunate victim.*

*Tornow admitted that this young woman was employed as a housekeeper by his
mother from about October 1909, until his mother died on November 13, 1910.
She continued to live and work at the house until Tornow took the pregnant Miss
Bauer to Aberdeen, on November 26, 1910.*

*During that time, there were many boarders, "but she didn't keep steady
company with any of them," Tornow said, adding "if she had, I would have
known it."*

*This testimony is certainly damaging to the credibility of Tornow, who repeatedly
denied he wasn't aware of the girl being pregnant, yet he admitted in court there was
no one else involved.*

*Tornow also detailed the sleeping room arrangements, though not until pressed
fully. He testified that his mother slept downstairs and "I slept upstairs at one*

end of the building as a rule, and Mary slept on the south end … right over my mother's room."

Agnew also induced Tornow to change his story that he did not object when his sister, Minnie, and her husband, Henry Bauer, the girl's parents, repeatedly objected to Mary being in the Tornow house when they sought several times to get the girl to come home.

Agnew asked Tornow if he ever seriously objected when she (Mrs. Bauer) requested Mary "to come home."

"No sir," Tornow replied.

Then a few minutes later, Agnew returned to that question again. "Did either the father or the mother request at any other time that Mary come home?"

Prosecutor Campbell objected that counsel should confine himself to the request being made in Tornow's presence, but Agnew argued that Tornow would not have known of the request, if he wasn't there.

Judge Ben Sheeks then instructed the witness to answer the question.

"Why, after my mother died (November 13, 1910), they did," Tornow said.

Again, Agnew hammered at the witness's credibility.

He wasn't through, not by a long shot.

He then attacked Tornow's relationship with Mrs. Kaatz. Tornow testified that he had known Mrs. Kaatz for about 10 years. He said he had been to her place in Aberdeen on a few occasions, having eaten there several times and even stayed overnight.

"Yet, you never knew what her business was … her reputation?" questioned Agnew. "You didn't know she was practicing medicine to a certain extent? Didn't you know that was a fact? … You didn't see she advertised as being a midwife? … that she advertised steam baths and gave medical treatment?"

Each time Tornow replied: "I did not."

Then Cloud wrapped up his story with the next testimony, saying Ed Tornow is expected to testify this afternoon of the fateful day when he brought young Miss Bauer to Aberdeen. Campbell is likely to call Mrs. Kaatz to the stand.

He concluded his story by saying "It is clear, the defense has a difficult task ahead with Tornow already casting a shadow on his testimony, and in part, making it difficult for Emma Kaatz to be believed."

———

"You all done?" the rewrite desk reporter asked.

"Yes, that's it for now," Cloud answered.

"Mr. Rupp wants to talk to you."

"Okay, put him on," the reporter said, wondering how he screwed up now.

"Cloud my boy. Great job! Just wanted to say that to you personally and to show appreciation, there'll be a room for you at the Washington until this is over."

"Sir, I don't know what to say," the ecstatic reporter said, almost at a loss for words. "Thanks a lot. That'll make the nights a lot easier.

"Gotta go, Cloud. Go get 'em kid."

———

Much of the next morning's trial consisted of Agnew going back over Ed Tornow's testimony of the previous day when he repeatedly said he had no knowledge of Mrs. Kaatz's reputation as a midwife, as an operator of steam baths or the medicines she dispensed. Tornow said the reason he had come to Aberdeen was to sell apples and other items. He said he piled them on to two crates for the train trip; then rented a cart to take them to the market, where he sold them. He testified that Mary Bauer came with him. They arrived in Aberdeen about 1 o'clock and went immediately to the home of Mrs. Kaatz, a couple of blocks from the train station.

Agnew: Now, you say that Mary Bauer confessed a certain condition to exist: that is, that she was pregnant. And she asked you to assist her in relieving her of her situation.

Tornow: Yes, sir

Agnew: She said that she had stood by you when you were in trouble and that she wanted you to stand by her.

Tornow: Yes, sir

Agnew: Was that a fact, had she stood by you in your trouble?

Tornow: Yes, sir She did.

Agnew: What trouble did you have?

Tornow: I had my mother to take care of.

Agnew: Oh, I see.

Tornow: Which I could not very well do alone.

Agnew: Did she have to keep that secret?
Tornow: No, sir
Agnew: This particular one, she said, she wanted to keep a secret?
Tornow: Yes, sir

Agnew then switched his questioning to the time after Tornow had returned to his ranch at Satsop and was confronted the next day, November 28, by his sister, Minnie, who had come to his ranch to see whether Mary came back with him.

Tornow said Mary wrote a letter to her mother, saying she had gone to Aberdeen and had figured on staying there a week. He said he told Minnie nothing about Mary being sick, except to say she was having trouble with the blood disease — erysipelas.

Tornow continued to testify that when they got to Aberdeen, Mary was going to see Dr. Stapp about the disease. Under continual questioning, Ed Tornow again maintained he didn't tell Minnie Bauer anything about Mary's pregnancy and that he didn't even know she was pregnant until Mary told him when they arrived in Aberdeen.

Tornow went on to affirm testimony of the morning that during the first day in Aberdeen, he went to the Chehalis Boom office to discuss the logging operation he and his brothers were involved with on the Satsop property; then to the Pacific Fruit Company, where he was unsuccessful in peddling his apples; then to some other smaller fruit stands, where he unloaded the fruit at a much-lower price than he had expected.

He also testified, as he did under direct cross from Campbell that he made a quick trip to Hoquiam via trolley to the Hoquiam Lumber and Shingle Company. There, he attempted to get some money for logs that was due him, though he hadn't done any logging for more than a year. The logs continued to come down the river, and especially after the big storm in October.

He said he arrived back at the Kaatz house about six o'clock and he and Mary ate dinner, then left to take in two short silent picture shows at the Rex and Starland, arriving back at Kaatz's house about 10 p.m.

Tornow said that he and Mary Bauer slept at Kaatz's house in separate rooms that night and arose about 8 a.m. He then spent around three hours at Adams & Smith electrical business, discussing the purchase of $200 in stock for an invention in which he had an interest.

It was when he was in that shop that Mary sought him out and related the news that she was pregnant, Tornow testified.

Tornow went on to say they went for a long walk through the dense and bawdy saloon and bordello district of Aberdeen, up to Market, down to Broadway, back down to Heron and back to the corner of H Street.

Tornow testified that during the walk Mary asked him to take her to see Dr. Stapp, but Tornow said he didn't know where his office was.

As they were standing on the corner across from the Finch Building at Heron and H, she just happened to look up and see Stapp's office sign.

Agnew: Well, what did you do then?

Tornow: She wanted me to go up and see Dr. Stapp and get some information from him.

Agnew: She had already told you what she wanted, hadn't she?

Tornow: Yes she told me she wanted to go and see him. But before I went up there, I wanted to know what she wanted to know.

Agnew: What did she tell you she wanted?

Tornow: In the first place, she wanted to know how long she would be sick.

Agnew: She wanted to know how long she would be sick?

Tornow: Yes, sir It was a case of doing the work.

Agnew: The case of performing an abortion, is that what you mean?

Campbell: Objection Your Honor. Leading the witness.

Sheeks: Overruled. I'll allow it. Mr. Tornow, answer the question.

Tornow: Yes, sir

Agnew: What else did she want to know?

Tornow: She wanted to know how much it would cost.

Agnew: Where did you go then?

Tornow: Well, I went across the street and she stayed. She said she would walk around the street while I went in.

Agnew: What did you do?

Tornow: I went up to the office room.

Agnew: How did you go up?

Tornow: I walked up. This was on Sunday, the elevator wasn't running.

Agnew: And when you got to Dr. Stapp's, you went where?

Tornow: Into a sitting room — a waiting room.

Tornow went on to testify that he didn't go into Stapp's private office, but the doctor came into the sitting room to talk to him. He asked the doctor about the charges and said he was told it would be $50. He said the doctor said Mary would be under the effect for 24 hours.

Tornow testified he asked the doctor "In regards to her health, whether it would injure her health any. And he said 'No, sir, not a particle.' And he said 'I will guarantee a safe cure, without injuring her health, for fifty dollars.'"

Tornow said the doctor asked where he was staying and he told him, "Mrs. Kaatz's, not at a hotel." He objected to that, saying "She is against any work like that." He said he would "fix it up with Mrs. Kaatz. You don't need to tell her anything about it."

Under Agnew's questioning, Tornow said Stapp wanted to do the operation at 8 p.m. that night.

Agnew: Was anything more said about payment?

Tornow: No, sir

Agnew: He didn't ask you whether or not you were going to pay it, or whether she would pay it?

Tornow: He asked me whether she would pay for it, or whether she had the money, that is what he asked.

Agnew: What did you say?

Tornow: I told him I thought she did.

Agnew: Didn't you know she had the money?

Tornow: I didn't know how much she had.

Agnew: Didn't you testify in your direct examination that the day before in Montesano you cashed a creamery check?

Tornow: Yes sir, and I gave her $25 that day.

Agnew: Now, where did you go after you got through with Dr. Stapp?

Tornow: Why, I went outside.

Agnew: And where did you go?

Tornow: I walked out on the sidewalk and went to the corner of the Finch Building. And as I turned the corner, I met her coming up the street.

Agnew: What did you do then?

Tornow: We turned around and walked down to Mrs. Kaatz's.

Agnew: About what time of day was this?

Tornow: It must have been along after five o'clock.

Agnew: What did you do when you got to Mrs. Kaatz's?

Tornow: She went in the house, and I went back to Smith's office.

Agnew: Did you have any conversation with her while you were going down the street?

Tornow: I told her what the doctor told me, while we were walking down the street.

Agnew: And what did she say?

Tornow: She kind of thought it was all right, but still she didn't know.

Agnew: She kind of thought it was all right, but still she didn't know? Is that all she said?

Tornow: Yes, sir. She didn't talk very much at the time, only asked me questions and I answered them.

Agnew: What were those questions and how did you answer them?

Tornow: She asked how much he was going to charge, and I told her fifty dollars. And she asked me how long she would be sick, and I told her she probably would be out from under the effects of it in 24 hours and up in three days.

Agnew: What else did you tell her?

Tornow: I told her she didn't have to go up there and didn't have to have the work done, if she didn't want to.

Agnew: You told her she didn't have to?

Tornow: Yes, sir

Agnew: What was the occasion for your telling her that?

Tornow: I told her the day before that the best thing for her to do would be go to Seattle and stay there until the time came, and go to the Orphan's home and leave the child there when it was born.

Tornow continued to testify as Agnew repeatedly went over his earlier testimony. When asked by Agnew if he thought it was a bad thing to have Mrs. Kaatz involved, if she was against that sort of operation, Tornow snapped back, "I didn't care if it did." He continued to say he had not heard of Dr. Stapp until he was walking with Mary that Sunday afternoon. He said he was positive he did not suggest the name of Stapp to Mary and it was Mary who accidentally saw his name when they walked that day.

Tornow: She saw it. She was watching for the name.

Agnew: You weren't watching for the name, but she was?

Tornow: She would not have noticed it, if she hadn't been.

Agnew: And she called your attention to it?

Tornow: Yes, sir

Agnew continued to probe for more cracks in Tornow's story, retracing the testimony from the time he left Montesano on November 26 until he returned home two days later. There was little deviation.

Tornow then testified that, after being told of Mary's death by a friend from the Satsop Valley, as he had no telephone, he arrived back in Aberdeen about 4 p.m., December 1.

He went directly to Mrs. Kaatz's house, and after a few minutes, took a short walk up to Whiteside's Undertaking Parlor. W.R. Whiteside had just recently purchased the business from W.J. Woods and Bowes & Randolph, consolidating it into one operation on Wishkah between Broadway and I streets.

Tornow said he went to Valentine Drake's to get a shave, and then returned to Mrs. Kaatz's. About 7 p.m., Police Chief George Dean and Coroner Paul Smits arrived to question him.

Agnew: What did you do then?

Tornow: We went up to the room and examined the room where she was in.

Agnew: What?

Tornow: We went up to the room that she died in.

Agnew: You went up with Chief Dean and Coroner Smits to look at the room?

Tornow: Yes, sir

Agnew: What was done or said in there? Did you hear Dr. Smits question Mrs. Kaatz about the room? Mrs. Kaatz was there with you when you went up?

Tornow: Yes, sir. I don't remember everything that was said there that night.

Agnew: Tell us what you do remember.

Tornow: Well, he asked her how Miss Bauer came to be down there and when she came down there. She told them the whole story. He wanted to know what kind of tablets were in the room. The coroner said he had seen them in the morning and now they were gone.

Agnew: He wanted to know what became of the tablets that had been there?

Tornow: Yes, sir. She didn't know whether anybody took them or not. Dr. Smits asked her if anybody had been in the room since he had been in there and told her to lock up the room. And, she said there had. And, he wanted to know who it was.

Agnew: Did she tell him?

Tornow: She said that Dr. Stapp had been in there since the Coroner had been there. Stapp told her to unlock the door and said he wanted to see the girl before she was taken out.

Agnew: Dr. Stapp wanted to see the girl before she was taken to the undertaking parlor?

Tornow: Yes, sir

Agnew: What did Mrs. Kaatz tell Mr. Smits about these tablets?

Tornow: She didn't tell him anything else about those tablets at that time.

After lengthy testimony, a tiring Tornow then became totally confused about when he told what to whom, and became rattled when he contradicted his early testimony a number of times.

Tornow finally said that he was kept at the jail on December 1 all night, not in a cell, but he stayed on a lounge. He said he had received a letter at home from Mary Bauer telling of her intentions and he said he left it on the counter, but when he and Chief Dean went up there together on December 2 to retrieve the letter; it was nowhere to be found. He said he had no idea what happened to the letter.

Agnew then asked Tornow to describe what happened when he was taken to the jail.

"They said …"

"Excuse me Mr. Tornow," interjected Agnew. "Who is they?"

"Campbell and Smits," he said referring to the prosecutor and Coroner Smits.

Agnew: Were they trying to get you to tell this story?

Tornow: Yes, sir

Agnew: Did they offer you any inducement to tell this story?

Tornow: No, sir.

Agnew: None whatever?

Tornow: No, sir

Agnew: Didn't they tell you in substance, if you told that story they would see that you didn't get punished?

Tornow: No, sir. They said nothing of the kind.

Agnew: Why did you tell it to them, then?

Tornow: They told me I would be arrested, if I didn't tell what I knew.

Agnew: Did they bring you up to Montesano at any time?

Tornow: No, sir

Agnew: Who was it that told you that you would be arrested if you didn't tell this story?

Tornow: Paul Smits.

Agnew: Tell me just exactly what Dr. Smits said.

Tornow: I don't remember what he said that night. He said he had a notion to have the whole cheese of us arrested.

Agnew: Arrest who?

Tornow: Arrest all of us.

Agnew: You didn't want to tell them the story at that time, did you?

Tornow: No, sir. I didn't want to break the promise that I made to Miss Bauer, at that time.

Agnew: You had already broke the promise to Chief Dean the night before?

Tornow: No, the next morning.

Agnew: When was it that Dr. Smits told you, you were going to be arrested unless you told this story?

Tornow: The night of December 1st.

Agnew: So you thought it over until the next morning and then told Chief Dean.

Tornow: Yes, sir

Agnew: What did Chief Dean say to you at that time?

Tornow: He said he wanted to know what all I knew about the case.

Under testimony, Tornow said Chief Dean questioned Mrs. Kaatz, asking if anyone else had been in the room since the Coroner was there. She said Dr. Stapp had been there and taken the pills.

Agnew: Now in your own language, tell what you did and what she said.

Tornow: I asked Mrs. Kaatz if Mary had asked her to go up to the office with her. And she said she did. I asked her if she went. And if she had gone up with her?

Agnew: What else did she say?

Tornow: I said "You were up in the waiting room?" And she says "Yes, I was." I think that was the question at the time.

Agnew: Did she tell you anything about being present while any sort of an operation was being performed on Mary?

Tornow: No, sir

Agnew: Was that all the conversation you had with her?

Tornow: It was that night.

Campbell then re-directed examination of Tornow.

He asked about the letter Mary Bauer had written and asked Tornow what was the date. Agnew objected, saying the letter itself is the best evidence of that. Judge Sheeks overruled and ordered Tornow to answer, to which Agnew called "exception." Tornow said it was November 28, 1910. Campbell dismissed the witness.

Then Agnew, who declined to re-cross examine, asked the judge for an aside and handed him a penciled note that read:

"The defense reserves the right, and moves to strike the testimony of this witness, on the ground that his testimony shows him to have been an accomplice."

Judge Sheeks denied the request, and then adjourned the court for the day.

———

Cloud slowly ambled up the steps of the Montesano, where he had heard Agnew was going to spend the night. He peered into the lower level restaurant and spotted the attorney alone at a table.

"Care if I join you, counselor?"

"No, not at all," the attorney replied.

"So, what do you think of that Tornow?" Cloud asked, breaking open a moment of silence.

"Off the record?"

"Well, all right, but I'd rather have it on the record."

"You know, I can't talk about the case in detail," the attorney said.

"On the record first. What was that little aside you had with the judge before adjournment today?"

"That I can tell you because since he replied, it will be in the court minutes. I penciled him a note, telling him it was my right and my request that the testimony of Mr. Tornow be stricken because the testimony he gave shows him to be an accomplice."

"And the judge's response, of course was denial?"

"Yes, with no comment."

"Then I take it that you believe that he is as guilty as Stapp?"

"That goes without saying," the attorney said. "You heard him today. Everything he said pointed in that direction. One thing I do know, from everyone I have talked to, he's the father."

"I agree with you that he's the father. Everything points to that, but is he an accomplice? I think that's going a little far, isn't it?" answered the scribe.

"You can't print a word of this, but I think after tomorrow, you'll change your tone on that," the attorney, said. "I'll tell you more later. Right now I got to go relieve myself."

Agnew got up and headed to the restroom, leaving some notes on the case in full view of the reporter.

"Did he intend for me to see them?" Cloud thought to himself? "Of course he did or he would have hidden them in his satchel."

He didn't have to see much to know what the attorney was talking about. He peered at the paper and could easily read upside down:

Kaatz, guilty as Tornow, Conspiracy. Poke holes in prosecution. Background, conversation with Stapp. Went with Bauer, saw operation, could have stopped it, Pills, Pills.

Cloud saw what he wanted and started to leave when Agnew returned.

"Gonna leave so soon? Thought you were gonna eat?"

"I was, but I probably better get going. Got to catch a ride to town. You know, they don't pay us reporters enough to take the motor car," he said chuckling.

"All right, Cloud. See ya tomorrow. And Cloud, be careful what you write. You know you're covering a trial. Just the facts."

"Yeah, I know," the reporter said, sliding his chair up to the table. "Yeah, but it sure is tempting."

It was nearly 7 p.m. when Cloud arrived back at the *World* office and sat down at his desk to pound out the next day's story.

He would have preferred to write more, but a note from the editor told him no more than five inches, unless there was something extremely compelling.

"Nothing too compelling, I guess, particularly since I have to deal only with the facts," the reporter said out loud. "I can do that."

He finished his five-inch article about Ed Tornow's testimony and the defense's cross examination, and concluded with the judge denying Agnew's request to have the testimony stricken.

He grabbed the two double-spaced typewritten pages and slapped a glob of glue on them.

"Cloud, 2-17-11. Stapp trial, 2 takes, lead to come mid-morning," he penciled on top and placed it in the wire basket on City Editor Bill Irvine's desk.

He knew there might be some critical testimony after the morning session when Mrs. Kaatz takes the stand.

Cloud looked at the clock on the wall and thought to himself. "Umm. 7:45, maybe she's still there. Dinner."

He hustled out the door and crossed the street to the police department. His heart sank as he opened the door and there was no Lindy in sight.

"Where's Lindy?" Cloud asked the man at the desk. "She didn't come in today. Under the weather, I guess."

His thoughts of a nice dinner and some late night companionship dashed, Cloud closed the door without a word to the desk clerk and headed to the Washington.

"Probably, better off. Gotta keep my mind on this trial," he said drifting off to sleep.

———

It was mid-morning when Prosecutor Campbell continued his direct questioning of Emma Kaatz.

After filling in the jury on her background, Campbell questioned Kaatz on each detail of the days of Saturday, November 26 and Sunday, the 27th.

She said Mary Bauer and Ed Tornow had stayed at her house Saturday after arriving about 3 p.m. She told of Mary and Ed leaving for about three hours on Sunday and returning about 5 for supper.

She said after supper, Tornow left for home with her son, Charlie, and she and Mary went to the doctor's office.

Campbell then questioned the woman in great detail about the specifics of Stapp's office and everything that occurred in that office.

Judge Sheeks then adjourned the court for a short recess, and Cloud dashed for the phone to call in the new lead.

"An Aberdeen woman, who was often a midwife, offered damaging testimony today in the continuing trial of Dr. Robert Stapp, the Aberdeen man, who is accused of malpractice in the abortion death of an Upper Satsop woman."

Cloud's story went on to describe briefly how Emma Kaatz had testified to being in the room when Dr. Stapp performed the abortion, how she found Mary Bauer dead at her house on Thursday morning, December 1, and then the damaging part about the doctor taking the pills and all but threatening the woman after that.

Court was already in session with Defense Attorney Agnew attacking Kaatz's credibility when Cloud returned to the courtroom.

She testified that she had known the Tornows and Mary Bauer for about nine years, refuting what Henry Bauer had said earlier about Kaatz having no acquaintance with Mary until 1909.

Kaatz also testified that she and Mrs. Tornow were good friends, but Minnie Bauer had earlier said "My mother didn't like her much."

Agnew then succeeded in getting the woman completely mixed up on her time frame.

She said Tornow and Mary Bauer had arrived at 1 p.m., differing from Tornow's testimony when he said he arrived about 3.

Cloud made a quick note of this important distinction, because Tornow could not have accomplished all that he needed to get done between 3 and 5 p.m. He wondered why Agnew didn't hammer this point more clearly to the jury.

"I guess he's got his reasons," the reporter noted.

Kaatz also testified that when she was at the Tornow's farm the night after the funeral for Mrs. Tornow (November 18), Mary had complained of the blood disease breaking out, but Coroner Smits said after performing the autopsy there was no sign of the erysipelas.

Agnew then continued to discredit the woman, who repeatedly denied she knew Mary was pregnant.

Agnew: You didn't know she was pregnant?
Kaatz: No zer.
Agnew: You didn't know until after you got up to the doctor's office after seven o'clock?
Kaatz: No zer. I didn't know a zing about it. I tot all the time she vas going to be cured for that blood problem.
Agnew: Erysipelas?
Kaatz: Yes zer. I think that's vat it's called.

Cloud jotted some notes to pursue. He hadn't known much about pregnancies and the complications or abortions. But he had done his homework and was prepared for the technical aspects of this trial. He had even studied erysipelas after it was brought up after the autopsy.

"Strange. Was it strange that this experienced midwife hadn't notice the changes, even slight changes, in appearance or build in this woman four months pregnant; Strange. Erysipelas produces red streaks on the skin and it normally lasts several months. None were present at the autopsy, but Kaatz says she thought Mary was being treated for that; Strange. If Mary wasn't pregnant, why did Kaatz jump to the conclusion that an abortion was being conducted?"

Agnew then tried to trap Mrs. Kaatz into a wrong, faulty description of Stapp's waiting room, but she talked only in generalities, and each time the attorney got specific, she said "I not know."

He then took Kaatz back through the sequence from the time she was with Mary Bauer at her mom's funeral until after the operation.

Then she dropped a bombshell when asked what happened when they returned home after the operation.

Kaatz: I said "Vat did you have dat done for?" and she said "My sweetheart deceive me and I no vant to go back to my mama."

Agnew didn't want this discrepancy to go unnoticed.

Agnew: You stated you never spoke to her after this operation was performed. You stated you never in any way talked in relation to this operation after you left the office.

Kaatz: It vas at home, like I zay. She zay "I could not go to my mother because my sveetheart run avay."

Agnew: Did she tell you this sweetheart's name?

Kaatz: No. She zay he vas cruiser. He vas der in June or July. He came der fishing or hunting.

Cloud jotted another note: Hunting season started September 1.

Agnew: A cruiser was up there fishing and hunting?

Kaatz: Yes. She zay "He come ver rest. And he promised to get married after Christmas. Four or five weeks before she come to my place, she never had answer from him."

Agnew then went in another direction.

Agnew: Do you remember a man by the name of Dr. Van Valkenberg?

Kaatz: Ya, he come ver treatment about December 13.

Agnew: And didn't you have a conversation with him about this?

Kaatz: Ya, I told him.

Agnew: Didn't you tell him that you were satisfied Ed Tornow, the uncle of the girl, was the cause of her condition?

Kaatz: Na zer.

Agnew: Didn't you tell him, on or about the 13th day of December when you were treating him, that you didn't know she was pregnant, but you went with her to Dr. Stapp's office, and you didn't go in.

Kaatz: Don't you zink I know ven any man comes to me ven I know zomzing. Do you zink I am going to tell a strange man vat goes on?

Agnew: Raising his voice and pointing his finger at the witness: Did you tell him that or did you not?

Sheeks: Counselor. Calm down. Mrs. Kaatz, just answer the question.

Kaatz: Ya zer. He asked me vat I knew about her and I told him few words about it.

Agnew: Didn't you tell him "the old son-of-a-gun of a Dr. Stapp was in that business all along" and that "you were going to clip his wings?" Didn't you tell him at that time "Stapp is out on bonds now, but when you get through with him he will be behind bars?"

Kaatz: Dat is not zee truth.

Agnew: You didn't tell him that?

Kaatz: Na zer.

Agnew: Didn't you tell him that Dr. Stapp came down and got tablets and told you to "Shut up" and "Come to his office and he would give you a piece of money?"

Kaatz: I don't know. The Coroner ask me who took the tablets and I say "Dr. Stapp did."

Later Agnew hammered again at the German woman regarding her testimony for the time between the night of the abortion and the death.

Agnew: You mean to tell me that you went to this doctor's office, and that you knew it was the purpose of performing an abortion, and that this girl was a friend of yours, and that you were interested in her almost like a mother, and you never went to see her once after she went to bed until she got up in the morning?

Agnew continued to pound, Kaatz broke down and lost her composure under the relentless questioning. She had obviously had enough.

Agnew: You continue to say that you never told anybody until you got on the stand, that you saw an operation performed?

Kaatz: I can't remember vether I did or not. I can't tell you. Does dat satisfy you? And vat else do you vant to know? I feel like coming down and fight, if you vant to.

Then turning to the judge, Mrs. Kaatz blurted out, "I will take an inkwell and throw it in his face pretty soon. He acts like he wants to fight."

Judge Sheeks: Never mind, just answer his questions.

Agnew: Coming back to the time …

Kaatz: You come back all you vant to.

Agnew: Coming back to the time that Dr. Smits said, "Where are those pills?" Where was it that he said that?

Kaatz: In zee room vere Mary vas.

Agnew: And you told him you didn't know?

Kaatz: I no like to tell, right avay.

Agnew: What did Dr. Smits tell you there? Didn't he say "You look here, old woman, you tell me where they went or I will make it hot for you?"

Kaatz: Ya zer.

Agnew: You don't remember telling Dr. Van Valkenberg afterwards that this old fellow, Dr. Stapp, had been practicing this for a long time and you were going to "clip his wings?"

Kaatz: Na zer. I tell him no zuch zing. He vas zuch a good spiritualist. I guess zome of the spirits took him from Aberdeen.

And the courtroom burst out laughing.

And with that, Agnew ended his cross examination, turning the re-direct over to Prosecutor Campbell.

Mrs. Kaatz testified initially to finding out that Van Valkenberg was a detective who she said was sent by Stapp. The "doctor" however, wasn't aware that the woman knew who he was. He had boarded there for nine days before Kaatz discovered him snooping through her bedroom.

Kaatz testified the "doctor" had a lame back "zo I made mustard plaster for him, den he complained of stomach ache and I fix poultice of onion, garlic and rye flour and all kinds of stuff in it. Ya, and I show him vat it vas like to come and deceive me, and I deceive him too."

"Crusty old lady," Cloud thought to himself.

In Campbell's final re-direct, Kaatz admits telling Campbell and Police Chief Dean a few days earlier that she was present at the operation.

"Ya, I told you I vas der and I guess I said it here today. That is all I know. I guess the court reporter has it in his book vat I said dis afternoon. I know nothing else," Kaatz said.

There was a short re-cross from Agnew, who went over the Van Valkenberg incident, then the telling of the operation to Campbell and Dean. The attorney again petitioned Judge Sheeks to strike all testimony of Mrs. Kaatz on the grounds of her being an accomplice.

Judge Sheeks again dismissed the petition and asked Prosecutor Campbell to call his next witness.

Coroner Smits took the stand and the rest of the afternoon dealt with technical information regarding the health of Mary Bauer, the condition she was found in, the abortion operation and the autopsy.

Smits testified to being called by Dr. Chamberlain, not Mrs. Kaatz's daughter as the woman had said. He also said he saw the pills and told Mrs. Kaatz to "let nobody in that room until the undertaker arrived." When he returned and didn't find the pills, Kaatz told him she didn't know where they were.

He said the appearance of the girl indicated that there might have been trouble with the circulation of the heart. An autopsy was performed immediately because he said, there "was nothing to indicate anything externally abnormal."

Smits said when he began the autopsy that evening, he examined the heart and found it showed degeneration of the heart muscle. "I also found an enlarged uterus with a fetus in it about four and a half months old; the placenta, or afterbirth, was loosened in two places; and the fluid surrounding the fetus inside the amniotic sac was out. The uterus showed congestion in spots."

At that point, Smits said he stopped the autopsy, notified the police, who then began their investigation, and called in a cadre of medical officials the next morning.

E.W. Boner then took charge of the cross-examination and, unlike Campbell, grilled Dr. Smits about the pills. After a lengthy series of questions, Smits recounted the exhausting, intense questioning he gave Mrs. Kaatz until she finally admitted that Dr. Stapp was in the room and took the pills.

Boner then built the defense for his client and questioned Smits in detail about the condition of Mary Bauer's heart.

Boner: And you found that the fibers of the heart had in fact degenerated?
Smits: Yes.
Boner: "Lost their force?"
Smits: Yes.
Boner: "In cases of this kind, what will cause death? What will precipitate the cause that will overpower the heart?
Smits: Great worry or great excitement.
Boner: You might drop dead?
Smits: When you have a condition like that of the heart muscle, any shock could do it, of any kind.
Boner: The heart fails to work, and in a few minutes it is all over?
Smits: Yes.
Boner: That was the condition of Mary Bauer's heart?
Smits: Yes.

The coroner testified that the water was gone, most of the placenta had been loosened from the wall by abrasions of the inner wall of the uterus. It was a puncture by a sharp tool.

Boner then probed Smits to say that a puncture of the sort that existed here would cause "considerable shock."

The attorney then attempted to grill the Coroner as to his view of Mrs. Kaatz's reputation, but ran into roadblocks from Campbell's objections before ending his cross-examination.

Campbell: Objection. Mrs. Kaatz is not on trial, your honor.
Sheeks: Counsel is right. Stick to relevancy, Mr. Boner.
Boner: No further questions, your honor, but I would like to call another witness.
Judge Sheeks: Prosecutor, are you going to re-cross this witness?
Campbell: No, your honor.
Judge Sheeks: Call your witness, he said to Boner.
Boner: The defense calls Dr. Harry Watkins to the stand.

Cloud read through his notes and background on this expert witness. H.C. Watkins was not a director of any hospital, but had been associated with Hoquiam General Hospital and had 14 years of obstetrics practice in Hoquiam. He had been one of five who participated in the autopsy after Coroner Smits suspended the operation and notified the police:

Watkins gave much the same description of the young woman as did Smits.

Boner then asked him for his conclusion.

Boner: Now, Dr. Watkins, you have offered details of expert testimony in this case, and there is no argument you are an expert witness, having witnessed many births, many operations and, as you say, "a good many abortions that failed." Would you give us your conclusion in this case after participating in the autopsy, and be specific please. The jury would appreciate that.

Watkins: My conclusion from this examination was that the abortion had been performed not to exceed 12 hours before death, and probably less. Also, the extent of the injury that occurred in that uterus, and to that fetus and placenta, I don't believe that woman could have walked at all, or very little.

Boner: Doctor would you describe for us the condition of the placenta, the uterus and the amniotic sac.

Watkins: The amniotic sac was punctured, the placenta was punctured, but the fetus was not. I expected the fetus to be punctured, too.

The doctor went on to say that he had "never seen a case quite like this one. I had seen several hundred women who had abortions. I had seen surgery done by Dr. Stapp, not in recent years. Dr. Stapp did good surgery. This was an incompetent job."

Boner thanked the doctor and Campbell began his cross examination.

Campbell: Are you informed as to the nature of criminal abortion?

Watkins: Yes, sir. I treat patients very frequently when those things occur.

Campbell: How are those criminal abortions performed?

Watkins: They are performed in many different ways.

Campbell: This was performed in one of those ways, was it not?

Watkins: I never saw such a state of affairs as I saw at that autopsy. I never heard of it being done before. I don't believe you can get a parallel case in the books, in precedence.

Campbell: Your opinion in this particular case is not based on any former experience, doctor?

Watkins: Oh, yes, I only have my own experience to follow in forming my opinion.

Campbell: You stated you never saw or heard of a parallel case.

Watkins testified when asked by Campbell how many abortions he had "cured," that he had treated "probably 200 to 300 abortions, some of them badly done abortions." He said in most cases, women can walk around soon after the operation, but added, it depends on the extent of the injury and the age of the pregnancy. He talked of treating women with a fetus four-to-five months old and said the woman was usually up and walking within a couple of days.

Campbell took this opportunity to leave the jury overnight with a key question, one the defense had pushed, that of an application of iodine for erysipelas caused the heart failure.

Campbell: Was there any indication of any iodine being used on the body of Mary Bauer when you examined her?

Watkins: I didn't notice any.

Campbell: Did you notice her arms and hands?

Watkins: Yes.

Campbell: If there had been iodine there, would you have seen it?

Watkins: I think I would have seen it.

Campbell: No further questions.

Judge Sheeks: We will recess until 9:30 Monday.

Cloud was glad that there was going to be a weekend recess. It had been a taxing week for any reporter, especially a young one. He would welcome the rest, maybe even a chance to spend some time with Lindy.

"I should be able to knock this story out quickly and get out of here."

He figured he'd lay a little levity on the reader this day after some heavy testimony most of the week.

"They'll appreciate the feisty old bitch," he said to himself, formulating the lead to his story in his head as he journeyed to Aberdeen on the train.

"After four days of intense testimony, a witness for the defense in the abortion trial of Dr. Robert Stapp exploded on the stand Friday, threatening to fight it out with Prosecuting Attorney William Campbell."

He went on to write about that incident and the other blowups before getting serious with the severe grilling the old woman received at the hands of the attorney.

He figured he'd close with a couple of paragraphs to balance the story, giving the defense its shot with Boner's cross examination of Coroner Smits to show that Mary Bauer could have died of blood poisoning. He concluded with Dr. Watkins' expert testimony that this operation was "incompetent."

Cloud pasted the four takes together and plopped it on editor Irvine's desk, glanced at the clock and headed out the door.

"Now that was a week," he thought to himself, "but it was fun."

He walked briskly toward the hotel. He grabbed a quick sandwich and a cup of soup at the cafe across the street from the hotel and bought a magazine at the cigar store in front. He strutted to the front desk at the Washington, very proud of himself. He checked in and headed to his room.

"Maybe I'll ring Lindy to see how she is," the reporter thought after taking a long shower. "Na, too late, I'll probably wake her if she is still ill."

He plopped down on the comfortable double bed to read and immediately fell asleep, the magazine falling into his lap.

17. A DAY OFF

February 1911

The light tapping on the hotel door fit perfectly in Dan Cloud's dream and he didn't stir until … the rapping became more vigorous and urgent.

"What the — What's that," he thought to himself, sitting up in bed. "It's only 8. I don't have to get up today. It's Sunday, isn't it?"

He ambled over to the door. "Who's there?" he said, almost in a whisper.

"Maid service, Meester Cloud," the feeble voice answered with a distinct foreign accent.

"At this hour? I'm not ready to leave yet. I don't have to get up today. Come back in a couple of hours."

"But, I can't Meester. I gotta clean this room early, something going on here later, I guess."

"Well, OK. Wait until I get some clothes on."

"Oh, meester you don't have to put clothes on for me."

"What the hell?" he thought to himself. "Uhhh. What did you say?"

"You don't have to put clothes on for me," she repeated.

"Now, you go away and come back in a couple of hours or I'll report you to the manager."

"Please meester. I want to please you. Let me in."

"No. Now do as I say and leave me be."

"But, meester, I already seen you without clothes."

"What are you talking about?"

"You're not married are you?"

"No, but I have a girlfriend."

Hearing this, the voice on the other side of the door dropped the accent.

"Oh, Danny. It's me, let me in before someone hears us," said Lindy.

It took Cloud but a second to open the door.

"Gotcha," said a beaming Lindy, holding a couple of bags.

"You sonovva bitch," he said. "You got me all right. Best prank anybody ever pulled ... and I love it."

"Danny, you've been working so hard. Today, you are all mine."

Cloud loved the sound of that. He wasn't too experienced in the relationship department. His life had been too busy to get involved. In the short time he and Lindy had been seeing each other, he had been the aggressor.

Now, she was making the rules. He loved it.

"And, Danny, you're my boyfriend. I'm glad you didn't open the door when I said I already seen you naked. Now, sit down and let's have breakfast," she said putting the bags on the table.

"Breakfast?"

"Yep. Brought it with me."

"Hmmm. Presumptuous young lady," he thought to himself.

"Well, dear. What are we having for breakfast?"

"Nothing too fancy. A bowl of fruit, little oatmeal, pastry and coffee."

"Sounds good to me."

The two gobbled up the breakfast and put the dishes out in the hall, even though it wasn't room service, but take-out Lindy had picked up from Hosmer's grocery down the street.

"What now, my dear?" he said grabbing the young brunette from behind, wrapping his arms around her waist and kissing the back of her neck.

"Now, you did it," you rascal. "We've got to have dessert now."

Dan knew what that meant and the two fell in deep embrace on the bed.

It had been a couple of hours when Dan heard a tapping at the door.

"Room service, Meester Cloud."

He bounded out of bed to save the embarrassment of being caught naked in front of the maid — this time for real.

"Uhh. Can you give me about 30 minutes?"

"Sure, I come back," the maid answered.

"Hey, sweetie. You awake?" he said nudging the contentedly napping young lady.

"I am now," she said, rolling over exposing her naked body as she pulled her man onto the bed.

"I told the maid to come back in a half-hour and I gotta take a quick bath."

"OK. I'll just lie here and watch you; I'll be ready, then I've got a great day planned."

"I'll hurry," he said, then again smiled as he headed to the tub. "Hmmm. I kind of like this. She's got something planned. Can't wait."

Dan was out of the tub in a few minutes and watched his lady slip into her clothes, savoring every curve she slowly covered up.

"Ready?" she asked Dan. "We better hurry. Got to catch the train. Oh, and grab your jacket."

"The train?"

"We can catch the 11 o'clock, if we step on it."

Still, she wouldn't divulge her plan as they walked the couple of blocks down to River Street to board the Southern Special.

"Where we going?" he asked, probing for some clue.

"South," she said, not giving an inch.

She went inside the depot and purchased two tokens.

"C'mon. We're going to the beach."

"What? It's February."

"I know and we'll have it all to ourselves."

That sounded enticing to Dan, but still cold.

They got off the train at Ocosta and walked about a half-mile arm-in-arm, down to Bottle Beach, a popular recreation area in the summertime.

Just as Lindy expected, they had the beach to themselves.

"There's some wood over there and we can build a fire," she said.

Dan grabbed a few pieces of driftwood and small roots for kindling. "The wood's nice and a fire would be great," but I don't have anything to light it," he said.

"Will this work?" Lindy said pulling a box of wooden matches out of her pocketbook, then handing them and a few napkins she had stashed in her pocket at the grocers to Dan.

"You think of everything, don't you," he said with a smirk. "Gonna have to be on my toes to keep ahead of this one," he thought.

Warmed by the fire, the young couple shared each other's life stories as they embraced one another.

Neither of them noticed the chill in the air on this early February day.

It seemed like a couple of hours as they enjoyed this special moment, Dan breaking away once to rekindle the embers and keep the fire going.

It was a 45-degree day, but he was warm as toast in Lindy's arms and she in his. They had their love to keep them warm.

"This is so nice," he said. "I could get used to this."

Dan's mind was a million miles away from the courtroom at Montesano, and he needed that.

Lindy had grown up in Aberdeen, and while the two were the same age — 23 — their paths hadn't crossed until Dan began going to the police station for his research.

Lindy was a bright girl, graduating at the top of her Weatherwax High School class. She wanted to attend college, but shelved that notion to care for her dad.

Her mom passed when she was just eight and her dad raised her, along with an aunt, when her father had to spend long days in the woods. He contracted an illness while Lindy was at college and recovery took nearly a year.

She didn't go back to school after a friend told her about an opening as clerk at the police department. It was very rare — almost unheard of — for a woman to occupy such a position, but she had met Chief Dean before and he was impressed with her knowledge and ability to get along with people.

"I was real nervous when I went to talk to them about the job and I forgot Chief Dean was there," she said, relating how she got the job. "He came in when they were talking to me, gave me a big hug and that was that. I was calm after that and I started that afternoon."

Lindy was fascinated by the several positions Dan had already had in journalism, and he was still young. He told her about the accident he covered as a youngster at the *Vidette*, then the investigation that uncovered a still in the woods. He also shared the story he unveiled at the *UW Daily* in college that exposed the financial administrator and ended up with his being fired.

She was mesmerized by this young man and he seemed rapt in her world as well.

"I could stay here all day," Dan said, "But, we best head back. I'll take you to dinner and maybe a picture show. I'm going to spend as much of this day with you as I can."

They doused the fire and walked back to the station at Ocosta, a burgeoning rail hub from Aberdeen to all points South.

It was late afternoon and approaching dusk when the Evening Special chugged into Aberdeen station.

They disembarked and walked briskly in the chilly early evening air toward the Washington.

"Let's go around this way and see what's on The Grand tonight," Dan said.

"Nothing too exciting," he noted, when they saw the poster outside the picture show. "Maxine Elliott in 'Samaritan.' Haven't heard much about that."

"Let's go back to the hotel," Lindy said, pulling the young man's arms that were locked in hers.

"We've got a little time before dinner," he said as they relaxed on the bed. "Let's just snuggle a bit."

"You sure that's all you want to do?" she queried.

"Probably not, but I am worn out after this great day. Let's see what happens."

It was almost 6 when Lindy nudged Dan in the ribs. "C'mon sleepyhead. I'm starved."

"Oh, wow. I died. You wore me out, sweetie."

"Yeah, I just woke up, too. Let's go see what's on the Washington menu, OK. My treat."

"No, I can't let you do that. It's expensive there, but you know, we're worth it. Let's go."

They both enjoyed fresh grilled Quinault salmon, mashed potatoes and gravy, red beets and cornbread with little wild blackberry pie for dessert. The one dollar and forty-cent tab would put a dent in Dan's wallet.

"I'm so full. Guess we've already had our dessert," Lindy said with a twinkle toward Dan.

"C'mon, hun. Gotta pay the bill," he said, moving toward the clerk's desk.

"You got my bill, Mr. Stahl?" Cloud asked the hotel desk manager, Ben Stahl.

"Nope, the tall man answered."

"Nope? What do you mean?"

"It's taken care of."

"What? Who?"

"It's on me," said Stahl. "We've been following your stories on the Stapp trial and we like having you here. This one's on us."

"I don't know what to say. I can't believe it."

"Well, you don't have to say anything, just keep doing the good work."

"Thank you so much," said the young reporter, grabbing Lindy by the hand.

"Wow, can you believe that?" he said. "Has this ever been a great day!"

"And it's not over yet," she said as Dan unlocked the hotel room door.

"Are you going to stay?" he asked.

"Welllll, maybe — with a little encouragement."

18. THE VERDICT

February 1911

Dan Cloud had to wait for the coach in Aberdeen, but he knew he wouldn't miss anything important. He had done his background research on the doctor and Cloud knew Defense Attorney Agnew would spend the first hour questioning Dr. Robert Stapp to give the jury those important details. He was well aware of the attorney's tactic to leave no stone unturned.

As he calculated, Agnew was deep into Stapp's history when Cloud opened the door and took the seat that was prepared for him, adjacent to Prosecuting Attorney Campbell.

"What a great day," Dan thought to himself as he sat at the table. "What am I thinking? I've got to get head my back in the game."

The doctor said he had been practicing in Aberdeen about 22 years, though he was no longer associated with any of the hospitals — either Sisters, also known as St. Joseph's, or General Hospital, downtown on Broadway. He related his experience in surgery and answered, under intense and lengthy querying, that he was familiar with women's injuries as they related to pregnancy and abortion.

Stapp testified that he had treated "many women, who had tried to do abortions on themselves, or who had asked others to try and failed." Agnew continued to delve into Stapp's expertise, which was primarily surgery as it related to obstetrics. He also said he had many years of experience with men's urology, such as prostate issues and its treatment.

Agnew then motioned to the chart that was displayed in the courtroom for the jury to see. It showed how the placenta had been punctured, the drawings being from the coroner's department on the Mary Bauer autopsy.

"You have seen the puncture of the placenta that has been introduced as evidence in this case?" the attorney asked.

"Yes, sir," the doctor responded as the court reporter entered the following transcription:

Agnew: Could that have been done by anything, except a curved instrument?

Stapp: It could be made with a straight instrument, but not under these circumstances. The puncture would have been made with a catheter, a piece of wire, a hatpin, or pencil lead. I've seen them all.

Agnew: Describe how a puncture like that would be made and what would be the result.

Stapp: The instrument would have to enter at the mouth of the womb, would have to separate a portion of the placenta, and then turn inward. That's the way I understand it. I don't see how there could be anything else, but an immediate hemorrhage.

Agnew: A violent hemorrhage?

Stapp: I don't see how such a condition could exist in a live person without an immediate hemorrhage or great suffering.

Agnew: Would you consider that a job like that would be in the line of surgery, or not?

Stapp: If it was done in a case requiring abortion, you mean?

Agnew: Yes, that's what I was asking.

Stapp: I think if a doctor did it, he ought to go and surrender his credentials.

Agnew, who had done his homework and was well-coached in the problems a female would suffer in a botched abortion, then questioned Stapp about the hemorrhaging that would occur, and to an even greater extent, blood poisoning.

The doctor answered clinically and tersely, and offered nothing except to answer the attorney's specific questions. Agnew must have been satisfied because he switched to a different line of questioning, asking the doctor to talk about how he spent his day on Sunday, November 27, 1911, starting when he went to the office.

Stapp said he arrived at the office about noon or a little before and had two men patients, one elderly, whom he had treated for many years. He said he left about half-past one and went to the Mecca for lunch, returning to the office about 2:30. He said he was in the office all afternoon and no more patients came in. He left at 5 o'clock or half-past 5 and went to the Washington for dinner.

Stapp: It was Sunday and I remained there every minute until half-past 10 or a little before 11.

Agnew: Tell us what you did there and who did you meet there and what fixes your mind on the time you were there.

Stapp: I met Mr. Abbott, a friend of mine, and we talked for 15 or 20 minutes. I don't remember exactly. They have a place you can get a cigar, and they have a dice game, called 26. I played that game.

Agnew: Describe the game.

Stapp: It's one player against the house. You roll the dice from a cup. The action is fast and you have a clerk count for you. It's hard to win, but I won a lot that night.

Agnew: Did anybody else play?

Stapp: Mr. Abbott was with me.

Agnew: Who counted for you?

Stapp: That would be Ben Stahl. He was cigar clerk that night.

Agnew: You say you won a lot?

Stapp: Yes. Ten dollars worth for three and a half hours. It was the biggest winning ever made in the house. That's one thing that makes it distinct in my mind. But, I didn't play all that time.

Agnew: How long then?

Stapp: Maybe three quarters of an hour, perhaps an hour.

Agnew: What else did you do?

Stapp: In the neighborhood of 7 or 7:30, we, Abbott and I, went to the dining room for our dinner. I know it was then, because you can't get dinner after eight. Then we went to his room and played cribbage for awhile.

Agnew: What time did you go home?

Stapp: I left the Washington about 10:30 or 11. I made a quick stop at the office, about 30 seconds, and walked home.

Agnew: During any part of that time, did Mrs. Kaatz or any other woman come to your office?

Stapp: No, sir.

Agnew: Did you have a conversation with Mrs. Kaatz or any other woman in your office that day?

Stapp: I did not.

Agnew: Did you perform any operation of any kind upon any woman that day?

Stapp: No, sir. I did not.

Agnew: Was any woman in your private office that day?

Stapp: No sir.

Agnew: Did you know Mary Bauer at any time?

Stapp: No, never.

Agnew: When was the first time you heard of her?

Stapp: When I picked up the Aberdeen Daily World on the evening of December 2nd, 1910.

Agnew: Did you know Mrs. Kaatz?

Stapp: Do I know her?

Agnew: Yes, do you know her?

The doctor testified that he had known Emma Kaatz about five or six years ago when she brought one of her boys to his office with a cut lip. He also said he had been to her house a time or two about five years ago when he was summoned to treat a boarder.

Agnew then asked Stapp if he knew Ed Tornow and he said he didn't. When asked when he first heard of Ed Tornow, the doctor replied: "Not until I saw him on the witness stand being sworn in." Agnew continued to question the doctor about the alleged conversation he had with Tornow.

Agnew reminded the doctor and the jury that Tornow had testified to being in Stapp's office for consultation about an operation on Mary Bauer. Still, Stapp denied any conversation existed. He said he had no contract or arrangement to perform an operation and had never met Mr. Tornow.

The attorney then asked the doctor what he did the next day, on December 1, to which Stapp replied that he was ill. "I had the grippe, my throat hurt and I had a headache and was in bed all day." The doctor stopped to think a bit, then said he wasn't in bed all day, saying he slept a bit, then felt well enough to go to the office about 2:30. He continued to deny ever being to Kaatz's residence, repeatedly said he didn't go there to view the body of Mary Bauer and said he didn't pick up any pills that were in the room. Stapp continued to deny any knowledge of Mary Bauer, and when asked specifically if he gave her any pills or any medicine of any kind, or if he gave pills or medicine to any other person, he replied: "Absolutely not."

Agnew released the witness, then after a short recess, Prosecutor Campbell began his cross-examination with a line of questioning designed to discredit Stapp's ability as a surgeon, not that he had a doubt the doctor had a history of credibility as a surgeon, but did he still have it?

Campbell questioned the doctor about his surgical practice and where he last performed surgery and when. He responded it was at Sisters Hospital last year for an abscessed pelvic cavity, which he lanced and the woman recovered.

Campbell then switched his line of questioning to target Stapp's ability to remember details. He asked him repeatedly about what he did last week and Stapp couldn't remember for sure. He then asked the doctor about a few days ago what he had for breakfast, for lunch, for dinner and what he did at the Washington.

Stapp continued to be evasive. "I don't know for sure" was his pat answer most of the time, though he did clarify that he ate dinner every night at the Washington Hotel.

Then Campbell said "But you can recount every detail of what you did on November 27, on the night of the 27th."

Stapp answered: "Yes, sir. I have gone over it and over it in my mind. I know exactly what I did and what time because of the distinction of what happened," referring to 26, the dice game.

The doctor was unwavering in his answers, saying he had "fixed it in his mind everything that I did from November 27th to December 2nd." When asked if he knew everything, he replied, "No, not everything, just on the days these people claimed this work was done. I got my mind centered on that and stuck to it."

Campbell asked him about every single day, from the 27th through the end of November and Stapp said he would have to check his diary, but when questioned about December 1st, he replied: "That one I know. That's when they say the girl died. I know I was home sick all day until about 2:30 and I was only at the office a few minutes."

The prosecutor continued to hammer at Stapp's memory, asking him where he ate dinner, but the doctor again was ambivalent, saying "I suppose I was at the Washington." When asked about what he had for dinner, again questioning his ability to recall, Stapp said: "I'm not sure."

At this point, Campbell asked the judge for an aside and Sheeks motioned the counselors to the bench. Campbell handed the judge a list of the doctor's past arrests for the last seven years, dating back to 1904 when he had a nasty divorce. He wanted to submit the list as evidence. Agnew asked to see the list, but the judge declined, saying "Not until after I make a decision." The judge called for a 15-minute recess.

Cloud couldn't help but wonder about this little discussion, but he knew neither attorney would divulge what went on. He knew he had to try anyway.

He followed Campbell out of the courtroom, down the hall to the washroom.

Campbell cupped his hands under the running water and washed his face to freshen up.

"Counselor?" Cloud asked the attorney, a bit startled by his presence. "Can I ask you what that was about?"

"You can, but I won't tell you, yet."

"Did you try to introduce new evidence?" the scribe asked.

"OK, I can tell you that much. That would be a yes, but that's all I can say. The judge didn't even show the defense what it was. You'll find out in good time. We better get back in there."

Judge Sheeks summoned the counselors to his chambers. "Mr. Campbell, I can't allow this."

"But, judge this goes to character. It goes to history and crimes committed."

"That's alleged, counselor. Yes, you are right, but this is past history, way past history, and while there were allegations, all were dismissed. I can't let the jury see this."

"Judge, can I see that now," Agnew asked.

"Sure, but I imagine you have seen it, anyway. It's the doctor's history of arrests for investigation of abortions," the judge answered.

"You are right, I've seen it, but I'd like to see it again to make sure that corresponds with the information I have," Agnew said.

"I object, your honor," Campbell asserted.

"You object to my giving information to Agnew?"

"No, your honor. I object to your ruling. You can show Agnew, if he wants it."

"I am going to overrule," the judge said. "I can't allow any of this, or the objection in court. It would cast too much suspicion for the jury."

"Here you go, counselor," said the judge, handing Agnew the copy of the information. "Now let's get back in there and get this over with."

Campbell had no further questions for Stapp.

Agnew stepped up for re-direct and didn't have any more questions for Stapp after the all-day hammering by Campbell. But, also, he didn't

want to leave the jury thinking his defendant was incompetent, so he
returned to have Stapp talk about the utensils he used in his office, with
a goal of restoring the doctor's credibility.

Stapp answered diligently, but again tersely, though he seemed
puzzled by the direction the attorney was taking.

After letting Stapp describe professionally the utensils he used in his
office and for what purpose — which he showed on the chart so the
jury could see — Agnew switched gears to question the doctor about his
recollection on what he did on the days from November 27 to December 2.

"I can't recall all of that," said the doctor.

Stapp forgot that he had submitted his diary for dates in question
as evidence, but Agnew didn't.

"These papers you submitted to me for evidence state it all, don't
they?"

"Oh, yes. I forgot you had them."

Agnew had Stapp look at the papers and then, for the third time,
despite Campbell's objections, reiterated all that he had done on those
days that was submitted as evidence.

Agnew then excused the witness, but Campbell wasn't done, asking
for a re-cross, which the judge granted.

Campbell asked Stapp "When you were figuring out those times, did
you also figure out who was in your office on all those times, doctor?"

Stapp said he couldn't figure out everyone who was in his office on
those days, but did say he could "call to mind that no one was there,
but who I knew who they were."

Campbell then excused Stapp and the judge ordered a lunchtime
recess before the defense called its final witness.

Cloud shook the cobwebs from his head after the exhausting
morning of nothing more than reiteration on both sides, and tried to
get his mind set on what happened.

He glanced at the jury, most of them yawning, and heard at least
one mumble, "At last."

"That was pretty boring today," Cloud thought as he ambled toward
the lobby phone. "One thing I can say for sure is that everybody is a
liar. Stapp is a liar, Kaatz is a liar and Tornow is a liar. I wonder what
the jury thinks?"

He spied the phone open, stepped to the box and called. "Hi,
beautiful," he whispered into the receiver.

"Hey, you. How's it going up there?" Lindy responded.

"To tell the truth, it was dull, real boring, mostly technical stuff and they went over and over it. I hope they wrap it up today. I don't know if there will be a verdict from the jury tonight. I doubt it. Well, I just wanted to hear your voice and tell you thanks for yesterday."

"Yeah, it is great to hear your voice and yesterday was so much fun."

"Well, I better get going. I want to grab a quick bite before I get back to the courtroom."

"Will I see you tonight?" Lindy probed.

"I don't know. If the trial wraps up and the jury gets the orders from the judge, I might have to stay here. I'll try to let you know."

"Until then," she said, hanging up.

""I better get down to the Montesano," Cloud thought, referring to the restaurant a few blocks away. "I can grab a turkey sandwich and eat it on the way back. I think I'll run all the way, gotta get the blood flowing again."

He looked up while taking a bite of his sandwich to see a tall, sturdy figure come out of the Montesano State Bank.

"That looks like Tornow, John Tornow," he thought to himself. "I know it is."

"Good afternoon, John," the scribe said, catching up with the big man, who was walking south away from the bank.

"What's that?" the big man answered, startled by the young scribe's approach.

"I didn't see you at the trial. Have you been there?" Cloud asked.

"Nah. Don't have any use for any of that stuff."

"You don't care what happens to the doctor? You don't care what happens to the man accused of killing your niece?"

"No. All I know is my sister's little girl is dead and my brother is responsible. He's the one they should have in jail. They can hang the doctor, but that's not justice. Ed's the one who should pay."

"Whoa! That's pretty strong stuff against a member of your family, isn't it?"

"No. I'll never forgive Ed. Minnie won't either and I'm sure Henry wants to kill him, too. Now, I got to get going,"

"Thanks for your time, John. Where ya headed?"

"Going to work. I got the boys; you know John and Will Bauer, with me up at Mack's in Elma as soon as this circus is over. We're also doing some logging in Mason County by my property. They're great kids. Gotta run now."

"They should have a verdict today or tomorrow, I imagine."

"The boys will tell me next time I see them. They should be up there by week's end."

Cloud was surprised at how composed the big man was, not like his first encounter at Minnie's place. But, he also was taken aback at his attitude toward Ed and the whole trial. Another thing rolling around in his mind. "My property? What did John mean?" That note went on his tablet to investigate. Cloud dashed up to the courthouse and beat the attorneys back to court. He sat at his desk, went over his notes and wondered what this final witness was going to say.

When court resumed, Agnew called Benjamin Stahl to the witness stand.

"Oh, wow. Mr. Stahl," Cloud said to himself. "What does he know? Sure was nice of him to pay for our dinner."

Agnew questioned Stahl about his residence, his work and how long he had been in Aberdeen. Stahl said he knew Stapp through business; said the doctor came in daily for dinner, about 5 or 5:30; said he was at work on Sunday, November 27th, his usual night off at the Washington. "I was clerking, helping them out," he answered.

Agnew went directly to the point, asking Stahl if there was "anything that fixes in your mind that it was your night off and that you were there on your night off, any circumstances at all?"

Stahl: Yes, sir. I had a theater ticket.

Agnew: For what?

Stahl: The Armstrong Musical Company.

Agnew: Was there anything special about it that you remember, anything that fixes in your mind it was that night?

Stahl: Yes, sir. There was a limbless girl staying at the hotel and she was in the show. I wanted to see her and I was off that night, so I got tickets.

Agnew: Did you see Dr. Stapp that evening?

Stahl: Yes, sir.

Agnew: Can you fix a time that you saw him?

Stahl: Well, I would say about 6 o'clock, maybe a little later.

Agnew: And why does that fix in your mind?

Stahl: I was off duty at the time and he asked me to count for him.

Agnew: Count for 26, the dice game?

Stahl: Yes.

Agnew: How long was he at it, how long did he play?

Stahl: Forty or fifty minutes, I guess. I had to go to the theater.

Agnew: Then, that's all you saw of him?

Stahl: Yes.

Agnew: Was there anyone with him?

Stahl: I believe Mr. Abbott was there. He was standing at the counter with him.

Agnew: What time was it when you left?

Stahl: It was 7:15 or 7:30. The show started at 8, so I know it wasn't any later.

Agnew: Was Mr. Abbott with Dr. Stapp when you left him?

Stahl: Yes, I think so.

Agnew: But, you don't know for sure?

Stahl: I can't say for positive. I was watching the time, so I could leave for the theater.

Agnew: Your honor. I am finished with this witness.

Campbell then rose to begin his cross-examination. He knew the defense had not been able to find Mr. Abbott, and Stahl was the lone person who could vouch for Stapp that night, but not after 7:30.

He asked Stahl to go back over his time at the Washington and the testimony he told the defense.

Campbell: So, Mr. Stahl, can you tell me how long it would take someone in relatively good health to walk from the Washington Hotel to the Finch Building, where Stapp's office was located?

Stahl: I suppose five, ten minutes at the most. It's only about four blocks.

Campbell: If Dr. Stapp had left the hotel immediately after you last saw him, what time would he have arrived at the Finch?

Agnew: Object. Judge, that calls for speculation.

Sheeks: I'll allow. Answer the question.

Stahl: 7:25 or 7:30.

Campbell: Do you know whether Dr. Stapp went back to his office immediately after you last saw him.

Stahl: I don't know where he went, or if he left.

Campbell: That's all, your honor.

Agnew: The defense rests, your honor.

Sheeks: Gentlemen, are you ready with your closing arguments?

Both counselors answer in the affirmative.

Campbell: Ladies and gentlemen of the jury, you have heard the testimony from Mary Bauer's parents, from her uncle, Ed Tornow. He testified he took Miss Bauer to Aberdeen to see Dr. Stapp and subsequently to have an abortion. You have heard the testimony from Mrs. Kaatz, the midwife, who said she took the girl to Dr. Stapp's office at 8 p.m. on Sunday, November 27. You heard Emma Kaatz say she didn't know she was taking the woman there for an abortion. She testified she thought Mary Bauer was being treated for the blood disease, the erysipelas. You also heard her testify it was the disease that she says caused Mary Bauer's death.

And then, ladies and gentlemen, you have heard the testimony from Coroner Smits and others of the condition of the placenta, the amniotic sac and fetus. You have heard the testimony describing in graphic detail how badly performed this operation was.

You have also heard the evidence that the defense brought to you from Mr. Stahl, who testified he saw Dr. Stapp on the evening of November 27, but he, Stahl, left for the theater a little after 7. You have heard no evidence that puts the doctor anywhere but his office during that time Mrs. Kaatz said she took Miss Bauer to his office for the operation.

There is also no evidence to deny that Dr. Stapp was at Mrs. Kaatz's house on December 1, the day the girl died, except the doctor's statement that he was sick until 2:30 that day. You heard Mrs. Kaatz say the doctor took the pills out of Miss Bauer's room after she was pronounced dead by the Coroner. You also heard the Coroner testify that he told Mrs. Kaatz not to let anybody in the room.

Now, hearing all this evidence, your only conclusion is to find this doctor, Robert M. Stapp, guilty of criminal abortion.

Defense Attorney Walter Agnew began his closing arguments.

Agnew: Members of the jury, there is no question that there was a crime here. We have a young woman in the prime of her life, who is now dead. You have heard the expert testimony that this was a botched abortion. That is not in question.

What we have here is a prosecutor in search of a perpetrator.

There is no evidence to prove that Dr. Stapp is guilty of this dastardly crime. He testified he didn't know the girl, never heard of her until he was arrested. He said he didn't know Ed Tornow, who claims to have taken the girl initially to the doctor for consultation. And, Dr. Stapp said, while he knew Mrs. Kaatz, he had not seen her and he had not given pills to her, as the midwife alleges. He also testified that he was home ill on the day the girl died. The prosecution has been unable to refute any of the testimony from the doctor.

We have a situation where a doctor with a solid and credible reputation as a surgeon is accused of the crime of abortion, but there is no evidence to substantiate that this good doctor was involved.

With that testimony, and the lack of evidence to tie this good doctor to this crime, ladies and gentlemen, your only judgment in this case, is to acquit and return Dr. Robert Stapp to his rightful and good place in our society.

Judge Sheeks gave the jurors their instructions, which were simple: return a unanimous verdict of guilty or not guilty of the charge of criminal abortion.

Cloud exited the courtroom and found the lone phone in the hallway unoccupied.

"Hi, Bill, Cloud here," the scribe greeted his city editor, Bill Irvine. "The jurors have the case, but I don't know how long they will deliberate. It's about 4, now. I'll hang here until about 8 to see if we get a verdict. If not, I'll try to hitch a ride into town, and if I can't do that, guess I'll shack tonight at the Montesano."

"Sounds like a good plan," the editor tells the scribe, brash beyond his relative lack of experience. "That kid's something else," Irvine thought. "Not many reporters I know have that kind of moxie, and I'm sure not many would have already figured out a plan like he has."

Cloud hung up the phone and started to decide where he would spend the next few hours. First, he had to notify the bailiff where he planned to be. While he had a plan for later that night, he wasn't sure about the next few hours.

He then realized he had been caught up in the moment of the trial ending and hadn't called Lindy to update her.

"Hi again, beautiful," he whispered into the mouthpiece, although there was no other person around.

"What's happening up there?" she asked. "Ya done?"

"No, but the jury is out, just went out, so I'm caught up here."

"Oh, no. You mean I might not see you tonight. How can I stand it?"

"Oh, don't be silly. You'll survive. I don't know what's going to happen here. It could be a couple of hours, it might be all night. I told the editor I would hang here until about 8, try to catch a ride into town or else stay here tonight. So, that's my plan. If I had to guess, I'd say I'll probably have to stay here."

"Will they stay out all night?"

"I don't know. I've never been to a trial before. I guess we'll both learn as we go."

"So, what do you think will happen?"

"I think they will find the doctor guilty, but you never know about juries."

"So, what are you going to do now?"

"Frankly, I'm not sure. I have to catch the bailiff before he leaves, so he knows where to find me, if the jury comes back. I better go and see if he is still here."

"OK, sweetie. I'll miss you. Hope you can wind things up tonight. Bye."

"Bye, honey. See ya when I see ya."

Cloud got lucky and ran into the bailiff, who was about to leave.

"What are you going to do?" the bailiff asked Cloud.

"I wish I knew. Never done this before, so I'm kind of lost."

"Why don't you head to the Montesano. You can catch dinner and maybe chat with the Bauers or others. I bet most of them are down there. I have instructions to call there when we hear something."

"Sounds good. Got nothing better," Cloud answered

"Maybe, I ought to book a room or tell them I might book one," he thought as he walked down Main Street to the two-story hotel and restaurant. As he walked into the restaurant, he spotted the Bauers: Henry and Minnie and their twin sons, William and John, and daughter Lizzie.

"Hi, folks. May I join you?" the scribe asked in the direction of Minnie.

"You're the reporter, aren't you?" Henry shouted, not allowing Minnie to answer him.

"Yes sir, I am. Guess we got some time before we get a verdict. Mr. Bauer, let me say how sorry I am for the loss of your daughter. I met your wife several months ago after I heard about Mary's death. I met Mary and Ed, Ed Tornow, right here in this restaurant before that and she seemed like a sweet young lady. So sorry."

"Thanks. This has been so hard on all of us," the patriarch said, wiping a tear from his eye and gripping his wife's arm in a rare showing of emotion.

Cloud never expected this softer side from Henry Bauer. In the trial, he didn't show one bit of emotion, only a couple of outbursts, the last of which, the judge had to remind him that "this is a courtroom, and I won't tolerate those outbursts."

"So, can I ask you what's the jury going to do? What do you think will be the verdict?" Cloud asked.

"He's guilty," shouted William. "Hang him," echoed his brother."

"I can't believe Uncle Ed," William added. "I can't believe he would do that."

"Now, boys, that's enough," chided Minnie. "We don't need to say anything more."

"I'll tell you one thing, Mr. Scribe. What did you say your name was, Cloud, was it? I'll tell you, I better never see Ed Tornow or any of them Tornows again. I wash my hands of them all."

"Now, Henry, John didn't do anything," Minnie said, referring to her big brother. "He's tried to help us."

"Maybe not, but he's a Tornow, and I'll have nothing more to do with them, not after this."

"Henry, let me remind you that I am also a Tornow. Do you want nothing more to do with me?"

"Of course not, Min. You're my wife. I don't mean you. You know what I mean."

"Do you mean we can't go with Uncle John fishing and hunting?" John Bauer asked.

"No. I don't want you hanging around him. He's nothing but trouble," Henry told his disbelieving sons.

"Papa, you are so wrong. Uncle John is a great guy. He's taught us so much when we were fishing or hunting, or just hanging in the woods," asserted William. "You have your opinions and Johnny and I have ours and we aren't going to stop seeing him. He's done nothing wrong. He's helped Mama so much when you are gone, and you are gone a lot. Besides, we are working with him at Mack's and in Mason County when this trial is over."

"Boys, I've told you how feel and I expect you to obey me," Henry said, suddenly realizing that the reporter was still at the table and a witness to this serious family argument.

"Cloud, would you leave us alone. We want to finish eating and get back and wait for the verdict."

"That's fine, Mr. Bauer" Can I ask you if you'll talk to me after the verdict?"

"I'd rather not. I think I've done more talking than I should have already. Remember, this is a family matter. Now leave us be."

Cloud got up and moved to another table and waited for the waitress.

"What can I get you, sweetie?" asked the attractive, young blonde.

"I think I'll have that special, open-faced, hot roast beef, isn't it?"

"Yep, and it's really good. Our cook makes terrific gravy."

"You got it. I'll have a tall glass of milk, too."

Cloud looked up after ordering and saw the defense attorneys, Agnew and Boner, huddled together at a small corner table.

He walked over to say his greetings.

"Good evening, counselors," Cloud said. "Quite a trial, huh?"

"Yes. Glad it's about over," Agnew said. "Always tough when you deal with a death and a respected member of the community."

"Well, how do think it's going to go?" Cloud asked.

"Depends, but I know one thing. I sure wish we could have found that Mr. Abbott. Our defense would have been stronger," offered Boner, a young attorney practicing with his father.

"If we lose this, we'll appeal," said Boner. "We've already decided. When that appeal is overturned, we might be able to submit new evidence and find that Mr. Abbott. We need him."

"Yes, he might have been able to provide an alibi for Stapp," said Cloud. "But, what if the appeal is denied? What will you do then?"

"Well kid, we can talk 'what ifs' all night, but I will say this. I will fight to the end. If the Supreme Court does not overturn the conviction on the appeal, we can then ask the governor for a pardon or a grant of clemency."

"I guess this is far from over, huh?" said the scribe. "So, you've read the stuff I've written, how do you think I've done for my first trial?" Cloud asked.

"This is your first trial? I'd say that you earned your wings," said Agnew, surprised that the scribe was a novice in covering court trials. "This has not been easy, lots of technical stuff."

"Yeah, but I don't think the average reader wants to know, or even should know, much of that," Cloud said.

"You sure this is your first trial?" Boner continued, almost in disbelief at the savvy of this young reporter.

"Yes, it is, and it's been a lot of fun, I learned a lot. There's my dinner, talk to you later after the verdict. Hey guys, how does it work if the jury is out until, say after 8? Will they stay out later or will the judge suspend deliberations until tomorrow? What usually happens?"

"It's up to the judge, but usually he will suspend it at about 8 p.m. until tomorrow," Agnew answered.

Cloud sat alone and gobbled down the hot beef sandwich, then decided he would top it off with a piece of warm apple pie and vanilla ice cream.

He got up from his seat and spotted the Seattle newspaper and *Colliers* magazine on another table. He picked up both of them and moved to the hotel lobby's comfortable sofa.

"That's more like it," he said to a dapper-looking gentleman sitting by himself at the end of the couch. "Those court seats get hard after awhile."

"How's the trial going?" the man asked.

"Uh, OK. Do I know you.?"

"Yeah. Ovie Nelson. We met the first day of the trial. You were talking with Ed Tornow."

"Oh, yeah, sure. Forgive me, it's been a long five days and it's my first trial. Got a lot on my mind."

"What are you doing here?"

"The jury just went into deliberations, so I'm waiting it out. And what are you doing this late?"

"Waiting for my boss. He should be here any minute."

"Abel, the attorney, isn't it? Isn't he your boss?"

"Correct."

Suddenly, Cloud's mind flashed to the words he jotted down when he was talking with Ed Tornow.

"Timber deal. Would this be the time to bring it up?" he wondered. He thought better of it and decided to let it go until another time.

Cloud excused himself and went to the washroom.

When he returned, he noticed Nelson and another man leaving the hotel lobby.

"Must be Abel," he thought.

———

Cloud plopped down on the couch and picked up the magazine. He wondered if anybody would mind if he took off his shoes and relaxed a bit on the comfortable sofa. He did just that, and in short order, was sound asleep, magazine in his lap and head back on the couch.

"Mr. Cloud, Mr. Cloud," the hotel clerk said, shaking the reporter slightly.

"What? Oh, my, I must have fallen asleep."

"Yes, you were out. The bailiff just called and the jury is expected back within the hour."

"Thank you. That's good news."

Cloud dashed into the washroom, freshened his face with cold water, then headed back to the courtroom, a few blocks north.

Cloud looked at the clock on the wall as he entered the courtroom. Eight forty-five, it showed. "Four and a half hours and counting," Cloud said to himself about the length of time the jury had been deliberating. I wonder what that means for the verdict?" he said muttering to himself.

Within 15 minutes, Judge Sheeks entered the courtroom and faced the jury.

"Foreman of the jury? Do you have a unanimous verdict?" the judge asked.

"We do, your honor," said the foreman, a mid-fortys good-looking man in suit and tie. He handed the judge a slip of paper.

"Dr. Stapp, would you rise and face the jury," the judge instructed then turning to the jury said, "What say you to the charge of the crime of abortion?"

"On this day, February, 19, 1911, in the charge of criminal abortion, so say we all, we find the defendant, Dr. Robert Stapp guilty," the foreman announced.

Cloud was in position to see Stapp's head drop slightly when the verdict was read, otherwise he showed no emotion. The reporter also heard a chorus of deep sighs, falling just short of cheers, coming from the other side of the room, where the Bauers were sitting.

With that, the judge thanked the jury members for their service and excused them.

"Your honor," said Agnew, rising to face the judge. "The defense will enter an appeal with the Superior Court."

"So noted," the judge answered, then instructed the bailiff to remand Dr. Stapp in the county jail.

"Mr. Foreman?" Cloud asked the jury leader, who was waiting outside the courtroom. "How did the jury arrive at its decision?"

"It came down to believability, and we didn't believe the doctor. He had no alibi for the time in question. We didn't believe hardly anybody in this trial, but the defense couldn't help the doctor, not with the witnesses they provided."

Cloud thanked him for his comments and hustled to grab the prosecuting attorney.

"Mr. Campbell, Mr. Campbell. May I have a minute?"

"Sure Dan. What can I do for you?"

"I won't keep you. We are all tired, aren't we? But how do you feel about this verdict?"

"I think we built a pretty good case for the prosecution and they had nothing but the doctor saying he didn't do it, didn't know the girl. I don't think the jury bought that for a minute. But, you got to remember, there are no winners here. A woman died and that's tragic. You have to remember that. Is it justice that a doctor was judged guilty? Perhaps, but is he the only guilty party? I don't think so."

"One more question. You going to Aberdeen tonight?"

"Yes, need a ride?"

"I sure do, thanks. I'm so tired. I really don't want to spend the night up here."

"Well, let's get out of here."

"Can you hang on just one minute. I want to try to get a comment from the Bauers. I see them down the hall."

"Sure, no problem."

"Mr. Bauer, I know you said you didn't want to comment, but quickly can you say if the verdict pleased you?"

"Mr. Cloud. I told you before 'no comment,' and that's all I want to say."

"Thank you, sir. I respect that, and again, let me say how sorry I am."

It was nearly 11 o'clock when Cloud walked into the *World's* newsroom.

"That little snooze at the hotel was good. I'm awake. If I'm smart, I'll write this story immediately and get a good night's sleep, my last night at the Washington.

Stapp
Guilty of
Abortion

Read the headline on the *World's* front page.

Jury deliberates less than 5 hours to convict Aberdeen doctor in death of Satsop woman

Read the second deck headline just below it.

MONTESANO — *Aberdeen doctor Robert M. Stapp was convicted Monday night of the crime of abortion in the death of Mary Bauer of Satsop on December 1 of last year.*

The jury members deliberated less than five hours before announcing their verdict in Chehalis County Superior Court before Judge Ben Sheeks.

James Jenks, the jury foreman and spokesman, said the verdict "came down to believability."

He said the jury didn't believe the doctor when he denied that he knew Mary Bauer and denied that he knew Ed Tornow, the 24-year-old woman's uncle, who brought her to Aberdeen for the abortion.

Jenks also said the jury did not believe the doctor when he denied that he talked to Tornow and also denied he talked to the midwife Emma Kaatz, who runs a boarding house on Hume Street. She is the same woman, who testified she took Miss Bauer to see Dr. Stapp on November 27th, but she said it was treatment for a blood disease, called erysipelas, and not for an abortion.

Defense Attorney Walter Agnew announced an appeal will be filed in Superior Court.

Ed Tornow, a Satsop farmer and uncle of Mary Bauer, testified he consulted with Dr. Stapp, who told him he would do the job for $50. Stapp told Tornow the woman would be up and moving in no more than three days.

Tornow and Kaatz testified that Kaatz took the woman to see Stapp that evening and returned with Bauer to her home to recuperate.

But, Kaatz testified Miss Bauer suffered from erysipelas, a blood disease that causes skin-reddening, and defense attorney Agnew alleged that is what led to her death on December 1.

In closing arguments, William Campbell, prosecuting attorney, told the jury not to listen to Dr. Stapp's repeated denials that he knew Bauer, that he knew Tornow.

"Don't listen to him saying he didn't perform the operation and that he did not give Miss Bauer pills for her blood disease. All you need to know is the doctor has no alibi for the time this operation was performed."

Defense attorneys Agnew and Elmer Boner counted on Stapp's reputation as a 22-year surgeon in Aberdeen, and what they say was a "lack of evidence to tie the doctor to the crime," for their defense.

After the verdict, Campbell reminded all "There are no winners here. A girl is dead and that's tragic. Is it justice that a doctor must pay for this crime? Perhaps some, but I doubt the girl's parents think it is justice. They lost their daughter and there is no justice that can equate to that."

Miss Bauer's parents, Henry and Minnie Bauer, who were every day at the trial, declined to comment and left immediately after the verdict was announced for the long ride up the Satsop Valley to their home. As the verdict was announced, there was a collective sigh of relief from their corner of the courtroom. The Bauers' twin sons, William and John, and daughter, Elizabeth, attended every day with their parents.

Stapp is free on $2,000 bond, but could still face charges of manslaughter in Superior Court, for which he is also free on $5,000 bond.

Stapp was originally charged with murder in the first degree, but the charge was amended prior to trial to criminal abortion.

The sentence for criminal abortion is one to five years.

Sentencing was set for April 8, but Boner is also filing an appeal to stay the sentence until after the appeal is heard.

19. DOC & THE DOG

Spring 1911

The small gathering rose to their feet as Superior Court Judge Ben Sheeks entered the courtroom. On one side, were a few of Dr. Robert Stapp's fellow physicians and family members. On the other, Henry and Minnie Bauer, their twin sons, William and John, and daughter Elizabeth. Also on that side of the room, though separated from the Bauers by several rows of benches, were two members of the Tornow family: Edward Tornow and his brother, William; also in the crowd was Emma Kaatz and her son, Charles.

It was a much smaller gathering from that which jammed the tiny court room during the criminal abortion trial of Aberdeen physician, Dr. Robert M. Stapp.

They had come to hear the sentencing and perhaps receive some measure of justice from the pronouncement when Stapp was proven guilty of performing a fatal abortion on Mary Bauer after her uncle Ed Tornow brought her from the Satsop to Aberdeen. She died at the home of midwife Kaatz on December 1, 1910, shortly after the abortion. The jury convicted Stapp of the criminal act on February 11, 1911. Sentencing was set for April 8, 1911.

"You may be seated," instructed the bailiff as Sheeks took his seat.

"The sentencing range for this crime is 1 to 5 years. I have listened to the arguments on both sides and arrived at my decision after careful consideration, thought and examining precedent.

"Dr. Stapp, before I pronounce sentence, do you have anything you would like to say?"

"Yes, Your Honor, I do. I am very sorry that a life has been taken in this case. For that I show remorse, but I continue to maintain my innocence in the death of this young woman. I can only hope and pray the one responsible for her death, if indeed anyone was responsible, will be found out and I will be freed and my good name restored. I am confident that when my attorney files an appeal, which he has told me he will do immediately, the real truth will be borne out."

As Stapp finished his comment, a slight groan could be heard from the left side of the room, where the families of the Bauers and Tornows were seated, prompting the judge to call for quiet.

"Mr. Stapp, I have taken into consideration your record of 22 years as a physician in Chehalis County," the judge said. "I have taken into consideration your reputation at the hospitals in Aberdeen as a surgeon. But, what you have been proven by the jury of doing, taking a human life — two human lives, if you will — during or after the act of an illegal criminal abortion, cannot be overlooked. The Prosecuting Attorney presented enough evidence to convince the jury, and while some of it may be, as your defense attorneys maintain, circumstantial, you are still guilty of a crime.

"I therefore, sentence you Mr. Stapp, to nine months in the county jail. You will not be eligible for release until January 1912. Bailiff you may remand Mr. Stapp immediately."

"Your honor?"

"Yes, Mr. Boner."

"I respectfully submit that the counsel for the defense will file an immediate appeal."

"So noted, Mr. Boner. No surprise there."

Dan Cloud, reporter for *The Aberdeen Daily World* and *Chehalis County Vidette*, watched Henry Bauer closely as the sentence was announced. His face was ashen, jaw dropping as if to say WHAT, after the words left the judge's mouth.

He saw a grin come over Ed Tornow's face, while behind him sat Emma Kaatz, her hands clasped across her face. Stapp's family showed no emotion.

Bauer rose and immediately left, closely pursued by Cloud.

"Mr. Bauer, I know you can't be pleased with that sentence. You must be disappointed."

"I told you I wasn't going to say anything after the sentencing, but I'll say this. "That's not justice. The doctor killed my daughter and all he gets is a few months in jail. What kind of justice is that?"

"I agree with you. It just doesn't seem right that a life can be worth only nine months in jail. And, it might not be that if the appeal is upheld," the reporter said.

Just then, Ed Tornow stepped into the foyer.

"Hey, Mr. Tornow, wait a minute, I want a word with you, if I might," the reporter shouted.

"You better get outta my sight and fast," bellowed Henry Bauer, raising a closed fist in the air and taking a couple of steps toward the younger Tornow, who was backing away from him.

"At least he's going to jail," shouted Tornow. "You gotta be glad about that."

"Get the hell outta here. You are just as guilty as he is. You should be going to jail, too."

At that, Tornow turned and started quickly down the stairs out of Bauer's sight. Cloud was in fast pursuit.

"Mr. Tornow, slow down a minute. I want a word," Cloud shouted as Tornow reached the front door.

"I'm very sorry Mary is dead, but I had nothing to do with it," said Tornow to Cloud, who was surprised that the young man found it necessary to convince him he was not guilty.

"She was my niece, but she was also my best friend. I spent a lot of time with her and she helped my family out. How could I have had anything to do with her death?" he said. "I spent day and night with her … er, uh, I uh, that's not what I meant."

"That's OK, Ed. I am not a cop, not a judge. You don't have to convince me of anything. I just want to know what you think of the sentencing. Was that fair?"

"Fair? I guess. The doc performed an abortion, that's a crime and Mary is dead. He's going to jail for what he did, so yeah, I guess that's fair."

Cloud couldn't help but be amused at the shallow thinking the younger Tornow displayed, even at a time when his niece was dead and he might be the father of the baby that was inside her.

"OK, Ed. Gotta run. Thanks and see you around," the scribe said, finding an escape route he dashed down the steps, down Broadway to Main Street.

"I saw the Bauer boys take off toward the Montesano," Cloud thought to himself. "Maybe they will have something to say about their sister's death."

He walked briskly the few blocks to the hotel and restaurant and saw the twins take a table near the window.

"Mind if I join you boys?" he said to the 18-year-old Bauer twins.

"No, I guess not," said William, the more vocal brother. "What did you think of that sentence?" he asked of the scribe, stealing the thunder with the exact question Cloud was about to ask.

"I was going to ask you the same thing," he said. "It surprised me a bit."

"Me too. Not much justice in that."

"Yeah. You'd think he'd get more than that for taking a life," added John Bauer.

"I know your father was upset and lashed out at Mr. Tornow in the courtroom hall."

"Yep. papa's got no use for that low scum. What he did to Mary. He's my uncle too, but he's so different than Uncle John."

"So, how come you boys are here and not with your parents?" Cloud queried.

"We're not going home. Heading to Elma, so no need to go all the way up the Satsop," Will answered.

"What's going on in Elma?" Cloud continued.

"Work. We've got a few months of work with Uncle John at Mack's," John chimed in. "We worked with him out there the last two springs. Good money and it's kinda fun too."

"Always fun with uncle. He shows those loggers how to work a good day in the field," Will added. "We've been out there since the trial ended."

"I wondered why you two were in woolen work shirts and dungarees. Now I know. You work a lot with your uncle?" Cloud questioned.

"The last few years we have, since we were 16 and he got us on with Simpson up at Mason County, then a few weeks at Mack's that year and last year too."

"I don't know much about Mack's. Tell me about it," Cloud asked.

"It was called Mack's Spur and still is, although W.D. Mack doesn't own it anymore," said Will. "It's about a 12-mile strip of land in between Schaefer's and Vance's. The mill is about two miles off the main drag; it kind of parallels Newman Creek. The property extends all the way to White Star, just a bit into Mason County. Mack started it in 1891, but sold it in '03 to W. E. Slade, then Mack died that year. A. J. West, who has a mill in Aberdeen, joined with Slade last year. All along, the area has continued as Mack's Spur."

"I'm surprised you haven't heard about it. It was the first logging railroad in the county to use a steam locomotive to transport logs," added John.

"Well, I have heard of Mack. He was mayor in Hoquiam for a time a few years ago, but I didn't realize he had a logging operation," Cloud answered.

"You have to excuse us," said Will. "Me and John gonna grab a sandwich and some juice and water and head out. We got about seven miles of walking ahead of us. Our grub is here, so we better hit the road. Here, John, fill these canteens and let's go. See you later Cloud."

"Sure, guys, thanks for the info and maybe I'll see you around again," said Cloud.

"He's a nice guy, isn't he, John?" Will Bauer asked his twin as they walked along Pioneer and headed to Elma.

"Yes, he is. Did you hear those guys at the courthouse talking about Uncle John?"

"Yeah, I did. They didn't know who we were or they wouldn't have talked that loud."

"Who were they?"

"Just some loud-mouth loggers, I figger. I didn't pay them no nevermind."

"Yeah, I didn't either, but I didn't like what they were saying about Uncle John. They said he was a crazy man and got locked up at an asylum."

"That's nonsense. You know that's not true. He couldn't have worked those logging jobs with us, if that was true."

"That one guy was really out of it. He said he escaped from the nuthouse in Salem by climbing over a fence and walking all the way back to the Satsop."

"How crazy is that? It would take some kind of super-human to do that. What's it to Oregon — at least 200 miles, isn't it?"

"Not quite, but I wouldn't think of walking it."

"Well, I don't want to talk about that anymore. We know it's not true, so let's forget it."

————

Back at the Montesano, restaurant, Cloud spotted Defense Attorney Boner just as he picked up a small chef's salad for an early lunch.

"Hi there, counselor. Can I join you?" Cloud asked.

"Sure, but I'm not here long. Going to grab something to go."

"I know you're going to appeal this decision, but did the length, or rather, the short length of the sentence surprise you?"

"I was a little surprised because of the verdict that it wasn't a bit longer, but they had nothing to go on, no direct evidence, really, just circumstantial evidence, and no corroborating evidence, so the judge had to go with the low range. Their witnesses were not believable."

"Everybody I talked to said they were surprised, that it wasn't justice for a life taken."

"Well, kid when is a jail term ever justice for a life. Life's worth more than that for sure, but the judge has to go by the guidelines the legislature sets."

"You got that right. Mrs. Bauer lost a daughter and that's the bottom line. She is never coming back, no matter how many years Stapp might serve. What's the basis of your appeal going to be, Mr. Boner?"

"I've got a bunch of bones of contention, several points I want to bring out, but I am not at liberty to divulge those until I file."

"I figured you wouldn't tell me just yet. I learned so much during this trial," said Cloud. "It's my first trial and I learned a lot about how to do my job, a lot about how to talk to the victims and a lot about the judicial system. It was challenging, but a lot of fun too. I am glad it's over, however. Now, I might be able to spend a little time with my girl."

"Ah, aha! So, you got you a honey, huh?"

"Yep. You probably know her, too."

"Oh yeah?"

"It's Lindy Fleming."

"Oh, yeah, the gal at the police department. She's a looker all right."

"We haven't been together much since the trial started, but I hope we can see more of each other now."

"Yep, young man. Gotta strike while the iron's hot."

"Speaking of that, I better grab a bite and head out to catch the train. I've got a story on the sentencing to write; then maybe Lindy and I can grab dinner. See ya later, counselor."

With his courthouse business wrapped up early, Cloud was able to catch the 1 p.m. train back to Aberdeen. It was his favorite time because when he could make it to that train, it meant a short day and he would be back in plenty of time to finish his story and spend the evening with Lindy.

As he relaxed on the train, he formulated his short story on the sentencing, so when he sat down to write, it would be mostly written in his head.

It didn't take him but a few minutes to pound out the story, although he wished he had been able to talk to Stapp, but the doctor was whisked out of the courtroom soon after the sentencing was read.

Next up. Lindy.

"Anybody here want to go to dinner," he announced as he opened the door to the police department.

"Sure. You buying," answered Sgt. Thomas Delahanty from behind his desk.

"I didn't mean you, sergeant. Where's Lindy?"

"She'll be right back. She's running an errand for me to the mayor's office."

Cloud grabbed her chair and had waited only a few minutes before Lindy returned to a surprise visitor at her desk.

"Oh, Danny, you rascal. You done already? The guys taking good care of you?"

"Yeah, Lindy. Where would you like to go to dinner? Dan's buying?" the sergeant said with a big grin.

"Guess I opened my big mouth too soon and asked if anybody wanted to go to dinner when I opened the door," Cloud admitted.

"Well, sergeant, where would you like to go," said Lindy, playing along with the "get-Dan-joke."

"Washington, of course. You big-time reporters can afford that, can't you?"

"Sure, but you and Lindy can't leave at the same time, can you?" Cloud answered, not quite sure if the sergeant was serious or not.

"No, better not leave the desk open that long. Chief wouldn't like that, so I guess you are off the hook this time, Mr. Reporter."

"Whew! I thought you were serious, sergeant."

"What do you mean? I was serious."

"Come on Danny. Let's get out of here. See you tomorrow Tommy. Hold down the fort."

"Sure kids, now you run along and have fun."

"I had a sandwich earlier, so I think I'm going to get pork chops tonight," said Cloud. "How about you?"

"Sounds good to me, too. I just had a salad for lunch and it was early, so I'm starving. Tell me about your day."

Cloud shared the sentencing story, the confrontation outside the room with Henry Bauer and Ed Tornow, the conversation with the Bauer boys and with the defense attorney.

"Never a dull minute in your life," Lindy said.

"Well, what should we do now?"

"I don't want to go home just yet. I haven't had much time with you and I don't want it to end."

"You don't know how glad I am to hear you say that. I feel the same way. I just don't always express it."

"I didn't see anything on the picture show that I wanted to see, so, you know it's a really nice evening. Let's just go for a walk."

"That sounds great, hon. Let's go down by the river. It's always pleasant there."

———

Cloud was grateful for the respite that his life was now enjoying after the Stapp trial. He was assigned to cover the city of Aberdeen, in addition to the county commission meetings. He had his big stories each week, but no murders or major events over the next few months. After covering the trial, the city council meetings were mostly boring.

It was nearing the end of August when he ran into Ed Tornow at the Montesano hotel and restaurant after a county commission meeting.

"What are you doing in this neck of the woods?" Cloud asked the youngest Tornow brother.

"Business. Been a busy day."

"What kind of business, if I may ask?"

"Timber and some other stuff," he answered.

"Did you make a property deal?" Cloud continued to probe, realizing this Tornow brother didn't have the sense to keep his mouth shut.

"Yeah, it's in the works. Just met with Ovie Nelson and it won't be long before I'll have some of my family's land."

"Really, how's that going to happen. I thought the land was held up in the probate?"

"It is, because they couldn't locate John and when they did, he told them to get lost."

"Sounds like he doesn't want any part of it."

"Yes, but we got him this time."

"Got him? What do you mean?"

"He's going to be committed. He's insane, and a crazy man can't be a property owner in this state, Nelson told me. When he gets put away, we will get an agent to sign off for him and then I can sell the family's property, and particularly that part in Mason County that he owns. The family is all in this with me. We want to get this thing settled and get out from under it."

"So, how are you going to get him committed. Did he do something that warrants that?"

"Yes, but I don't have time to tell you now. I just came from the sheriff's office and he has my statement. Go over there and you can get it all."

"OK. I'll do that. Good to see you again."

"Yeah. Take care. Things are going to different real soon. You'll see."

Cloud ordered a bowl of soup and a half of a chicken-salad sandwich; then headed up the street to Sheriff Ed Payette's office.

"Sheriff, how's it going?

"Cloud, haven't seen much of you lately. What brings you in today?"

"Ed Tornow, that's what."

"Oh, that kook. Yeah he was here, filed a petition to have his brother, John, declared insane."

"I just ran into him at the Montesano and he told me he's 'got him this time.' What did he mean by that? He said he gave you a statement."

"He just left here. You don't miss much, do you? That's good. I'll get you a copy of his statement. It's pretty descriptive about shooting of a dog, if you can believe it."

Payette went into the back room, where the new mimeo machine was located.

"Cloud, come here a minute. I want to show you this new toy."

"Sure, what toy you talking about?"

"It's called a mimeograph. You put the original document here on this drum and the paper you want to copy it to on this tray. You roll the drum and presto, a nice clean copy in no time."

"Ewwww! What smells?" Cloud asked.

"It's the chemicals in the purple ink. Only bad thing about it, but it does the job and much faster than anything we had before. Anyway, here's your copy of Ed's statement. Let it dry a minute or two, then read it over and I'll answer any questions."

"Sure, sheriff."

Cloud took the duplicate copy and the warrant and began to analyze it.

The warrant, signed on August 10, 1911, by Ed Tornow, asked that John Tornow be declared insane and is unsafe to be at large. It commands the sheriff to take John Tornow into custody and keep him until he appears in court to answer said charge.

"I was standing on my porch with Rex, my dog, when my brother, John, came walking down the path to the house. He was shouting incoherently and I asked him what was bothering him. He came right up to me face-to-face and said he was told, I had shot his dog," wrote Ed Tornow.

"I did shoot his dog, but it was a mangy hound and kept holding me up in the woods. I looked after Cougar when John was gone, but rarely took him with me on hunting trips. He was too old — 14, I believe.

"He was going crazy. 'Shot my dog, did you. I'll show you,' John Tornow said, and raised his rifle to his hip and killed my beloved Rex. I had only had him about three years. He was a trusty hound. Shot him right through the heart. Poor Rex, at least he didn't know what hit him.

"Then he pointed his finger at me and shouted 'I am going into the hills and nobody better come after me or I'll kill them. I want nothing more to do with you.'

"That was last week and he frightened me. That was a crazy man standing there. No doubt in my mind. I want him committed. Nobody is safe with him out there."

"Sheriff, do you think this actually happened?" the reporter queried.

"I don't know, but guess I'll take Deputy Fitzgerald with me and we'll see if we can find him. Ed told me the vicinity John was known to be in last. Did you ever meet John?"

"Yes, a couple of times, once at his sister's house and again here when I was having lunch one day. He's not crazy, that I could tell, but he does have a mean streak. At Mrs. Bauer's place, he had found out his niece was pregnant and Ed was the likely culprit. He was hot."

"Yes, he can belligerent, if crossed."

State of Washington,} ss.
COUNTY OF CHEHALIS.

In the Superior Court, holding Terms at Montesano.

IN THE MATTER OF

John Tornow

WARRANT.

INSANE.

The State of Washington to the Sheriff of Chehalis County, Greeting:

WHEREAS, *Ed Tornow*

having made affidavit in the Superior Court for Chehalis County, State of Washington, holding terms

at Montesano, that *John Tornow*

is insane and unsafe to be at large, all of which appears to us of record,

NOW, this is to command you, the said Sheriff, to take the said *John Tornow*

, and him, the said *John Tornow*

safely keep, and have him forthwith in this Court, there to answer to said charge, and abide such further order
as the Court may make in the premises.

HEREIN FAIL NOT.

WITNESS, the HON. MASON IRWIN, Judge of the Superior Court

for Chehalis County, State of Washington, and Seal of said Court,

this _10th_ day of _August_ A.D. 1911.

CLERK.

Washington State Archives

The warrant that Ed Tornow took out in August 1911, attempting to declare his brother, John, insane. The sheriff found no cause for the warrant.

"Do you know anything about a land deal Ed is trying to pull off?" the reporter asked.

"I know the probate is being held up until John signs off on it. That's all I know."

"I guess, from what Ed says, he and the brothers are trying to get him declared insane so they can take control of the property, and Ed says John owns a lot of property in Mason County, as well as one-sixth of the homestead. He also has a couple of plots in Aberdeen."

"I didn't know all that, so it sounds a lot like there might be collusion there," the sheriff offered.

"Do you think there's enough to get him declared insane? Shooting a dog is not really a crime, is it?"

"Probably not, but the death threat, if it really happened, is cause?"

"Thanks Sheriff. When do you think you'll get out there?"

"Sooner, rather than later. I like to clean things up as quickly as possible, you know that."

"I'll be waiting to see what you find out."

It was less than a week later when the phone rang at Cloud's desk.

"Sheriff Payette here," said the voice when the reporter answered.

"Hello, Sheriff. Got any news?"

"Yes and No. I found Tornow and he's no more insane than you or I. He wasn't where Ed said he was, but I ran into a timber cruiser who had seen him over near the Oxbow on the Wynooche, and that's where I found him. I had no problem with him. He even invited me in when he saw I was a sheriff. I sat down and talked to him for about an hour. I asked him about the dog incident and he told me pretty much what Ed said. Cougar had been his trusty companion for 14 years and he wasn't much of a hunting dog anymore, but he was still good company. He told me he was angry and upset with his brother, but the dog wasn't the only problem he had with Ed. He told me his 'good for nothing sibling' — that's his words — had taken advantage of the family. He had gotten his niece pregnant and was responsible for her death. He told me Ed wants to get rid of the property and John said he is not signing any probate."

"Did he talk much about living in the woods?" the reporter interjected.

"Yes. He said he has spent a lot of time in the woods the last two years, in particular, and since his work at Mack's Spur in Elma is now over for the time being, he wanted to retire to the woods, where he loved its silence. He said he can live alone in the woods, finding food 'just about anywhere' and he just wants to be left alone. He's a naturalist, a conservationist and that's all there is to it."

"What was he living in?"

"It was pretty crude lean-to, but it had a couple of rooms. He showed me how he stored food in caches and water in a bucket under the ground and covered. He had elk meat drying and hides too. He's the most resourceful guy I have ever met."

"Did you tell him why you were out there?"

"Sort of. I just told him some people were concerned about him. I didn't mention the insanity warrant, but you know what? He knew about it. I guess he gets some information from newspapers."

"Not from mine. I didn't write anything until you made your decision."

"I guess he heard about it from someone who had been in Montesano. Maybe he has a mole delivering information to him. Anyway, he knew there was an insanity warrant out for him."

"You don't think he was putting on an act for you?"

"No, I don't think so. I don't believe he could have kept it up for that long and I did get pretty specific with my questions about him. Like I said, he's no more insane than you or I."

"I guess that pretty much puts that issue to rest, doesn't it, sheriff?"

"I would say so. I stopped by the Tornow homestead and told Ed of my findings. He was pretty upset and was actually sobbing a little. I didn't stay long. I don't trust that guy."

"Yes. His track record isn't very good. His plan failed and that probate is still ongoing. No telling what he might try next."

20. TWIN TRAGEDIES

September 3, 1911

C rackling sounds from the weight of the men walking through the unspoiled foliage was the lone sound they could hear. With each step into the dense brush, they searched for any sights or clues of the missing twin boys.

Fall had come early in 1911. It was only September 3, yet already the forest had been hit with frosty mornings. That, coupled with a particularly wet August and a windy start to September, signaled the men that fall was in the air.

The Upper Satsop was home to wild and majestic trees — giant cedars, towering firs, Sitka spruce and strong hemlocks. Alders graced the valleys with vine maples on the slopes. Huckleberries, blackberries and salal grew wild in thickets.

Lowlands offer a haven for skunk cabbage, moss-covered downed logs and impenetrable underbrush.

The Satsop has three forks; the middle one was known as the Tornow branch, likely because of its proximity to the homestead. Six to seven miles west of the Satsop's west fork lies the Wynooche River, and in between is the rugged Oxbow country, so-named because of the U-shape bend in the Wynooche River.

In summer, the Upper Satsop and Oxbow country had unrivaled beauty, but in late autumn, winter and its early gloom and dankness prevailed, exacerbated by the incessant rainfall, which averages more than 100 inches annually.

William and John Bauer were husky, good-looking men, standing nearly 6-feet tall and weighing about 190 pounds. They were 19 years old and knew every inch of the Upper Satsop.

They were experienced woodsmen and fishermen, learning the traits early in life from their Uncle John Tornow. Even though they had reached manhood, they were known by friends and neighbors as the "Bauer Boys."

They hunted frequently in the area, and unless they had planned ahead, they always returned home by late afternoon.

Sunday, September 3, they left early in the morning and hadn't returned by 6 p.m., prompting their father, Henry Bauer, to round up some neighbors to search for the boys. Henry said he sent the boys out to hunt a bear he believed had ravaged one of his cattle.

"I heard about three faint shots early in the day, from over there," Gus Maas told Henry, pointing to the ridge about a mile and a half away, when he reached his neighbor's homestead. "Sure, I'll tell my boys to get ready and we'll join you."

"I think the Halls and Mullers are coming too. They're going to meet us at the bottom of the ridge on this side of the river," Bauer added.

The party of six spread out and searched the first ridge without finding a single clue to the cow, a bear or the boys. The men slogged through the forest litter of the Upper Satsop's dense valley floor and found nary a footprint.

As darkness approached, a frantic Henry Bauer called the party together and decided it would be futile to search through the night.

"Sheriff, I'm worried sick," said Bauer, who had stopped at the Muller homestead to telephone Ed Payette. "My boys haven't come home from hunting and six of us searched until dark tonight. They went bear hunting and they are always home by supper. Can you help?"

"Sure, Henry. I'll send McKenzie and he can get some guys together first thing in the morning. Stay at your place until he gets there. I'll give Colin McKenzie my bloodhound pup to take with him," the sheriff said.

Neither Henry Bauer nor his wife, Minnie, slept that night, feverishly awaiting dawn and the arrival of the deputies.

It was still dark when a motor car arrived at the Bauer homestead and four men got out. A few minutes later, two others arrived on horseback and joined the men inside, where Henry consoled his wife the best he could.

"You know the boys," said Henry. "They are strong and they can take care of themselves," he said embracing his wife. "We'll find them."

"I know, Henry. But, I'm so worried. It's not like them to not come home like that. I worry that something might have gotten them. That bear or something … or even worse," his wife, said sobbing.

"Now, don't you worry none," the husband said, calmly. "These men are the best trackers around."

"Henry, get me some of the boys' clothing from their room. I want the hounds to get a good sniff on and we'll get out of here," Deputy McKenzie ordered.

McKenzie stopped at Maas's ranch on the way in to pick up his bloodhound, Ol' Red. It would be a little cramped for the half-mile drive to the Bauers with Red and Mac, Sheriff Payette's bloodhound pup.

McKenzie and Red were familiar with each other. Just a year ago, McKenzie had borrowed the dog, one of Maas's seasoned bloodhounds, to track down a Chilean fugitive, Louis Albert Salazar, who had murdered Ah Fook, a Chinese gardener in nearby Hoquiam.

McKenzie had been a photographer in Aberdeen when his studio was razed in the Black Friday fire of 1903. The blaze wiped out virtually all of downtown, and in the process of escaping his studio, which was also his home, McKenzie suffered a broken back when a wall fell on him. He was able to flee, barely.

It took several years for McKenzie to regain his health. When he was finally back to full strength, he decided to take up bounty hunting to provide additional cash. He proved to be quite good at it, too. The ruggedness of the wilderness didn't seem to bother his back. With each trek, McKenzie was deputized in order to make an arrest. When a reward was offered, he was paid handsomely, with no questions asked.

When the murder in Hoquiam took place, McKenzie went into action, tracking the fugitive throughout the Northwest for more than a month, until he got a tip that Salazar had found his way into British Columbia.

That's when McKenzie procured Ol' Red from Maas and set off on his own to continue his pursuit.

What Salazar didn't know is that he had made his escape directly into the backyard of McKenzie's homeland. The former B.C. resident scoured every fishing camp along the Fraser River and soon discovered his man was in the vicinity. On March 15, 1911, he caught Salazar, who was helping at a dock and had nowhere to go when McKenzie approached.

He brought the cuffed fugitive back across the border and down to Chehalis County for incarceration and subsequent trial. The man confessed the murder to McKenzie, then pleaded not guilty when facing Judge Mason Irwin. The jury, in rapid fashion, convicted the Chilean of first-degree murder on April 7 and a week later, Irwin sentenced him to life imprisonment in Walla Walla.

Payette, the sheriff, knew the search for the boys would be in good hands with McKenzie in charge, along with his other seasoned tracking veteran, Carl Swartz, who was a couple of years older, but less-experienced than the 31-year-old McKenzie.

Swartz was the lead deputy on a recent search that took him and his posse about 50 miles into the west Olympics to arrest a notorious elk poacher who had ravaged for months the Forks area on the north Olympics coast. Swartz finally bagged his quarry near the Bogachiel River, which emptied into the Pacific Ocean, despite being told the suspect was a dangerous man with much ammunition. But the deputy surprised him as he napped and made the arrest. In his possession were dozens of antlers. The man, knowing his time was up, told Swartz of his crimes with his lips.

He was convicted and sent to prison for 10 years.

"I thought you might be in on this, Colin, when I heard the boys were missing. Ya think they were done in?" Maas asked McKenzie.

"I don't know. That would be a lot of tragedy for the family. Just last year their daughter, Mary, I think it was, died in that abortion in Aberdeen. That was just before Christmas, wasn't it?"

"Yeah, it was, but don't jump to any conclusions," McKenzie said, straining to hold back Ol' Red, who was champing at the bit to get going.

"Any news yet?" Maas asked Bauer as the men gathered to plot their search.

"Nuttin'. Not a word. Me and Min got no sleep last night, but we got to get outta here and find my boys. Someone said here last night that the boys were probably just lost and not to get too excited.

"They not lost. They don't get lost out there. I just know something …," said Henry, his voice trailing into a hush.

"Don't you worry, Henry. We'll find 'em. We got the best trackers in the Northwest and Ol' Red," said Maas. "You know Colin, don't you?"

"Yeah, deputy. Glad you're here," said the distraught father.

Just then his wife entered the room. "Henry, I was just talking to Elizabeth Maas. She said she was on her porch yesterday about 3 and heard two, maybe three shots. Maybe it was the boys."

"Yep, Gus heard it too — probably over on the second ridge," he said. "Well, if it was, then they ain't too far away, are they? I gonna go get some of the boys things for the dogs. Got to get going now."

"Oh, Henry. I am so scared," sobbed Minnie, embracing her husband, in a rare public display of affection.

"We'll find 'em, dear. I know we will."

As Henry left the room, Gus Maas embraced Minnie and both sobbed.

"I just wish John was here. He'd know where the boys are. Probably go right to them," said Minnie, talking about her brother, whom she hadn't seen in several weeks until two nights ago. She was awakened about 3 a.m. by a noise in the kitchen and found John gathering provisions as he had often done since he went into seclusion. Fortunately, Henry didn't hear a thing. He would have been furious.

When he was working in the area, John would often visit his sister when he knew Henry was going to be gone. Henry didn't care for the Tornows, especially Ed and John, since well before his daughter died less than a year ago. Bauer had severed Tornow family ties completely.

John's visits were less frequent since his dog was shot by Ed last month and he vowed to go to his beloved woods and announced "Nobody better never come after me or they might get killed."

There was no reason for John to go to his homestead. The parents were both dead and all the brothers had left. The Tornow siblings — brothers Fred, William, Albert and Ed, and sister Minnie — had signed off on the probate that was set up to sell the property. But not John. He was nowhere to be found, and he wanted nothing to do with it. The boys also knew when they saw the probate that John was the benefactor of a major portion of property in Mason County.

Minnie remembered how John would hide in the old cedar stump at the edge of the property, and when he saw Henry leave the house, he would come in and get some home-cooking and she would cut his hair.

After the deaths of her parents, she would comfort her brother and assure him things would be well. Oh, how she wished John were here.

"Henry, you stay with your wife in case the boys return, then fire two shots into the air, then a second or two later, two more, so we know," the deputy admonished Bauer.

"You don't think I outta go with ya?" Henry queried.

"No, we have enough men. We'll be back by nightfall, hopefully sooner."

———

The posse found a shallow spot to ford the Middle Fork of the Satsop, then spread out to cover the first ridge. It was fruitless. Nary a track was discovered as the men trudged along the underbrush and up the first ridge, within a mile of the Bauer homestead.

Crossing the ridge was a bit easier through a dense forest, but less underbrush, though still fruitless as the search passed noon.

Then as they headed up the second ridge, finally a break.

"It looks like a bear, probably a female, has been around here, sheriff. And it's been hit. See that blood," said Swartz.

"If that's a bear, I don't even want to think what might have happened to the boys. Hold the dog down and see if Red can pick up the scent. Maybe the boys were here," said McKenzie, whose group had met up with the other men as they began to ascend the second ridge.

Suddenly, Red picked up a scent and Gus let him run. "He's got something," said his owner. They sped up the search and caught up with Red at the base of a little creek. They saw the dog on the other side.

"Look, Gus. He stopped. He's gone crazy. I can't figure it out," said Swartz. "What's there? I don't see anything."

"He won't go any further. There's got to be something here," answered Luther Mullinix, another member of the search group. "Let's look closer. Check every piece of ground, carefully."

The searchers saw nothing but little heaps of leaves and bark, nothing at all unusual, yet the hound wouldn't stop his baying and clawing at the earth.

Suddenly, Swartz stumbled across a well-concealed fallen log when he had been looking ahead and all around, but not at his feet.

"Oh, crap. That hurt," he bellowed when he struggled to regain his feet. Then he stopped dead in his tracks. At the base of a ravine lay a badly wounded she-bear, apparently paralyzed from a rifle shot.

She was in dire straits and near death. At her side was the offal of a heifer.

The searchers theorized the animal was eating when surprised by a gunman or gunmen and never knew what hit her. Since she had been hit farther up the ridge and bled for a bit, the men believed the animal might have fallen down the ravine, where she lay near death.

They also believed that the dog had picked up the scent of the bear and not of the boys.

The men cautiously approached the dying animal and mercifully, McKenzie put her out of her misery with his carbine. With the animal now dead, the men carefully dissected the bullet that caused the initial injury to the animal.

It was determined to be a .30-30, likely a Winchester.

"Hey Gus, didn't Henry say that was what the boys were shooting?" queried Swartz.

"I believe he did. In fact, yes, I know it was because their Uncle John gave them those rifles when they turned 16. They're just like his. I guess that means Tornow could have shot the animal, too."

"Well, I think we can say that they were here, likely shot the bear. But what then? What happened to them? Why didn't they go get the bear? Where are those boys?" said the puzzled McKenzie.

"This is real strange. I thought maybe one of the boys fell victim to the bear, but both of them, not likely. And if so, their bodies would be around here, wouldn't they? They'd be in plain sight and they are nowhere to be found," Colin continued.

"Guys, let's go back up this incline to where we first saw the blood. I want to go back over that area carefully," said McKenzie.

"Yeah, good idea. And where's that hat one of the Bauer boys wore. Maybe the hounds can pick up the scent again," said Lem Nethery, another of the searchers.

The men walked up the short hill to the flat above and back a few hundred yards to where they first discovered blood on the forest floor. They carefully held the hounds back, so they wouldn't be attracted to the scent of the injured bear.

"Carl, wasn't this the area where Tornow was said to have spent some time?" McKenzie asked Swartz.

"I think it was. Let's climb that knoll and see if we can find anything. He is known to camp near a river and the Middle Fork is pretty close."

The men decided the next order of business was to try and locate the camp. It wasn't long before they found it, no more than 100 yards from where they spotted the bear.

"Look at this," said McKenzie. "That hanging beef is still wet. And look at these hides. Somebody has been here recently. I'm sure this must be Tornow's place. Let's look all over this site, there might be a clue."

The men scoured every inch of the hand-hewn, crude, log lean-to, but didn't find anything significant; except it appeared the occupant was using it as a smokehouse and had been jerking beef that was found hanging high on a line tied between trees to keep it away from bears.

"If it was his, where did he sleep? There's no sign of a bed," noted Mullinix."

At that moment, Swartz stopped dead in his tracks at the base of a cedar just outside the lean-to's opening.

"Look at that," he said. "Isn't that a bullet hole in the tree?"

"It sure is, Carl," McKenzie agreed. "Give me a boost and I'll see if I can get the bullet out."

"Got it, and it looks like another one shaved off some bark," McKenzie said, examining the bullet, once back on terra firma. "It looks like it could be a .30-30, maybe from the boys."

"Or Tornow?" snapped Swartz in reply. "Remember, he had one too."

"OK guys. We can speculate all we want, but we need more. Let's keep looking," said Maas. "Colin, bring Mac over here and let's try to give the dogs a good sniff."

Maas rubbed the hat they brought with them all over Ol' Red's face and did the same with Mac. The hounds just stood there and didn't move; then Red suddenly took off down a small ridge into the brush with the men in pursuit. Mac was close behind his new friend.

Swartz could detect no reason for the dogs' actions, overlooking the pile of leaves that seemed to be exactly as they fell naturally from the canopy above.

"There's got to be something here," he said. "The dogs wouldn't be goin' off like that for no reason. Let's see if there is something under these leaves," he said without realizing he was alone in the search as the others had continued probing along nearby fallen logs.

"Oh, God, no," Swartz bellowed after he had removed a thin layer of moist leaves. "It's John. He's been shot. He's dead."

The others came rushing over to witness the grisly scene. "He took it in the heart and in the shoulder," said Swartz, choking back tears.

It was just after noon when the body of John Bauer was discovered. But where was the other twin?

"Colin, look at this. It looks like the body was dragged here. He was killed somewhere else. See, those leaves and brush are kind of tromped down. It took a good-sized man to do this. Those boys are pretty big," said Maas.

"I am going to look around a little more to try to find the other body, then I'm going back to Henry's and give them the bad news and go up to Mullers and call Ed," McKenzie said.

Two hours of searching revealed nothing more, so McKenzie and Maas left the party and headed back to the Bauer homestead.

"We'll just search around a bit more and head back, so we can get home before dark," said Swartz.

One hour after McKenzie left, the group decided to extend their search, and this time it was Payette's pup that made the discovery. "Follow him closely," said Swartz when the hound suddenly took off; the hound stopped about 50 feet from where John Bauer's body was found.

It was a similar location to where the first body was discovered. A loose patch of fallen leaves. This time, they didn't ignore the dog, but began to toss the leafy cover aside and immediately found the body of Will Bauer, shot once through the heart.

The remaining searchers sat down on a log in a moment of quiet and to gather their thoughts.

It was Swartz, who finally broke the silence as he carefully stood and marked the spot with a mound of dirt to easily locate it in the morning when the coroner arrives to examine the bodies.

"Guys, we know now we have a murderer to find, a double murderer. Be careful, you don't become the next victim."

21. THE MANHUNT BEGINS

September 5, 1911

It was a long and somber trek back for the remaining searchers, who scarcely said a word as they recounted in their mind the horrific findings of the day. Before they reached the Middle Fork of the Satsop, dusk had settled in and the small group double-timed it across the valley and up the small incline to the Bauer homestead.

"Carl, glad you guys are back," greeted McKenzie as he walked away from the gathering at the house and met the returning searchers. "I can tell from your body language that you found the other body." Right?"

"Yes, Mac." I'm afraid you are. About two hours after you left. Not far from the other one. How's Henry taking the news?"

"Not well, Minnie either," McKenzie answered. "Their daughter, Lizzie, was here, but Min sent her over to Maas's after we told her. Said she'll figure out how to tell her later. That poor girl has lost a sister and two brothers in less than a year. There's quite a gathering in there and sheriff is here too. He figured when he hadn't heard anything, he might as well grab the motor coach and head up. That reporter, Cloud, is with him."

"Well, I'm not ready to talk to the *World* guy, yet," said Swartz.

"Yeah, all I told him was that we found one body and you were looking for the other one. No details yet, haven't even told the sheriff anything. He just arrived about an hour ago."

"Well, let's go in and get this over with," said Swartz, walking toward the back door. "I've been on a lot of manhunts. It's never easy, but this one is the worst ever. Tears me up when kids are involved. What were these guys, not even 20, you think?"

"Nineteen is what Henry told me, but, you know, he wasn't sure. At least that's the way it sounded," answered McKenzie. "He was pretty distraught when he told me."

The men entered the back door and found Henry and Minnie at the dining room table. They didn't need to say a word. Their faces told the whole story. Henry held Minnie's hand; then embraced her as she broke into uncontrollable sobs.

"Folks, I wish I had better news for you, but about two hours after Mac left, we found Will's body. I don't know how much Mac told you, but I can share the details with you, if you like," Swartz said. "I'll give you a few minutes to gather yourself and we'll come back in. Cloud, come outside with us, please."

"I know you haven't been doing this for long, but you gotta give them time to process what happened," McKenzie told the reporter, his arm around the young man's shoulders.

"Yeah, I know that. Sheriff talked about that when we were driving up here. I respect that he has enough confidence in me to bring me along. I can see how this has affected them, and having met them a couple of times — Mr. and Mrs. Bauer, I mean — makes it easier. I just said my condolences. I haven't asked them anything, yet, just observing. Mr. Bauer did tell me about the boys leaving to hunt that bear and about the cow

Washington State Archives

John and William Bauer and their dog.

disappearing. He pointed out the ridge where they went, so I do have some background."

"Well, son, sounds like you have been given a good briefing, but we want to talk over the details with the Bauers first, then we'll talk with you. Why don't you take a walk down to the river or something. It's straight down there and the moon's out, so it'll be a nice, quiet walk," said Sheriff Payette. "We'll wait until morning to go back and recover the bodies. The coroner will be here early. I got to get over to the Mullers and phone Deputy Quimby. I want to get a posse going as soon as possible."

"Sure, sheriff. No problem. One thing, though. Where we going to sleep tonight?"

"I haven't thought that far ahead yet, but we'll likely grab some blankets and find some hay in the barn. I want to get an early start and we'll have to get a couple of pack horses ready. Not much time to sleep tonight."

"I'll do whatever we have to do to find the killer," the reporter said. "One thing, when you call the office, would you have the deputy call my folks. They might be worried about me. I did tell them I'd be with you when I left, but I know if I didn't come home tonight, they'd be worried. Oh, and he better call my editor, Mr. Irvine, Bill Irvine, and tell him what we know for tomorrow's paper. I have no way to contact him."

"Sure, give me the numbers and I'll get it done," said the sheriff. "Smart kid and thoughtful too," he said to himself as the reporter ambled down the hill.

Before heading inside, Payette took a minute to gather his thoughts for the day ahead, then collected the searchers. "Guys, I just want to thank you so much for your help today," he told them. "As you know, we've got a tough job tomorrow. If you are available, I want to leave before sun-up and I'd appreciate your help. If you can't make it, that's OK, too, and I thank you for your help today."

"I'm in," said Mullinix.

"Me too," echoed Nethery.

Two others who accompanied the group said they weren't available.

"Good, that's gives us four and I'm sure Maas and Muller will be with us and Henry too. I'll see if Quimby can round up another six or so and join us later tomorrow. I'll deputize you all in the morning. Now, get a good night's sleep and I'll see you early. If you don't have time to get home and back, you can join the rest of us in the barn tonight."

"Sheriff, I think we are ready to hear more," said Henry Bauer as he approached Payette in the backyard. "It's going to be hard, no matter what, and I think we want to get it over with."

"Sure, Henry," said the sheriff, his arm around the grieving man's shoulder. "I'll get Mac and Swartz. I haven't even had time to hear anything yet from Carl. His report will be new to me, too."

The men gathered around the table and told the Bauers of the ghastly details they uncovered that day.

"Thanks, sheriff," Henry responded. "That wasn't easy and it won't be tomorrow, either. I'd like to go with you guys to bring out the bodies," Henry said. "You be all right, honey?" he asked Minnie in uncustomary endearing words.

"Sure, Henry. You go. I got to go get Lizzie and tell her. Poor girl. Two brothers and a sister taken from her in, what is it? Just 10 months?"

"Yes, how terrible, how tragic," the sheriff responded. "Nobody should have to endure such heartache, and in such a short span. Wasn't it November when Mary died?"

"December 1," Minnie answered, breaking into tears.

They all sat in silence for a few minutes before Minnie got up.

"Where's my manners? I'm sorry folks. I gotta feed you all. It's after suppertime."

"Now, Minnie, don't you even think about that," the sheriff responded. "You got enough on your mind."

"Just you never mind. No problem at all. I've got some leftover chicken we didn't eat last night. There's plenty, 'cause I fixed for the boys too. My chicken's their favorite," she said, unable to choke back tears.

The sheriff moved to embrace her, but she held out her arms. "I'm all right. Really, I'm all right. Give me a hand peeling some potatoes and it'll be ready in no time. I'll put the chicken on top of the woodstove and it'll get warm pretty quick."

"I can't believe you, Min. We've just lost our boys and you're thinking about food," said Henry, walking away from the table.

"Henry, I'm hurting too. I'm not thinking about food. I'm thinking about our guests. They are here for us, and when we have guests, I want to take care of them, no matter how I feel. Mama taught me that. So many times she was hurting, but she always fixed meals for her family and guests. And besides, I'd just as soon keep busy than sit idle and start my mind to racing."

It was still dark when Coroner Ray Hunter and two men, who would join the posse pulled down the long driveway to the Bauer homestead. They approached a man near the barn getting the horses ready.

"Who are you guys? What do you want?" the man asked curtly.

"I'm Coroner Hunter and these men are deputies Howard Philbrick and Con Elliott. We're here to help take the bodies out. And you?"

"I'm Henry Bauer."

"Oh, I'm so sorry for the news of your boys, Mr. Bauer."

"Thank you. I want to get going and get this over with. It's going to be a tough day."

"Sheriff, I thought you'd be up long before now," said Cloud, rising from the hay and leaving the barn.

"I did too, but we better get moving. I thought I heard Henry get the horses an hour or so ago."

The sheriff gathered the men together in the Bauers' backyard and briefed them on what lay ahead.

"It's going to be a tough day for all of us," the sheriff said. "Mac, you know the lay of the land better than me. Brief the guys on what's going to happen."

"Sure boss. First, we head down to the river, then go upriver until we can ford it. We found a pretty good spot yesterday. We got wet, of course, but it's easier for the horses, and we'll dry off quickly once the sun's up. We have some fairly tough terrain and brush to go through to get over the first ridge. Then we go down into a little valley, more like a meadow, then about halfway up the next ridge. We'll take the horses as far as we can, then we'll have to tie them up and carry out the bodies on stretchers. We marked the spot where the bodies are, so we could find them again. We'll talk more as we get closer. One thing I forgot. Henry, do you have any wooden poles and canvas in the barn that we can use for make-do stretchers? Can you take Lem and get those for us?"

"Sure, sheriff. I think I can find something that will work."

After Henry returned with the poles and canvas, Sheriff Payette gathered the men in a group and deputized several of them — all but Cloud, Henry Bauer, the coroner and attorney.

They were off on their sad journey well before sun-up.

"Cloud, I know we haven't had a chance to talk yet, but I won't leave you out of the loop. Can you write while we walk?" the sheriff asked the reporter.

"That's OK. You can talk all you want. I don't need to write it down. I'll remember it right here," he said pointing to his head. "When we get there, I'll get a visual and take some notes."

"Here's what we found," the sheriff said as he related the gruesome discovery. "What I am telling you is exactly like Mac and Carl briefed me. It might change a little when we get there and try to recreate what happened."

"I understand," Cloud answered. "Can I interrupt you if I don't understand something?"

"Sure, kid," the sheriff said.

Cloud didn't like being called "kid," but in relation to the others, he was just that. He knew the sheriff meant it more as a salutation, an informal one at that.

"They didn't find even a trace until after noon when they started up the second ridge," the sheriff explained. "That's when they looked down into a ravine and saw a badly injured she-bear, helpless and hidden in the deep thicket."

"If the bear was hidden, how did they see her in the ravine?" Cloud queried.

"Good question, boy. The dogs. They had two bloodhounds with them. Ol' Red belongs to August Maas and Mac is mine. They are experienced trackers. The dogs got a good sniff and led them right to the bear. She had been shot and was paralyzed. McKenzie finished her off."

"Did the bear kill Mr. Bauer's cow?"

"We think so, because some of the cow's innards were next to the bear. They didn't know then where the rest of the animal was."

"Do you know what the bear was shot with?"

"Yes, I was just coming to that," the sheriff said. "It was a .30-30, Winchester rifle."

"Isn't that what the Bauer boys shot with?" the scribe asked.

"Yes, their uncle, John Tornow, gave each of the boys their rifles last Christmas. It's also what we know he liked to shoot. Strike that. He gave the boys the rifles for their 16th birthday."

"Then what happened?"

"Hold on, Dan. I can't even catch my breath. "The guys decided to head back up the ridge where they first spotted the blood."

"Spotted blood? What blood?" the reporter asked.

"The bear's blood. I think I forgot to say that before," the sheriff answered. "They saw the blood in the brush midway up the ridge and they didn't know at that time if it was an animal or maybe the boys.

After disposing of the bear, they went back up the ridge to where they saw the blood.

"After an hour or so with no clues, they decided to try and find out where the shot came from and headed up the ridge, then one of them spotted a lean-to. When they got up there, they saw some beef hanging high and it was still wet, so they knew someone had been there and recently. They looked around the lean-to and saw a bullet hole in a tree and dug it out."

"I bet it was a .30-30," the scribe interjected.

"Yep, sure was," the sheriff answered. "They also saw where another bullet had chipped off some bark on the same tree.

"The searchers had one of the boy's hats and rubbed it in the dogs' noses. The hounds suddenly took off."

"Do they have any idea who might have been in the cabin?" the reporter asked.

"Well, it's pure speculation, but the boys' uncle, John Tornow, had gone up into the area several months ago. We don't know much about that, but we do know it's the general vicinity. We do know he was known to have several of these lean-tos in the lower Olympics. But again, that's pure speculation."

"Sheriff, do you think Tornow's demented, crazy or what?"

"Not really," the sheriff answered. "You remember it was just a month ago that his brother swore out a warrant for him, but I found it unwarranted. Still, he did utter those threatening words that nobody better come after him. We have to look at all possibilities."

"That sounds pretty threatening, doesn't it?" the scribe responded.

"Yes, it's kind of incriminating, but again, I caution you about making presumptions."

"I told you last month I met him a couple of times and I think he kind of took to me. I liked him. I liked his gruffness and I saw his compassionate side when Mary died. He was concerned for Minnie and the boys."

"I've heard that about him, too," the sheriff answered.

"Sheriff, I heard some people talking at your office when I was waiting for you saying that Tornow had been in the insane asylum in Salem."

"I heard something about that when the warrant came out, but I investigated it, made some calls to a sheriff I know in Portland and also a friend with the Oregon Mental Health Department and both said they could find nothing about a Tornow being in an institution in Oregon. They both said, if that had been the case, they would have complete records of it. So, I caution you about reporting anything, other than what I have told you. Remember, just the facts."

"Sure, and thanks for telling me that about your investigation, because with the information that you have now, even if it is speculation, people are going to talk. So, can I say that John is a suspect?" Cloud asked.

"Right now, I think what you can print is that, and you can quote me, suspicion falls toward the uncle. We definitely want to talk to him, to ask him where he was on Sunday afternoon."

"That sounds fair, sheriff. You told me that they found some meat hanging outside the cabin. Was that meat dry and perhaps had been there several days, or was it wet and maybe fresh?"

"First off, let's not call it a cabin. It really wasn't that at all, just a lean-to or some call it a wickiup. I think Carl said the hanging meat, a hindquarter, was still moist. That raises some questions because it could be rather fresh and maybe the cow from Henry Bauer's or it might be that way from precipitation. It rained a little Sunday night and it was definitely dewy in the morning. And where is the rest of the meat?"

"He probably took it with him, or part of it, anyway," said the reporter. "So, sheriff, where did you leave off in your description of what you found?" Cloud asked.

"Beats me kid," Payette answered, huffing a bit as they climbed an incline, pushing through dense brush as they went. "Tell me what you remember and maybe it'll come to me."

"Sure, sheriff. "Let's see, you told me about the cabin ... er lean-to, I mean. And the bullets they found in the tree. Who found those, again? Didn't you say Swartz?"

"No, it was Mac, McKenzie. Swartz boosted him up there. You know what was real strange about that lean-to? There was no sleeping place, no matted leaves or cot or anything. But there were some hides, nice ones, so whoever was there left in a hurry, I suspect."

"Yes, sheriff that is strange, but maybe he has another lean-to where he sleeps," Cloud said, trying to imagine the scenario. "Where did they find the bodies?"

"The guys rubbed a hat from one of the Bauer boys on the dogs' faces. Mac said they didn't move for a minute or two, then bolted through the brush and stopped near a fallen log about 100 or so feet away in fairly dense cover."

"And there the bodies were?"

"Not exactly. Mac said there was nothing there when the dogs stopped, except for a pile of fallen leaves. The guys gave up and went in another area, but Swartz stayed there. He said he couldn't figure out the dogs' behavior, if there wasn't something there to attract them."

"Yes, I agree," Cloud said. "My dad's dog is like that. If he stops running, it's gotta be for a reason. And another thing, leaves don't usually fall in piles, do they?"

"You're right kid. In fact, we've caught up with the rest of them, so I'll let Carl tell you what he found.

"Carl, can you join us here for a minute?" the sheriff hollered to Carl Swartz. "I'd like you to describe to Mr. Cloud just what you found when the dogs stopped running and started baying."

"Sure, Ed. How ya doin' Cloud? This is quite an education for a greenhorn, isn't it?"

"Yes, it is Mr. Swartz, but I'm not exactly a greenhorn. I've been doing this for a couple of years now, since I got out of school."

"Yes, I know, Swartz answered. "But, how many murders have you covered?"

"Well, sir, this is my first one."

"See, that's what I mean by greenhorn."

"OK, I guess you're right when you put it like that."

"That said, I know Ed, Mr. Payette, wouldn't have brought you along, if he didn't think he could trust you, if he didn't think you'd make it."

"Yes, I really respect him for that. So what did you find? Sheriff stopped at the point where the dogs stopped in front of a pile of leaves."

"The other guys didn't see anything other than a pile of fallen leaves on either side of this fallen log. I guess they expected to find fresh dirt or something because they went up the ridge. I stayed right there. I knew the dogs had to have stopped there for a reason. I started throwing leaves aside and about a foot or so down in the leaves, I came across John's body."

"What was your reaction when you saw it?"

"I think I said 'Oh God, no.' I called out to the other guys. I didn't move the body, but I could tell he had at least two wounds, one in the breast near his heart, and the other was near his shoulder. They were clean shots and there was very little blood. But there were rags the murderer stuffed in the shoulder wound to absorb the blood. Then I looked off to the left and it appeared the leaves were smashed down, and I saw a small path where the dirt was clean, like it might be if a body were dragged across it."

"So, they probably weren't killed where you found them?"

"It appears so, but at this point, there was no them, just John's body. We looked all around, but couldn't find William's body. After a couple of hours, Mac, Colin McKenzie, decided he better head back, so he could get up to Muller's place and call in his finding. It was tough on us that the Bauers didn't have a phone."

"So, how long after he left did you find Will's body?"

"It wasn't long, a couple of hours, I guess."

"And did you find his body in the same place as John?"

"Fairly close, just about 50 feet apart. John was in the leaves on the right side and Will was on the left, but since the log had fallen into dense underbrush, it was tough to find. You'd think that the brush would have been tamped down, but that wasn't the case until we came up the other side of the ridge and saw where the brush had been pulled aside, likely to get the body up there close to the other one. Will was shot once in the heart. The coroner can probably figure that out for sure, but I think Will was likely killed first and death was instantaneous."

"This doesn't sound like the work of a deranged man, does it, Mr. Swartz?"

"Well, kid. You might be young, you might be inexperienced, but one thing you are not, is stupid."

———

It was mid-afternoon by the time Coroner Hunter, the posse, the sheriff and the reporter arrived back at the Bauer ranch, where the coroner applied formaldehyde to help preserve the bodies.

The coroner, in the presence of Prosecuting Attorney W.A. Campbell and Constable Rube Quinn, conducted the autopsy soon after the bodies were returned to the Bauer home. Henry and Minnie decided they would have a small service in a couple of days at their ranch, then have the boys' bodies buried in the Grove Cemetery, where Mary is interred not far from her grandparents, Frederick and Louisa Tornow's tombstones.

The coroner confirmed what those in the search party already suspected: William had been shot in the breast, a .30 caliber bullet going directly through the heart. John was shot twice, the first bullet entering his right side just above the waist and passing straight through the abdomen and going out of the left side. Another bullet, believed to be fired at close range, entered at the top of the right shoulder, passing through the heart and lodging near the backbone.

The coroner said "Will was shot first and died instantly, but the murderer probably found John alive and went to where he was lying and finished the terrible deed."

Hunter continued his forensic analysis, noting that both boys had been dragged about 50 feet to their burial spots. "The Bauer boys were about 190 pounds each and stood 6 feet tall, so the murderer had to be a man of great strength, and Tornow, we know, is a man of great strength."

The reporter spent a few minutes talking to the search party before the sheriff beckoned him it was time to leave.

Cloud boarded the motor coach with the sheriff and headed to Montesano.

"Try to get a few winks. You've got a long night ahead of you," the sheriff told Cloud as they started the long road back to the county seat.

Cloud slept soundly as Payette pulled into Montesano.

"Tell you what kid, I'm gonna take you home. You probably won't be able to catch the train yet tonight and it won't take that long," the sheriff said to the reporter, who moved with his family to Aberdeen a month ago.

"Sheriff, that's mighty nice of you. I'm dead tired, and I know you are too" the scribe said. "That nap was great."

"Nap? You slept the whole way."

"Sorry, I wasn't much company. I'm exhausted. That was grueling and it was emotionally tough too, but I am so grateful for the opportunity."

"That was quite an experience for a young reporter and you did fine. I was a little surprised you didn't shed a tear. We all did. It was an emotionally challenging time."

"I wanted to, and it was hard not to, especially when you guys came out with the bodies. What a waste, two lives taken so young. Do you mind if I shed a tear now? I've kept it in for a long time."

"Not at all kid, just go ahead and bawl, if you want. You'll have a great story to write. When do you have to get your story done?"

"Usually, I'd do it at night, but I just can't do it tonight, so I'll be there by 7 or so in the morning."

When Cloud arrived home, his parents rushed to greet him.

"This is Sheriff Payette," he said, introducing his mother, Lucy, and father, Daniel.

"Pleased to meet you folks. You've got a fine son. I think he learned an awful lot up there. Nothing like hands-on to help a young man learn his trade," the sheriff said.

"Thank you, sheriff. I didn't know what to think seeing a sheriff's automobile pull up in front."

"We had quite a difficult experience, but I'll let Dan tell you about it."

Cloud decided he better communicate with his editor and see if the plans for him to come in early in the morning would work out.

"Is this Bill Irvine?" he asked the voice on the other end.

"Sorry, to disturb you at home, Mr. Irvine. This is Dan Cloud."

"Yes, I know. I recognize your voice. Where have you been?"

"I've been with Sheriff Payette. Didn't the deputy call you?"

"Yes, but that was two days ago."

"I went with the sheriff, so I had to wait until he was ready to leave and we just got back home. I am dead tired and I would appreciate it if I can come early in the morning and do the story. I guarantee this will be the story of the year. I've got everything for a great, great article and I'll get some current stuff from the sheriff in the morning."

"That's fine. I know you work quickly, so that shouldn't be a problem."

"Thank you, Bill. I'll see you in the morning."

Cloud gobbled down a plate of pot roast, potatoes, carrots and biscuits, then headed off to bed.

"Danny, aren't you going to tell us what happened up there?" his mother queried.

"I'd love to, but I have to go in real early. Get me up no later than 6, better make it 5. I've got a lot to write about."

"Did they find those boys?" Cloud's father asked.

"Yes, but they were both dead."

"I figured as much. Do they know who did it?"

"Not for sure, but they suspect the boys' uncle John Tornow. Now, I'd like to get to sleep and you can read about it in tomorrow's paper."

Cloud grabbed a cup of coffee and sat down at his desk at the *World*. He had been formulating in his mind exactly how he wanted to write his story.

Since he had been in the woods for two days, the *World's* readers didn't have much of the story. When the editor was called Monday, it was after deadline, so nothing appeared until a few paragraphs in Tuesday's edition, which left more questions than answers. The short article said the boys had been missing since going bear hunting on Sunday and that John's body had been found. At that point, the search remained for Will's body, and of course, for the murderer.

"I remember what my editor told me about reporting on a continuous story," Cloud thought as he began to formulate how he would tell this story. "Give the reader 'what happens next, the most current news first.' This story surely follows that principle."

With that in mind, he made a quick call to the sheriff's office and surprisingly found the sheriff answering the phone.

Payette told the young reporter that a posse left earlier in the morning and he would be taking another posse into the Upper Satsop in a couple of hours. The sheriff detailed the plans as best he could, without tipping his hand.

Thus, Cloud had the freshest information for his comprehensive story.

He was now ready to write.

It was a most complete report, filling in the reader on all the juicy details, or at least most of them.

The Aberdeen Daily World reporter Dan Cloud accompanied the sheriff and his posse to retrieve the bodies of John and William Bauer on Monday and Tuesday, September 4-5. Here is his report:

Equipped for a month's stay and prepared to penetrate deep into the Olympic Mountains, if need be, two posses left Montesano today in search of John Tornow, the alleged slayer of his twin nephews, John and William Bauer, of the Upper Satsop on Sunday.

Sheriff Ed Payette sent deputies Colin McKenzie and Carl Swartz, along with four others, to scour every foot of the vastness of the headwaters of the Wynooche and Satsop rivers to try and pick up the 31-year-old Tornow's trail. The sheriff said Tornow is the suspect because the boys' bodies were discovered on Monday afternoon near a lean-to that could have been occupied by Tornow. The man was believed to have been in the area and was the likely occupant of the lean-to.

"All the evidence, though not conclusive, points to Tornow being the suspect. He is the man we want to talk to," said the sheriff.

Two posses search

A second posse of six men, under Payette's leadership, was to leave about 7 this morning. He said the posse is equipped for a stay of two or three weeks. The posse was to have driven by automobile directly to the home of Henry and Minnie Bauer, the boys' parents, in the Upper Satsop. The machine will be abandoned at that point and the chase will be taken up on horseback and on foot, scouring the country in all directions with the Bauer home as base of operations for supplies. Included in this posse is Officer Ed Tribbets of the Aberdeen police force.

The authorities expect the chase to be a long, hard one, for Tornow knows every foot of the woods, having been raised in the Satsop and having been an inhabitant of the woods from childhood.

Payette said he cautioned the men in both posses to be extremely wary of Tornow because he "is a skilled marksman, in addition to being believed to be demented by some, and the two taken together, added to his ability in woodcraft, make him a desperate character."

It is thought that Tornow has probably taken the trail back to his old cabin in the Wynooche district where he wintered last year. He has had by now a two-days' head start and is strong and hardy and accustomed to following all kinds of paths in the woods. The sheriff said Tornow likely has his own provisions, part of which was a half of a beef, the other half of which was discovered hanging in the lean-to near where the boys' bodies were found.

He said Tornow is wily and resilient. "Even if he were not provisioned, a man who has been able to remain in the woods for as long as he has and never come out for provisions, should be regarded as not only able to take care of himself, now that he is a fugitive from justice, but also as a particularly hard man to track."

The sheriff said the chase for Tornow will be difficult and no doubt lengthy. "The hunt for the bandit Harry Tracy will have nothing on this" is how he described it.

Tracy was the Portland bandit, who, along with his brother-in-law David Merrill, was responsible for about 11 deaths and countless robberies of saloons, banks, trolley cars and businesses in the 1898-1899 era. Media called Tracy, a member of the Butch Cassidy gang, "King of the Bandits."

The Portland sheriff heard that Tracy was headed to his mother's place near Vancouver, Wash., where he was eventually captured at a nearby butcher shop. He was sentenced to 20 years in the Oregon Penitentiary and Merrill to 12 years. Both escaped the second day they were there. A few weeks later in Southern Washington, Tracy shot and killed Merrill in a dispute. The hunt for Tracy continued for 58 days, at the time the longest manhunt in Northwest history.

He was finally corralled at a ranch in Eastern Washington, about 8 miles from Creston. He had obtained a job as a ranch hand there when another worker recognized him and called officers. When authorities arrived, Tracy was chased into an adjacent wheat field. One shot from the posse broke his leg and another struck him in the shoulder. Expecting the end was near, Tracy put his own .30-30 in his mouth and pulled the trigger.

Other suspects

While much of the suspicion is centered on Tornow, not all the searchers believe he is the only suspect.

"That's a crazy man who killed those boys," said posse member Howard Philbrick. "And Tornow is known to be demented. I don't know that, just what I've heard."

"I'm not so sure," said Swartz, who sat down to talk with a reporter after arriving at the Bauer home with the boys' bodies on Tuesday. "From what I saw in the woods today and yesterday it is not the work of a deranged man. Those bodies were skillfully buried, not the work of an idiot."

"I've known the man and his family quite a while," said Maas. "I knew the family — his parents, Fritz and Louisa — more than John, but I've had dinner at their place and once or twice John was there. Real quiet, doesn't say too much, but I did hear him talk about the boys. He loved those boys. No way do I believe he killed them — unless they were shooting at him, and I don't think that was the case. His sister said he loved the boys more than his own siblings."

Hearing Maas talking to the reporter, Luther Mullinix, another Satsop neighbor, who was in on the search, chimed in: "I've hunted with him and his brother, the older one, a few times. The young one is too lazy. John's actually a fun guy. He knows how to hunt and when you go with him, you know you aren't coming back empty-handed. That was several years ago. He told me he didn't like being around people that much. He knew me and my family, so it was like hunting with friends, for him.

"I like him and we had fun together. He had a great rifle, knew a guy up at Matlock — Lathrop, I think his name was, Charles Lathrop. The guy worked at the rail camp, but also was a trapper. He put Tornow in touch with a guy at Shelton who made him a custom U.S. Winchester .30-30. He didn't like the sight on it, so he removed it, melted nickel and made a new sight. He didn't miss much with that rifle."

Mullinix also said there were other men and other circumstances to consider and not just limit the suspicion to Tornow.

"So you don't think Tornow did it?" Cloud queried him.

"There is not enough evidence right now. I also heard tell one of the brothers found out John was going to get a big share of his mama's property after she died. They still haven't settled up on that yet. Been almost a year. Never know. But bad family blood runs deep, they say. Coulda been a set-up that backfired. Them brothers were always at it. And I don't trust that young one at all. He did shoot John's dog."

Mullinix hardly took a breath as he spouted off one theory after another.

"And that Bauer guy, John's brother-in-law, the boys' dad, he's been trying to get even with the Tornows too. He never did care for John, even though he's family. Since his daughter died last year, Bauer's been going around blamin' that family for it. He still thinks one of the Tornow boys got the girl in trouble with a baby."

"It's hard to believe Bauer's the kind who'd do away with his own boys to frame Tornow. But then the other day I read where a divorced man in Centralia killed his kids 'cause he was jealous of his wife taking them away from him," Mullinix continued. "Fella said if he couldn't have them, then neither could she. And another thing, I heard one of the guys say that maybe the boys were sent out to get Tornow. I don't think so. They idolized their uncle, and if they were sent to get him, wouldn't they have been more concealed when shooting at him? We believe where they were killed, they were in plain view of that shed. No way the boys did it!"

"Lord, Lute, you sure let your mind run wild, don't you," the sheriff snapped.

"Maybe so, Ed, but it's something to think about. He sure had enough reasons."

Whether the shooting was an accident or the work of a deranged mind, Tornow was their suspect and the man they most wanted. He likely headed into the foothills or the high country. He didn't need a map, that's for sure. He knows every inch of that country by heart.

Sheriff determined

Payette is noted for his sagacity and daring in the woods. His determination, once he has taken the trail of the criminal, is to see it through to the end. The men under him have been selected for their knowledge of the woods and on the records of their past performances in similar pursuits.

Deputies McKenzie and Swartz are skilled woodsmen and familiar with the Harbor country. They have made trips into the depths of the forest. Swartz arrested an elk poacher on the upper reaches of the Humptulips on the west side of the Olympics and brought him back without difficulty, though he had been warned that the game law violator was dangerous. Swartz caught him with elks' horns and, before arresting him, heard from his lips the story of his illegal hunt.

McKenzie, a well-known photographer in Aberdeen, had broken his back when a wall fell on him in the Black Friday fire of 1903 that destroyed most of downtown Aberdeen. He had done some tracking before, but became a bounty hunter and deputy sheriff last year. His tenacity and skill rose prominently to the front in his search and capture of Chilean Louis Albert Salazar, the murderer of aged Hoquiam gardener Ah Fook.

Fook was killed November 12, 1910, and soon after McKenzie was on Salazar's trail. The fugitive headed into Eastern Washington; then McKenzie heard the man had taken up residence at a fishing camp in British Columbia. No bigger mistake could Salazar have made. He ran into the land that McKenzie knew so well. It was his homeland. McKenzie scoured every fishing establishment along the Fraser River and finally caught his quarry on a short fishing dock and brought him back for a trial and subsequent conviction.

The men in the first posse, the one led by McKenzie and Swartz, are Deputies Philbrick, Henry Hildebrand, Con Elliott and Ed Bonnell. Their destiny is a secret, but it is believed that they are proceeding along a general line north from the scene of the attack, and without any specific clue.

The finding of the bodies of the murdered boys yesterday was due to the training of the bloodhounds belonging to Payette and Upper Satsop resident August Maas. When news of missing lads reached Payette on Monday afternoon, he immediately dispatched a posse, headed by McKenzie and Swartz, who brought the sheriff's pup, Mac, along. When they reached the Bauers, a neighbor, Gus Maas, had his hound, Ol' Red, a veteran tracker that McKenzie used on the Salazar hunt.

As the sheriff explained and this reporter later saw for himself, the lads had apparently been attracted to a lean-to, where it was believed Tornow might have been staying. The boys were in pursuit of a bear that their father said likely made off with one of his cows.

When the posse reached a point midway up the second ridge east of the Middle Fork of the Satsop River, and about a mile and half from the Bauer homestead, they spotted blood on brush where they were tracking. They then spotted a wounded she-bear at the bottom of a ravine.

The finding of the wounded bear first gave the men the impression that the animal had made away with the boys. After a while, one of the posse members climbed to the top of a small knoll and found a lean-to believed to be Tornow's, and also found a fresh, moist hindquarter of beef hanging high outside the structure, indicating a recent occupant.

Curiously, no sleeping cot or mound of leaves was found. McKenzie then discovered bullet holes and an embedded cartridge in a cedar outside the lean-to. He dug one bullet out and then found another that scraped bark off the tree. He said the bullet was a .30 caliber, the same caliber the group found in the wounded bear. It is also the same caliber of the Winchester the boys were carrying, and also the same as Tornow was known to shoot.

So, the logical question is who shot the bear? Officers don't know since the victims and the suspect carried the same type rifle. No weapons were found, save for a small knife on John Bauer's person.

After this discovery, the men put the dogs back to work, rubbing the noses of the hounds with a hat that was owned by one of the Bauer boys. At first, the dogs didn't move, then almost in unison, according to McKenzie, they took off running, stopping about 50 feet away at the edge of a small pile of leaves next to a concealed fallen log.

Swartz finds bodies

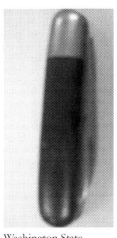

Washington State
Archives

**Knife found on
John Bauer**

Most of the posse conducted a search of the area, then unable to find anything, headed off in another direction.

Not Swartz. He said he figured the dogs stopped there for a reason and he began tossing aside leaves. "I had removed a lot of leaves, then saw some fresh dirt and dug down about a foot. I struck something hard and pulled off some more dirt and leaves and I saw the body. It was John. He had been shot in the shoulder and heart."

Swartz said he called the other posse members over to look at his discovery, then covered the body with leaves to try and keep it that way until the coroner could examine the body the next day. The coroner would want to look at unspoiled evidence. Swartz said it appeared, with the brush broken and leaves smashed and parted in a pattern along the path, the boy had been killed somewhere else and the body dragged to the burial site. He said it was a cleverly concealed site.

Swartz and the other searchers continued to look for the other body, but an hour of scouring the area revealed no other clues. At that point, McKenzie made the decision to return to the Bauer homestead, then go to a neighbor's home to phone the sheriff with the discovery. He took two men with him, while Swartz, Mullinix and Nethery stayed behind to search until just before dusk.

Swartz said it was frustrating, but he continued his pursuit. "I figured they were both killed and had to be buried in the same area," the deputy related. "It wasn't more than an hour or 90 minutes at most, that we found him."

The deputy revealed that he had climbed down a short knoll to reach the backside of the brush where the log had fallen. When he climbed up the other side, he spotted smashed brush and trampled leaves squished into a pattern that indicated something had possibly been dragged across them.

"The other body was buried in the same way," said Swartz. "Will was shot only once — right through the heart. I figured he must have been shot first and died instantly with that shot."

Coroner Randolph F. Hunter later Tuesday confirmed that was likely the scenario.

He and the deputies advanced the theory, after an inspection of the scope of the crime, that the boys, unaware of Tornow (or someone else's) presence, followed a bear to a point near the lean-to and there shot at it. They were likely midway down the ridge and shot up at the bear. It is supposed that their bullets whistled over the head of a man in the camp, lodging in the cedar behind the lean-to. What remains to be discovered is whether the boys wounded the bear with another shot or perhaps Tornow wounded the she-bear ... or was there another shooter?

The murder followed. If it is indeed Tornow, then he is an excellent shot and the boys didn't have a chance. It is argued that Will was killed first and then John. The killer likely moved to a point to see that John was still alive and ended his life with a close-up shot to the heart that lodged near his spine. He had been shot earlier in the shoulder.

Some raised the question why the second shot to John's body was not in the head to make sure. Instead it was to the shoulder and lodged near the spine. Perhaps the boy turned as the shooter fired. Perhaps the coroner was wrong in his assessment and John was only wounded, then killed with the shot to the heart.

The coroner also confirmed the shots that killed the boys were from a U.S. Winchester .30-30, the same caliber bullet that was pulled from the tree behind the lean-to. It was also the same type of rifle the boys carried, and the same that Tornow was known to have shot. It was also the same caliber that felled the bruin.

Swartz was able to figure out, based on blood spatterings, smashed leaves and somewhat furrowed earth, that the boys were killed about 100 yards from the lean-to. Where they fell was in plain view of the lean-to. The burial sites were not.

The deputies said once the boys were dead with a few feet of each other, the bodies were dragged to a secluded spot. One was buried on each side of a well-concealed fallen log in dense underbrush about one foot deep in fresh soil well covered by a small pile of fallen, moist leaves.

While this is more or less conjecture since nobody witnessed the crime, it tallies, the officers think, with the evidence that is at hand.

After killing the boys, the murderer cut the buckskin thongs which held their watches and robbed the boys of their timepieces, then took the boys' weapons and their outer coats.

The crime was committed within a mile and half of the Bauer home, which is about 20 miles northeast of Montesano and within a few miles of the place the suspected murderer was raised.

Tornow went into the woods nearly two years ago, saying before he left that he never expected to leave the forests again alive. The sheriff noted that Tornow had an altercation with his brother, Ed, a few months ago at the homestead. He came home and discovered the brother had shot his old, mangy dog, Cougar. John then shot Ed's dog, Rex, and said he was going to the woods and "nobody better come after me or I will kill him."

It was only a month ago, the sheriff took a warrant that Ed Tornow had sworn out to declare his brother insane. "I found him, sat down with him and talked to him. There was nothing wrong with him that I could detect. His speech was a little slow, but he answered all my questions and he told me about the dog incident. He said he didn't care much to be at home, never did. He wanted to be in the woods and left alone to enjoy its solitude and beauty were the words he used. I couldn't argue with that. I said goodbye and left."

The sheriff also noted that rumors that Tornow had spent time in the insane asylum were false, according to his investigation.

The sheriff noted that the site where he went with the warrant was not the same, not even in the area where the activity of this weekend took place. That campsite was in the Lower Wynooche, not the Upper Satsop, where the boys were murdered. He said Tornow had several camps throughout the areas.

What is known is that Tornow did not attend the funerals of his father in 1909, nor of his mother in November 1910, nor his niece, Mary Bauer, in December 1910. Or if he did, he wasn't visible to those gathered. Family members said he was working in the woods and there was no way to get in touch with him. If he had been institutionalized, it would likely have been noted on his parents' property estate probate as John was to have received a sizable portion of that estate.

All members of the family signed off on the probate, except for John, It remains unsettled at this date.

Payette also related another incident in which someone had claimed he saw Tornow and reported that he was dying and destitute. The sheriff sent a professional tracker, J.B. Lucas, to locate him, but he said he couldn't find any trace of Tornow.

Tornow is known to have some money, which he inherited from an estate in the Tornow family. He also has some additional money at the Montesano State Bank and owns a couple of lots in Aberdeen. He also has some money on his person, having sold several pelts in the last few months in Montesano and Matlock.

He appears to spend money only on provisions and ammunition. When he was working near Elma at Mack's Spur and White Star, he frequented Commissioner Wilson's mercantile at Satsop, but Wilson said he hadn't seen Tornow in quite some time.

Cruisers confront Tornow

The sheriff said this morning that a timber cruiser came into his office in Montesano and told of running into Tornow about a week ago.

"Mike Scully and his compassman, Earl McIntosh, cruiser for Schafer Brothers, hired by Attorney W. H. Abel, bumped into Tornow unexpectedly where he camped about a half-mile from where the murders took place. Scully said he came upon Tornow, who was sitting by the fire. The two men stumbled on Tornow's camps a number of times, but never did find where he slept. Scully said he startled Tornow when he said 'Well, I found you this time, didn't I?'"

He said Tornow's answer was to pick up his rifle and demand what the men were doing there. Scully told them they were cruisers and marking timber. 'Where is your Jacob's staff?' Scully said Tornow asked, indicating he didn't believe him. He said it was in his rig and told McIntosh to retrieve it.

The sheriff said Tornow seemed to be satisfied once he saw the staff, the vertical rod that holds the compass, an essential tool for surveyors and assessors.

"Scully said he and McIntosh decided to do their cruising in another section of the forest and return to that area at another date."

The sheriff added, according to Scully, that Tornow showed he would suffer no interference and his disposition showed him to be a dangerous man, and not one to clash with.

John Tornow, 31, is the brother of Minnie Bauer, mother of the dead twins.

The Bauer home is devastated. Of the four Bauer children a few months ago, only one, a daughter, Elizabeth, who goes by Lizzie, 23, remains alive at the family home. Death has tragically taken a daughter, Mary, at 24, last December and now the boys, who were 19. Mary, who Ed Tornow had moved into the family home to care for his mother, her grandmother, became pregnant. Ed took her to Aberdeen for an abortion and she died a day later. Dr. Robert Stapp of Aberdeen was convicted of the botched abortion. His case is now being appealed to the State Superior Court.

The Bauer household is now desolate and the parents of the ill-fated children are distraught with grief.

Cloud sat back in his chair, hands clasped behind his head, and smiled.

"Whew!" he sighed. "Not bad, not bad at all. I think I got it all in there. Now to give this to Irvine," the obviously satisfied reporter thought to himself.

Irvine was called out on another assignment, so the copy went directly to the publisher, Werner Rupp.

"Cloud, come in here, please," Rupp bellowed across the room. His usually gruff voice sometimes gave the impression something was amiss. Usually, it was the opposite. When Werner Rupp was on your side, you were a friend for life.

Dan had been accustomed to being called into the big man's office, but it didn't happen often.

"Have a seat. This is great stuff, kid. You earned your stripes on this one. Congratulations. I changed very little of your copy. I liked the pace, the lead with the new stuff, even though it was a double murder. That was the perfect way to handle it."

"Thank you, sir. Mr. Irvine told me about leading with the fresh stuff, then catching the reader up with the events in sequence."

"Well, you did it. I don't care how long it is, and this sucker is long, but it's worth it. And you know, it doesn't read like it's that long. It's compelling, it's gut-wrenching, it's tragic, and it's like a novel, only shorter, a lot shorter. Great job. You know, you got more education this week than you could get in four years of college. Nothing like learning from the bootstraps, getting in there, getting your hands dirty and learning how the authorities do their job. You'll remember this the rest of your life. Now get out of here and get some breakfast."

Those were the accolades Cloud was hoping to hear, now he could relax.

"Hmmm. Wonder what Lindy is up to," he thought to himself. "She's not ready for lunch yet, but I think I'll see if she can go and I'll wait an hour or two."

It had been several days since the two had been together.

"Hey, beautiful. How ya doin'? Hungry yet?"

"Hi Danny, you old rascal. I've been wondering about you. Chief told me you had gone with the sheriff. How was it? What did you learn?"

"I learned a lot and it was a tough two days, then I had to go in very early and write my story this morning. I just finished and thought how nice it would be to have lunch with my girl."

"Well, your girl would love to have lunch, but you'll have to wait for about an hour. I can't get away until then. Can you find something to do for an hour? Then you've got to tell me all about it."

"Sure, I'll probably go back to the office and take a nap. I can also check in with the sheriff's office and see if there is anything new. See ya soon, babe."

———

Cloud walked back to the World building from the police station and found the publisher still in his office.

"Dan, come in here. I want to talk to you," Rupp summoned the scribe.

"Sit down and relax," said Rupp, who had the dual roles as editor and publisher as well as president of the World's publishing arm, Grays Harbor Publications. His arms grasped the shoulders of his young protégé.

"That was a helluva story you wrote. I was impressed. I think you deserve a full-time position. You're practically working that anyway and we'll need someone to stay on top of this story. This is the story of the year, or any year, for that matter. So, what do you say? Up for that?"

"You bet I am, Mr. Rupp. "Thanks so much. I've worked really hard for that and I was hoping I'd get the chance. I love this work, I love this job. Mr. Irvine will be surprised."

"Not exactly. He's the one that pushed me to make that decision, although I'd been thinking about it since you did that Stapp trial.

"I want you to stay on top of this story. We should have something for the reader every day for a few days, even if it is no news, just a continued search. We'll take a look by the weekend and see where the story leads."

"That's exactly the way I was thinking, boss. As you know two posses are on the hunt now. There likely won't be too much to report, and reporting won't be easy. Not much access to phones up there. I know the Bauer ranch is where they go for provisions, but there's no phone. I think the other posse is headed into the Wynooche area and the closest phone up there is at Simpson's Camp 5, and it's still a long way from the headwaters of the Wynooche."

"Well, you've got a pretty good network of authorities at Montesano, so that's your best source. Be sure to check on a funeral for the boys. I want you there, if at all possible. I'll clear it with the coroner."

"I already checked on that, but there wasn't much expected. A minister, family and a few neighbors. I think they were planning it for tomorrow. I'll check with Montesano on it and see what they know. I'll be there, for sure," the reporter said. "The sheriff told me they were going to bury the bodies tomorrow at the Grove cemetery right after the funeral."

"So soon? I guess they want to get it over with. That family has got to be distraught," said Rupp. "I guess I'd feel the same way, were it my kids."

"Yes, Mrs. Bauer is taking it pretty hard. Can't really talk without tearing up. Henry isn't showing that much emotion, but he does try to console his wife."

"Those are good observations, Dan. That's the sign of a good reporter, and you'll only get better. There's a big raise in it for you. You've done such a good job on this and you've been working almost non-stop for three days on it, I'll start you full-time retroactive to last Monday. Now, did you ever get your lunch or breakfast?"

"Not yet. I'm waiting for my girl to get her break so we can go. That's why I came back here, and I'm glad I did."

It was the first time he had used the phrase "my girl" in front of another.

"Hmmm," he thought. "I like the sound of that."

22. SOLEMN FAREWELL

September 7, 1911

"Hi, Lindy. You ready to have lunch with the *World's* new full-time reporter?"

"Oh, Danny. That's terrific. I know you have been working hard for that. I am so happy for you. Yes, I can go. Let me just tell the chief."

"George, can you come here a minute," Lindy said after running down the hall to Chief George Dean's office.

"Sure, Lindy, what's up?" the chief answered.

"I want you to meet the *World's* newest full-time reporter."

"Really, Dan. That's terrific. I know you have worked hard for that and, my boy, you sure deserve it," he said, eschewing the handshake for a warm embrace. "I'm sure we'll see a lot more of you."

"Chief, OK, if I take my lunch break now?" Lindy asked.

"Sure, and why don't you two take a little extra, but not too much time," the chief said, winking at Dan.

"Thanks Chief. We're going to the Washington today."

The two lovebirds hustled out the door and the few blocks south to the Washington Hotel's restaurant, Aberdeen's finest eatery.

"You know what? I am going to have the prime rib sandwich. It's so good," Dan said, "and you should too, my dear. I had it a couple weeks ago when Mr. Rupp brought me here. Come to think of it, I bet he was planning to make me a full-timer at that time."

"OK, you talked me into it," she answered with a twinkle.

"This is just what I need, a few minutes alone with my girl and a great lunch. Tomorrow is going to be a really tough day, and a long one," Cloud said.

"Why's that, Danny?"

"The funeral and burial. It was so hard not crying when the boys' bodies were brought out. I wanted to be a man and I didn't quite make it. But, I didn't let them see me. Tomorrow is going to be just as bad, just as emotional."

"But, Danny. It's OK to cry. It doesn't mean you aren't a man," the wise police clerk said, reaching across the table to touch her man's hands. "Funerals are so sad and when kids are involved, it's even tougher."

"You are so smart," the reporter said. "The boys' mother cried when we got back with the bodies, the guys bringing out the bodies cried when they started to remove them, even the sheriff had a few tears, but you know what? The father didn't. He didn't show much emotion. I thought that was a bit strange."

"Maybe, but different people show their grief in different ways."

"I hope the posse had some luck finding whoever did this. They all think it was Tornow, the boys' uncle, but I am not so sure. I think I am going up to Montesano this afternoon and maybe catch a ride to the Upper Satsop to the Bauer home and stay up there tonight. If I didn't do that, it would be hard to get there by mid-morning when the funeral is scheduled."

"Sounds like a good plan. I've got a feeling that I won't be seeing too much of you until this is over."

"You know I want to try and see you whenever I can, but Mr. Rupp told me this is my story and he wants something every day for a few days, so yes, I'll be spending a good deal of time in Montesano."

With that, the reporter walked Lindy back to her job and he headed home to tell his parents the good news.

"Mom, mom, where are you?" Cloud hollered after not finding his mother in the kitchen or living room.

"Up here, Danny. What's up? You sound frantic."

"Frantic? No, excited. I got promoted. I'm now a full-time reporter."

"That's wonderful, son. I know that's your dream, what you have worked so hard for and I am so proud. Both Dad and I are."

"I just wanted to run over here and tell you. I've got to get to Montesano to the sheriff's office. I want to catch a ride to the Upper Satsop tonight. The funeral is tomorrow and the burial too and I have to be there."

"Ok, son. I'm so happy for you and I'll tell Dad as soon as he gets home."

"I want to catch that 1 o'clock train or the later one will put me up there pretty late."

"When do you think you'll be back?"

"Probably tomorrow night. I'll have a tough story to write. I think after today, I'll be able to do a lot of writing from the office here — unless something big breaks."

"OK, see you tomorrow."

Cloud hopped on the afternoon East County Special, and before it had pulled out of the station, he had dozed off. The long week, late night and early rising had taken a toll on the young reporter.

"Here already?" he asked the conductor, announcing the train was pulling into the Montesano station.

He walked the five blocks up Main Street to the sheriff's office and opened the door.

"Hi, Mr. Cloud," said the dispatcher, Josephine Gleason, whom everybody called "Jo."

"Afternoon, Jo." Sheriff in? No, that's right. He's off with the posse, isn't he?"

"Yep, sure is. Deputy Royce is in charge."

"OK. Is he in?"

"Sure. I'll get him."

"Hey, there Danny. I hear congrats are in order," the deputy said entering the waiting area, where the reporter usually met with the sheriff.

"Uh. Yeah," Cloud said, somewhat stammering at the thought the deputy knew about his promotion already.

"You don't sound too excited about it?"

"Oh, but I am. I am just surprised that you knew about it. I only heard myself a few hours ago."

"Well, Mr. Irvine called me a couple days ago and asked me what I thought about you, then I talked to him this morning on another matter, and he told me he was going to promote you."

"OK. That makes sense. Now, down to business. Anything new on the Tornow case? I guess we are calling it that because he is the suspect."

"Well, a couple of things. "I guess there is not going to be a reward offered. The county commissioners turned down the sheriff's request. You can call Commissioner Wilson for the exact reasoning. I guess it makes sense, but if this hunt goes on very long, I think you'll see a difference of opinion on that.

"We are also getting a lot of inquiries for help from all over. Sheriff's offices Seattle to Portland are offering men to assist. Sheriff said to thank them, but for time being, we have enough men."

"Really, that's great that so many want to help. Then the sheriff figures the capture will come rather quickly?"

"He sounded that way when he left, but he did take quite a few provisions with him. We also got this strange note that was on the door at the office today," the deputy said, handing the reporter a hand-scribbled paper.

"Can I use this?" the scribe asked, glancing over the faint writing on a small sheet of paper.

"I don't see why not. But, don't use any names, just say we are investigating a cryptic note that suggests there might be more suspects."

"Are you going to check on it?"

"Yes, when the sheriff gets back. I put in a call to Joe Campbell, the guy who is supposed to know everything, but he wasn't there. How about these two trappers, Howard and Murphy? What do you know about them? And the guy who wrote this, Wesley Schumaker?"

"The only one I have heard about is Murphy. He has been here to sell skins before. I don't know anything about any of the others. But remember, you can't use any names."

"Yes, I know that. I need to call Commissioner Wilson, but do you know if any deputies are going to the funeral tomorrow or even tonight?"

"I think Deputy Quimby is planning on going and he is leaving tonight. He's got a relative in Matlock. You might be able to hitch a ride with him."

"Great, is he due in soon or should I call him?"

"I think he said he'd be in by 3 or 4, but you might try to call him."

"OK. I got to catch the commish and get my story done for tomorrow's paper. Not too much new, but the reward denial and maybe this note and tell the readers about tomorrow's funeral, then say no real new news from the posses."

One quick call to Commissioner Wilson gave him all he needed. With that information, Cloud dialed his City Editor Bill Irvine. He had typed some notes and phoned Irvine to dictate his story for Thursday's paper:

Cloud's next story highlighted the fact that the county commissioners declined to offer a reward of $500, due to what Commissioner Wilson said is the "belief that Tornow's capture will be quick without any additional expense. Wilson also declined to give the sheriff the approval to seek a reward from the state. He said the commissioners' decision was unanimous with Wilson, Willis Hopkins and George Davis all denying the request.

The article also cited a note that was received in the sheriff's office that opened the door to other possible suspects.

The note read in part, though names are not being published at this time: "I think you had better arrest BLANK and BLANK, those two trappers. Call up or come over and see BLANK. He knows that these two men threatened to kill both boys if they ever came in the woods where they were. The bullets that killed those boys were not from their own guns, and BLANK knows the gun that shot those boys used copper-nosed bullets."

Deputy Jerry Royce, in the sheriff's office, said the note was signed by a Hoquiam man and the office would be investigating. A call to the one man the note said knew the information, went unanswered.

Royce said the office had been flooded with offers of help from "sheriffs from Seattle to Portland," but the sheriff declined, saying he had enough help right now, indicating he expected the suspect will be caught sooner rather later.

The Bauer family decided to hold a private funeral this morning (Thursday) with burial to follow at the Grove Cemetery near Matlock.

Leading the posse into the Wynooche lowlands are Sheriff Ed Payette and Deputies Colin McKenzie and Carl Swartz. They are hoping to use the logging camps' phones to get word out on their search. No new information has been communicated to the sheriff's office.

"That's it, Bill," Cloud told his editor. "I should be back in town tomorrow evening to write my story on the funeral. I'm going to catch a ride to the Satsop with Deputy Quimby in an hour or so. Talk to you tomorrow."

———

The Bauer home was crowded. Guests jammed the living room, spilled over into the parlor and dining room. A few others waited outside when Deputy Giles Quimby and Dan Cloud arrived a full hour before the ceremony was expected to begin. The Bauer boys were well liked in the area and most of their friends and neighbors were there.

Cloud looked around for familiar faces and found only a couple. He sidled up to Bauer's neighbor Gus Maas, who was on the search party to bring out the bodies. "Sad day, isn't it Mr. Maas."

"Yes, it is, son. A parent should never have to bury his son, let alone two sons. That's just so sad. These boys were good kids and didn't deserve this."

"Where are the Bauers?" the reporter asked.

"Upstairs with the Reverend. I guess going over details of what he might say, and I think they are just avoiding people until they have to come down."

"Could you point out people to me, so I know who is here?" Cloud asked.

"Sure, I know almost everybody. Starting over at that corner, are Mr. and Mrs. Schaletzke, their two kids, Walter and Ewald; Mr. and Mrs. Spalding and their son, Odine; next to her is my wife, Lucy and our daughter, Elizabeth. She's a couple of years younger than the remaining Bauer daughter, Lizzie. Then there's Albert Kuhnle and his wife. On this side in the living room is Margaret Carstairs, the boys' teacher at the Elizabeth School, then it is Charlie Kohlmeier and his wife and two kids. Then over there are the Hollatzes, Julius and Anna, and their children, Annie, August and Herman. They were school chums of the boys. I'm not sure of that family in the back. It might be the Helin's. Their kid, August, went to school with the boys. The other two are the Andersons, Addie and Frans. They went to school with the boys too."

"I can't believe all these people are here," said Cloud. "Mr. Bauer told me it's so crowded in here and not everybody is here, yet. I think they will have to spill into the dining room. Too bad they didn't have it in a church or something. Thank you for your help."

Tombstones of the Bauer twins in the Grove Cemetery south of Matlock.

"Sure thing, kid. Not too many young reporters get the education you have had this weekend and this week."

"It's something I'll remember all my life," the reporter said as the Rev. T. F. Allen of the Matlock Lutheran Church slowly led the Bauers down the stairs.

"Folks, we have quite a large group here. The ceremony won't be very long, then we'll all adjourn to the cemetery for burial," the minister said. "The Bauers request that all who can make it to the cemetery are invited. It would be a good idea to pile into as few vehicles as possible. There's not a lot of parking over there."

———

It was nearly dusk when Cloud opened the door to the World office and was greeted by his editor.

"Back so soon?" Bill Irvine asked.

"Yes, it was very emotional, but I had a fast trip back and I caught the *Harbor Queen* at Monte into Aberdeen, otherwise I'd have to wait until 5 for the last train. The steamer was wonderful I could sit back and relax and think about what I was going to write."

"That's good thinking kid. Good journalists always make good use of their down time to formulate their story. You are learning well."

"It's because I have a good teacher. You're the best, Bill."

"That's enough of the plaudits. Bet you are going to have a stemwinder of a story."

"Stemwinder? What do you mean?" Cloud asked.

"That's what Mr. Rupp says when a reporter has an unbelievable story. He calls it a 'stemwinder.'"

"Well, I think the one I had yesterday was a 'stemwinder.' Now that was almost unbelievable. Tomorrow's will be rather emotional, gripping, a tear-jerker."

"OK. I'll let you get to it."

It wasn't much more than an hour until Cloud leaned back in his chair and summoned the editor over for his review. "I can't believe how quickly that story took shape. It kind of wrote itself," the scribe said, handing the four type-written and glued story-takes to the editor."

More than two-dozen people gathered Thursday morning in the house of Henry and Minnie Bauer of the Upper Satsop for the funeral service for their two twin sons, John and William, who were murdered last Sunday, while they were hunting a bear.

Everyone there agreed it was the most somber event ever held in these parts.

The large group included many neighbors and school chums of the boys, who graduated from the Elizabeth School last year. Their teacher, Margaret Carstairs was also there.

The service was officiated by the Rev. T. F. Allen of the Matlock Lutheran Church, who led the Bauers downstairs to the waiting crowd. Mrs. Minnie Bauer and her daughter, Elizabeth, 23, wore black, including a netted veil. Mr. Henry Bauer wore a dark suit with no tie, but a white shirt. They had been in seclusion most of the morning, having been distraught since the boys went missing Sunday afternoon.

The minister spoke briefly, committing the "souls of our departed brethren far too early in life into your hands," he said looking upward.

His message, quoted in part, came from I Corinthians, speaking on the definition and power of love:

"And though I have all faith, so that I could remove mountains, but have not love, I am nothing ... Love suffers long and is kind; love does not envy; love does not parade itself, is not puffed up; does not behave rudely, does not seek its own, is not

provoked, thinks no evil; does not rejoice in iniquity, but rejoices in the truth; bears all things, believes all things, hopes all things, endures all things. Love never fails."

Rev. Allen's blessing for the gathering was heartfelt and powerful:

"Give the family and friends strength to endure this unspeakable situation and offer forgiveness when, and if, the suspect is apprehended."

He then asked all those in attendance to join him in saying the 23rd Psalm. *"I hope you can find comfort in the words from the Psalmist David, the minister said. I know I did."*

"The Lord is my shepherd; I shall not want. He maketh me to lie down in green pastures; he leadeth me beside the still waters. He restoreth my soul; he leadeth me in the paths of righteousness for his name's sake. Yea, though I walk through the valley of the shadow of death, I will fear no evil; for thou art with me; thy rod and thy staff they comfort me. Thou preparest a table before me in the presence of mine enemies: thou anointest my head with oil; my cup runneth over. Surely goodness and mercy shall follow me all the days of my life; and I will dwell in the house of the Lord forever."

He wrapped up his message with these words of comfort:

"The golden gates were open wide. A gentle voice said come and angels from the other side welcomed our loved one home."

Minnie Bauer then turned to the minister: *"I want those words on the boys' tombstones. That says our feelings so well."*

"I'm sure we can do that," replied the minister. *"Now I'd like to ask if any of you would like to say a few words."*

Neighbors spoke about how wonderful and talented the boys were, but all of those who spoke had trouble finishing their comments, without breaking into tears, their voices choking.

These boys were well thought of by the community. The speakers had glowing words about the young men and all told how sad it was they were *"taken from us at such a young age, and this way, too."*

They told about the terrible tragedies that have been inflicted on this family in such short time. The Bauers' daughter Mary died last December in an illegal abortion. An Aberdeen doctor is serving time in jail, but appealing his conviction. They issued words of comfort for Minnie and her family and offered their support.

Some talked about the suspect, John Tornow. Neighbors mostly defended him.

"I know John didn't do this like they say he did. He dearly loved those boys, taught them everything they knew about the woods and survival," said their teacher, Margaret Carstairs, who also taught Tornow 13 years ago when he was a teen.

"I saw John and the boys together many times," said Charlie Kohlmeier, a close neighbor and longtime family friend. *"It wasn't that long ago, a month or so, he was by*

This postcard was sent by Henry Bauer to Chris Muller thanking him for helping on the search for the Bauer twins.

my place with them. They were heading off to fish and hollered at me. I was in the field, but they always greeted me. Just great kids. It's hard to believe they are gone. It's harder to believe John did that to them. I don't believe it. I won't believe it."

When the service was over, the minister invited all guests to accompany him to the burial site at the Grove Cemetery, a short distance north. The boys were buried alongside the tombstone of their sister, Mary, and one row behind their grandparents, Daniel Frederick and Louisa Tornow.

As the pallbearers moved to pick up the caskets, Minnie Bauer rose and started to speak. Everybody froze as she offered a foreboding premonition, one that left everyone wondering and thinking.

"John is watching every move made here. His keen eye is covering every detail and he knows as well as you or I what is going on here. He will see my two boys taken from the house and borne to their final resting place. He will hear the echo of the pastor's last words as my boys are lowered into their graves.

"John Tornow is my brother. I know him better than you do. From some well-hidden place he is even now watching us. When the ceremony is over, he will leave, for he knows now, that he is a fugitive and a price will be placed on his head. John will kill many before he is taken, and I do not think he will be taken alive.

"I know John better than you think. My boys, please don't go out alone. If you value your life, don't go even a short distance from the house," she said turning toward the pallbearers and to those who were to continue the search. *"Something gives me warning that the man who killed them is not far away. After the funeral, John will leave for the north, but not until then."*

23. THE HUNT INTENSIFIES

September 8, 1911

When Cloud contacted the sheriff's office the next day, the deputy didn't have much to report. "I can give you what the sheriff told me, but they haven't made much headway at all," Deputy Royce said.

"He was able to get a phone call in from the Hall Ranch, said they were turning over every stone and hadn't covered much ground. I think he means they are spread out with their four men over a small amount of the forest."

"Did he say where the search is concentrated?"

"Just, generally. He said they are still in the Upper Satsop with his posse, but Carl Swartz is taking his men into the Decker settlement, then head further north. McKenzie's group is already up in the Wynooche Oxbow area. So, between the two posses and the men Ed Payette has with him, they are still covering a lot of territory."

"Thanks that's helpful," Cloud responded. "Can you tell me who are in the posses?"

"Not really, because, when Ed's group met up with Swartz, they split up. I do know that Ed Tribbets is with Swartz. Hildebrand is with him too, and I think Joe Watkins is another, but I'm not sure of that."

"So, when do you expect the next information to come in?"

"I can't say for sure, but I don't expect anything before about Sunday," the deputy answered.

"OK. You know I don't have a Sunday paper, so I'll call you Sunday evening for a report on Monday."

"Sounds good. Talk to you later."

Cloud hung up, then jotted off a few paragraphs for Saturday's paper to keep the reader up to date on what had happened, even if it was virtually nothing.

"That's all I got for now," said the reporter, handing the one-page story to his editor. "I won't have anything until sometime Sunday, hopefully, and I'll have a new report for Monday."

"Sounds good," said Irvine. "I think, since it's a slow day for the hunt, I'll have you make the beat calls. I think you already know how to do that. Just stop at the police station and check with George Dean for anything from the cop shop, then go over to fire and see if Bill Tamblyn has anything to report. When you get back, and if there's time, you can take the company rig and do the same in Hoquiam."

"Sure, boss. I can do that. It'll be good for a change of pace."

———

On Sunday afternoon, one full week after the killings, Cloud telephoned the sheriff's office and Deputy Giles Quimby answered.

"Hi, is Deputy Royce there?" the reporter asked.

"Not today," Quimby said. "Can I help you?"

"This is Dan Cloud, the *World* reporter."

"Oh, sure. I heard you are a full-timer now. Congratulations."

"Thank you. What do you know about the hunt for Tornow?"

"I know it all. Jerry told me everything he knows before he left last night and then I talked to McKenzie this morning. In fact, he is in Aberdeen now getting supplies."

"I need to write a story for tomorrow's paper and get the readers up to date on what is happening. Can you give me that info?"

"Sure, Dan. Be glad to tell what I know, or what I think I can tell you. Some things might be proprietary. In other words, the sheriff might not want to tell everything he is doing for fear that word might get out to Tornow. You know what I mean?"

"I can appreciate that. By the way, do you know where McKenzie might be here in town?"

"No, I don't. I'm not sure what he was picking up and what he already had. You might try that livery at the east end of town. I think he said something about getting horse blankets. One stop he'll probably make is at Roscoe Conrad's grocery just down on Heron from your office. They have the best provisions for food, if you are going to spend some time in the woods.

"You might also check with that real nice general store, Huotari's, on F Street. I know he likes that place, or if he has time, he might go to F.G. Foster's in Hoquiam. You probably know they have the best stuff for woodsmen."

Cloud dashed downtown, but was unable to track McKenzie, so he returned to the office and made a phone call to Foster's, but they hadn't seen him either. So, he sat down to write his article for Monday's paper.

He told the readers there were two posses and Deputy Colin McKenzie had returned to Montesano and Aberdeen to gather provisions for a long search. John Tornow, the alleged suspect, had at least a two-day's head start on the posse, which spent last Sunday through Thursday searching, then collecting the bodies and attending the funeral.

"Not only does he have a head start, but Tornow has lived in the woods most of his life and knows every inch of the territory from the Upper Satsop to the headwaters of the Wynooche and even further north," the sheriff said this morning.

Tornow is the lead suspect because he had been known to be in the area and the lean-to had several food caches and provisions that might have belonged to him. He is also known to have a .30-30 Winchester, the same caliber rifle that killed the boys as well as wounded a she-bear.

When he was in Aberdeen yesterday, McKenzie picked up Thomas Morgan of this city to join his posse, which will be headquartered at the Hall ranch 38 miles from Montesano near the Middle Fork of the Satsop River. Ed Tribbets of Aberdeen is also in the posse led by Swartz.

McKenzie's posse will meet up with Payette, who along with Swartz is in charge of the other group. From the ranch, the posses will combine forces and proceed slowly to the headwaters of the Wynooche, about nine miles distant from where the Bauer boys were killed. It is believed Tornow is now camped in that area, according to information Quimby received from Payette via telephone from the Hall ranch late Friday.

It is the plan by the two posses to travel about two miles apart and to keep within striking distance of the ranch, the sheriff said.

"Footprints reported by posse member, Joe Watkins, were followed for several miles and officers have every reason to believe that the suspect is near the Wynooche headwaters," Quimby said. It is probable that one, and possibly two men, will remain within sight of the Hall ranch, as it is the opinion of the sheriff that should Tornow decide to come out of the Wynooche wilderness, he would pass that place.

Tornow is known to have wintered at various camps in the Wynooche headwaters area last year, or even the last two years.

———

Several days passed before there was anything new to report on the Tornow story, and then it was all about fear and trepidation.

On Thursday, the sheriff's report said that two cruisers were believed to have met with foul play in the vicinity of the West branch of the Satsop River. Alex McKay and Doug Shelton, employees of J. A. McGillicuddy, are now 14 days overdue.

McGillicuddy said he will leave tomorrow in search of them. "Anxiety for their safety is keener because of the possibility of their meeting John Tornow." The cruisers' chief said both men are experienced and familiar with the woods, so it is strange that no word has been received from them. The fact too, that a man answering to the description of Tornow was recently seen in the vicinity, adds to the fear that they may have been killed.

———

"Dan Cloud, here," the reporter said as the sheriff's office dispatcher answered the phone Friday afternoon.

"Hi, there. This is Jo. How is it going with you?"

"I'm good, just checking in to see if anything new has come in on the Tornow case."

"Sure, and there is something new. I'll call Deputy Royce in. He can tell you all about it."

"Thanks, Jo."

"Hey, Cloud. How are you? Have I got some new stuff for you."

"Really? They caught Tornow?"

"No. Nothing that earth-shattering, but you know the cruisers I told you about earlier in the week. Well, they are fine. In fact, I guess they not only saw Tornow. They were apparently in his camp and had supper with him."

"Are you kidding me?"

"Naw. Not a bit. You can get the whole story from them, if you can get here tomorrow morning. They are supposed to be in here about 8."

"That's pretty early, but if I get up before dawn, I can catch that 6 a.m. paddlewheeler. Can you hold them in the office until I get there?"

"I'll see what I can do. If you catch the steamer, I'll have Jo meet you about 7 and bring you up here."

"No need for that. It's just a short walk and I'll be so excited, I'll probably run all the way."

"OK. See you tomorrow."

"Yeah. I got to clear it with the boss, but I think he'll be all for it. We can get it in tomorrow's paper, if I get the information that early."

Cloud hung up the phone and immediately went to Irvine's office.

"Bill, have I got some news for you."

"They caught Tornow?"

"No. That's what I asked too. Those two cruisers that we wrote about in Friday's paper, well, they are fine. In fact they not only saw Tornow, they were in his camp and had supper with them."

"Really? What did they eat?"

"Oh, crap. I forgot to ask about that, but I can. They are going to be in Montesano at 8 tomorrow morning. I figured I can catch the *Harbor Queen* at 6 and meet them. If I can get all the data for a story, I can call you with it before 10."

"Be sure to find out what they had to eat," the editor said, half joking.

"Really?"

"Yes. I want to know, and if I want to know, so will the reader. They will want to know everything about how Tornow exists in the woods, including what he is eating."

"You got it, Bill."

The *Queen* arrived a few minutes after 7 in Montesano and Dan raced up Main Street to the sheriff's office. The cruisers, McKay and Shelton, arrived, as expected, at 8. They grabbed a coffee, as did Cloud, along with Deputy Quimby, then all four went to the conference room, where the cruisers related their story. Jo was also there to record the information.

It took a little more than an hour for them to relate their harrowing tale, and both cruisers still appeared nervous as they talked and answered questions from the deputy and Cloud. It was enough time for Cloud to type out a quick story and call Irvine with the breaking news for Monday's paper.

"I knew they were after me. I saw six of them the day they started out, and damn them. I came pretty near taking a shot at them."

"Let me stop you right there, the editor said. "Usually, it's not a good idea to start a story with a quote. You kind of lead up to it, then hit them with the whopper."

"Yes, I know, but I figured this quote is so compelling, and it also tells the reader that Tornow knows he is a wanted man. It's also the first time we have Tornow actually talking since the boys were shot. I figured it's so strong, we can break the rules. And he also says he almost shot at them."

"Well, kid. You have a strong argument. I like your moxie. You win this one. Go on."

Cloud continued to dictate his story to the editor.

Such was the statement made by John Tornow, uncle of John and Will Bauer, the 19-year-old twin sons of Henry Bauer, a Satsop River rancher. The boys were murdered in the woods near their home September 3, and whose murder Tornow is the suspect.

Tornow made his statement to Alex McKay and Douglas Shelton, two timber cruisers in the employ of Jerry McGillicuddy, who were making a cruise of the timber for the county last Thursday night. Tornow was seated between the two cruisers when he made it. The men were within six miles of the bereaved Bauer home.

Tornow was begrizzled, hungry and tired. He looked the hunted man that he is. Two posses are now out in search of him, and his statement was made undoubtedly in reference to the searchers who have unquestionably been very close to him or his camps.

McKay was the speaker during much of the interview, saying the three sat down to a "hastily prepared and quickly eaten meal of roast beef hash and mustard greens. Tornow grasped the rifle, (which is believed to have ended the Bauer boys' life) in his one hand and gulped the food with the other," McKay remembered.

"Tornow came into our camp about dusk Thursday night," said McKay. "I did not recognize him at first and then he asked for food and we invited him to join us. He looked different from the last time I saw him. He had a long beard and tattered clothing. He did not seem at all excited, and I thought he was just a hunter who had been lost in the woods. Not once did he let his rifle drop to the ground. We said nothing to him about the murder of the Bauer twins. We reported the incident soon as we reached the city."

After hearing the description given by Sheriff Ed Payette of Tornow, the cruisers say they are certain the man at the camp was Tornow.

"I do not hesitate to say that we believe Tornow was in the immediate vicinity of the Bauer home at the time of the funeral nearly two weeks ago," said Sheriff Payette, who called the sheriff's office this morning and talked to McKay. "It is probable that he left during the day for the north country, but returned to the scene of the crime later."

Payette is now endeavoring to get in communication with Deputy Sheriff Carl Swartz and his posse, who are at present, within 12 miles of the Bauer home. It was evidently Swartz and his posse who Tornow referred to in his conversation with McKay and Shelton.

It is now the theory of the sheriff that Tornow is still in the vicinity of the Bauer home and is probably on the lookout for two posses in search of him.

The cruisers say they asked no questions as to the posses mentioned by Tornow, but it is their impression that the fugitive has provisions hidden in the vicinity of his former camp within two miles of the Bauer home, and which was destroyed by the first posse sent out to look for the boys.

Considerable anxiety was felt for a time last week for the safety of McKay and Shelton. There was relief from all who know them, including their boss, Jerry McGillicuddy.

McKay said they were delayed in reporting their condition because of an injury to Shelton. Much fear was expressed for them, but both cruisers were in good condition this morning.

However, they did say that grave fears have been felt for the safety of cruiser J. P. Moriarty and his compassman L. T. Carpenter, also of McGillicuddy's employ, who have not been heard from since August 4. They had been cruising the west half of Township 21 in Range 7, the area where Tornow, the alleged slayer of the Bauer boys, is said to have had a winter cabin.

McGillicuddy and several other cruisers have searched the area a couple of times without finding a clue.

"That should do it, Bill," the reporter said.

"Good job, again. Really good stuff, here."

"Thanks, boss. It's been a long day, and it's only 10."

"I was going to ask you if you wouldn't mind swinging by the commission meeting at 11. We don't usually cover all the meetings, unless there's something big to report, but since you were a *Vidette* reporter and we stole you from them, they don't have a replacement yet."

"I'll just grab another cup of coffee and head across the street," Cloud said. "Hopefully, it's rather uneventful, and I'll be able to catch the 3 p.m. train back."

"Appreciate it, Dan. Just check in with the clerk and she'll give you a rundown of what's expected. I think you'll like her too. Her name is Jessie. See ya later."

"Yep, later."

Cloud sat back, gave a big sigh, and thought to himself, "Guess that's the life of a journalist. "Guess that's what my life is going to be like from now on."

The reporter walked into the commission meeting room, picked up a hastily printed agenda and a separate listing.

HOUSES FOR SALE

He started to set the listings aside and concentrate on the agenda for the meeting when he glanced down the list and his eyes fell on a line.

Henry Bauer ranch, Upper Satsop, by Horn & Carter of Satsop. 120 acres, many fruit trees, horses, cattle, farming implements and other equipment. Large 2-story home and outbuildings, barn.

"Whoa. That's news," he said so everyone in the room could hear him. "I think I've got time to make a call on that."

He stepped up to the clerk's desk and asked to use the phone. "Hi. You got a phone number for a realtor, Horn & Carter of Satsop?" he asked.

"Yep, I'm Jessie. I can get it for you," said the attractive, young clerk, brushing her auburn hair off the side of her face with three fingers.

"Thanks. I'm Dan Cloud of the *World*. I owe you one," replied the reporter with a big smile.

"I'll hold you to it," said the clerk, clearly smitten by the young, dark-haired reporter.

"Is this the office of Horn & Carter?" he asked when the voice on the other end only answered with a "hello."

"Yes. Can I help you?"

"I hope so. I am interested in the listing you have for the Bauer ranch on the Upper Satsop. I'm the reporter covering the story on the murder of his two boys. Did Mr. Bauer say anything about where he was going? What he was going to do when the ranch sold?"

"You'll have to ask him about that. I'm not at liberty to talk to you about where he might be going. Sorry."

"That's all right. Just curious. I don't doubt that he is ready to leave the area."

"You got that right. They are still distraught and having lost three children, they want to get a fresh start somewhere else."

"Thanks for the info. Have you had many inquiries on it yet?"

"It hasn't even been advertised, and yes, we've had a lot of interest."

"Can I check with you regarding the sale? I'd like to know when it sells and I'm not always in Montesano."

"I can take your name and number and call you when, and if it sells," said Fred Carter, a partner in the real estate firm.

"I'd appreciate it. And I know it will sell. That's a fine ranch."

"Yes, it is. It's going to command a good price. We are listing it all over the Northwest.

"I'm sure it will. I'd love to have it," but I don't have any money, and neither does my family."

"Too bad, kid. It would be a great investment."

"What is the listing price for it?"

"It's $15,000 for the ranch. We don't have a listing for the tools and animals. They will likely sell individually or at an auction."

"Thanks, and hope to hear from you soon."

Cloud hung up the phone and went back to the commission room. It wasn't a long meeting, a discussion about land-use issues, a report from George Watkins, owner of the Montesano Hotel, about recent renovations, including the new entrance to the adjoining café on Main Street.

Of most interest was a report on the status of the old courthouse, replaced by the spanking new structure last February. Cloud remembered when he covered the Stapp trial in February, it was the first full trial in the new edifice.

His report appeared in Tuesday's edition of *The Aberdeen Daily World* and Friday's *Chehalis County Vidette:*

The county commissioners have lost considerable sleep recently while trying to figure out a way of economically and successfully ridding the courthouse grounds of the old buildings, which since the completion of the new edifice late last year has assumed the proportions of a white elephant and an eyesore.

The first published call for a purchaser drew a blank; the second resulted in several propositions to dismantle the old structure for a big cash bonus, which were turned down. A call is now being made on the windows, doors and fixtures. If these can be sold, the prisoners, now idle in the county jail, will be turned loose on the structure, the written report noted.

When the wreck is over, the lumber, brick etc. will be sold for what they will bring.

"At first, it was planned to dynamite the old trap and complete the demolishing by judiciously setting a match to it, but the scheme was abandoned," Commissioner Wilson told the audience.

The old building will probably shelter its present occupants for a month or more as it will take that long to furnish the new one.

———

Cloud was sitting at his desk at the World office late Wednesday when the phone rang.

"*Daily World*, Dan Cloud speaking."

"Hey there, greenhorn," said the voice.

"Deputy Swartz, that must be you. Where are you?"

"I'm in Montesano right now, but I've got a story for you for tomorrow's paper. In fact, I'm going to be in Aberdeen in the morning. Can we have coffee and I can give it to you."

"Sure, what's up?"

"I know you talked with McKay and Shelton the other day and had a big story on their encounter with Tornow."

"Yeah, sure did. We had lots of comment on that one."

"Well, here's the story. It's all bogus, all lies."

"You mean they made it up?"

"They sure did, admitted it to me today. I'll give you the details of what they said in the morning. What's the deadline for the paper?"

"I've got to have it done by 10. Can you get here that early?"

"Sure. Quimby will let me take the motor coach. I'll be at your office by 8. Is that enough time?"

"That should work. I'll be here. Give me a minute, let me check with my editor to make sure it's OK with him and he doesn't have anything for me to do."

Cloud returned seconds later and told Swartz he would meet him at 8.

"Let me be clear, here," the editor queried the young reporter, "You talked directly with these two shysters and everything you wrote was a direct quote from them?"

"It sure was, Bill. It was only McKay doing the talking. And deputy Quimby and the clerk, Jo, were taking it all in. We are clearly covered on this one."

"Just checking, Dan. We've got to be careful what we print, how we attribute it, and it sounds like you did it perfectly."

"That's right. Swartz said McKay is lying, but he didn't tell me why. That will come tomorrow."

"I can't wait to hear this tale," the editor said as Cloud stood up to leave.

Cloud was at the office before 8 in the event the deputy arrived early, and he did.

"Let's walk down to the Washington, my treat," the reporter said at the rare opportunity to play host.

"Good, I haven't been there in a while."

"The two men enjoyed a Western omelet with biscuits and honey and country potatoes, as they talked. When finished, they walked back to the World office and Swartz left the reporter.

"One more thing, deputy."

"What's that Dan?"

"Can we drop the greenhorn crap?"

"Sure, you've earned your way out of that. See ya later."

Cloud sat down to quickly write this piece of fiction:

The statement given out by cruisers Alex McKay and Douglas Shelton, and printed by The Aberdeen Daily World in Monday's edition, concerning their encounter with John Tornow, is absolutely false. "At no time during our trip to the vicinity of the Wynooche headwaters did we meet Tornow or anyone else matching that description," McKay sheepishly confided to Deputy Sheriff Carl Swartz, who met with a World reporter.

Swartz, who had led one of the posses in search of Tornow, said this morning that the cruisers came into the sheriff's office on Wednesday and admitted they made up the story.

"There is absolutely no truth in the statement made by those two cruisers, Swartz said. "McKay said they made up the story because, in McKay's words, 'it

was up to me to tell some kind of story, inasmuch as we knew that considerable anxiety was felt for our safety.'"

Swartz and Sheriff Ed Payette are livid with this development when informed about the lie on Wednesday. "The statement made by these two cruisers has resulted in severe criticism by the sheriff," said Swartz. The published reports of McKay and Shelton's alleged interview with Tornow has "caused a feeling of unrest on the part of the cruisers now in the vicinity where Tornow is supposed to be hiding," the sheriff said today.

Deputy Swartz, who is in charge of the posse of four men camped near the Hall ranch on the West Fork of the Satsop, reached Montesano yesterday and was in Aberdeen this morning to secure more men for his party.

Swartz said he has "valuable information from cruisers working in that locality" and is of the belief that Tornow is near, or in the vicinity of, his cabin on the headwaters of the Wynooche.

Two days later, the sheriff said he had recruited a standout football player out of Tacoma, who had come to Aberdeen in search of a job.

Ray Mahaffery, a crack football player, who, as center with the Tacoma high school team that fought a scoreless battle with Aberdeen last November, has turned man-hunter.

Swartz was to pick up Mahaffery later today and said the football star will join his posse.

The deputy said he met with Mahaffery, who indicated he wanted a job. He didn't care what. "He said he 'wanted something that required a little nerve.'"

Swartz described a kind of roundabout way he found out about Mahaffery. "I was on the phone talking to Sergeant K. G. Church at the Tacoma Police station, about the need for men to join the hunt. At the same time, Mahaffery and his dad walked into the Tacoma office. The football player's dad had been a principal when the sergeant was a student in Port Townsend. The young man went to the Tacoma office to see about a possible job and he overheard our conversation.

"I want a job and don't care a rip what it is, as long as it is honest," the young man said, when his father interrupted the conversation between Church and Swartz.

Church told Swartz about the situation and the deputy said he told the sergeant to put Mahaffery on the phone.

"I want a man to join our posse in search of John Tornow, who is accused of murder," Swartz said he told the young man. "If you want a job at $2.50 per day, here is your chance."

The deputy said he explained the hardships and dangers of the job, but Mahaffery said he was equal to the task.

The young man accepted the job and will join the posse tomorrow when it convenes at a designated site on the West Fork of the Satsop.

Main Street in Montesano, looking north in 1910; the Montesano Hotel and restaurant are on the right.

24. THE REWARD

October 3, 1911

Nearly one month has passed since the killing of the Bauer boys and the two posses are no closer to catching their suspect, John Tornow. Sheriff Ed Payette has added several bodies to each of the posses, one directed by Colin McKenzie and the other led by Carl Swartz, with no results.

Payette said via telephone from Camp 5 in the Wynooche area, that he believed Tornow has enough provisions to last the winter. He said bad weather has hampered the search as well as false reports.

With that information, he once again implored county commissioners to issue a reward for the capture of Tornow.

Not only has the board got the ear of Payette, but several citizens as well spoke up and demanded action during the clamorous open speaking session of Monday's commission meeting.

That prompted a motion from a commissioner to vote again on the reward. This time it passed.

After the commission meeting, reporter Dan Cloud called in this report for the *The Aberdeen Daily World* that was published Tuesday, October 3:

After nearly a month during which two well-equipped posses have been searching the Upper Satsop and Wynooche areas for John Tornow, suspected slayer of his twin nephews, John and Will Bauer, the Chehalis County Commissioners relented to pressure and issued a $500 reward for the capture of Tornow.

The commissioners made the decision at Monday's meeting, granting $400 for the capture of Tornow, dead or alive, and added $100 more on the grounds that he is suspected of "being insane and too dangerous to be at large," commission President C. N. "Bud" Wilson said.

It was one of the most important meetings in many years as Sheriff Ed Payette had pressed the board two weeks ago to consider issuing a reward. After two weeks without any clue to Tornow's whereabouts, Payette again pushed the commission.

There was some discussion; most of it regarded the alleged insanity of the fugitive.

Tornow has been sought by two posses since the September 3 slaying of the Bauer boys, but, as Commissioner Hopkins pointed out, "There is little evidence to tie Tornow to the crime. Tornow, however, is believed by some to be demented and a search for him on this account was made by the sheriff in August, but was dismissed as not the case."

Wilson said the sheriff told him Tornow was known to have frequented Simpson Camp 5 to obtain provisions several days ago.

"That doesn't sound like a murderer to me," Wilson noted, "but I think we can consider a reward to talk to him about the murders and also on the insanity angle. It might draw more people toward the authorities, and maybe give us more clues, if there was a reward."

Commissioner George Davis made the motion to issue the reward "based on Tornow's insanity, and giving him the benefit of the doubt regarding the murder." The vote was unanimously approved by all three commissioners.

A near-packed chamber room rose and unanimously applauded the decision. Commissioner Wilson called for order or he would clear the room. The audience quietly took their seats.

Meantime, the sheriff said "We still have evidence that Tornow is in the immediate vicinity. The two posses are doing everything they can under the circumstances to find him. As long as we continue to believe he is in the area, we will continue to be on the lookout."

Ed Tribbets of the Aberdeen Police force had been with the posse for three weeks, but returned to his job in Aberdeen last week. Thomas Morgan, also of Aberdeen, is still with the posse, directed by Colin McKenzie. They are searching the Wynooche Oxbow area and are possibly gearing up to head further into the Olympics.

Tribbets told the *World* reporter today that the posse had followed several different trails to no avail. "We had some leads we followed up on, but they went nowhere. We left the area when we heard about the cruisers' tale, but when we found out that was a lie, it set us back a good week."

The Aberdeen man said he thinks people are giving Tornow help, getting him supplies and provisions. "We are pretty sure he was at Camp 5 and got some stuff, but we weren't anywhere near there until yesterday when the sheriff gave his phone report. I was glad to hear that the county finally issued a reward. With a little incentive, we might get some help or at least some clues."

He said at least one posse will remain in the Wynooche area through the winter and will likely get provisions for three months from Camp 5 in a few days. "The weather is getting bad up there already. We had several days of torrential downpour and that wipes out all tracks. It's almost impossible to search in that goo. Best we can do is to keep slogging along and try to find his camps, and he has several. Every time we find one, we destroy it. We did find several caches in the area we knew he frequented last year. They had some food, a few hides and one even had, like a well dug to hold rainwater, I imagine for drinking or washing."

The posses were equipped for a month, and that time will be up in two days.

Tribbets said the false reports have to be investigated because "you never know if it is true or not, until you do. But each time you head in a different area, you lose ground to the man, if it isn't true."

He pointed out one such report of a dead horse found on the Tornow homestead, which currently has a leasing tenant. "The horse found at the homestead was dismembered by a single stroke of a hunting knife. Sheriff said we needed to get down there. It could be Tornow returned to his former home."

Payette sent three posse members, including Swartz and Tribbets to camp out in that vicinity and keep a close watch on the place. Tribbets said the men stayed there for three days and saw nothing. "We didn't believe this dastardly act was the work of Tornow. From what we have been told, he is more of a preservationist and I don't believe he would do such a thing to an animal, unless the animal was sick or distressed and our investigation of the horse saw nothing to indicate that."

Swartz then contacted the tenant at the former Tornow ranch, who was renting it pending the estate settlement. "Swartz said he was satisfied that it was not Tornow, rather the animal was gored to death by a bull. He said the horse was owned by S. S. Morse of the Montesano creamery used by the tenant to haul milk to the creamery. He said the animal was found dead by the creek and it looked like it had been cut open by an axe or a knife. It was likely the only weapon the man had at the time to put the animal out of its misery. This probably led some to believe it might have been done by Tornow."

H. H. Pennell of Montesano and a member of the Swartz posse, agreed with Tribbets' account, saying he hopes there are no more false alarms. "It really hurts our search," he said, "particularly that tale told by the cruisers. If I get a hold of them, they'll wish I hadn't. That McKay had better not be cruising in my area."

He said the posses have put in "endless hours on the search, and have employed all their secrets and woodcraft in an effort to stay ahead on the trail of the fugitive. It is the belief of those in his posse group that Tornow likely lingered near the scene of the crime out of reach of his pursuers for a couple of days before heading north.

"I know the sheriff believes he might be jerking beef somewhere for the winter months before heading to his winter campsites. It makes sense, and it is our hope that we can get to his winter camps before he does."

Pennell said he believes "Tornow is a wily one. This guy might just outsmart us, but we are equal to the task. We have already found a couple of his camps and destroyed them. He just keeps on going. I think we are going to give it a few weeks, then a group of us, myself included, will go as deep into the Olympics as the weather will allow."

The group did run into one man who has known the fugitive for many years. "I am perhaps more acquainted with Tornow than anyone in Chehalis County," said Sol Foss, who lives in the Satsop area. "I most certainly believe he is a dangerous man and I am sure he is in possession of the fact that he is wanted for murder."

Sheriff Payette said the office has had offers of help from many individuals, including one man who contacted him from Shelton. "He said he offered, in his words, 'to go into the woods and get Tornow.' He asked if there was a reward and I told him (at that time) that the county was asked to issue one, but declined."

Payette said the Shelton man was a "woodsman of many years and had hunted with Tornow several times in the same area that he is said to be inhabiting."

The sheriff said the man seemed credible and that he would likely join the search in the coming days.

"The more people we have who know this area and who know this man, the better off we are," the sheriff added.

After calling in his report, Cloud walked down to the Main Street Café to grab a sandwich before heading back to Aberdeen.

"Isn't that Mrs. Bauer?" the reporter said to himself, glancing out the window. "Sure it is," he said, rising from his seat and heading out the door. "I'll be right back, Dorothy," he signaled to the waitress behind the lunch counter.

"OK, Dan, no problem," she said.

"Mrs. Bauer, Mrs. Bauer," he shouted to the woman walking down the opposite side of the street.

"Oh, Hi, Mr. Cloud. How are you today?" Mrs. Bauer answered.

"I'm fine, and you?"

"I'm OK, but sad. We are going to be leaving the area and I love it here," Minnie Bauer said.

"Yes, I saw where you have your ranch up for sale."

"Yes, it is, and I think we might have a buyer. A Seattle man who is traveling now, but he'll be back in a couple of weeks."

"I can understand you wanting to leave this area. You have had to endure quite a bit of tragedy in the last year."

"I don't really want to leave, but what Henry says is true. We don't have anything holding us here. He wants to leave and so does Lizzie. They are fed up and we want to get a fresh start."

"Where will you go?" Cloud queried.

"California. Henry has a friend there who is going to put him to work until we can get enough to buy a ranch. We are leaving by the end of the year, and sooner if we sell the ranch. We'll be set for a while. Henry is down there now and might find us a place before he comes back next week."

"That sounds like a fresh opportunity for you. I wish you the best," said Cloud.

The two stood, silent for a few seconds, each wondering if the other would ask the question.

Cloud finally broke the silence. "Have you heard anything from John?" he asked.

"No, but I know he is well and keeping busy with those deputies chasing him. I know this. I know he knows where I am and I expect he might try to contact me before we leave."

"Where you are? You are not at your ranch?"

"Not since Henry left about 10 days ago. I am at the Maas's place. Lizzie loves it there and that family has done so much for us."

"And, you think John knows that?"

"I know John knows that, and that's all I am going to say about that. Now, I best get my chores done and get back home. I have to meet Lucy Maas in a few minutes. She's got the family auto."

"Nice to see you, Mrs. Bauer, and good luck to you."

Cloud headed back across the street to the café, where his sandwich and, by now, cold soup awaited him.

"Dan, wait a minute, I'll get you a hot bowl of soup. Was that Minnie Bauer?" Dorothy asked.

"Yes, yes it was. She's leaving us, going to California."

"Too much heartache in the Satsop for her, I guess."

"Yes, she said her husband is down there now and will be back in a week or so."

"Here's your soup. I gave you a big bowl this time."

Cloud enjoyed the bean and barley soup, then had Dorothy pack the ham and cheese sandwich for his train ride home.

One thing kept nagging at him as he sat quietly on the train.

"How did John know where his sister was staying, and how did she know he would contact her."

25. MISFORTUNES STRIKE

October 16, 1911

I
t has been more than six weeks since the Bauer twins were slain about a mile and a half from their Upper Satsop home, allegedly by their uncle, John Tornow. Two different sheriff's posses have combed the Satsop and Wynooche headwaters, chasing down one errant clue after another.

All misguided traces were investigated, yet each time they proved fruitless and enabled the elusive fugitive to escape deeper into the woods; the net the posses had thrown out to surround Tornow had developed more and more holes.

A few weeks ago, two timber cruisers reported they ate supper with the 31-year-old Tornow; then a couple days later, they walked into the sheriff's office in Montesano and said they made up the entire story. They had been missing about 14 days, and one of the men, Alex McKay, said, "I figured I had to say something because we were missing so long."

Sheriff Ed Payette was back in Montesano today and was still talking about how damaging that story was to their search.

"Those two cost us so much time," the sheriff told Dan Cloud, *The Aberdeen Daily World* reporter, who journeyed to Montesano for the interview.

"I am thinking about filing a false report against these two," the sheriff said. "It's my belief that because of their story, Tornow is not behind bars in my jail today. We were hot, on what we thought was, his trail in the big Wynooche canyon. We had evidence that he was in the canyon and we were closing in. Then, when the report came in, we hot-footed it down to the Satsop area. My posse camped out there and we waited without a result."

Payette said after two days, he went on to the Hall Ranch and called Montesano. It was then Deputy Quimby gave him the news of the false report.

"You can't believe how pissed off I was," the sheriff said. "I was seething. I figured that not only cost us time and gave it to Tornow, but it was costly financially, too."

A week later, the report of a dead horse found on the Tornow homestead led Payette and two posse members to investigate that incident only to discover the horse was likely gored to death by a bull.

That was more time lost, and more gained by Tornow.

When the sheriff and his group returned to the Lower Wynooche and met up with McKenzie's posse, the deputy told him that he had some evidence to suggest that Tornow took off into the Olympics and might have gone to the west side in the Mt. Olympus area.

"He said an old timer, William Sherwin, told him …"

"William Sherwin? You mean 'Billy the Bear?'" Cloud interrupted the sheriff.

"Yeah, that guy. He told Colin that from what others told him, you could expect Tornow to head for his winter digs. Sherwin told McKenzie that he knew for a fact that Tornow had a couple of shacks in the Olympics and he had spent some time there last winter."

The sheriff told Cloud that his plan was to beat Tornow to the sites, although the Olympics are rather expansive.

"Do you think Billy can be trusted?" Cloud queried. "We — my Dad and I — were hunting in the Wishkah Valley last year and ran into him. He was full of wild, unbelievable tales, talked about a Wildman swinging through the trees. Dad said he couldn't be trusted. You know, sheriff, he just might be in cahoots with Tornow. He might have said that about the Olympics to throw the deputies off track."

"Yes, we know about Billy's reputation and you are right. He could be sending us on a wild goose chase. But, I had a plan I thought would cover all bases. I sent McKenzie along Donkey Creek to Humptulips and into the Quinault area. He was going to try to go toward Mt. Olympus on the west and I was going to head up the east side with my posse."

Mt. Olympus, at just a shade under 8,000 feet, is the tallest of the Olympic mountains and would be quite a trek for anyone, but now it was approaching winter and the snow would soon make it too treacherous to travel, even at the mountain's base.

"That was the plan, but we kept getting sidetracked," the sheriff said. "Darn MacLafferty trial."

The sheriff explained that last week he had to pull both McKenzie and Swartz off the posse detail to testify in the MacLafferty case. The Aberdeen physician was charged with a criminal operation in the death of Goldie Ness of Aberdeen. The deputies gave testimony for two days before being relieved of their duties and returned to their posses as soon as they were excused. The doctor was eventually convicted.

"It was a bit of a setback, but the other members of the posse continued their pursuit. They just didn't push any further into the mountains," the sheriff noted.

"Then I caused a bit of a setback when I fell as we were climbing a pretty big mountain on the east side."

"You fell? I was going to say something about your limping that I noticed when you got up, and I see you have a couple of bruises on your hands and arms."

"You should have seen me a couple of days ago. I wasn't going to say much about this, but I guess it's good for people to know how dangerous this search has become. I was nearly killed. I'm lucky I am here today. In fact, I really thought I was a goner. All that and nobody was shooting at me."

"Start at the beginning and don't leave anything out," the reporter said.

The report on the sheriff's mishap was recounted in Cloud's article in *The Aberdeen Daily World* and the *Chehalis County Vidette* the week of October 16.

Sheriff Ed Payette returned to Montesano last Saturday, showing visible evidence of a terrible trip in the Olympic Mountains in his search for John Tornow, the suspected slayer of his twin nephews, John and William Bauer, on September 3.

Payette had a noticeable limp as he walked across the room to talk to the reporter. His arms and hands showed numerous abrasions and he had several bumps and bruises.

"I was acting on a tip that Tornow was heading into the Olympic Mountains," said the sheriff. "I sent Deputy Colin McKenzie to the west side and I took two men and we headed up the east side of the Olympics. We were really high, about

6,000 feet, and we ran into some deep snow. We had to climb across many gullies and ravines, but we had to turn back because the snow was too deep."

The sheriff went on to explain about his adventure crossing a glacier, which he said he thought might be a shorter route to lower ground.

Sheriff Ed Payette

It was shorter, but not the way Payette had figured.

"We decided to cross this glacier at about 6,000 feet and I thought I had a good foothold. But, then I didn't. I started to slide down the glacier and just kept sliding. I thought it was all over for me, and it would have been, if it hadn't been for a big boulder that broke my fall. The guys figured I had to have slid about 1,500 feet. The guys were frightened that I had slid all the way down. They said they couldn't even see me and didn't know I was hung up on the rock until they got down several hundred feet."

The sheriff explained it was about 30 minutes that he was clinging to the boulder before he heard the voices of the other posse members and called to them. He said he was afraid to move and he couldn't stand or even crawl. He was dazed from the fall.

"When the guys reached me, I was a bloody mess and my leg was really banged up, a sprained knee, the doctor told me yesterday."

The other two helped the sheriff to his feet; then formed a carrying seat to tote the sheriff, but he was too heavy and it was dangerous to walk down the mountain in that situation. After about an hour, as storm clouds approached, the men and the sheriff reached a path that had been used by others and he was able to limp along as they gingerly and slowly descended the mountain, which was about 80 miles north of Montesano.

"If that rock hadn't broken my fall, I'd still be sliding," the sheriff said, choking back tears. "I was pretty lucky. Thank God the glacier was fairly smooth and icy. That was an awful trip. Another time we had to wade through ice cold water up to our waists. That's treacherous country up there. If there's any more terrible country in the nation, I'd have to be shown it," said the sheriff, who grew up in Missouri.

"There is no doubt in my mind, that if we had been able to cross the divide, I am positive we would have been able to take Tornow," the sheriff said today. "As it is, he is probably well entrenched in the Olympics and will likely remain there through the winter. I'll tell you what, I know Tornow is a skilled woodsman, but if he is up there in the Olympics, more power to him. I couldn't last up there, from what I experienced."

"Will McKenzie stay out and or is he coming back?" asked Cloud.

Payette said McKenzie will continue with his posse of just three men until the rigors of winter drive them back, then they will likely return until early spring, adding he didn't know how high McKenzie might be able to get from the west side. "He knows about our mishaps and he is supposed to contact me no later than Friday before heading into the high country.

"From the clues we have been able to find, we are almost positive he is in the Olympics. We were investigating some of those clues, when we got the report about the cruisers. We know he wintered up there last year and we have a pretty good idea where the shelter is. We even found one small cache near the base of that glacier and we took those items."

The sheriff said the cache included some dried beef, well preserved in the cedar stump, a few strands of elk hairs, some tanned strings of hide, perhaps for a belt or maybe a headband, and a small knife.

"That's the method he uses at his lean-tos, though the shed we found at that cache had collapsed from the snow. We are pretty sure he has moved on to even higher ground."

The sheriff said he knows Tornow is a skilled woodsman and is capable of living in "those terrible conditions for many months, even in the deep snow. We know he has food and other supplies in caches. He can subsist on a meager diet that the woods provide. We're also pretty sure there are mountainfolk, who have helped him out. Now, you know what we are up against."

Despite the setbacks and unfortunate incidents, the sheriff is confident Tornow will be in jail eventually.

"I'll get my man. You can count on that. It might take some time, but we'll get him. You can bank on it."

Later that week, Cloud received the information he had been expecting from Fred Carter, chief agent for Horn and Carter Realtors in Satsop.

"Mr. Carter, Dan Cloud, *Daily World*, calling. Any news on the Bauer ranch yet?"

"As a matter of fact, yes. It has been sold and they will be leaving the area."

"Can you fill me in on the details?" the reporter queried.

"I can give you what is public information and what the *Vidette* will print."

With that information, Cloud, still a correspondent with the Montesano paper, published this report in the October 20 *Vidette*:

The Horn and Carter Real Estate Co. of Satsop this week sold the Henry Bauer ranch, comprising 200 acres, to E. W. Mills of Seattle, for $13,500. Mr. Bauer also arranged with George Sell of Montesano to dispose of the stock on his place and will sell his implements, farming tools and other equipment.

Since the deplorable tragedy in which their 19-year-old twin sons, William and John, lost their lives on September 3, the Bauers have been despondent and Mr. Bauer made the decision to put the ranch up for sale.

It has been a tragic 10 months for the Bauer family, who also lost their 24-year-old daughter, Mary, in December 1910. She died after an abortion in which Aberdeen's Dr. Robert Stapp was convicted of the criminal operation. He was sentenced to a nine-month jail term, but his attorney has filed an appeal.

When contacted a few weeks ago, Mrs. Bauer said her husband was in San Diego, Calif., searching out options with a friend, who had promised work and a place to live for the Bauers until they could obtain funds to purchase their own place.

Mrs. Bauer said the family was hoping to leave before the end of the year, "and earlier, if the ranch sold."

Carter confirmed that Henry Bauer was in San Diego and Minnie and their daughter, Elizabeth, would follow soon. He said Minnie and Lizzie are staying at a neighbor's in the Upper Satsop.

———

After attending an uneventful county commission meeting, Cloud stopped at the courthouse clerk's office to check on any late, breaking news. He had been expecting a decision on the Stapp appeal from the Supreme Court of Washington.

"Good afternoon, Jessie," he greeted the clerk.

Before he could ask for any news, Jessie interjected.

"I've been calling your office. I forgot you were coming here today. Mr. Boner wants you to have these papers on the Stapp appeal being denied."

"That's a surprise. Not that it was denied, but the decision coming so quickly. Thanks, Jessie. Do you know where I can reach Mr. Boner or Mr. Agnew?"

"You can't. They went hunting in Eastern Washington. Left yesterday and will be gone a week."

"I guess I'll have to write that up with no comment from them. Mr. Campbell's still here, isn't he?" he queried about the prosecuting attorney.

"Yes. In fact, I just saw him this morning."

"I'll stop at his office."

Cloud found the prosecuting attorney in his office and knocked on the door as his secretary was not at her desk.

"Mr. Campbell, may I ask you a few questions about the Stapp appeal denial?"

"Sure, Dan. Have a seat."

"First, I imagine you are pleased with the decision."

"Yes, but we fully expected it. Boner's arguments were way off base and the court saw it that way as well."

"Were you surprised a decision was reached this quickly?"

"Yes, but only because it's a state court, and nothing happens that quickly when the state is involved. I wasn't surprised because of the decision. To me, it was quite clear there was no evidence for an appeal."

"What happens next?"

"I really don't think Boner will take it past the state court."

"So, Stapp will remain in jail until January when his term is up?"

"I would expect so, but you never know."

"Thanks, Mr. Prosecutor. You have been a big help since I have nothing from the defense side. Boner and Agnew went on a hunting trip to Eastern Washington."

"You bet. Glad to help out. Can you figure out the language in that paperwork?"

"I think so, but if I have some problems, can I call you?"

"Absolutely."

"One thing I've learned is not to get too technical. The average reader doesn't understand that lawyer language."

"That's smart kid. By the way, you are doing a terrific job. Keep it up."

Cloud hustled out the door and caught the 3 p.m. train.

He took his seat and pulled out the papers on the trial denial.

"Why can't they talk English?" he thought to himself as he perused the decision papers. "This isn't going to be easy."

After arriving at his desk, Cloud wrote this article for the October 28 edition:

Aberdeen Dr. Robert Stapp, convicted in February of criminal abortion, may have reached the end of the line in an effort to gain his freedom this week when the Washington State Supreme Court denied his attorney's latest appeal.

It was a quick decision and a thorough one as the court denied all of Defense Attorney E. W. Boner's appeal arguments.

"I am pleased with the decision, but it wasn't unexpected," said Prosecuting Attorney W. A. Campbell. "Boner's arguments were way off base and the court saw it that way as well."

Boner and Assistant Defense Attorney Walter Agnew are in Eastern Washington on a hunting trip and unavailable for comment.

Stapp was convicted of the criminal act, which was reduced from manslaughter, in the death of Mary Bauer, niece of wanted fugitive John Tornow. He was sentenced in April to nine months in the county jail. He won't be scheduled for release until January, 1912.

Miss Bauer was taken to Dr. Stapp's office in Aberdeen from her Upper Satsop home by her uncle, Ed Tornow, on November 26, 1910. The abortion was performed the next day and Mary Bauer passed away at the home of midwife Emma Kaatz on December 1.

In his appeal, Boner contended that the conviction may rest on the uncorroborated testimony of an accomplice or accomplices.

He filed six motions of contention:

1. The trial court erroneously denied appellant's (Dr. Stapp) motion for a directed verdict in his favor;

2. There is no evidence showing appellant's connection with the crime charged, save the testimony of two witnesses (Ed Tornow and Kaatz), who, it is insisted, were accomplices in the crime, and whose testimony the court should have held to be unworthy as a matter of law;

3. Appellant was a witness in his own behalf, and in fact, his testimony and surgical experience he attested to, qualified him as an expert witness.

4. Contention that Prosecuting Attorney William Campbell's cross amounted to prejudicial misconduct. The issue in question was when Stapp was discussing his last surgery, which he said was at Sister's Hospital. He said he performed an operation for a pelvic abscess. Campbell then asked "Was it a man or a woman?" Boner's contention

is that it was prejudicial and amounted to an impression that Stapp performed a criminal operation;

5. New evidence has been discovered. The court read the submitted affidavits and found no grounds to consider an appeal;

6. Boner contended that the trial court erroneously refused to instruct the jury that the testimony of the two witnesses that the court relied upon to connect the appellant with the crime, were accomplices and the court failed to give the jury proper cautionary instructions relative to discrediting such testimony.

All six contentions were unanimously denied by the court.

Campbell was asked what happens next.

"I really don't think Boner will take it past the state court. If there was some ambiguity, perhaps. But, the state court quashed every one of the talking points."

———

A few days later, excitement was rampant in Montesano with new clues that the fugitive's capture might be soon.

Optimism for that belief rested in the reports to the sheriff that evidence of Tornow's appearance showed up in the Wishkah Valley, high up in the valley.

This information came just as Sheriff Ed Payette was healing from his fall down the mountain and ready to take up the hunt once more.

Cloud corralled a new source, W. H. Blossom, manager of the American Express mailing company in Aberdeen. Blossom returned from a hunting trip in the area and encountered deputies, Carl Swartz and Stephen Scott, whom Blossom had met at Jack Winslow's camp in the Wishkah Valley. They indicated there was strong evidence that Tornow was in the area and his capture would be imminent.

It's logical that Tornow might be in the Wishkah vicinity because he knows that territory as well as the Wynooche and the Satsop valleys. As a younger man, he worked there for Cy Blackwell on the splash dam and other logging operations higher up in the region, all the way to Humptulips, 30 miles northwest of Aberdeen.

The reporter met with Blossom, who had returned to Aberdeen and said "I learned from the deputies that Tornow was positively known to be somewhere in that part of the country, and it would be just a matter of time before he is finally caught."

Cloud wrote this report for *The Aberdeen Daily World* and the *Vidette* the week of October 27:

From an official source of unquestioned reliability, it was learned that a recent outrage committed in the Wishkah Valley country is laid at John Tornow's door. He is suspected of killing his two nephews nearly two months ago and is being sought by two posses.

A party of four trappers living in a shack, awoke at midnight to find their home in flames. Some person had started a fire in the middle of the door to their shack and fled. The trappers managed to escape the flames, but were compelled to leave their guns, ammunition and supplies behind, and these were all consumed by the fire.

One of the men, a little slower to move than the others, nearly lost his life in the blaze but managed to crawl outside, though slightly scorched.

According to the trappers and the officials, there is no one in that country, who would do such a deed as this, except for Tornow. The theory is that he is endeavoring to terrorize that entire section to the point where the trappers and hunters who live there will seek other quarters.

There is much indignation among the inhabitants over this outrage and efforts to capture Tornow have been redoubled.

One hunter, who has a shack in the vicinity of Winslow's camp, reports that he was aroused at midnight recently by a man he is certain was Tornow. The stranger carried a rifle in a menacing manner and demanded salt with alacrity and left without further parley. The unusual hour at which the request, for such ordinary commodities such as salt and pepper, was made, convinced the hunter that his visitor could be none other than Tornow.

This impression was also strengthened by the stranger's manner, which plainly indicated he had not the slightest intention of being denied his request.

Sheriff Ed Payette said that an effort will be made at once to unite the two parties of searchers under deputies Swartz and McKenzie and the hunt for the alleged slayer of the Bauer boys will be renewed with vigor.

After filing his story, Cloud headed to the police station to meet Lindy for dinner. It had been several days since he has seen his lady.

"Hi, beautiful, ready for chow?"

"Yeah, and I am starved," she answered.

During dinner at the Mecca Cafe, Cloud shared the contents of his latest story with Lindy, who often queried him about how his day went and about his most recent articles before they appeared in the paper.

"You know what you should do?" Lindy asked her beau after he had told her of the Bauer ranch sale.

"What's that?"

"You should go and talk to Mrs. Bauer before she leaves here. If she's gone, you'll never find out about John."

"What do you mean, find out about John?"

"Didn't you tell me two weeks ago that she knew John would find her and talk to her before she left? Didn't you say she knew he would?"

"Yes, Lin. You are right. I almost forgot about that. What do I mean, almost? I did forget about that. I'm glad you remembered."

"Hey, Danny. I've got an idea. I'm off tomorrow. Why don't I see if I can borrow Daddy's auto and I'll take you up there?"

"Are you sure you could do that?"

"Well, it won't hurt to ask. I've shared a lot of what you told me with Daddy and he is really interested in this story. I haven't driven the car that far before, but it shouldn't be a problem."

"I'm so glad you are that interested in what I do to do that for me?"

"I'm interested in everything you do, Danny. You are the most interesting person I know and like it or not, you are a big part of my life."

"I like it, I like it," he answered smiling and grasping his girl's arm, lovingly planting a lingering kiss on her hand."

"I'll go to the desk and give Daddy a call. I think they'll let me use their phone."

"All righty, then. How about a picture show?"

"I'd like to, but it's been a long day and I am quite tired tonight. Besides, if Daddy says OK, we want to get an early start, don't we?"

Mr. Fleming reluctantly gave his consent for Lindy to take the car, which the family had only owned for a year.

"I had to promise I would do all the driving. He does not know you that well. Actually, he doesn't know you at all. But that's nothing against you," said Lindy. "I don't think he minds if I take it. He taught me how to drive and I've taken it before, but only for short trips. The longest one I made was to the beach. This is a lot farther than the beach."

Matlock grocery and post office in 1900.

Dan rose early and met Lindy at her east Aberdeen home at 7 a.m. He greeted her parents and the two left for their long journey into the Satsop, Dan vowing to return for a longer visit soon.

"Is it OK if I stop at the sheriff's office and make a quick check in at the courthouse? It's not out of the way," Cloud asked as the smooth-running Tin Lizzie approached the Montesano city limits.

"Sure, what do you want to do there? It won't take long, will it?"

"I usually call them in the morning, but since I won't be in the office today, I'll just pop in and see if there's anything new."

Dan and Lindy walked up the steps to the courthouse and approached the clerk.

"Hi, Jessie, how's it goin'?" Cloud asked the clerk. "Got any marriage licenses today? I can make a copy here as I'm heading up the Satsop today. Oh, Jessie, sorry. This is my girlfriend, Lindy."

"Hi, Jessie, nice to meet you."

"You hang on to this guy. He's a keeper," the clerk said."

"Holy … ." Cloud stopped short of finishing the sentence. "Look at this license: "That youngest Tornow brother is getting married."

"What?" said the clerk and Lindy almost in unison.

"Here's the listing in the licenses. Jessie can you get me a copy of that license? It's public record."

"Just a minute, I'll run across the hall to the records and get a copy."

"I can't believe that," said Cloud, turning toward Lindy. "Just a month after his nephews were killed and only two months after shooting John's dog and taking out that search warrant."

"I think he fooled everybody," said Lindy, who was kept up-to-date on the Tornow family whenever Dan had any news.

"I never heard of this woman, Sadie Baldwin before," said Cloud, still shaking his head in disbelief. "I wonder if she knows what she is getting into?"

"Here you are," said Jessie, handing the reporter a copy of the marriage certificate on file.

"Thanks. This is a shocker. I didn't even know he was seeing anybody after that incident with the Bauer girl," said Cloud.

"He did get that girl pregnant, didn't he?" the clerk asked.

"That's what everybody says," Cloud answered. "Henry Bauer all but said that in the doctor's trial. Makes you kind of wonder about this situation, doesn't it?"

"Yeah, you gotta wonder," the clerk said.

"It says Ed Tornow took out a license to marry Sadie Ruth Baldwin on October 30 at Porter. I wondered where he went after the house became vacant," Cloud said.

"We better get going," said Lindy. "Got a long drive ahead of us."

"You mean, you've got a long drive ahead of you," said Cloud.

"See ya later, Jessie. Thanks for your help."

"Nice to meet you, Jessie," Lindy nodded as they turned to head out the door.

"Same here. Take care of that guy."

"You know how to get there, don't you Danny?"

"Now's a good time to ask me that," he said smiling. "Yes, I know, I think, although I haven't driven there before. We stay straight on Pioneer until we get to Brady and turn left. There's a little grocery there. It's going to be a nice sunny day. Do you know how to drop the top?"

"I think so, but I bet you could figure it out. We have to be sure to remember and raise it again before we get home."

With the roof of the shiny Lizzie lowered, the two headed east out of Montesano and were at the turnoff to the Upper Satsop in a few minutes.

The rough road that cars used to travel between Brady and Matlock was full of chuckholes, so driving was slower than it might ordinarily have been. It was also muddy from the weekend rains. The road was improved by the county two years ago. It was almost a half-hour before they reached the Tornow homestead, which Dan pointed out on the left.

"Just a little more to go," he said as the car motored along the dirt path into a far denser forest. "I have to keep an eye out for that turn. It's not marked at all and it's not very wide."

"Well, we aren't going very fast on this road," Lindy said. "You should be able to spot it."

"That's it, ahead. Turn left and it's just a little ways down there on the left."

The car pulled up in front of Gus and Lucy Maas's house and the two climbed out. They knocked on the front door and Lucy answered.

"Oh, hello, Mr. Cloud. "I wondered who that was parking a nice, new auto in front of the house. What can I do for you?"

"Lucy Maas, this is my girl, Lindy Fleming."

"Hi, Lucy, nice to meet you."

"Lucy, is Mrs. Bauer here? She told me she was staying here with her daughter until they moved to California."

"Yes, I think she might be outside with her daughter. Walk around the side and you can probably see them."

"Thanks. I'll do that."

Danny and Lindy went down the stairs and around the side of the house without seeing the Bauers.

"Let's go out to the back. Maybe they are out there," Cloud said. "I think I see them."

"Minnie. How are you doing? Getting ready to go to California, yet?"

"In about a month, Mr. Cloud," she answered. "What are you doing all the way up here?"

"We came to see you before you left. Oh, excuse me. This is my girlfriend, Lindy Fleming. We came in her car."

"Howdy, Lindy. That's a mighty fine, nice man you got. Excuse my manners, got a lot on my mind these days. This is my daughter, Elizabeth, Lizzie we call her."

"Nice to meet you, Mrs. Bauer and Lizzie. 'Lizzie,' that's what my auto is called — 'Tin Lizzie.' Mrs. Bauer, I'm sure sorry for your loss," responded Lindy.

"Thank you, that's sweet of you," said Minnie, wiping a tear from an eye with the corner of her apron.

"Mr. Cloud, nice to see you again and Lindy, nice to meet you. If you excuse me, I have chores to do in the barn," said Lizzie.

"You go right ahead," said Cloud. "I've been telling Lindy all about your family; she knows all that happened. In fact, it was her idea to come up and talk to you before you leave," he said, turning toward Minnie. "I see that the ranch has been sold, so you'll probably be able to get your own place in California."

"You don't miss much do you, Mr. Cloud?" Minnie said with a smile. "That's the sign of a good reporter."

"I try to stay on top of things. That's all," he answered.

"What I really want to know, is if you have heard from John? There's a rumor that he might be in the Wishkah area and that's not far from here."

"He was here. I know it."

"You know it?" Cloud asked.

"Yes. I didn't see him. I didn't talk to him, but he was here."

"So, how do you know that?"

"He took the stuff I left for him."

"You left stuff for him? What kind of stuff?"

"I left a burlap bag full of potatoes, carrots, icicle radishes that he loves, onions and a razor. I wanted to see him, so I could trim his hair. I thought I heard a noise on the porch the other night, but when I got up, I didn't see anybody. In the morning, when I looked out, the sack was gone."

"When was this?" Cloud asked.

"Two nights ago, no three nights. It was the day I got the call about the house selling."

"That's wonderful about the house. You got a real good deal for that."

"Yeah. We're satisfied, but we wanted to get out of here and we took a lot less."

"Did you know that your brother's getting married?" Cloud asked, changing the subject.

"Married?"

"I guess you didn't know."

"We stopped at the courthouse on the way up here and picked up the licenses to print. I just happened to glance at the list and saw Ed's name, so I asked the clerk to get me a copy of the license. Here, take a look," he said, handing the license to Minnie.

"I heard he moved to Porter, but I have had no dealings and not even seen him since Mary's death. He knows how I feel about that situation with him and Mary. I didn't even know he was seeing anybody, let alone marry them. I never heard of this Sadie woman. I wonder if he got her pregnant, too. I'm sorry, I shouldn't jump to conclusions."

"I don't know, but it won't last long, I figure. He's so irresponsible, I'm told. I've had very little contact with him."

"I don't know how he's making a living, probably spending the little bit of money Mama gave him. He's probably spending money from the will before we even get it."

"The probate for the estate is still unsettled, isn't it?" Cloud asked.

"Yes, and with John on the run, I don't think it will ever be settled. I was so mad at Ed for filing that warrant to have John called insane. I almost wanted to get rid of him, myself. That guy hasn't done a day's work ever. Papa tried his best to get him involved, but he finally gave up. And, Mama didn't have any luck either. She said it was easier to let it go or do it herself, if she could, than to fight with him."

"Sheriff told me the family was all in on the warrant idea, but sounds like you weren't."

"No. No way would I ever buy into that. It was Edward and Fred. I don't think the other boys knew anything about it. Maybe Will, because he and Ed were close. Besides, no way is John insane. I know my brother better than any and I know he is a little slow in the education, but he can't be matched for his knowledge of the wilderness."

"You told me earlier in Montesano that you knew John would know where you were staying. How did that come about?"

"Pretty easy, really. I know he was still in the area, so before I left the homestead, I put a note in the cedar stump where John always hid and waited for Henry to leave. I knew he would go there first, if he came to the ranch, and he did. I just said simply 'come to Maas's, I'm there. Min.'"

"Pretty clever. I thought maybe you had a vision or something."

"I did have a vision. I had lots of visions."

"You said you were planning to leave for California in a month?"

"Yes. I'm looking forward to getting there, but I'm not looking forward to the trip."

"What's your plan for travel?" Cloud asked.

"Well, I'm not sure yet. Henry said if we sold the place, he would try to book passage on a boat for us, but I'm waiting for him to arrange it. He's supposed to call the realtors and they will take care of it from here before they send him the money from the sale."

"That sounds exciting. I've not even been on a transport ship. Just a steamer and I like that," the reporter said. "But, that's only from Aberdeen to Montesano. California's a long trip. Well, we better be heading back. That road to Montesano is a mess after the weekend rain. Lots of washouts."

"One thing, Mr. Cloud. What I told you about John, don't print any of that and don't tell anybody. That's our little secret because I like you and I trust you."

"Sure, Minnie. Between you and me, I don't think John did it and I like it that he is able to stay hidden from the posse. I don't want to do anything that would compromise that. Besides, I print facts and we don't have any facts as to his whereabouts, do we?"

"Thanks and I know he didn't do it. I just wish they would try and look for someone else. They are wasting time."

"I wish you the best in your new opportunity," said Cloud, moving toward Minnie. "Can I give you a hug? You have been through so much. Stay in touch. You can always reach me through the paper."

"Sure, I'd like that. You too, Lindy. Come here."

The three of them locked in a tight embrace and all three let the tears flow.

26. A WINTER'S TALE

Winter 1911-1912

Being a full-time reporter covering Chehalis County government in Montesano, as well as the John Tornow search, kept reporter Dan Cloud busy. Since late October, he had not written much about the man suspected of killing his two nephews on September 3, and he had done very little as a correspondent for *the Chehalis County Vidette.*

Just prior to Christmas, the *Vidette's* editor/publisher W. D. Crow did write the following editorial in the December 22 edition:

Where is John Tornow, wanted for murder? Many reply by pointing to the forests that crowd the skyline on all sides, and with a careless wave of the hand, say emphatically "there." No doubt they are right. Somewhere under the dripping trees, Tornow is undoubtedly watching the trails that lead to his hiding place, his rifle in the crook of his arm, his finger on the trigger guard.

These forests are vast, covering an unbroken area equal in extent to the territory of Germany, one of the most populous nations on earth, smothering rugged mountains, where every canyon harbors a tumbling stream of water. These great, silent forests, stretch far beyond the reach of man. Somewhere Tornow is hiding. Find him.

For many months, Sheriff Payette has attempted to comb these 10,000 square miles of vast, untracked woods, confining his efforts to the localities where Tornow is known to have spent his winters during the last several years of his nomadic existence. No definite trace of the man has yet been found and the search has dwindled to the daily vigilance of two men, Deputy Sheriff Colin McKenzie and an assistant.

Far back in the shadow of the foothills of the Olympics, 60 miles from home, the men have built a shack, and every day, rain or snow, are out in the timber, clambering over hills, crossing icy streams, struggling through dense underbrush, cautious, apprehensive for the man they search is as well versed in woodcraft as they, possessing the decided advantage of being the pursued, a crack shot, preferring death to justice, and capable of administering the former.

Last week they received their winter supplies and they are now out of touch with civilization. The snows of winter will soon envelop the mighty Olympics. The men are buried for the winter. If Tornow is in their territory, it is hard to imagine he will escape until spring without brushing against them. Whose funeral will it be?

Sheriff Payette scouts the idea that Tornow is dead by his own hand. Some unknown, and as yet unseen, man dwells in the Olympics, and occasionally wanders into the region now patrolled by McKenzie. The sheriff spent three days with his deputies last week in the hills and returned from there Friday evening. He was told by McKenzie that the latter and his assistant frequently encountered evidences of the presence of the nomadic hermit. During a snowstorm some five weeks ago, they tracked a man along a trail of but an hour old to the river, where he had no doubt gone to fish. The trail entered the water, but the point not found where it left it.

The two deputies are engaged in hazardous employment. There is hardly a doubt in the world that Tornow knows they are there. He is one of the keenest woodsmen the state has ever known. Besides, it is thought he has friends who have helped him. It is possible he is playing a waiting game, depending somewhat on the others to force the issue.

As the winter months wore on, reports of Tornow were scarce, but those that did come in to the sheriff's office ranged far and wide.

The Daily News at Port Angeles, on the north coast of the Olympic Peninsula, published a report of a couple of trappers who spotted the elusive hermit deep in the Hoh River Valley, 112 miles north of Aberdeen. This time, however, Chehalis County Sheriff Ed Payette let the north Peninsula authorities assume command.

Although it appeared unlikely it was Tornow, the Jefferson County sheriff, under a request from Clallam County, sent two deputies to investigate and found it wasn't likely Tornow, but the legendary John Huelsdonk, known as the mythical "Iron Man of the Hoh."

Huelsdonk became a legend soon after the turn of the century. Stories of his superhuman strength, incredible marksmanship and boundless energy became widespread from Port Angeles to Aberdeen. From time to time, he would sport a long beard. His 5-foot, 10-inch frame was a bit shorter than Tornow, but his weight was nearly identical, 200 to 220 pounds, depending on the time of year.

He was mostly a farmer and lived with his wife, Dora, primarily on the Hoh River homestead. But, to supplement the meager income farming produced, he worked logging camps seasonally until an accident mangled his hands so severely he couldn't swing an axe or wield a hammer. So, he adjusted. He packed supplies for timber cruisers or trail crews, carrying double loads of 150 pounds or more for double pay.

It was likely in this light that he earned the nickname "Iron Man." According to reports from his neighbors along the Hoh, a survey crew once encountered him carrying a huge cook stove up the trail. When they commented on the weight of the stove, Huelsdonk responded: "Oh, the stove isn't bad, but the hundred pounds of flour inside keeps shifting around ... ."

Much like Tornow, it was as a hunter, that he became a legend. One trapper said there is a photo of him at the little store at the Hoh standing next to a half-dozen cougar pelts nailed to the wall. A Hoh Indian the sheriff knew said the "Iron Man" once shot a hawk in the eye from across a hay field. The same Indian said because of him, the grey wolf is nearing extinction on the peninsula.

So, there is Huelsdonk in the West Olympics and Tornow in the East Olympics. Much the same individual in their abilities, reliance on the wilderness for survival, respected by everyone, feared by some.

Payette said he would like to meet Huelsdonk one day, but was grateful he didn't make the long trek to investigate another wild goose hunt.

———

On his next trip to Montesano for the weekly county commission meeting, Cloud was intercepted as he left the train by Commissioner Wilson.

"Hi, Dan. Hey, got some news for you, if you are interested."

"I'm always interested in news, you know that, commissioner."

"Well, for this one you need to see Jessie. She's got a stack of paperwork. We got a settlement on the Tornow estate probate."

"Finally. What's it been a year, isn't it?"

"Longer than that. Mrs. Tornow died in November 1910, and today is February 10, 1912."

"That long. I lost track because nothing transpired for so long. What was the holdup? Wasn't there a will?" the scribe asked.

"The real holdup was John. You know, his brother tried to get him declared insane, but that didn't work. Then the Bauer boys were killed.

It took a while for the court to declare he was a fugitive after that incident. Once he was declared a fugitive, the family asked the court to appoint Ben Cheney to act as agent for him. Once the paperwork for that was concluded, it was easy."

"There was a will, wasn't there?"

"That's a curious thing. All the children — they're the heirs apparent — maintain there was, but we conducted an exhaustive search and none could be found. Their attorney, Ovie Nelson, thought there was one made out years ago when Frederick was still alive, but it wasn't in their file. What should have been fairly easy, turned out to be a nightmare."

"Is everybody happy with the way it turned out?"

"I think so. All the kids got their share, and that's the way it should have been."

"Thanks, commissioner. I'll pick up the paperwork right away. I'll see you in the chambers in a few minutes."

Cloud walked up the stairs to the courthouse and was met by Jessie's smiling face.

"Hi, Dan. Here's your meeting agenda."

"Thanks, Jessie. Also, I'd like to get a copy of all the details on the settlement of the Tornow family probate."

"Sure, Mr. Wilson told me you'd be wanting it. I got it all packaged for you."

"Awww, you're a jewel, Jess."

"Anything for you, Dan. Here you go."

Cloud walked into the meeting room with a stack of papers an inch thick.

"This is going to take a while to decipher," he thought to himself. "I hope nothing important happens in this meeting."

Cloud returned to Aberdeen and began to wade through the papers in the Tornow estate. While there was a mound of documents, he determined that only a couple were necessary to wrap up the case for the reader. Normally, there wouldn't be a story, but when Tornow became a fugitive, the probate was elevated to public news. What had lingered for 15 months, he summarized in a few paragraphs.

After nearly 15 months, the estate of Frederick Daniel and Louisa Anna Mary Tornow, parents of the fugitive outlaw John Tornow, has been settled with each of the six children receiving one-sixth of the property.

That includes John Tornow, suspected killer of his twin nephews, William and John Bauer, on September 3, 1911. His share will be deposited in the Montesano State Bank.

"John's situation was the holdup," related C. N. Wilson, administrator for the estate. "He couldn't be located to sign the paperwork; then months after the Bauer boys were killed and he was the presumed suspect and thus a fugitive, the family asked the court to name an agent for John. Superior Court Judge Ben Sheeks appointed businessman Ben Cheney to act on his behalf, mostly to sign papers. It was a quick settlement after that."

The Tornows owned four sections of real properties, all of which have been sold:

The South half of Northeast quarter and Northwest quarter of Northeast quarter, Section 36, Township 19, North, Range 7 West;

Southeast quarter of Southwest quarter, Sec. 1;

North half of Northeast quarter, Sec. 12;

Northeast quarter of Northwest quarter of Sec. 12, all in Township 19 North, Range 7 West.

It was determined that property in the first listing (including the homestead and barns) were worth $4,800; the homestead sold for $3,800 to W.S. Valentine, a farmer from Montesano, who narrowly outbid the Bauers' neighbor, Julius Hollatz, who bid $3,000; the second listing of properties was appraised for a combined $5,575, but sold at auction for only $2,900 to A. J. Jackson of Montesano.

In addition, the following items were among those sold at another auction: all the farming implements, among which were a couple of wagons, hay mower, buggy, scythe and several harnesses; all house furnishings, including living, dining, bedroom and kitchen furniture and a cook stove; plus 25 cattle, two horses (one 24 years old), 45 chickens and two ducks.

The Tornows also had $1,873 in certificates of deposit at the Montesano State Bank.

One other interesting asset was a long-overdue debt of $200 due nearly a year ago from Emma Kaatz, who ran the Aberdeen boarding home, where Mary Bauer died in December 1910, following a criminal abortion in which Dr. Robert Stapp of Aberdeen is now serving time. There was no indication what the debt was for, just that attempts have been made to collect it to settle the estate.

Once all the assets were totaled, the debts, including funeral costs, taxes, appraisals, and fees from all physicians and other medical personnel, were subtracted.

This resulted in each of the six children receiving $1,664.89. The order was signed by Judge Ben Sheeks and approved by the commissioners: Wilson, James Gleason and J. W. Pettijohn. Payments were made to the following Tornow kin:

Mrs. Henry (Minnie) Bauer, 44 of San Diego, Calif.; W. M. Tornow, 38, of Elma; Albert Tornow, 37, of Centralia; C. F. (Fred) Tornow, 35, of Portland, Ore.; John Tornow, 32, of Satsop and fugitive at law; and E. W. (Edward) Tornow, 30, of South Bend.

John Tornow's portion is to be held at the Chehalis County treasurer's office for a period of 120 days, then deposited in his account at the Montesano State Bank.

One month later, the next information about the fugitive outlaw was printed. Nothing had transpired on the search, except Payette did send Assistant Sheriff Fitzgerald, and sheriffs' deputies, Dan Pearsall and Jack Winslow, into the Oxbow. Their search provided nothing on the hunt for Tornow, just frustration and dead ends.

A couple of days after the New Year, Cloud went to Montesano to meet with the sheriff after Payette told him he had some news, perhaps the final news report for the winter, pending any unexpected turn of events.

"I'll tell you what, Dan. This has been so frustrating," Sheriff Ed Payette said, greeting the intrepid *Daily World* reporter as he took a seat in the sheriff's office.

"I can't believe it has gone on this long. We would get close, then another false alarm and, we'd have to start all over, or at least curtail our search; then the snow caused all sorts of problems in November and into December."

"Yeah, it's been frustrating for me, too — in a different way. My editor wants something almost weekly now, but I haven't had too much to write about."

"Here's something new for you, and it will probably be the last report for a while. I pulled McKenzie off the search a couple of days ago. It wasn't getting anywhere and he was bogged down by the snow. In fact, I expect him here any time now. He had met up with a local attorney, Dan Pearsall, when he came down from Humptulips and crossed back over to the east side of the Olympics."

"I'd like to talk to him, and Mr. Pearsall, too, since he has been in that area."

"Sure, why don't you go get some breakfast at the hotel and be back here within the hour."

"Sounds like a good plan, sheriff. I'll give my editor, Mr. Irvine, a call and let him know what I have coming. May I use your phone?"

"Sure, Dan, you can put the nickel in the piggy bank," the sheriff said jokingly.

It was a little more than an hour before the weather-beaten deputy McKenzie arrived at the sheriff's office.

"Colin, here's your paycheck. It's more than I told you because of the hazards you endured," the sheriff said. "The commissioners approved it at last meeting, though it wasn't easy. The skinflints don't want to spend a dime on anything."

"Thank you, Ed. It's most appreciated. You just don't know what it was like up there," the stocky McKenzie said. "Dan, good to see you again. Haven't seen you since the funeral."

"Well, you've been pretty busy, I hear," the reporter answered. "Mr. Payette was telling me earlier how frustrating this search has been."

"Yes, I never thought it would go on this long," said the deputy, about 25 pounds lighter due to the meager diet of the past three months, as well as the rigors of wilderness life.

"Yes, it has been long, longest in state history," Cloud informed the deputy. "We set a state futility record in early November. Sheriff was a prophet when this search started. You remember when you said 'This hunt will have nothing on the search for Harry Tracy?' You knew what you were talking about," he said, turning to Payette.

"I do remember that. It was 58 days, if I recall correctly before that killer was caught in a wheat field in Eastern Washington. He took his own life. What are we now? Over 100, I think."

"Yes, you are right again. It was 58 for Tracy and we are over 100, way over it. Today is day 120, that's four full months."

"Four months of grueling, hard and frustrating work," chipped in McKenzie.

"Mr. McKenzie, did you have any mishaps on your side of the mountain?" Cloud queried.

"If you mean, did I fall 1,500 feet down a glacier and get snagged on a rock? Nothing like that," he smirked, smacking Payette on the back.

"Sure, Mac, just rub it in," the sheriff smiled back.

"It was relatively mishap-free. I was lucky in that way. One of the guys, that football player, Ray Mahaffery, we had for a while, did sprain his ankle pretty bad and he had to leave. That's really all, considering the hazards we had to endure."

"I guess you were pretty lucky. Tell me about the conditions now. We have a good idea about this side of the mountains, but the sheriff said he hasn't had a report from your side for several weeks until the other day."

"Snow's bad, real deep, two to three feet in some spots and about 15-16 inches most everywhere. I really didn't want to come out, but it makes sense. We hadn't been following any kind of clues or even false reports on that side of the mountain, like we had earlier on the Wynooche side. We were just spinning our wheels and getting nowhere."

"Sheriff said you met the attorney, Pearsall, coming out of the Upper Wynooche?"

"I had stopped at the river before heading back down and he was camped there. He said he had spent several days hunting on the Weatherwax Ridge, about 30 miles from here. He had to leave because the snow was too deep and it had started snowing heavily again when he left. He said the trails were all unbroken, no signs or clues of anyone. He said there's no use in trying to hunt for anything in those conditions."

"Did he say anything about meeting up with anybody there who might have seen Tornow or any other strange men?" Cloud questioned.

"Yes, he did. He said he didn't run into anybody, who had seen him, Tornow, or anyone else. Pearsall showed me several mink pelts and a small dressed bear he said he shot and lugged down the mountain."

"Sheriff, how long do you think Mr. McKenzie will be off the search before it resumes again?"

"I'll answer that, Dan," said McKenzie. "When the weather clears. If it clears early next month, I'll be out there. If it's not until spring, I'll be there. You can count on me being back on the search with a full posse as soon as it's possible, as soon as it's safe to travel."

"So, you believe Tornow is still up there, up in the high country?"

"Yes. I think he got to the high country and his winter camp ahead of us, probably when we had to backtrack to chase that dead horse story or those two yahoos who made up that tale about feeding him."

"You think he's going to stay there all winter?"

"Let me just say this. If he comes down through those conditions on either side of the range, then he's a better man than I am."

"Thanks, Mr. McKenzie. You've been a big help and I hope you enjoy your time out of the woods."

"I will, Dan. See you later."

"Sheriff, any more wild tales cross your desk recently?" Cloud asked.

"Just one, a real wild one."

"What's that?"

"A drunk, named Frank Glick, stumbled in here the other day and insisted he not only drank with Tornow at a Main Street saloon last week, but he declared emphatically that he intimately conversed with the man and discussed his situation."

"Did you believe him?"

"Not really, but he did say that he had known Tornow for years. Glick said he berated him for appearing in such a bold manner in a public place. He said Tornow just laughed, bought him a drink and left via the side door."

"Did you investigate that at all?"

"A little bit. I went to the saloon and talked to the owner, who was behind the bar. He said Glick is always coming up with some crazy tale. I told him about the Tornow story. He said 'That's a new one.' I asked him if he, meaning Tornow, was in the bar, and he said he doubted it. He said he didn't know Tornow, but others in the saloon did know him and would have surely pointed him out, if he had been there. I just shrugged it off as a drunken tale."

"You'd think if someone in there had seen him, he'd jump at the shot to get that reward, don't you think?" Cloud answered.

"You'd think."

"And another thing. Everything I have heard from the family members, mostly Minnie Bauer, John doesn't touch alcohol."

"Yes, that's what I've heard too," the sheriff said."

27. SHOCKING DISCOVERY

March 1912

The search for the elusive John Tornow, suspected killer of his two nephews, stretched into its sixth month before the first signs of spring made their appearance. The milestone was reached on March 5 when there was still snow on the ground in the Upper Satsop and Wynooche forests.

That didn't stop the intrepid Colin McKenzie from heading back into the woods to search for Tornow. The hunt had been mostly dormant during the long, cold winter months and McKenzie was champing at the bit to get back on the trail.

On February 28, the sheriff received a call at his office from a Simpson logging camp. It was Frank Getty.

"Sheriff, me and Louis Blair came across a dead elk carcass near the Oxbow," the caller said. "I am pretty sure it was killed by Tornow."

"What reason do you have for saying that?" Sheriff Ed Payette questioned.

"There's a couple. The carcass was near a lean-to that could have been Tornow's. But get this; whoever killed the elk had taken the meat, the hide and the brains. But the teeth were still in the animal's head."

"That is strange," the sheriff answered.

"Yes, it is. Trappers and your usual hunters would take the head, and especially the teeth. They are valuable trade items. And the brains. We use them for tanning the hide, nothing better."

"Well, you would know that, wouldn't you?" responded the sheriff, noting that Blair and Getty were successful trappers as well as watchmen for the power company on the Wynooche.

"My theory is this, sheriff. I say it was Tornow. He took what he needed, but he knew being a wanted man, he couldn't seek a market to trade the teeth. It also means he's probably back in his own territory and out of the Olympics, or at least out of the high country."

"I'll get Colin in here. He's anxious to get back out on the trail."

McKenzie and his new companion, Alvah Elmer, wasted little time in getting to Payette's office, arriving as the sheriff did at 7 a.m. the next day. Payette filled them in on the information he received from Getty and they set out to resume the search, agreeing to team up with Getty and Blair where they discovered the carcass. The sheriff also helped them acquire provisions to last "as long as it takes," according to Payette.

Elmer was an expert woodsman, who was employed as a game warden for Chehalis County. He was regarded as an excellent marksman, who "knew the Satsop and Wynooche wildernesses better than most timber cruisers," the sheriff said.

Deputy Carl Swartz, who had directed one of the earlier posses, said he was worn out and wanted to rest a few more days before resuming the search.

Deputy McKenzie, 33, immediately called the man he wanted for his partner. He had hunted many times with Elmer and he knew his 42-year-old friend from Hoquiam and a fellow Knight of the Pythias was a better shot than he was, and McKenzie believed he was pretty good.

Washington State Archives

Game Warden A. V. Elmer sits outside the cabin he and Deputy Colin McKenzie occupied in the Oxbow.

"I am as good a woodsman as Tornow any day, and I can shoot as straight," boasted the stout, bespectacled, lion-hearted McKenzie before he left the sheriff's office.

"I know you are good or I wouldn't have you two out there," the sheriff added. "Just the same, we are not hunting a normal wanted man. Some people call him the 'Wildman of the Wynooche.' They are probably right. This man is cunning, he's smart, he knows these woods like no other man. Be careful, be wary of an ambush and don't do anything stupid."

The sheriff knew he didn't need to register the admonition with these two, his longtime good friends, but the words of warning seemed to come flowing out. It was his obligation as sheriff.

"I know sheriff. We will be careful. He fooled me once, but he won't fool me again," McKenzie vowed.

That was the last conversation, the sheriff would have with his two friends before they headed north into Tornow's domain.

The two deputies went to the Oxbow area, met with Blair and Getty and took off after their quarry.

That was two weeks ago and nobody, save for one individual, and maybe Tornow, has seen the deputies since.

More than a week ago, Getty shared his concern with Payette.

"They were camped at a cabin near where we found the carcass," the trapper informed. "They found some tracks that looked like they could have been Tornow's. Another trapper said Tornow had a pair of moccasins with the big toe cut out. That was the kind of tracks they were following, not caulked boots that we had spotted earlier. I think he might have been trading shoes to keep us guessing. He's a sly guy. They told me they were going out for the afternoon and would be back by dark. Colin said he was taking only a couple of boxes of raisins because he expected to be gone only a few hours."

Getty told the sheriff he and Blair went looking for the deputies when he had not heard from them in two days.

"We went to the cabin and found their two hounds baying outside. Both had been tied up and they had gnawed their way through the ropes. I fear for them, sheriff. I suspect the hounds broke loose and went to look for them; then not finding them, returned to the cabin as bloodhounds are trained to do. They are smart, well-trained dogs."

Payette said he feared the worst, until he received another call from Getty the next day, saying that they might still be alive. "I ran into a trapper named Ackey, who lives up by the powerhouse on the Wynooche River. He said he saw McKenzie the day that his disappearance was first made public. That was 10 days ago. Anything could have happened between now and then."

Getty told the sheriff that many residents in the Wynooche Valley believe Tornow left that area, and if McKenzie and Elmer are dead, it could be the work of poachers or they might have even drowned in the Wynooche rapids.

That's not what Payette thinks. "I believe he is still in the area and I caution each of you to continue to be vigilant and careful in your pursuit."

After getting the call from Getty, Payette sent out another small posse, headed by his capable assistant sheriff, A. L. Fitzgerald, to aid in the search. He reported back with nothing, no clues, no tracks, thankfully no bodies.

When the 10th day that the deputies had gone missing arrived, the sheriff, believing the deputies were dead, approached the county commissioners with a proposal to approve a $5,000 reward for Tornow, dead or alive.

Colin McKenzie

"I am sorry to say that I believe McKenzie and Elmer are dead. I had been hoping they would make their way out and get to Simpson's Logging Camp 7, but that hasn't happened. They have gone missing and nobody has heard from either of them since February 29 or March 1. It is not impossible that they are still alive, but I think improbable."

The sheriff, in consort with Prosecuting Attorney William Campbell, asked the commissioners to approve the reward request, which he would then take to Gov. M. E. Hay.

Once again the commissioners declined to expand the reward, above the initial $500. Their reasoning was to wait until official word from McKenzie and Elmer arrives or their bodies are found.

Commissioners questioned Payette on the rumors circulating throughout the Satsop and Wynooche areas — that two unidentified bodies were found somewhere near the headwaters of the Wynooche.

"I've heard those rumors and they are absolutely false. I traced them to the source and there is no truth to any bodies being found in the water. The source couldn't say where they were found and couldn't even provide a description of the bodies. I found no credence to those rumors."

Payette said the missing men were not only deputies, but his good friends for a long time. "I have had a close bond with McKenzie and Elmer for many years. This has been weighing deeply on me."

Two days later, Payette's world came crashing down.

Daily World reporter Dan Cloud sat in Payette's office as Deputy Sheriff Giles Quimby related the tragic news everyone had dreaded. Cloud wasn't the only journalist as reporters from many Northwest newspapers descended on the county seat once news circulated that the bodies had been found.

The following is Cloud's lengthy and comprehensive article that included several decks of headlines as newspapers of the day often published with banner stories:

**Price for Tornow
Dead or Alive**

Commissioners offer $4,000 for capture of murderer

*Governor will be asked to increase amount by $2,000;
Posse leaves Montesano to bring in bodies of McKenzie
and Elmer and to organize determined hunt for slayer;
Funeral here Sunday*

Determined to bring in, dead or alive, John Tornow, slayer of his two nephews, William and John Bauer, and now deputies Colin McKenzie and A. V. Alvah Elmer, a posse of 15 men, under the leadership of Sheriff Ed Payette and Deputy Sheriff A. L. Fitzgerald, left Montesano shortly after 9 o'clock this morning for the Oxbow country of the Wynooche Valley.

That is the location where the bodies of the deputies were discovered, and from which the posse will return with the bodies; then they will develop a plan to search the country for Tornow.

Meanwhile, the board of county commissioners in a special session in Montesano this morning, rescinded its previous action as respects the offer of a reward of $2,000 for the slayer of the Bauer twins and $2,000 for the slayer of deputies McKenzie and Elmer. The commissioners also decided to ask Gov. M. E. Hay to post a reward of at least $1,000 in each instance on behalf of the state.

Elmer's .25-20 carbine is on display at Duffy's restaurant in Aberdeen, courtesy of the Wieland family.

If this should be posted, the total price on Tornow's head will be $6,500, and this amount, it is believed, will be sufficient to make attractive to some hardy spirits the peril involved in capturing Tornow.

No word is expected from the posse that left the county seat today until tomorrow night at the earliest when it is likely an escort will return with the two bodies. It is nearly 50 miles from Montesano to the scene of the latest murders and the traveling is rough. Automobiles can be used for about 30 miles and the rest will have to be made on foot. Only a brief inspection will be made of the bodies, which were left after their finding yesterday by Fitzgerald, just as Tornow had left them, and then the return trip will begin.

The posse has orders to shoot Tornow on sight, and to shoot to kill.

Shortly after 5 o'clock this morning, the Aberdeen posse left the city for Montesano reaching that place about 6 o'clock. The party was comprised of W. R. Whiteside, acting as coroner, Dan Pearsall, as Deputing Prosecuting Attorney, Arthur Salmon, Eugene McGillicuddy and Robert Shean. The men are all well-armed and provided with equipment for the woods. No provisions were purchased in Aberdeen as this detail is under Sheriff Ed Payette.

No difficulty was experienced by the sheriff in securing members for the party from Aberdeen. Last night several residents of Montesano also volunteered to join the posse.

Twelve days after their disappearance, McKenzie and Elmer were found dead yesterday, stretched in shallow graves. Deputy Fitzgerald, who headed a posse sent out last week to search for the missing men, made the discovery. Both men had been shot. Their graves are not 30 feet from Tornow's winter camp, and there is every evidence to show that they walked straight into a trap prepared by Tornow.

Fitzgerald says that neither man could have had a chance for his life, and the signs at the scene of the killing show that the men were in reality assassinated, not killed during a fight. Death probably came to the deputies a week ago last Saturday (March 9) when they left the camps of Louis Blair and Frank Getty, two trappers in the Oxbow district of the Wynooche Valley, with a promise to "be back for supper."

Neither man was seen alive after that by anybody, but Tornow. The graves of the men form a "T," McKenzie being buried at Elmer's feet. They both lie in shallow trenches, and it was due to the soft earth that the discovery of the bodies was made.

McKenzie and Elmer must have been shot in their tracks without even seeing their slayer. The camp is so cunningly planned, that anyone approaching can easily be picked off by Tornow, protected by logs and windfalls. The posse, which left today, will attempt to locate him before bringing out the bodies.

The story of Deputy Sheriff Fitzgerald, who along with George Stormes and Getty came into Montesano last night, shows only too plainly that McKenzie and Elmer did not even have a fighting chance for their lives.

Fitzgerald told reporters the deputies left Montesano Saturday morning. In the company were Deputy Sheriff Swartz, who wasn't feeling well, George Stormes, a former Army officer, Deputy Cole, a soldier of fortune, C. C. Carpenter and Getty. He said they met several others at the Oxbow, including George Clemons, Gene McGillicuddy and Louis Larson, a Wynooche Valley farmer.

The deputy said, because of heavy snow, they were stranded in their Oxbow camp until Tuesday when they went about 2½ miles below the elk carcass that Getty and Blair found earlier. It was this carcass that spurred McKenzie and Elmer to intensify their search for Tornow.

"From the carcass, we travelled directly east in the direction the boys had told Getty and Blair they would go," the deputy said. "We followed a creek leading eastward and covered the entire section. We struck in by a smokehouse where trappers smoke their meat and a little later found Tornow's trail. We followed this some distance and came upon other unmistakable signs showing that the man had recently passed that way. He couldn't have been more than 20 minutes ahead of us.

"Then the dog which McKenzie and Elmer had taken with them and had been left at the Oxbow, broke loose, and caught up with us. He caught Tornow's scent and went after him. We lost track of the dog. An hour or so later, Swartz and myself were standing together and we heard a shot. We thought the dog was dead and Tornow had shot him. It wasn't until the dog came back into camp Wednesday morning that we knew he was alive.

"Frank Getty had his dog along, and Wednesday morning we noticed that he was continually whining. This seemed to mean something to us, and we agreed if he did it again, we'd let him run and we'd go in the direction that his attention was riveted. This was down in a gulch. The dog whined again and we went down.

"We hadn't gone but 50 yards when we found tracks made by McKenzie and Elmer, their footprints where they had stepped on logs with their caulked boots, showing plainly. We followed on down about 250 feet and found other signs which meant that we were either close to Tornow or the missing men.

"We came out to a cleared place and right onto Tornow's shack. If he had been there, he could have killed the entire posse before we could have seen him. His shack is cunningly placed between windfalls, which crisscrossed and formed a sheltered spot. We went over to the camp and looked around. Tornow had been smoking a great quantity of elk meat there, and the skin of the elk which he had killed near the Oxbow camp, was stretched over one side to keep out the wind. Tornow had his bed made under one of the windfalls. Around the camp, small brush had been piled to make the hiding place more safe and secure. It was from this camp that Getty and Blair had seen the smoke, which they reported to McKenzie and Elmer.

"Then we searched high and low for Tornow, and beat through the woods and spread out in a kind of dragnet. We couldn't find him, and at 11 o'clock, started back to the shack, intending to go on to where they found the elk's carcass.

"Stormes started to go under a windfall, and noticed a little fresh hole in the ground, 30 feet away from the place where Tornow had made his bed. It was there that the men were buried," Fitzgerald said, his voice choking.

"The earth had been dug out in two shallow trenches — really one grave — and Elmer was lying under the windfall, while McKenzie's body was at an angle from it. Stormes called us over and showed us the earth. There was only one thing to do and one of the men started digging with the butt of his rifle. He uncovered Elmer's shoes. We dug further and uncovered Elmer's face and head with a little work with the gun stock. So far as I know the bodies are still fully clothed. We covered Elmer up again carefully, and didn't disturb McKenzie's remains. They are buried underneath a foot of earth. We don't how they were shot.

"It was too awful. You can't imagine how we felt there in the woods, knowing how our friends had been murdered," the deputy said. "I imagine that both men had been shot from the front, as they were crossing the cleared space to Tornow's camp. Doubtless they saw the smoke and were creeping up on their man. Tornow would watch unseen. There was no chance for them to see him for he could hide among the windfalls. I doubt either of them knew how the other died. Tornow was a sure shot and undoubtedly shot to kill. Possibly one heard the first shot, and may have seen the other fall on the ground.

"We decided to come in immediately and get help. The ground is very rough and we could not possibly have brought out the bodies alone. When we got to Camp 7, we phoned to the sheriff's office, and Deputy Royce came up in the machine and got us. He made the trip of 50 miles in two hours and three quarters.

"We don't know where Tornow is. Undoubtedly he killed McKenzie and Elmer a week ago last Saturday. We intended to try and locate

Tornow and then come back to Montesano for reinforcements. The spot where the bodies lie is two miles east of the Oxbow and a quarter-of-a-mile off the trail.

"I think that Tornow has gone east, but he will undoubtedly come back soon, for there was a large quantity of smoked meat hanging at his camp."

Fitzgerald said the group had to leave Swartz at the logging camp. He might possibly be coming down with typhoid fever. He said the posse was all played out, didn't have much to eat and had traveled over difficult terrain. It will take at least a day to get back to the site where the bodies are buried. It is about 40 miles to Camp No. 7 from Montesano and a good 20 miles west of there to Tornow's camp.

"McKenzie and Elmer were led to the camp, I believe, because they knew the gully in which it was located was the only place in the vicinity where hardwood for smoking meat could be procured," the deputy said.

The killing or capturing of Tornow will now be but a matter of a few days, thinks Sheriff Payette. He says, "It's improbable that Tornow will ever face trial for his crimes. No man hunting for him is likely to take chances of capturing him alive. He is a maniac, a thorough woodsman and more cunning than the best woodsmen because of his insanity," words the sheriff disputed only a few months ago.

———

Colin McKenzie was born in Pictou, Nova Scotia, in July of 1879, being at the time of his death, age 33. Shortly after graduating from common school there, he was forced to make it on his own, despite being from a large family. He worked at various odd jobs until he came of age, then headed west to join a brother, R. F. McKenzie, at Vancouver, British Columbia. A few months later, he arrived in Aberdeen.

He was a lover of the woods and spent many days hunting and fishing the northwest's natural resources. After coming to Aberdeen, he continued to pursue life in the woods. He became a photographer and enjoyed long excursions and adventures in the upper country.

In 1898, he was engaged with Dell Castle in the shipping express business in Aberdeen. In 1903, in the Black Friday fire that leveled 13 blocks of downtown Aberdeen, he injured his back while helping

Chief Koehler and other firemen extinguish the conflagration. A large cornice fell on him as they were rushing into a burning building on F Street. The wall fell on both him and Koehler, but the chief was able to break free. He pulled McKenzie from under the wall and believed he was dead. But McKenzie suddenly moved; Koehler revived him, though his back was broken. McKenzie spent several months in St. Joseph Hospital, hovering between life and death. Doctors figured he would be a cripple the rest of his life.

They didn't know the little guy's resiliency. A friend of Colin's, Dr. Caryl Smith, a successful orthopedic surgeon in Portland, had recently moved to Aberdeen. The retired physician put McKenzie on a rigorous rehab treatment schedule and a miracle happened. McKenzie not only recovered, he was walking, even hiking within the year.

After recovering from his injury, McKenzie opened a small studio on Wishkah Street. He was soon able to expand the business, and his photography became highly sought after in the county. He was considered one of the top photographers of Native Americans in the West.

When Payette was elected sheriff, he immediately lured McKenzie to become one of his deputies. In his execution of duties, he was always found to be a faithful and courageous officer, the sheriff said. On more than one occasion, his fearless adventures have brought words of praise.

Perhaps the most notable was in 1910 when he doggedly pursued Louis Salazar, a Chilean, who murdered Ah Fook, a Chinese gardener in Hoquiam. McKenzie tracked him into British Columbia, snagged him without incident at a Fraser River fishing camp and returned him to Montesano for trial. He was convicted and sentenced to life in prison.

At the first call for volunteers to join the posse in the search for Tornow, McKenzie was at the head of the line, and directed one of the posses to look for the Bauer boys. He has tracked Tornow for the past six months since the boys were shot. He pursued Tornow into the snowy Olympics, tracking him from the west side of the range. Only when the snow became too deep, did he return to Montesano for the winter months. He was back on the trail three weeks ago.

McKenzie had aspirations to run for sheriff and announced his intention to do so when filing opens this summer.

McKenzie, perhaps had a forewarning of his fate, evidenced by a remark made to the sheriff's office by Mrs. T. H. Hill, an old acquaintance in Aberdeen. "Just before leaving on his trip, he bade us farewell and entered the sheriff's automobile," said Mrs. Hill. "As the machine was about to start, Colin got out and returned to the house. With tears in his eyes, he grasped me by the hand and said, 'Something tells me that I may not see you again.' Taking the ring from his finger he gave it to me requesting that I keep it in remembrance of him."

The Hills, who live on Wishkah Street in Aberdeen, were warm friends of McKenzie. While he was still suffering from his injuries, they encouraged him to come to their home. From that time, the three had been inseparable. They had also given him a watch, while he was recuperating.

"The death of Colin has been a terrible blow to me," said his brother, Rod McKenzie, who arrived today from his home in Vancouver, British Columbia. "There were eight children in our family, and Colin was always the favorite boy. Both mother and father were planning to surprise Colin with a visit to the West Coast this year."

Rod McKenzie said he was waiting for word from his parents in Nova Scotia before making any definite plans as to the disposition of the body. Should the body be in condition, he said it will probably be sent back to the McKenzie home.

McKenzie was a member of Wishkah Lodge No. 44 Knights of Pythias and also a member of the D.O.K.K. (Dramatic Order of Knights of Khorassan), a service division of the Pythias. He also was a member of the Knights of Maccabees, the lodge which helped care for him during his injury. He was not, as much as can be determined, a member of the local volunteer fire department at the time of his death.

Alvah V. Elmer was a fearless officer and has singlehandedly gone into situations where the most bold and experienced officials have declared that it was plain suicide to go. He leaves two brothers, Wesley Elmer of Hoquiam, who is a logging foreman employed by the Stearns Lumber Company, and Floyd Elmer of Eastern Washington. Alvah worked and lived for a time at Stearnsville, the company's logging camp.

Like McKenzie, Elmer was unmarried. It was Payette's policy when selecting posse members for dangerous work to pick only single men.

He also was a member of the Knights of Pythias lodge in Hoquiam. He was a resident of Hoquiam for the last nine years and was immensely popular on Grays Harbor, where he was known as the best game warden the county ever had. He was known as an expert woodsmen and marksman, especially with a revolver, and McKenzie had said he was "elated to have Al as my partner" when it came time to resume the search for Tornow three weeks ago.

On the same day as Cloud's story appeared in the *World*, the paper's publisher, Werner Rupp, wrote the following editorial. When this was written, news of the deaths of McKenzie and Elmer was known, but the editor did not know that the commissioners had backed off their previous decision to reject the request for a $4,000 reward and to approve the funding for the same price. Rupp wanted to be sure the newspaper was on record.

Here is his editorial, appearing on March 21:

MIGHT OFFER REWARD

When Sheriff Payette asked that a reward of $5,000 be placed upon the head of John Tornow, dead or alive, it was rather broadly hinted that the then assumed disappearance of Deputy Colin McKenzie had political significance because McKenzie had already announced himself for sheriff. The county commissioners decided not to offer the reward until after the bodies of McKenzie and Elmer should be produced as evidence of the need of offering such a reward. Far be it from us to question the superb wisdom of the commissioners, but we would respectfully invite their attention to the ghastly evidence of the truthfulness of Payette and the realization of his worst fears.

Question is raised in some quarters as to whether or not Tornow is guilty of the Bauer murders and of this latest crime. Every suspicion, however, points to him as the murderer. At all events, some man of murderous instincts is free in the woods and he ought either to be killed or be brought to justice before he can perpetrate another murder. One more or less will make little difference to him now. It makes considerable difference to this community. The man who killed the Bauer twins, killed McKenzie and Elmer. There can be no doubt of that in the mind of the man who has followed this case from the onset, and there is every reason to think that Tornow is the murderer of the Bauer twins.

It may be that this murderer's body will be brought in before the commissioners can have a chance to offer a reward for it. But, really, that is most unlikely. This hunted man is familiar with the woods, and will have a big advantage over any posse that undertakes to trail him down. If he is captured at all, it will be by some trapper and because a price is set on his head. No man is now going to undertake the risk of bringing in this man or engaging in an encounter with him unless a monetary reward of sufficient size to be an attraction and to outweigh in imagination the peril involved is offered.

It seems reasonable to suppose that if the county commissioners had offered a reward of $1,000 for Tornow after the murder of the Bauer twins, both McKenzie and Elmer would be alive today. In the meantime, the commissioners ought to make humble apology to the memory of Colin McKenzie for suspicions they entertained of him as "grandstand player." He wasn't. He was a straight, honest boy, who died trying to do his duty.

While Cloud was in Montesano interviewing Deputy Quimby for the story on the deaths of the deputies, his editor, Bill Irvine, was working on another angle. The following story also appeared in *The Aberdeen Daily World* on March 21:

Tornow Insane
If he is guilty,
Says brother

Brother of murderer says family
Has been unable to locate
Accused man

PORTLAND, Ore., *March 21 — If John Tornow is guilty of the crimes of which he is accused, he is mentally unbalanced, believes Fred C. Tornow, of Portland, a brother of the fugitive. Fred Tornow is a member of the firm of Cusack & Tornow, timber dealers.*

"I have not seen my brother John for three years," Fred Tornow told The Aberdeen Daily World today. "At that time, his mind was unbalanced and he was treated at the Mountain View Sanitarium. The report that he escaped from the sanitarium, however, is incorrect. He was released as cured. If he has committed the crimes that are charged to him, it must be the result of mental trouble.

"I do not know whether my brother has been living as a hermit in the woods since that time or not. Such a report reached me and my other brother, E. W. Tornow, a logging man in South Bend, Wash. Ed went into the mountains to find John, if possible, but was never able to verify the report that he was living there. People told us several times they had seen John living in the woods, but when my brother tried to run down these reports nothing definite could be found out."

When Cloud called his editor before heading back into Aberdeen, Irvine informed him of the short item that he wrote.

"But, that's not true," Cloud said of the sanitarium angle. "The sheriff said he investigated that and found it was false. There are no records of Tornow being anywhere in an institution in Portland or anywhere in Oregon."

Irvine said "That's OK. I have Fred Tornow on record. He's the one saying it, not me. He's the only one making that statement, but a lot of papers are going to pick it up as the gospel."

"We hear all about those Wildman stories, a maniac in the woods. His brother doesn't go that far, does he?" Cloud said.

"No, not at all. He just says mentally unbalanced. Hell, that might fit us all at times. A crazy man, a lunatic, a maniac? I don't think the brother thinks quite that way. I think some of those guys in the woods are spinning some wild tales. That's why we always print only the facts, never conjecture or opinion, unless you are going to attribute it to someone. If the sheriff wants to say his opinion, if Fred Tornow wants to state his, then I'll print that."

"Thanks Bill. See you before long."

Cloud was the most prolific of the reporters covering the Tornow story, but another, Fred Boalt of the *Tacoma Times*, could be labeled a "tireless scribe." He had been making many long trips — about 60 to 70 miles each way — into Tornow country since the disappearance of the deputies went public. Boalt's reporting not only informed the residents of the state's second-largest city, but his writing style was a little unusual for the day and he had a big following in Tacoma.

Cloud was young and still feeling his way. He wrote like a veteran and was an excellent interviewer as well as reporter. Boalt was a veteran of many years in Tacoma and was given free reign to publish more prose. He was a wordsmith, accurate and thorough. The day after the bodies were reported, he joined the posse on the sad journey to bring out the bodies.

Boalt was the one reporter to see the pain on McKenzie's face; the lone scribe to witness how the bodies were buried in a shallow, leafy grave at a "T," angle, a "T" for Tornow. He was there when Sheriff Payette said "without a doubt, the man who killed these two also killed the Bauer boys. The burials were similar."

In the previous three days, Boalt had written long, descriptive stories of the hunt for Tornow over the last six months. It was through his reporting that Tornow became the "Beast-Man."

He was a contemporary of legendary *San Francisco Examiner* and *New York Journal* publisher William Randolph Hearst, whose "Yellow Journalism" style pushed the boundaries of news writing and news gathering through bold, screaming headlines, daring writing often without attribution, and purple prose. Others called this style "Sensationalism." Whatever, it is called, the style sold newspapers.

Witness Boalt's descriptive report on the finding of the bodies that appeared in the March 21 edition of the *Tacoma Times*:

BRAVE MAN-HUNTERS
FOUND "BEAST-MAN"
AND THEY BOTH DIED

And now the end.

"I am as good a woodsman as Tornow any day, and I can shoot as straight," said Colin McKenzie, the lion-hearted.

He and Alvah Elmer, the "dead shot," found the beast-man.

And, A. L. Fitzgerald's party later found the bodies of McKenzie and Elmer. The expressions on their faces told the story of how they died.

The trappers had sent word that the elk beyond the Wynooche were restless, sure sign that they were being hunted. McKenzie and Elmer, working on this shadowy clue, found the carcass of an elk. Their woodcraft told them much.

Whoever had killed the elk had taken the meat, the hide and the brains. But he had not taken the teeth. He had taken the meat for food, the hide for clothing, the brains to tan the hide. Why had he left the teeth, the most valuable part, for elks' teeth are used in making fraternal pins and always bring a good price? The slayer had no use for the teeth because he was an outlaw and could not seek a market for them.

So, McKenzie and Elmer worked through the wilderness, using the carcass as a base, and keeping in touch with another posse, the members of which were Getty, Larson and Blair.

On March 9 of this year, McKenzie and Elmer said goodbye to their comrades to explore a creek tributary to the Wynooche. Sometime between then and the 20th, they met the beast-man.

A giant tree had fallen, and where the trunk split at the base, there was a gap resembling a whale's mouth. Beyond the fallen tree's roots was a hummock, 20-feet high mound of dirt thrown up when the tree fell.

The gap in the trunk was the beast-man's lair, the hummock his watch-out. He had walled the side of the gap with elk hide, in which he had cut peepholes. He had set brush outside the hides. One might have passed within five feet of it without distinguishing it from other thickets. From the watch-out, the beast-man could see in any direction.

Elmer, the "dead shot," never had a chance. The beast-man watched them come, and marked little Elmer as the first to die. When Fitzgerald's party found the bodies, the face of Elmer was serene and smiling.

Not so McKenzie's. He saw the beast-man, who had just slain his comrade. To reach Tornow, he had to stoop and go under a fallen log. He might have got away unscathed. He might have run. But that was not McKenzie's way.

What he said to the beast-man and what the beast-man said to McKenzie then, the world will never know, unless the beast-man tells. McKenzie went forward, courting death. He could not shoot because of the intervening log.

He went forward, running, stooping, hurling defiance. He reached the log and stooped still lower to pass under it. And so, bent over, he came within range of the beast-man's rifle.

The ball smashed into his shoulder and ranged almost the length of his mighty body.

When Fitzgerald's party found his body, his hands were clenched and his face, grim in life, was twisted into a grimace of hate, which was not good to see.

It was on the 20th that the bodies were found. The hound stopped and the hair on its back stood erect.

"Get on!" shouted the deputies, but the hound only stiffened.

One of the men felt the ground yielding beneath his feet. He dug with his heel. A few inches below the surface of the ground he found — a human hand:

They found McKenzie, and at his feet, Elmer, the bodies forming a letter "T."

"T" for Tornow.

Later they found the lair, empty of course.

That is the whole story of the man-hunt for John Tornow up to date, though the future may add tragic chapters.

Sheriff Ed Payette summarized for Boalt the task confronting him.

"Tornow lives on elk meat, one elk keeping him 30 days. He has only to kill one man a year to give him a fresh supply of clothing and ammunition. Even now, he has enough cartridges from his victims to last for years.

"You must remember, too, that the advantage is all with Tornow and against the deputies. He isn't looking for them; they are looking for him. To find him, they must move about. He has only to hide and wait, and shoot them as they come.

"There can be no such thing as a systematic show of force in this hunt. It must be each deputy for himself as soon as the woods are entered.

"We are not underrating Tornow now. He has proven that he can and will shoot. His woodcraft is almost uncanny. I sometimes think he 'senses' us long before he sees us. Some of the boys swear he can see in the dark like a cat.

"We will get him, of course — some time. But we will not take him alive. We will get him as he got McKenzie and Elmer. I know he is mad: I know he talks with spirits in the woods; but even so, it is not easy to keep the official mind. He killed McKenzie and Elmer, as good men as ever lived, and as game. They were our friends, you understand. Yes, we will get Tornow, but, if I know the temper of the boys, he will not be taken alive."

Boalt went on to say the Tornow homestead is deserted.

"The doors of the great barns are wide open and the stock gone. A few chickens wander about the barnyard, a few cattle roam the fields untended. The brothers have scattered. They are afraid the beast-man might return. Mrs. Bauer, her husband and daughter have moved to San Diego. The Tornow estate is to be sold.

"The Satsop winds through wood and meadow to the sea. Beyond it, broods the forest, mile on mile. Far away the snow-clad mountains scrape the sky. Between are valleys which the feet of the man never trod. Through them nameless rivers flow.

"Somewhere between the Satsop and the mountains, somewhere between the inland waters and the sea, the beast-man awaits his chance to strike yet another blow at the world which always called him 'queer.'

"Woodsmen are a superstitious folk. The trappers swear that a hound follows at the beast-man's heels — a crotchety, cross-grained surly brute, the one creature in all the world which saw John Tornow's passion and understood."

Each newspaper strived to find a different description of the fugitive outlaw, but for the most part, the information was force-fed from the sheriff's office.

The *Grays Harbor Washingtonian* described Tornow as a "devil."

Witness this lead, the opening few paragraphs of the story that appeared in the "Washie" on March 22.

> *Colin McKenzie and A. V. Elmer, deputy sheriffs of Chehalis County, are dead, the victims of a devil of the woods.*
>
> *Their bodies are buried side-by side-in a shallow grave, far up in the wilds of the Wynooche Valley, two and one-half miles south of the Oxbow, where they were roughly interred by their slayer.*
>
> *John Tornow roams the woods north of Grays Harbor in the vicinity of the Oxbow, on the Wynooche, a prey on mankind and sought by the officers of the law, who may also fall victim to his deadly aim before he is himself slain or captured.*

Quimby told Cloud he expected Payette and Whiteside to return with the bodies by evening, or if not then, by mid-day tomorrow. Cloud received the approval from Quimby to travel with the posse that would leave Thursday morning to bring out the bodies. He knew he was a day late for the breaking news, but getting up to the site the next morning was paramount. Cloud's editor, Bill Irvine, agreed and suggested Cloud stay at the Montesano Hotel that night. He borrowed a bunk roll from Quimby and retired to the hotel.

He met the posse and teamed with a chap, who knew Tornow for years, a former school chum. Cloud felt the hair on the back of his neck stand up when this man offered a stern word of caution for any who would take up the search. Cloud was happy when Quimby handed him a rifle from a backroom cache, although he desperately hoped he wouldn't have to use it.

"Tornow won't wait very long to inquire into a man's business if he has killed the deputies," said James Empey, a timber cruiser, who is thoroughly acquainted with the territory the fugitive is known to have roamed and made his home the last three years.

"He will probably shoot before noticing whether a man is a trapper, timber cruiser or deputy sheriff. It is anything but safe in that part of the woods at present, and will be as long as Tornow is at large."

Empey also attested to what is well known about the fugitive's marksmanship. "Tornow is one of the best shots in the country. I understand that he has plenty of ammunition, and he never has to shoot but once to kill. Add this accomplishment to a more intimate knowledge of the woods than any other resident of the district, for this reason, the ability to travel at night, the help that caches of food in different localities furnish, and anyone who goes after that particular man is taking his chances."

Then the new friend told Cloud and others gathered around him a tale that bordered on the supernatural.

"I'll tell you a story about Tornow you won't believe. If I hadn't seen it with my own eyes, I know I wouldn't. We wuz kids — 16, I believe — Torn, Cash and me, Emp. We were pals. We shortened our names. John was Torn, I was Emp and Cash, that was Jeremiah Plenny. We called him Cash because he was always flipping a coin in the air. Got on our nerves sometimes. This one day, a beautiful day, too nice to go to school, we ditched, got my pop's rickety buckboard and went to Lake Nahwatzel near Matlock.

"We wuz duck hunting, got a few early, then nothing. We were sitting in this blind soaking in the sun. Torn said we ought to head back, Cash was flipping that coin when a teal darted out of the reeds about 50 yards away and only a few feet off the ground. Torn grabbed that coin out of midair and backhanded it at that drake. Bang it hit the water. Faster than you could say 'Jake get that bird,' our dog Jake was in the water, had the bird in his mouth and brought it to us. That coin was lodged in the drake's eye. Never knew what hit him. Cash and I sat there with our mouths wide open. That was good eatin' too, didn't have to pick out any lead.

"We did get in trouble at school the next day. Old Lady Carstairs, the schoolmarm, she knew what we did, why we weren't in school. She called us to the front of the room the next day and asked us 'how was hunting?' Before we could think of some lie to make up, Cash blurted out 'how did you know?' She said 'I didn't, but now I know.' We told the story about the coin and the duck, but she didn't believe a word of it and the other kids just laughed. We had to stay after and do extra work. But it was worth it."

The trip with the posse was made in incredibly short time. Leaving Montesano at 7 a.m. Thursday, the group of 11 men reached Camp No. 7 by noon, where the horses were left and the party had a bite to eat. The walk through the woods with two pack horses began, the posse reaching Oxbow camp at 6 o'clock that evening. The party was on the trail at 6:15 Friday morning, dug the bodies out and prepared them for the trip. Acting Coroner Whiteside examined the bodies, temporarily embalmed them and sewed them into canvas bags. The bodies were placed sideways on packhorses, which brought them to the dead wagon at Camp 7. They arrived in Aberdeen at the Whiteside Funeral Home by 12:30 p.m.

Cloud phoned Lindy from Montesano and arranged to meet her for a late lunch. He felt he needed a quiet respite with his girl before launching into another of the big stories coming his way.

"Hi, sweetie. Am I ever hungry," he greeted the police clerk.

"Oh, Danny. I'm glad you are back. I was so worried with that maniac up there. I was so glad to get your call."

"I need some time to collect my thoughts and get a bite to eat before going to work. I can't make today's deadline, anyway."

"And in what order do I come in those priorities?" she snapped back with a smirk.

"First, of course. Now let's get out of here."

"Just checking. It sounded like I was an afterthought."

"You know that's not true," he said, reaching to hold her hand and planting a warm kiss on her lips."

"Hmm. Nice," she smiled, giving him a warm embrace."

The two enjoyed a nice lunch at the Washington. Dan ate a prime rib sandwich and a bowl of clam chowder, figuring it might be late when he finished his story.

———

When Cloud wrote about the recovery of the Bauer boys' bodies and the funeral, it was as tough a story as he ever had to tell, at least emotionally.

Until now.

This was even more difficult, far more graphic reporting. He also saw the bodies of McKenzie and Elmer up close, and Sheriff Payette didn't allow him to see the bodies of the Bauer twins.

Cloud sat for a while at his desk, staring off into space, trying to gather his thoughts when Irvine walked in.

"Having trouble getting started?" he asked.

"Sure am, boss. This is a tough one, real stressful."

"Follow me, kid."

"What?"

"Follow me outside."

"OK. Whatever you say."

The two walked outside and down the alley, where a large picture window gave visitors a glimpse of the newspaper's press as it rolled.

"Now, on the count of three, I want you to cut loose with the loudest scream you ever made. I want you to do that three times."

"Anything you say boss, but I don't understand."

"Just do it. One, two, three."

The two men let out three blood-curdling screeches, one after the other.

"How does that feel?" the editor asked.

"I can't believe it. I feel great."

"I was like you. I had never heard of that before until Mr. Rupp took me by the arm one day and did what I did to you."

"It's amazing, like a load has been lifted. I'll remember that."

Cloud repaired to his desk and pounded out one of the best stories he had written to date. Boalt had his style, now Cloud was developing his own. His first-hand report is in the March 23rd issue of the *World* with the following headline bannered across all six columns:

No Chance for Lives; M'Kenzie Brutally Slain; "T" Meant for Warning

**BODIES SHOW
TWO DEPUTIES
ASSASSINATED**

Elmer never saw murderer and death came instantly;
McKenzie died in agony, second shot fired at close
Range being necessary to dispatch; Buried in "T"
Shape as warning is conclusion of posse

Deputy Sheriffs Colin McKenzie and A. V. Alvah Elmer were assassinated. They had no chance for their lives.

Elmer probably never saw his murderer. He died instantly.

McKenzie died in agony.

And then, his bloody work done, John Tornow, alleged slayer of the two men, closed the eyes of his victims, straightened their arms at their sides and went to

great pains to bury the bodies in such a manner that they should form a "T," the first initial of his last name, and to serve as a ghastly warning to others who might venture into the woods looking for him.

These are the conclusions of members of the posse, under Sheriff Edward Payette, who went into the Oxbow country of the Wynooche Valley on Thursday to reclaim the remains of the murdered men, and who returned last night with their task achieved.

McKenzie saw his slayer. This is proven by the look of agony on the face of the dead officer, the sheriff said. Elmer's face is tranquil, and there is no doubt but that he did not even hear the report of the gun, which caused his death.

Elmer was shot first, and but once, the ball from a .30-30 rifle entering his breast, plowing its way through his heart and coming out under the right arm pit.

McKenzie was shot twice. The first ball broke his collarbone, and the second ranged downward through his neck.

Elmer was probably killed just after he straightened up after stooping to walk under a fallen tree, and McKenzie was hit as he straightened up. Then, he was dispatched as he lay on the ground, the supposition being that his murderer approached to within a few feet of the wounded man to send in the last and fatal shot.

McKenzie did not die instantly. The face of the corpse was distorted and there was every evidence to show that he died in agony.

These facts are indicated by the location of the wounds and circumstances surrounding the location of the scene of the tragedy, according to Payette and Whiteside, acting as coroner for R. F. Hunter.

Washington State Archives

Members of a posse gather for a photo during the search for Tornow after he had killed deputies A. V. Elmer and Colin McKenzie. Charles Lathrop is on the far right.

Tornow buried his victims after taking certain articles of clothing more decently than could be expected of a maniac. The bodies were in good shape and were exhumed from only a few inches of earth that covered them.

Tornow buried the men in what is supposed to have been in accordance with a strange vagary of his diseased mind, in the form of a "T," Elmer's feet being close to McKenzie's side and his body extending at right angles from that of his companion. The men were buried almost on the spot where they fell.

The murderer stripped Elmer's body down to his underclothes. McKenzie's body was robbed of his woodsmen's shoes, paraffin trousers and hat. Arms and ammunition of both men were taken and pockets rifled. From McKenzie, Tornow took a .30 caliber Luger pistol, a Colt .38 caliber automatic pistol, equipped with a patent adjustable rear sight. Elmer carried a .25-20 Marlin carbine and one small compass, which Tornow took, along with all the ammunition carried by the men.

The sheriff theorized Tornow was on one side of his camp, and standing on a log, hidden by two small fir trees, growing out of the roots. He could see the men easily through a cleared space about 30 feet wide, on the far side of which they were standing. He evidently aimed through the slit in the log, picking off Elmer, then McKenzie.

The murderer's movements were traced by the posse, who found the shells which had been ejected from his rifle in reloading.

So cunningly was the camp arranged, that Tornow could move to and from his campfire unseen, from nearly any direction, yet at the same time keep a sharp lookout for intruders.

Those invading his camp were forced to walk on logs to make progress and all could be easily seen from his point of vantage.

Deputy Fitzgerald said the bodies were found in the North quarter of the South quarter of Section 18, Township 21, Range 7 West, and not 150 yards from the place where the elk's carcass lay. Heavy woods lie between the Oxbow trail and the scene of the murder.

In a cache found in Tornow's camp, were Elmer's hat, McKenzie's socks stolen from a cache that McKenzie had made, Tornow's old clothes, and about 50 pounds of dried meat. The cache was under a log and at the head of Tornow's bed, which was made from rotten wood covered with ferns. A fire pit stands in the center of an almost triangular space formed by windfalls and to one side is a well, a few feet deep and hollowed out with a stick to catch water.

Tornow is at large, believed to be wearing a small, yellow waterproof hat which he took from the body of McKenzie, woodsmen's caulked boots and paraffin pants he took from his victims and a blue woolen bobbed shirt, that Elmer had worn.

No posse has yet gone out to search further for the man. "Trappers are getting out of the woods around the Oxbow camp as rapidly as possible," the sheriff said. "Tornow is in control of the country, where the tragic deaths occurred, and likely will remain so. Anyone going into the country is warned to keep watch for, above all things, clusters of windfalls or fallen logs, in which Tornow has a habit of building his dugouts.

Seventeen men, including members of the first posse, which went out in the search for the deputies, trappers and other posse members added later, were involved in the search and recovery of the deputies' bodies.

The bodies were brought out Friday evening on horseback to the Neeby ranch. The posse then took them to the Shaughnessy ranch, where they were met by auto and arrived back in Aberdeen that night.

Among the posse members returning with the bodies last night were Sheriff Payette, deputies Royce, Swartz and Fitzgerald. Also returning were Carpenter, Pearsall, Whiteside, Getty, Shean, Stormes, Larson, Blair, McGillicuddy, Salmon and Cole. And the *World's* reporter.

Payette indicated he would suspend the posse the rest of the week, as many of the searchers were friends of the slain deputies and would like to attend their funerals. He is also awaiting word from Gov. Hay on the addition of a reward by the state for the capture of Tornow. The governor is in San Francisco, but due back any day.

Both funerals are scheduled Sunday in Aberdeen with elaborate heroes' ceremonies. The two deputies were both members of Pythian lodges, McKenzie at Wishkah No. 44, where the ceremony will be held, and Elmer at the Hoquiam lodge.

Meantime, on the same day as Cloud's story appeared in the *World*, was the revelation of a hoax that was perpetrated on two Harbor newspapers the day before.

"Snapshot" of John Tornow is Very good fake

The joke seems to be on the Grays Harbor News, a Hoquiam paper and the Grays Harbor Post, published in Aberdeen, which have printed "snapshots" of John Tornow, alleged murderer, within the last two or three days. The cut was first published in the News and later in the Post.

It is pronounced a fake, pure and simple, and the Washingtonian newspaper says "It is the ingenious work of Dr. Nail and Charles Davis, of the Harbor Engraving Company and Bert Pierson, the well known candy manufacturer of

Washington State Archives

The fake photo that the *Grays Harbor News* and *Grays Harbor Post* published, saying it was John Tornow. It appeared in March 1912.

Hoquiam, the three originators of the "stone man" hoax which had the people of the Harbor going during the Hoquiam carnival last fall.

The picture is that of Jack Ross, an old time friend of Pierson, and was taken while Ross was clearing Pierson's ranch near Humptulips. False hair and false beard, furnished by Pierson, who is an old theatrical man, gave Ross the haunted appearance of a genuine wild man, but a baseball bat held in his hands as he is crouching on the ground is scarcely calculated to inspire the hearts of those who view the "Tornow" picture with terror.

The picture was taken last fall soon after the murder of the Bauer boys at Satsop. The men in on the secret had a great deal of fun laughing over the fake, but didn't dream of palming it off on an unsuspecting press.

Day before yesterday, when the news came that the bodies of Elmer and McKenzie had been found, the joke was too good to keep, and the Harbor Engraving Company let the News know that the picture was in existence. With visions of scooping the other papers of the Harbor, the News jumped at the bait, and published a fake alongside a cut of McKenzie in Thursday afternoon's issue.

The Post was favorably impressed and also used the cut; doubtless wondering why other newspapermen of the Harbor were so slow to pass up the opportunity of publishing a genuine photograph of a real live murderer.

Friends of Ross recognized his face easily when the picture was published and word of the hoax passed from mouth to mouth until it was known all over Grays Harbor last night.

What was evident to those following the Tornow story, is that the man who was first a loner, then a fugitive, is now a "Wildman," yes, even a "Beast-Man."

28. DEPUTIES REVERED

March 26, 1912

Thousands, including many standing outside two Aberdeen buildings on Sunday afternoon, turned out to honor the memory of slain deputies, Colin McKenzie and A.V. Elmer, in impressive ceremonies. The two officers of the law were assassinated by John Tornow high in the Wynooche wilderness more than two weeks ago.

Citizens of all classes paid tribute to the dead men, where devotion to duty cost them their lives.

McKenzie's funeral was conducted by Wishkah Lodge, No. 44, Knights of the Pythias at the Pythian temple on First Street. Elmer's service was conducted by the Hoquiam lodge of Masons at the Whiteside Funeral Home.

In both instances, the rooms were packed to capacity long before the funerals started. Elmer's service was at 2 p.m., McKenzie's at 3, and more than 1,000 people assembled outside the temple in the street to pay tribute.

The caskets of both bodies were weighted with flowers from sorrowful friends and lodge members of their various fraternal orders of which the deputies had been members.

The Masons of Hoquiam were in charge of Elmer's funeral at the Whiteside chapel. A great throng gathered outside waiting to honor the memory of one of Tornow's victims. The Rev. T. W. Beard officiated. A long cortége followed the body to the gravesite in Aberdeen's Fern Hill cemetery.

Knights of Pythias conducted the funeral of McKenzie; Pythians met outside the lodge and marched to the Whiteside parlor, whence the body was escorted to the hall, and there an inspiring service was held.

The ceremony was in charge of J. E. Stewart, Chancellor Commander of the lodge. The Rev. F. W. Greene, pastor of St. Andrew's Episcopal

Church, provided the message that highlighted McKenzie's fealty and duty as officer of the law, while the church's choir, under the direction of W. O. McCaw, sang two beautiful hymns.

Greene, a personal friend of McKenzie as well as pastor, delivered a stirring eulogy from Luke 17, noting in particular "They have done that which was their duty to do."

After the service the body was escorted back to the undertaking parlor by pallbearers, Police Chief George Dean, S. A. Randolph, Robert Shean, C. T. Smith, Delbert Cassell and F. W. Loomis.

Many squadrons of police officers from throughout the county as well as hundreds of Pythian officers in full regalia from as far as Seattle and Portland were on hand.

The body was shipped to Vancouver, B. C., for interment at the Mountain View Cemetery, said Colin McKenzie's brother, Rod McKenzie, whose home is in Vancouver. McKenzie's parents live in Nova Scotia and were unable to attend the ceremony.

Accompanying a brief story on the funeral, the *Vidette* published Montesano resident Mary Philips Sutherland's tribute to the deputies:

OUR HEROES OF PEACE
Not to the beat of the heart-thrilling drum,
Not to the blare of the band,
But slipping away from life's busy hum
Into the silent land;
Hearing her voice, duty's call they obey.
Knowing chances but few for return.
With death stalking them like a fierce beast of prey.
Silent, relentless and stern.

Heroes of peace in honoring you
We honor each worker who strives.
The leaven of earth is the men who prove true
To the tasks that come into their lives.
With eyes that were clear to the danger ahead
But calmly accepting the same
As the day's work required, though the wilderness spread
Death broadcast, you played out the game.

McKenzie and Elmer were names singled out
To show us our heroes of peace;
But countless the number at work all about,
Quietly staking life's lease
Against duty's demands; a day's work each day
Are the steps in the pathway of life
That silently leads at the end of the way
To the crown that life grants for the strife.

———

The autopsy was performed on both deputies on Saturday with some new revelations as to the shooting of the two officers. Whiteside conducted the autopsy as Coroner Hunter was not available. His examination revealed that McKenzie had been shot three times and Elmer twice. Every indication, he said, "points to Tornow having used Elmer's rifle in firing the second shot into Elmer's body and the third and fatal shot into McKenzie."

Tornow shot at least one of his victims as he lay writhing on the ground. This is made certain, the deputy coroner noted, by the fact that the third shot fired into McKenzie's body entered at the back part of the neck, just over the right shoulder, and was fired at such close range that the powder burns were left on the flesh and part of the clothing driven far into the wound. The hole made by the bullet was so large it was impossible to determine from what caliber gun it had been fired.

Further, Whiteside said, McKenzie was first shot in the left shoulder, badly smashing the collar bone as the bullet ranged down through the heart and into the right lobe of the liver. This shot was with a .30-30, rifle, the same caliber, which Tornow is believed to have used to kill the Bauer twins. The second shot entered the left side, smashed through a rib and lodged in the right side near the 10th rib. When this bullet was extracted during the autopsy, it was proved to have been fired from a .25-25 caliber rifle, the same carried by Elmer.

The third shot is also supposed to have been fired from Elmer's rifle. It hit McKenzie in the back part of the shoulder nearly as high as the neck, severing the jugular vein and coming out on the right side about the seventh rib. This shot probably killed McKenzie instantly.

The coroner said there was some dispute over whether the first shot pierced McKenzie's heart. If this is not true, then death didn't come until the third shot, although the first two wounds could undoubtedly have been fatal.

Elmer was shot in the heart the first time. The bullet entered his body just over his heart, and came out under his left arm. The second shot seems to have been fired after Elmer had turned in a different position, for it entered the left side a little away from the first wound, and crossing diagonally over the path the first bullet took, coming out under the right arm.

Whiteside said the autopsy tends to show that Tornow fired from an elevated position on a log from behind some bushes, first at Elmer, then at McKenzie. Elmer fell, and McKenzie must have struggled on the ground. Tornow then, must have run out along a log and fired the second shot into Elmer's body as he lay on the ground, taking the rifle from him, then, firing twice more at McKenzie.

———

On the day of the funeral, the *Tacoma Ledger* printed a poignant editorial decrying the murder of the two deputies who died as brave heroes while doing their duties as officers of the law:

TWO CHEHALIS COUNTY HEROES

Colin McKenzie, deputy sheriff, and A.V. Elmer, game warden, murdered while in pursuit of a desperate Chehalis County outlaw, will be remembered in Southwest Washington as men who died for the law. John Tornow, with the blood of his two youthful nephews on his hands — a man who has lived all his life in the woods, and is known as a dead shot — is their supposed slayer, and is still at large in the deep woods, from which he may never be taken alive.

His life or death, freedom or imprisonment, is in itself a little thing compared to the lives of the two brave officers slain in his pursuit, but they were ready to face death for the protection of their fellows, the noblest cause in which a man may die.

When Tornow, a former inmate of an asylum, fled into the forest last fall, after slaying his nephews, there were many who gave chase. As the weeks and months dragged on without his being found, these returned to their ordinary pursuits, and, except for McKenzie and Elmer, the chase was practically abandoned. Several times, in their expeditions into the woods, these two officers were gone longer than expected, and their friends were alarmed for their safety. Always they came back. However, on this last expedition, even after they had been missing nearly two weeks, the hope was clung to that this latest alarm would prove as needless as the others. Elmer was an expert woodsman and both men of the fiber to give good account of themselves.

The finding of their bodies in the shallow graves scooped for them by their slayer, reveals a tragedy indeed. But it should only spur others on to accomplish what they so bravely attempted — the capture of the monster roaming the Chehalis County woods.

We have been taught to revere the men fallen in battle to give the nation liberty and preserve the Union. The officer of the law serves in a common cause. He gives his life that thousands of others may feel safety and security; that his fellows may be guaranteed life, liberty and pursuit of happiness. We have been given much false honor to the outlaws of old time. Let us honor the men who give their lives running down the criminals of today.

One day after the funerals, interesting developments began occurring in the search for John Tornow. Sheriff Payette received word that Tornow was at Pacific Beach last winter, the coastal community some 20 miles west of Aberdeen. He received mail there, but it is not known whether it was delivered to him by a friend or sent to the dead letter office. There is a trail heading from the Oxbow country through Humptulips

Plaque in the Grays Harbor County Courthouse honors slain deputies A. V. Elmer and Colin McKenzie.

and from there to the ocean beach, so the trip from the headwaters of the Wynooche or Satsop rivers would not be a hardship for him.

Payette said he was sure Tornow was receiving help and was being furnished with supplies by one or more friends The sheriff also said he is certain the fugitive has not been outside the territory to get provisions, as he has scouts at various outposts to report any findings.

Meanwhile, the undertaker said Tornow was likely watching them take out the bodies of McKenzie and Elmer, an eerie thought. "I have no doubt that Tornow saw us take up the bodies and prepare them for burial," said Whiteside. "The country is so wild that an inexperienced man can see but for a little distance. Tornow's eyes are so trained in the woods and he can easily see twice as far as any man sent in against him. More than that, his hearing is acute, as is that of all men who live long in the woods, and he is able to hear an approaching party long before they come in sight."

Payette wants the county to pay for the funerals of the deputies. "The state pays for funerals of its soldiers, and I believe that the county should bear the expense of the funerals for those deputies killed while performing their duties. Popular opinion is that the relatives and friends of Elmer and McKenzie should be relieved from payment of funeral expenses."

Two days after the funerals, Payette received the word he had been anticipating from the governor, but his plea was only partially granted. He had requested $1,000 for the Bauer boys' killer and $1,000 for the murderer of the deputies. Gov. M. E. Hay issued a reward proclamation, saying he believed the reward would be an inducement to get trained woodsmen involved in the search.

"Whereas, the said John Tornow, alleged slayer of William and John Bauer and deputies, Colin McKenzie and A. V. Elmer, is said to be hiding in the Olympic Mountains and terrorizing the territory with his murderous mania ... I hereby declare by the power invested in me, to offer a reward of $1,000 for the capture of said John Tornow."

That brought the price on the head of the "Wildman of the Wynooche" to $5,000.

With that in mind, Payette set about putting together a posse to take up the search. He said seven or eight men, all friends of the deputies, will go, with the sanction of Payette, into the woods in search of Tornow.

Payette said he didn't want any "tenderfeet involved, only experienced woodsmen familiar with the country they have to traverse, will be allowed to invade the locality where Tornow is known to be possibly hiding."

As evidence of his seriousness, he sent out via mail and by telegram, bulletins to many, many sheriff's offices, not just in the Northwest, but as far as Los Angeles, Calif., Phoenix, Ariz., Lima, Ohio, and Houston, Texas. The bulletin detailed the crimes, reward money and one other note: "I am seeking bloodhounds to aid in the search, not just any bloodhounds, but vicious, man-eating hounds. Please wire or call if interested."

He said the reward money — $2,000 by the county for the slayer of the Bauer twins, $2,000 by the county for the killer of the deputies and $1,000 by the state — has brought "people out of the woodwork" to participate.

Payette said he has been besieged by offers of help from sheriffs and deputies all over the country to countless folks with no experience at all. "Everybody wants a piece of that pie," the sheriff said. "I've had calls and telegrams from officers as far as Houston, Texas; Lima, Ohio; Biloxi, Miss.; and Laramie, Wyo. My sheriff's files are filled with all these letters of assistance. Of course, most are not worth the paper they are written on, but some are. I'm listening to everyone at this point."

Washington State Archives

A sheriff's officer holds bloodhounds used in the search for Tornow.

Payette was recently made aware of a dangerous situation surrounding the Simpson Logging Co., which is expecting to lay new railroad tracks in the vicinity of where the deputies were slain and have had timber cruisers in that area this week. He was told the workers are nearly done with the logging and preparation, but are doing it with a wary eye.

"The job boss said he wasn't worried," the sheriff noted. "He didn't think Tornow would bother them, if he is in the area. He's after deputies and posses, not loggers, the man told me. I just told them to hurry up and finish and get out of the area. I couldn't be responsible for their health."

Meantime, the *Grays Harbor Washingtonian* in Hoquiam sent a reporter to South Bend, about 28 miles south of Aberdeen, to interview Ed Tornow, who had recently married and moved there from Porter.

Their story had some interesting comments from John's youngest brother in their May 4, 1912, edition:

SOUTH BEND — *E. W. Tornow, brother of John Tornow, the presumably crazed slayer of his twin nephews, and later of the two deputies, Colin McKenzie and A. V. Elmer, who got too close to his hiding place in the woods north of Grays Harbor, is of the opinion that it is useless to pursue him; that the fugitive will simply not be taken alive, and that the only hope of capturing him is to keep a watch for him when he comes out of the woods after supplies. Mr. Tornow and his brother, W. M. Tornow, are carpenters here and the former has just completed a bungalow for himself near the Broadway schoolhouse.*

"My brother John has always been a lover of the woods since he was a boy," said E. W. Tornow. "Once while out on a trapping expedition he had the measles and did not know what was the matter with him. He caught cold and became seriously ill. He was sent to a sanitarium in Portland and his mind was affected apparently at that time. Though they treated him well at the sanitarium he took a dislike to it and declared that once he was again in the woods he would never be taken alive into such a place. I made a search for him seven months ago, but would not think of going into the woods after him at this time. He will be harder to run down than Tracy ever was. He has always been a crack shot since he was a boy, and he has the advantage of his pursuers because he can watch their movements and get the drop on them. I warned Deputy Sheriff McKenzie of his probable fate, but he was confident of his ability to get my brother. As for the killing of his nephews, John and Will Bauer, I think someone besides him was implicated."

Payette said that was the first time he had heard anything about Tornow being in a sanitarium as a younger man. "I know from the family that he had measles as a youngster and that affected him some, but never heard anything about later. I think you have to consider the source. Edward is the one who took out the warrant against his brother. He'd do just about anything to disparage him," the sheriff told Cloud when he called about the *Washingtonian's* article.

In the weeks after the funeral, word of "Tornow sightings" were popping up all over the Northwest.

In one instance, a bedraggled, weather-beaten, armed stranger, caused a wave of excitement at a wharf in Seattle when he stepped down the gangplank from a boat that arrived from Shelton. The crowd at the wharf became frightened, thinking it might be the wanted man.

Two policemen on duty, immediately drew their revolvers and pounced on the unsuspecting man, who protested indignantly. "Don't resist or it will go hard with you," the officer told the suspect, who was cuffed and led away.

At the police station, where the man was being booked, a friend arrived to say that the man's name was James G. West, a trapper from Shelton, and not the fugitive hermit.

West was irate. "If I was an outlaw, do you honestly think I would come into town in this outfit," he demanded. The policemen, and all those at the headquarters, humbly apologized for their gaffe, then drove the gentlemen trapper to a nearby hotel. They paid his bill.

In another situation, a day after the Seattle incident, Tornow was believed to have stopped at the home of Manley Baker at Cedar Flats, six miles west of Olympia. Baker said the man volunteered no information, only asking for something to eat. He even said he would cut wood to pay for his food, so Baker let him. The farmer described the intruder as young, with long, matted hair to his shoulders. He wore three coats and three pairs of trousers. The man appeared thin. He said the man was about 34, quite tall and when food was put in front of him, "he ate it ravenously, almost like an animal, rather than a human being."

Baker said he hadn't heard of the murderer, but his appearance frightened his wife and two children. He thought nothing of it until he was talking with a neighbor, who informed him of the Tornow circumstances. Baker notified the police, but said he didn't know which direction the man left, saying "when he finished cutting wood, he just disappeared."

The *Chehalis County Vidette* was the first to publish a picture of Tornow. The cut, published April 5, 1912, was taken from a photograph and shows the outlaw with his brother, Fred. John is about 18, and while the photo is quite dark, it shows the outline of the young man, his brother, a bicycle and several dogs. It was taken at the Tornow homestead in the Upper Satsop Valley.

It does offer pure evidence that the photo that appeared in the *Grays Harbor Post* and *Grays Harbor News*, was a definite fake. The *Vidette* says "all who knew Tornow will recognize him and know this picture is genuine."

Polson Museum collection

John Tornow, left, is shown with his brother, Ed, with their dogs and a bicycle in a rare photo of John prior to his death.

Incidents occurred almost daily throughout the end of April, and on numerous occasions posse members felt they had Tornow in their sights, only to come away disappointed and even more frustrated.

On April 13, Aberdeen attorney Dan Pearsall and some friends were hunting in the headwaters of the Wynooche. Pearsall said he may have seen Tornow, called out to a gentleman he believed was Jack Winslow, a member of his party. Whether it was Tornow or not, the man turned and ran away when he heard Pearsall's voice.

Aberdeen taxidermist George Newman, who was with Pearsall's group until he was scalded with hot coffee and had to return home, reported the hunting party and posse have joined forces and are now high above the Oxbow near the Wynooche headwaters at another big bend in the river.

Newman said Pearsall had become separated from the hunting party and was atop a ridge when he called down into a gulley to the man. He said he doubted it was Tornow, even though the man turned and ran. "Some people in our group had concerns about Pearsall's story, or at least doubted it was Tornow. If it had been him, he would have likely shot, not run. Others say it could have been him. Tornow might have realized he was in a disadvantage, being in a gulch, and would more naturally flee to a safer location."

Newman also reported that the posse is certain they found Tornow's fire. He wasn't specific how they knew it was his, only to say there are certain peculiarities which led to their theory. They believed Tornow had shot an elk to provide meat as they found no food caches at either one of two shelters they discovered. But they did find about 40 pounds of meat hanging on one of the smaller wind shields, they believe Tornow erected.

Two days later, Pearsall and Jack Cross returned to Montesano and declared emphatically that Tornow was still in the Wynooche area.

"There seems to be little, if any chance for failure. He may get one or two of them, but he will be taken," Pearsall stated to Cloud.

They brought back a burlap sack full of items they had procured from four different shelters Tornow had occupied. In the bag were several items Tornow had taken from McKenzie and Elmer, along with Tornow's old shoes that were evidently replaced by those taken from the deputies, and a rough-hewn paddle Tornow could have used to dig the graves of his victims. McKenzie's handcuffs and keys, along with Elmer's axe and holster, were also brought back. They also returned with hides from two black bears.

Only one posse is now out on the search, but it numbers about a dozen men, including several friends of the deputies. Among them are some who had been with the original posse searching for the deputies, including Larson, Stormes, Cole, Getty, Winslow and a new

Washington State Archives

This structure in the Wynooche area is typical of the lean-tos built by Tornow.

face in the group, Charles Lathrop, a railroad man and trapper from Dayton, west of Shelton.

Lathrop was recruited because he had hunted with Tornow and knew his traits as well as what he looked like.

Pearsall said he and Cross and two members of the posse continued north and within four miles of their camp found another site, which they believed was occupied last fall by Tornow. Here, they are also found fresh tracks. He said the camp was constructed similar to that of the first one.

The next day, Pearsall and Cross joined the hunters, who had now hooked up with the posse. After taking up the trail only a short time later, the dogs treed a bear, a small one. Winslow and Cole were with Pearsall and Cross. While looking for the bear, the party became scattered, but Pearsall said a single shot would be fired when the dogs were found. He said, while waiting with Cross, they heard a shot about 300 yards away.

"We figured it was from either Cole or Winslow," Pearsall said. "But, it wasn't. When the four of us met, we found out neither one had fired a shot."

"Do you think it was Tornow?" Cloud asked.

"Maybe, but there's more," the attorney said. "While we were sitting on a small knoll awaiting our companions, I fired a shot in the air as a signal. Several hundred yards away, we saw a man emerge from the underbrush. He was well concealed and we believed it was either Cole or Winslow. I called to him and he took off in the brush. We later found out neither of our guys were in that vicinity. We just couldn't see very clear because of the dense forest and poor light."

"Did you go after him when your other members returned and you found out it wasn't them?" asked Cloud.

"No, because it was a while before they returned and the mystery man was long gone," Pearsall answered.

Payette said the entire stretch of country in the upper Wynooche is inhabited only by Tornow and members of the posse. Pearsall said the "party's camp is cunningly located on a small hillock and it is practically impossible for any person to enter that district without being seen by the man-hunters. All of the posse and hunters are experienced woodsmen and not afraid of anything. Between these two groups, they have traveled the country immediately from the place where Elmer and McKenzie's bodies were found until they know the entire district like a book."

Payette said the plan is for the party to maneuver about that district and keep careful watch for Tornow's campfires. As soon as one is discovered, the party will take observation of the location of the fire, and during the early morning, close in upon the camp. It is believed with this strategy, the outlaw can be taken alive.

About a week later, several members of the posse, including two from Aberdeen, were awaiting a connection near the Wishkah River, west of the Wynooche, when they heard four shots they figured were about a mile away. The group didn't have time to investigate the rapid-fire gun shots, but reported it immediately upon arriving at a nearby camp.

By the first week of May, newspapers throughout the Northwest had editorialized on the situation.

A letter to the editor published by the *Vidette* in its May 3 edition, is an example of what the slain deputies meant to the communities of Grays Harbor. The letter is from Prof. Eldredge Wheeler of Montesano to the editor of the *Grays Harbor Post*, which published an opinion piece on the deputies in its April 27 edition. The *Vidette* noted that Prof. Wheeler, "who has more than any other man in Chehalis County, worked to perpetuate the memory of Capt. Robert Gray and other heroes, whose names are inseparably linked with the history of the Grays Harbor country, was a warm, personal friend of each of the dead deputies. In his letter, Wheeler offered some suggestions which this paper believes should be taken up by the public-spirited citizens of this harbor country."

Editor of the Post:

Some weeks since, the people of this country were shocked to hear of the tragic deaths of two brave deputies, who in performance of their duties, lost their lives in an attempt to capture the outlaw, John Tornow.

These men are laid to rest, one in your city, and the other in British Columbia, and I suppose that a modest monument will mark the last resting place of each, yet it is sad to know that neither leaves any members of a family here, who would sometimes strew the graves with flowers and give the loving tribute of tears.

In the performance of duty, these men met death. Not in charge of battle, fighting under our flag, but met it just as bravely in the dense forests of this county. No soldier on the battlefield died more bravely. No soldier fought in a cause more worthy.

I feel that the citizens of Chehalis County should not let time efface the memories of these men. They died for preservation of order in attempting to capture a desperate man.

I wish to suggest that this is a fitting time, that the friends of these deputies, as well as those who feel that their memories should be perpetuated as an example of

noble heroism, unite to procure and to place in a suitable place, a memorial tablet of bronze to commemorate the heroic virtues of A. V. Elmer and Colin McKenzie.
Sincerely yours,
Eldredge Wheeler

Wheeler said he would establish a committee for the memorial and accept donations through either newspaper. The *Vidette* also told Wheeler that Elmer did have a local brother, Wesley of Hoquiam.

Also on May 3, a letter arrived at the sheriff's office from posse member Winslow that they are hot on Tornow's trail.

"We have found fresh tracks of Tornow and we intend to stick here until we get him," Winslow wrote in a letter that was delivered by Pearsall to the sheriff.

This word was a welcome relief for Payette. The posse members were instructed to give a weekly report of some kind, but the sheriff hadn't heard from anyone in almost two weeks. When Deputy Sheriff Fitzgerald was in Aberdeen two days ago and reported he had no information, Payette registered much concern. At that point, the sheriff and his deputy decided to wait three more days before sending out more men to search for those already on the hunt.

Payette said there are still seven men taking up the search. "They are well-armed and have provisions to last several months, but I need to hear from them, to know they are safe." He also said he has to try and monitor the territory because, since the announcement of the reward became public, it has driven many woodsmen further into the wilderness.

The sheriff said, if Tornow is not captured by the summer, he plans to organize a more systematic search of the entire district.

Later on the same day, Payette received a call from Cougar Smith, a rancher living seven miles below the Oxbow. Smith believes Tornow is in the vicinity. Smith stated he heard a rifle shot fired Wednesday evening among his cattle grazing near his ranch buildings. He did not make an investigation, except to note that none of his cattle had gone missing. He reported the matter to the sheriff as quickly as possible.

There is no certainty the shot was fired by Tornow, but Payette took immediate steps to investigate.

Not much new information was reported for the next two weeks until the *Washingtonian*, in an interview with Sheriff Payette in its May

17 edition, reported that Tornow had been driven out of the Oxbow
and Satsop areas east into Mason County.

*He was seen and recognized by loggers at an abandoned camp of the
Simpson Logging company near the county line Wednesday afternoon, and struck
northeastward into the timber from there.*

*The posse of seven woodsmen, which has hunted the man for several weeks, is
already on its way to take up the hermit's new trail, it is believed, and Sheriff Lou
Sanderson of Mason County, with a posse, will join in the hunt at once. Deputies
A. L. Fitzgerald and Carl Swartz left yesterday for the Oxbow district to find the
posse and start them on the new scent.*

*Wednesday afternoon a party of men from the Simpson Logging Company's
Camp No. 1, west of Shelton, went to camp No. 5, which was abandoned last
Sunday, and as they approached, Tornow, armed with a rifle, came out of one of
the buildings, crossed the clearing and disappeared into the timber to the north. He
was recognized by the men, by whom he is known. The direction he took would carry
him into Mason County.*

*Yesterday morning Supt. Berry of the logging company called Sheriff Payette
and told him of Tornow's presence. At once, Deputies Swartz and Fitzgerald left by
auto for the Oxbow country, where the posse has been trailing Tornow. They should
have arrived in the vicinity in time to find the posse and get them started across to
where Tornow was seen, 20 miles to the east, Sheriff Payette believes.*

Sheriff Payette believes Tornow has found it too hot for him in the
Oxbow country and has sought to throw off his pursuers by slipping
away, and that he probably went into the abandoned camp in hope of
finding something to eat. For several weeks, the fugitive has been hard-
pressed by the seven expert woodsmen who have continually sought
him.

Several times, they have been close after him, but never quite up to
him. Numerous times they have come upon his camps, once with his
fire still burning, and at other occasions after the man had been gone
only a few hours. He has been driven away from his camps and from
his caches of meat. The elk herds have been carefully trailed by the
pursuers in the hope Tornow would be driven to kill an elk for food
and his whereabouts could be located. The men have been constantly
on the go, from early morning to late at night and often far into the
night, seeking traces of the fiend of the woods.

The posse has a large pack of dogs and with the new trail to start from, high hopes are entertained of running the hunted man to earth.

———

As the hunt for Tornow entered its ninth month, the Board of Chehalis County Commissioners made a decision that the search would be abandoned by June 15, despite the pleas of Payette and the posse, which is now in the Oxbow vicinity and requested the manhunt continue at least until July 1.

The commissioners told Cloud the posse has been too great an expense to the county and that continuing the search would be without result.

"What that means," said Sheriff Payette, "is that Tornow will be practically free from molestation in the vast territory to the north. During the past month, there have been no confirmed signs of the fugitive. There have been reports of strange men appearing and some fresh tracks, but nothing official.

"It's likely all the fresh tracks and strange men are owing to the reward and the many bounty hunters out there. Only a few experienced hunters and trappers, who have lived in the upper country for years, will know what they are doing, and we have picked up a few of them for our posse. For the others, it's my opinion that should a capture be attempted, the game will be played between Tornow and some hardened woodsmen familiar with the conditions in the timbered districts."

The sheriff also said he gave little credit to the report that Tornow crossed over into Mason County. "Sheriff Sanderson checked it out and found nothing."

The sheriff said he is disappointed that the search will be discontinued. "I firmly believe we should continue. Look at it this way, June and July are relatively dry in the high country and you'd think that would undoubtedly force him from the hills to the valleys in search of food and water."

"Makes sense, sheriff," Cloud responded.

"Ask any hunter or trapper and they'll tell you during the dry summer months, elk and bear seek more sheltered portions of the woods. This being the case, Tornow would likely find it to his advantage to live near the streams, where he would be given a better chance to secure game and fresh water."

The sheriff said Jack Winslow will remain in the Oxbow area through summer and fall as fire warden for timber owners. "He has been with the posse for several months and is an experienced woodsman, thoroughly familiar with the country, which is supposed to be occupied by Tornow," the sheriff said.

———

About a week later, a well-known criminologist, W. E. Graham, stopped by to chat with Cloud and share his opinion on what his experience has shown about the patterns exhibited by criminals, such as Tornow.

Graham, who lives in Denver, had been visiting his sister, Mrs. T. I. Pemberton in Aberdeen. He is one of the top sleuths in the Western United States. He said he had made no investigation of the Tornow case, and knew only what he has read in the paper. But, he upholds the opinion of several officers that, if the outlaw is captured, he will be caught within a short distance of the Tornow home.

"It has been my experience that the criminal, who successfully evades capture, will eventually return to this former haunts," said Graham. "This however, might be an exceptional case. I have studied criminology, and I find that this condition prevails in almost nine cases out of 10. Should the search for the man be given up, and is considered unsuccessful, the criminal is more than likely to come back to his former home. The same condition is true with a person committing either a murder or a robbery.

"After leaving the scene of the crime, and after discovering that his capture is only a matter of time, he becomes curious and wishes to view it again. In other words, convince himself of the thoroughness of his job. I do not say, mind you, that Tornow will return, but I do say that the chance for his capture is just as good in the immediate vicinity of his home, as it is in that dense wilderness. Time will tell whether my theory is correct or not."

Graham had left Cloud's office only a few minutes when the phone rang. It was Sheriff Payette.

"I know you weren't at the commission meeting today and I wanted to advise you of an appointment I made," the sheriff said. "I presented to the board the name of George Stormes to be the new game warden for Chehalis County, replacing Elmer. The commission concurred."

"That's great, sheriff. You couldn't have made a better choice. He hasn't been in the county long, has he, but he has sure been active? In fact, it was George who discovered the bodies of Elmer and McKenzie, wasn't it?"

"You are right, Dan. He was one of them. Good memory. He has been with the posse about five months, but he knows the area very well, like a book. He is capable in every way of filling that position."

The sheriff then told Cloud about a misfortune that Stormes suffered after the position was approved by the county commissioners.

"I guess he was celebrating or something and he was hurt in a motorcycle accident, not serious, but painful."

"What happened?" the scribe asked.

"As I understand it, he and Deputy Fitzgerald hopped on Fitzgerald's motorcycle and set out for the coast. Near Cosmopolis, the machine fell from the graveled road and both men and the machine tumbled into a ditch. They were able to right the machine and get it back on the road. A few hours later, when they were eating lunch, George collapsed from pain in his back. A physician was summoned, but George said he was OK by the time the doc arrived. He said he was much improved when I talked to him an hour ago."

"Thankfully, he wasn't hurt bad," said Cloud. "Thankfully, too, he'll be on horseback as game warden and not on one of those machines."

"One more thing, Dan. The commissioners won't reconsider their decision to stop all funding for the posse, so they will be out there two more days, then I'm pulling all seven of them in. They won't be getting paid anything after Saturday."

"Thanks, sheriff. I know it's been a source of frustration for you, but I guess I can see the commissioners' point. There's a lot of money going out for the posse with no result. I guess you have to draw the line somewhere. I'll continue to check in with you, and of course, I'll be at most commission meetings."

"OK, Dan. Hey, how's that good looking girl you had with you the other day?"

"Lindy? She's fine. In fact, I'm going to write this stuff up and get out of here. I'm sure she'll be glad the search is suspended. We'll be able to spend more time together."

Dan hung up the phone and called Lindy to let her know of his plan to write the story and then pick her up."

"I'll be ready, dear. I can't wait to see you. Hurry it up, please."

Cloud quickly recapped all that the sheriff told him earlier about Stormes' appointment, his accident and the conversation with the criminologist. He wished all of his stories were as cut-and-dry as this one. Within a half-hour, he was out the door and on the way to meet Lindy.

They enjoyed a nice dinner at the Washington and Dan suggested going to the Grand to see "Camille" with Sarah Bernhardt. "I had hoped you'd ask me. I've been wanting to see that," she said. "I'm surprised you know about her."

"Well, I don't know about her, but I heard the guys at your office talking about it. Thomas, Sgt. Delahanty, said 'Don't miss it.'"

"She is probably the most famous actress in the world, right now and she has been doing it for 40 years. Most of her acting was in France for silent films, but the last 10 years or so, she has been acting in American theaters."

Dan shared the news that the search would be suspended by the weekend with Lindy. As he talked, she beamed across the table at her man.

"I'm glad to hear that. It's been going on for so long and no results. So, maybe I'll see more of you, do you think?"

"That's the plan. You'll probably see a whole lot more of me."

"Promises, promises. That's all I get. Now let's get going, or we'll be late for the movie," she said, hustling Dan toward the door.

"Then, we'll work on your promises."

29. CONSPIRACY THEORIES

Summer 1912

True to his word, Sheriff Payette pulled the posse out of the search, and now it's been six weeks since any word of Tornow has appeared in the local papers, or any papers, for that matter. The last word was a brief notation from Deputy Sheriff Jack Winslow saying he was virtually certain the outlaw had fled the Oxbow country and was not within many miles of that area.

Winslow didn't know where the fugitive might be, but said, after talking to attorney Dan Pearsall and Deputy Sheriff Jack Cross, "We have covered pretty much all of the territory where we knew he had camped and found no signs of him. We hadn't seen a clue since we found the campfire burning some time ago. We talked to many hunters and trappers, who had been in the Oxbow territory and not one of them said they had seen anything or even heard anything about him."

Then Dan Cloud, the erstwhile *Aberdeen Daily World* reporter, unloaded a stunning revelation after sitting down with a couple of foresters from the Quinault country, who shed an entirely different view on John Tornow from what had been published in the *World* thus far.

Following is his report in the *World* on July 24, 1912.

WARDENS THINK TORNOW FREE OF MURDERS' TAINT

Quinault Woodsmen Question
Guilt of Fugitive

Factors in Slaying of Bauer
Twins and Deputies

Analyzed; Hermit Not
Vindictive; Poachers May be Guilty

Holding to the belief that John Tornow, supposed slayer of his nephews, the Bauer twins and Deputy Sheriff Colin McKenzie and game warden A. V. Elmer, is not now in the Oxbow country of the Wynooche Valley north of Montesano, and has not been since the deaths of the deputies. Forest fire wardens in the Quinault country take radically different views regarding the supposed outlaw than are generally entertained.

In a recent statement at Humptulips, one of several fire wardens in that section, declared that, if John Tornow was to make his appearance at the county seat and deny responsibility in any of the killings, no jury could be found that could conscientiously give a verdict of guilty against him.

The wardens base their views on the alleged declaration of Tornow that when he went from Montesano after taking some of his money from the bank, he said he would never return and he proposed to live the life of a hermit.

One of the wardens, who said that he had worked alongside Tornow, describes the man as practically inoffensive, queer in his notions and actions, but without any of the malice or vindictive spirit which have been attributed to him.

They account for the killing of the Bauer twins, if done by Tornow, as an act of self-defense. They argue on the theory that the Bauer boys, who were hunting, may have tracked a bear and in shooting possibly sent several bullets wild and into the cabin of Tornow or near where he may have stood. Tornow, believing he was being made a target, returned the fire. The wardens are not willing to admit that Tornow maliciously shot to kill the two young men.

Summing up their opinions in the McKenzie-Elmer case, the wardens say that they would much rather believe that the deputy sheriffs were killed by men, who had been violating the law with respect to the killing of elk and other game, and of killing cattle, rather than by Tornow.

The wardens say there are more desperate men in the wilds of Chehalis County than even Tornow might eventually prove himself to be, noting that "Elmer was feared and hated by men, who had made a practice of killing elk and stealing cattle. These men were only waiting a favorable opportunity of getting even. I would rather meet Tornow in the woods today, and take my chances with him than to take a chance with any of those men I speak of, if I came across them with an elk or the carcass of some rancher's cow."

The fact that the shoes and the clothes of the deputies had been taken, proves nothing against Tornow. He is a man of immense stature and could not wear the shoes of either McKenzie or Elmer. He would require at least a No. 10. The clothes would have been far too small. Then regarding the peculiar marking of the deputies' graves, "from what I know of Tornow, he would not have shown the vindictive spirit or the fatal idiocy involved in placing the bodies in the form of a 'T;' that 'T' indicates to me more than anything that Tornow did not kill them."

"That's interesting and everyone is entitled to their opinion," said Sheriff Ed Payette when contacted after the interview. "I do hold some credence to what they say, because of their experience in dealing with poachers and other law violators on a regular basis. But, for us, we stand by our belief that he is the alleged suspect, and all information we have studied, all the evidence points in Tornow's direction, nowhere else.

"We have spent a lot of money and more than 10 months in the woods searching for this man. Don't you think, we would stop what we are doing, if we felt he might not be guilty? I think not."

"That should get tongues to waggin'" the scribe said to himself after preparing the story for the press.

Later that week, Cloud decided to travel to Matlock to attend the monthly community meeting and Sunday brunch at the Grange.

"Hi, Dan. What brings you all the way up here?" queried August Maas when seeing the scribe walk in the door.

"Just curious. I know you guys have these monthly meetings and I am curious about what you think or have to say about the search for John."

"Talk to Ed. You know Ed Schaletzke, don't you?"

"Yes, I met him at the boys' funeral. Why, what's he know?"

"He runs our meetings and we always talk about the search. I think you'll be surprised."

Dan Cloud walked to the other side of the room where Ed Schaletzke, the close friend of the Tornow family, was conversing with two other gentlemen.

"You're Dan Cloud, aren't you?"

"Yes, and you're Ed Schaletzke, right?"

"Yep, that's me. I met you at the funeral."

"Yes, I remember now, but I met so many people that day."

"What can I do for you?"

"Well, I wanted to come up here and find out what the community folks have to say about this search for John Tornow, and since you have monthly Grange meetings, I figured this would be like one-stop shopping."

"I'll tell you, Dan, we would love to get our opinions out about this witch-hunt. Nobody really listens to us. So, I run this meeting and what I'm going to do is turn it over to you and you can ask all the questions you want. Get ready to be surprised."

"Thanks, Mr. Schaletzke. That sounds like it will work out well."

With that, Schaletzke moved to the podium and announced he was turning the meeting over to Dan Cloud. "Now give him a big Matlock greeting," he announced.

After a generous applause, Cloud stepped on stage, then took a seat on the ledge.

"Thanks for this opportunity," said Cloud, addressing the gathering of about 70 people at the Grange hall, just down the street from the Matlock Grocery, the hub of the tiny community.

"Folks, I'm interested in hearing what you think about this search for John Tornow, or as Ed Schaletzke told me, a 'witch-hunt.' First, let me ask this. How many believe John Tornow killed the Bauer boys?"

Only two hands went up.

"How many think he is the killer of the deputies?"

A few more hands went up, but clearly the majority of the room believed him to be innocent of killing anybody.

"That's interesting. Now, I'll ask and you can stand, say your name and share who did it."

One-by-one, the community members stood and spouted their opinions on the murderer or murderers.

"Bauer, the Tornow brothers, Ed Tornow, unknown trappers, poachers, Abel, the shyster lawyer. It's a conspiracy. It's a land deal gone bad. It was a set-up."

"OK. Now tell me if you would try to help out Tornow, if given the opportunity."

About two-dozen raised their hands.

"Now, tell me if you have ever left any supplies or food for Tornow."

About a dozen raised their hands.

"I've done it many times and I'll do it again," said Charlie Kohlmeier, standing before the group. "We all loved the family and we still love John. We don't believe he did the things he is suspected of doing. I've left him food. I've left him ammo. I've left him clothes — large clothes."

"And he's taken all these things?"

"Yes, sir. He sure has. Many times, so those stories about him not being in this area are pure bullshit. I guess I better say bull crap for the papers."

"Yes, he was at my house just last week," said Herbert Hearing. "My little girl, Dora, woke up and told me she heard a noise. I went out and saw John taking a burlap bag full of potatoes I left for him. He gave us some wonderful elk steaks. I gave him a thumbs-up, went back in and calmly told my girl 'don't worry, honey, it's just John Tornow. Go back to sleep.' We don't fear him."

"He was at our house before Minnie left for California," said August Maas. "Minnie didn't talk to him, but knew he was there because the sack she left for him was gone."

"John has been a friend of this community, all of us in this room, for many years. We know of his love of the woods and his ability to exist in it," said Albert Kuhnle. "We are not afraid of him, like others in the Wynooche might be. This is his home. He grew up here and knows all of us."

"Has anyone ever harbored John Tornow since he became a wanted man?" Cloud asked.

The room was silent, then a gentleman near the back slowly stood up.

"I have, once," said Chris Muller. "It was early this spring and he had just come out from being in the upper country. He said he was returning to the homestead for one last time. I told him the place had been sold. It was late in the evening and I offered to let him stay in the barn. He didn't hesitate. I think it might have been the first sheltered rest he had in months. I cut his hair and he took a bath. He and I are nearly the same size, so I gave him some clothes and would have given him boots, but his feet are too big, then I retired to sleep. He was gone when I got up in the morning. I haven't seen him since."

"Folks, I thank you so much. I have a much better picture of what you think, and I admire you for your faith in John. I trust you are right," the reporter concluded.

————

Over the next few weeks, Tornow (or folks who might have resembled him) turned up in various locations in Chehalis County, and even farther east in Olympia in Thurston County.

On August 8, Frank Miller of Tacoma, was hunting bear along the Deschutes River, southeast of Olympia, when he was startled by a sudden "ping" of two bullets that came dangerously close to him. He scampered into the dense woods that lined the river, got back under cover, returned to his camp and reported the incident to the sheriff as soon as he could. He told the sheriff, according to the *Olympian* newspaper, that he was sure it was Tornow, though he never saw the shooter.

Sheriff Fennell made a trip to the scene, inspected the area for two days and reported finding no evidence.

Six days later, a more plausible appearance may have occurred when four men returning from playing ball in Matlock, reported a long-haired, bearded man appeared out of the brush not 200 yards from the old Tornow homestead in Satsop. They were in their automobile on Sunday afternoon and paused long enough to get a good look.

"We yelled out, almost in unison, 'That's Tornow,'" said Francis Gleason, son of James Gleason of Satsop, who called Sheriff Payette. The young man said "the creature was standing in a hollow and they couldn't see his lower body," but he said he was recognizable as one who had been in the woods a long time. Gleason said his limbs were clothed in rags. He could not see his shoes."

Francis Gleason states the man was not carrying a rifle, but he didn't know if he might have a revolver. Young Gleason said they did not stop the car, but hurried on and told his father, a well-known rancher and county commissioner.

"I know it's Tornow. I've seen him and what my son and the others describe, it sure sounds like it is him," said the elder Gleason, taking over the phone call. The next morning, James Gleason and Payette went to the spot, where his son saw the man and carefully traced the steps along a trail to the homestead, but saw nothing of the fugitive.

Payette said "Tornow might have been emboldened by the fact that he has not been pursued lately and perhaps was attracted to his old home again, not being aware that it had been sold and a new tenant was now leasing it from the new owner, William Valentine."

If it was Tornow, it was the first any man has seen him in a couple of years. Like all previous tales, this one ended in another dead end.

Meantime, Dr. Robert Stapp's time in the county slammer was coming to an end. Prompted by a petition signed by a host of community leaders, Gov. M. E. Hay signed a pardon for the convicted Aberdeen doctor to free him as of August 27, 1912.

Stapp was convicted of performing a criminal abortion of Mary Tornow, niece of John Tornow, who is accused of murdering her brothers, William and John. Mary, 24, was the daughter of Henry and Minnie Bauer. She died on December 1, 1910, following that operation and Stapp was convicted and sentenced in April, 1911, to nine months. However, his attorney, E. A. Boner, filed several unsuccessful appeals, including the final one to the state Supreme Court.

Boner fought to keep Stapp out of jail and was successful until January of 1912 when Stapp finally began serving his sentence.

The governor's pardon comes after he served seven months of his sentence, two months short of his sentencing release date.

In early August, a petition signed by 35 civic leaders, including Judge Ben Sheeks, Prosecuting Attorney William Campbell, all three county commissioners and Sheriff Ed Payette, was sent to the governor's office requesting the pardon for "the reason that we deem him sufficiently punished for the offense in light of all the circumstances surrounding the case brought out by the evidence, and for the further reason that the doctor is needed at home to provide for his family, which consists of a wife and son. No good purpose could be served by detaining Dr. Stapp longer in the county jail; he has already served seven months and we trust that clemency may be extended in this case and that Dr. Stapp may at once be pardoned."

The law requires the superior court judge before whom the defendant was tried, the prosecuting attorney, the sheriff and commissioners all to sign the petition. Stapp's attorney, E. A. Boner, made several unsuccessful appeals for the doctor's release.

———

A few days later, the sheriff's office was abuzz when a Wynooche Valley resident Louis Larson, a trapper and hunter, who had been with the posse in the search for deputies McKenzie and Elmer, reported he was frightened by a man, who looked a bit like Tornow when he rounded a bend in the trail near the Wishkah Falls and came face-to-face with the stranger. The intruder then took off into the brush. When word of the incident circulated in the upper country, many thought it might be Tornow.

The next day, Payette sent Deputy Carl Swartz to investigate and bring the man in for questioning. Larson took the deputy to the site where he was frightened and found the man a short distance away. He was easy to track because the man could be heard singing in a rich baritone voice, and not a bad one at that. When Swartz returned, he had red-haired William Sherwin with him. He protested mildly being brought in to the sheriff's office.

Sherwin, who has lived in the Wynooche upper country, about eight miles from the Weatherwax ranch for about 10 years, is known by authorities and others in the wilderness as "Billy the Bear." He has a paralyzed right arm caused by a stroke, and had lost his left hand in a mine accident. He decided to make light of the situation, telling Swartz "At least I get to ride in an automobile." While his struggle for existence has been pitiful, he has to be admired for his tenacity.

Sherwin answered the description of Tornow similarly, except for the reddish hair. He had tattered clothes, long hair with no hat, and he was barefooted. "I don't blame Larson for being scared of me. Most anybody would be frightened. I am not a pretty sight, but I meant no harm. I desperately want to go back into the woods and be left alone," he pleaded with the sheriff.

Swartz said Sherwin had a wind shelter, secured with poles and skins and was protected from the weather. He also had about 10 pounds of beans, but the meat he had in his camp was spoiled.

"I have known Sherwin for years," said T. H. Hill, who brought Sherwin new clothes, shoes and a hat. "He has a good education and comes from respectable parents in Pennsylvania." Hill said Sherwin came by his moniker many years ago in Pennsylvania when he was out of work and acquired a small bear, which he raised. "The story goes that he wrestled the bear for profit in sideshows until the bear hurt him, then he quit and sold the bruin." Hill said Sherwin used to lie down with the bear to sleep. When asked why, Billy said "so some damn hunter wouldn't kill him."

He was known as "Billy the Bear" from that time. The reason for his seclusion is that he is sensitive of his physical condition, Hill said. "He is always happy, however, and never complains. I believe the county should look into providing some kind of aid for him."

Payette said he will make an effort to have the county bestow a small monthly allowance on Sherwin. He said the man protested vehemently to being sent to the county poor farm. The sheriff then instructed Swartz to return the man to his beloved woods. "I think we can afford a $10 monthly stipend for food stuffs," the sheriff said, "but he'll have to come here to get it." The county later agreed.

Also the same week as the Sherwin incident, Payette took a $5 greenback from Gene McGillicuddy, who received the bill in change at his place of business. "Later, I saw some writing on it and when I turned it over, I read the name of 'Tornow' on one corner and 'Oxbow' in another corner," McGillicuddy said.

McGillicuddy called Payette to report the incident. The sheriff said it is a misdemeanor to deface United States coins or currency, and whoever the person might be, Tornow, or someone who wrote it for the purpose of creating suspicion that Tornow placed his name there, is guilty of a crime.

The sheriff took the bill to the county courthouse to compare the writing on the bill with a sample of Tornow's writing. He said there should be a sample there, but he didn't have an answer yet.

It seemed there was no end to the Tornow saga, and while the posses had been called in by the sheriff, that didn't stop the stories from escalating.

On the one-year anniversary of the bodies of the Bauer twins being found, a stranger contacted Cloud to state unequivocally that Tornow did not kill the boys, saying he wasn't even in the area when the evil deed was done. The man also said Tornow is innocent of the killing of the deputies.

Following is Cloud's recap of that interview that appeared in the September 6, 1912, edition of *The Aberdeen Daily World*:

TORNOW DID NOT
KILL FOUR MEN,
SAYS STRANGER

"John Tornow is innocent of the murder of the Bauer twins and Deputies Colin McKenzie and A. V. Elmer. Tornow was 22 miles from the Bauer home on Sunday, September 3, 1911, when Will and John Bauer were slain near the home of their father on the Satsop River. Tornow is now less than 10 miles from

Elma. He is being supplied with food and ammunition by an Elma merchant. He is clean-shaven, wears good clothes and his hair was cut less than two weeks ago. Last week a new pair of hunter's boots were taken to him."

F. M. Potter, proprietor of the Potter repair shop on East Heron Street in Aberdeen, will, if necessary, make an affidavit to the effect that only a few days ago, a stranger, well-dressed and evidently familiar with the history of the tragedies, made the above statement to him.

He does not know the man, he says, but had seen him several times on Heron Street before the interview, which brought the foregoing statement.

"I was standing on G Street, near a tailor shop and talking about Tornow when the stranger approached," said Potter. "I had just inquired of my friend if Pearsall, Scott Stevens and others were going deer hunting or after Tornow. It was then that the man volunteered the information, which I believe should be immediately investigated. I am sure that he knows something about Tornow. He was not under the influence of liquor. He was dressed as a woodsman. I did not pay much attention to him at first. After hearing his remark, I resumed conversation with my friend. Wishing to question the stranger again, I turned around, but the man had gone. I have not seen him since."

The stranger went on to say, in our conversation, that "Tornow was well provided for and that, if necessary, he could take a posse of men into the fugitive's resort in less than four hours after leaving Elma."

"He told me that Tornow had several razors and that his clothes were in good condition. Potter said he wasn't able to question the man about the fact he said Tornow was not within 22 miles of the Bauer home on the day of the murders. The man also didn't talk about Tornow's part in the killing of the deputies, except to blithely state "he is not guilty of those crimes."

"For some reason, I hold a certain amount of faith in the fellow's story and would like to see the matter investigated," Potter continued.

Potter related the information of the stranger's conversation to Sheriff Ed Payette, who said he would investigate and keep the notes in his file, in the event Tornow is caught and brought to trial.

"If this man is right, and can prove where Tornow was, it would go a long way to vindicate him of the crime," the sheriff said.

"Hey, Bill. What do you think of that story?" Cloud asked his editor, Bill Irvine. Usually, the editor is aware of what his reporters are writing about well in advance, but this time Irvine was unavailable until he came to the office after Cloud had written his article.

"I'm glad you got that angle, that's good newspapering. I've talked to a lot of people who think he didn't kill anyone and now we've raised that question a couple of times in the last two months. What do you believe? You are close to the sources."

"Well, I definitely won't go as far as to say he didn't kill anyone. I am pretty sure he killed McKenzie and Elmer, either that or someone has gone to extreme lengths to make it look like that. I don't buy that. He was a desperate fugitive and had a lot of people chasing after him. He knew after the boys were killed, he was a wanted man. It was a case of preservation of life from then on. As for the boys, I think he probably killed them too, but it was an accident, perhaps self-defense like the fire wardens said in my story the end of July. The boys shot at the bear they wounded earlier, but missed, the bullets went overhead and lodged into a tree behind where Tornow was standing in his lean-to. He didn't waste time, picked up his rifle, took cover and fired two quick shots, killing both boys. When I went in to get the bodies, the deputies were precise in what they believed happened. We walked through the scenario. It seemed clear to me then, but now there are enough conspiracy theories out there to give some doubt to the veracity of his killing them."

"The hardest thing for a newsman is not to interject your opinions into a story, but I have never seen you do that. If you had, I would have known how you feel about the case. That's why I asked that," the editor said.

"You are right. It is hard when you think there might be some truth to a particular belief. But, I learned in school, and you emphasized to me so strongly, to stick to the facts and you won't get hurt or get the newspaper in trouble. I appreciate that."

"You mentioned conspiracy theory? What's that all about?

"Well, for one, I really want to try to get the bottom of that land deal that was never made between the Tornows and the Schafers. I think there's more to that than we know now. Another thing, the year the boys were killed, that new cruiser law went into effect. If you remember, prior to that, timber cruisers assessed taxes based on fallen timber that had the landowner or company's logo burned or branded into the ends of timber ready for the mill, or in some cases, even at the mill. There were a lot of problems with that, even though it had been done for years that way. Pirates could come along, hijack the timber, cut off the end and put their brand on it. That all changed when the

Bureau of Land Management got the Legislature to change how they assessed timber."

"That's right. I forgot about that," the editor said, almost chagrined he didn't remember how important that was to small woodlot owners.

"Standing timber became the rule of the land," Cloud said. "It was devastating to small woodlot owners. The cruisers only had to look at what might be marketable and taxes were assessed well before timber was cut and prepared for the mill. Can you imagine the squabbles folks had with the cruisers doing the assessing? I'm sure there were payoffs and some cruisers padded their wallets to not assess some standing timber as marketable. It was purely subjective because there are degrees of marketability, making some timber more valuable than others."

"You've done your homework on that, haven't you?"

"A little, but I think there's more to it than what meets the eye."

"How so?"

"Well, I find it quite interesting that there is a little-known rider or amendment in the assessment law that grants new woodlot owners — those who have created new small lots within the past 18 months — forgiveness for 36 months before they have to pay a tax on standing timber. So, do you know what happened? Well, I found out that lawyer for the Schafer Company, W. H. Abel, he took advantage of that loophole. Nothing illegal, but it probably took a savvy lawyer to discover it"

"Really, what did he do?"

"He created the Dallas Land Company, forming many small lots out of a huge amount of property the Schafers owned. That's thousands of acres, the big company wouldn't have to pay taxes on. That includes the land adjacent to the Tornow property, which he subdivided into smaller lots. Abel has tried for years to get an easement from the Tornows to transport their timber through the corner of the Tornow property. It would ease the path to get the timber to the East Fork of the Satsop for transport to the mills. Abel tried to get it from Old Man Tornow before he died, then he ran into John when he tried to confront Mrs. Tornow. I know John told him where to go, just like his dad did. The younger one, Ed, he wanted to sell, but the old man was smart and put in a clause when he gave that property to John, that John had to sign off on any sale, and that wasn't going to happen, while he was alive. It also took Mrs. Tornow out of the decision-making situation."

"So, that makes sense why Ed took out that warrant to have John declared insane before the boys were killed. With him out of the way, that could pave the way for the easement or even a sale."

"Yes, and he also could have been written out of the estate probate and John had a lot of property. He had one-sixth of the homestead property in Section 36 and one-sixth of the properties in Sections 1 and 12. These are in Chehalis County. Those show on the family's probate. He also was sole owner of a property in Mason County that his father had purchased from a man named Cedric Anderson in 1898. Interestingly, that property doesn't show in the probate. John also purchased two small lots in the Stewart Addition along the Wishkah River in East Aberdeen."

"Wow, what a convoluted mess," the editor said.

"When that guy wrote the letter to the editor that said 'People should let family matters be family matters, and this is definitely a family matter,' it makes a lot of sense."

"It sure does, but there's a lot more. I told you about the land that Fritz Tornow bought from Anderson? Well, get this. The Dallas Land Company, through Abel, filed suit on that portion, but he filed it against John Tornow on the former Anderson property. I'm not sure why, except with John being a fugitive, the property might not have been fully paid off and it might revert to the previous owner. Also, as a fugitive, John lost his legal right and a conservator was eventually appointed, but a conservator can't sign off on property. It happens by default in good time. Just guessing, but I think that makes sense."

"Sounds logical to me," the editor responded.

"But, this becomes even messier," Cloud continued, "because Anderson sold the land on September 25, 1912, to a man named A. J. Jackson, who then sold the 167 acres to Dallas Land the next day. Jackson was the high bidder when the estate went to auction on the Section 1 and 12 properties. Dallas Land filed suit against John Tornow on October 3, 1912. I still don't know why Dallas did that when they already owned the land. I'm not even going to speculate on what Abel had on his mind with that deal."

"That's really strange," said Irvine, who had become transfixed by the oddity of this land case. Are you going to tell me there's more? Have you talked to Abel about this strange transaction?"

"I did try to talk to Abel, but he wouldn't reveal his reasoning. His former assistant, Nelson, Ovie Nelson, gave me the basic facts and

I tracked the rest from the assessor's office. What I did learn from Nelson is that Abel knew, that without Tornow's signature on the deed, the transfer of land wouldn't be complete for another 90 days when it would then be complete by default. Nelson also said Abel and Dallas Land swapped property back and forth, apparently, according to Nelson, 'depending on how Abel felt that day.'

"Here's what I think the reasoning might be. I believe Abel was covering his bases in the event, John eventually was proven not guilty in court and the judge regranted him his property. I think Abel wanted to be sure that he won the suit and the property couldn't be taken away. Just speculation, mind you. Or maybe, just maybe, Abel knew more about who killed the boys than anyone thought?"

"We could sit here and guess about this situation all day, couldn't we?"

"Oh, and here's another theory. Some people I've talked to believe the brothers, particularly, the youngest, Ed, is responsible for the boys' death, either that he did it or had it done. John shot his dog after he had shot John's beloved hound, Cougar. At that last confrontation, Ed was furious and John said he was going to the woods and he would kill anyone who came after him; then came the warrant."

"That makes a lot of sense too," the editor said.

"Ed had been sent off the homestead by his dad, only to return after his death," Cloud said. "Ed not only left again after the boys were killed, but he also got married only one month after the slayings and moved to South Bend. He was told he wouldn't get any property from the estate settlement, only a few bucks in the bank. He did, however, get one-sixth of the homestead, like the others. That's $1,664.89, an enormous amount of money for an unemployed laborer. I figured out that a good schoolteacher was paid about $507 a year. Then again, with John out of the way, John's money in the bank as well as all his property shares would be divvied up into one less share."

"I guess there are conspiracy theories. So what are we to believe?"

"You remember after the deputies were killed and you talked to Fred Tornow? You wrote a short story that John was insane, if he was guilty as charged, and that he was released as cured from that Mountain View Sanitarium?"

"Sure, but the sheriff said it wasn't true."

"That's right. Fred and Ed were the only brothers working on getting John declared insane, so they would get more of his property and the family estate. That could be why he came out with that statement, only I'm not sure why Fred said he was released as cured, rather than going with the escape rumors. Don't you think Minnie would have talked about the sanitarium, if there was one? It would explain some of his actions, if that were the case. She never admitted he might be a madman or demented."

"Can this get any more crazy?" the editor asked.

"It sure can. In fact, the more I talk with people, the more theories arise. One of the biggest one is Mr. Bauer. We know from that Stapp trial that there was a great chasm between him and the Tornows from the time Mary Bauer went to live with her grandmother and take care of her; then she ended up getting taken care of by Ed Tornow. When she became pregnant, Henry Bauer was furious with Ed. He also had a major dislike for John Tornow. He, John, taught the boys all they knew about woods life and how to exist on the resources. Bauer was a farmer and didn't have the knowledge about woods subsistence. He was jealous of his brother-in-law. John knew this and timed his visits to his sister, Minnie, when Henry was out on the property. Minnie told me he often waited in a large cedar stump for Henry to leave, rather than face a confrontation and stir things up between them. He cared for Minnie that much. And he definitely cared for the boys as much."

"The more you keep talking, the more I think Tornow might be innocent," the editor said.

"It gets you thinking, doesn't it? But could Bauer have killed his own sons, or even had them killed in a set-up to frame Tornow? I don't think so. I'm pretty sure he didn't do it by his own hand, because Minnie testified that they were home together on Sunday, the day the boys were killed. But, she also said she was in the house and Henry was in the barn or out on the property. She said she didn't keep track of him and didn't need to, except to feed him breakfast. She said he didn't come in for lunch, but if he was back on the far property, then he wouldn't have to come back, he would have taken some food and water with him.

""There are still some who say the boys were sent by their dad to take out Tornow — that they were on a 'John hunt' not a bear hunt — and it went horribly wrong. I don't believe that because I saw the boys a few months before that and they talked so highly of their uncle and even worked with him on several logging jobs. Unless they had a vicious argument, I can't see that happening, and we don't know if

that happened or not. Even if there was a dispute, I can't see the boys
agreeing to do it, just because dad ordered it. In fact, when I had lunch
with them at the trial, the boys stood up to Henry and said they were
not going to obey him and would continue to see John. They were even
working with him after the trial.

"What really adds fuel to the fire," Cloud surmised, "is that Henry,
and later Minnie, beat a hasty retreat out of the state and down to
California. Less than six weeks after the boys were killed, he sold his
ranch. Minnie said he decided he had had enough of Chehalis County,
but if you ask me, it also sounds like a guilty man. He's home free
because the sheriff is considering only John Tornow as the suspect."

"I never thought about that, but it could be, I guess."

"You know, Bill. I said earlier that I thought John killed the boys,
likely on self-defense. But, think about this for a minute. What is John's
main tool to survive in the woods?"

"That would be a knife, wouldn't it?"

"Yes, he used it for everything. So, if he killed the boys, why did he
leave a knife on John Bauer's body?

"He did that?"

"Yes, when the sheriff's deputies examined the bodies, they found
a knife. I saw it, but didn't give it much of a thought — until later."

"You know, Dan, with everything involved in this situation, I bet
people will debate this for the next 100 years."

30. NEW BLOOD, NEW RULES

January-March 1913

A s the new year began, Chehalis County was preparing to induct a new sheriff. Ed Payette chose not to run for a third term. "I am exhausted and totally frustrated by my inability to bring to trial the fugitive outlaw, John Tornow," he told *The Chehalis County Vidette* when filing for the position opened.

Payette had made numerous trips in the past 15 months with innumerable posses into the Upper Satsop, Wynooche Valley and Lower Olympics in search of Tornow, the accused slayer of his twin nephews, William and John Bauer on September 3, 1911, and deputies, Colin McKenzie and A. V. Elmer, on March 9, 1912. Payette nearly lost his life last October when he tumbled down a glacier, surviving only when he became snagged on a boulder, then was rescued by posse members. He was back on the hunt less than three weeks later.

County commissioners told the sheriff the budget for chasing the outlaw was going to be slashed considerably by the first of the year. That was all Payette needed to give up the hunt. "Let the new sheriff deal with that," Payette told commissioners when apprised of the budget.

Undeterred, a blacksmith from Elma, decided to throw his hat in the ring.

"I am going to rid those hills of that Wildman John Tornow," Schelle Mathews shouted during his campaign, championing that vow as his one and only platform.

During his campaign, Mathews also told the electorate that he would change the approach to catching Tornow. "If elected, I will not squander the taxpayers' money. You won't get much information from me."

Mathews, born in Minnesota, had been in the Elma area since the first of the century. The 38-year-old had served as deputy for several years under Payette, until resigning in 1911. Since then, he had managed his own blacksmith business out of his home in Elma.

Mathews also had a kin connection with the sheriff's office, having married Amanda Quimby, the sister of Deputy Sheriff Giles Quimby.

Chehalis County residents liked the smooth-talking, but no-nonsense, assertive Mathews, and they bought into his campaign promise even more. While he had solid support, he rode the coattails into office of a near-Republican sweep of the ballot in November. He collected 3,475 votes while his opponent, Franklin Fry, had 966 votes.

Since the election on November 4, there was little to report on the search for Tornow. Payette pulled his posse off the search last June. Only an occasional possible appearance was reported to the sheriff's office.

Then, one week after the election, the lame-duck sheriff was informed of another possible Tornow appearance when a Satsop rancher, Ed Schaletzke, reported one of his bovines was missing. While searching for the cow, the rancher said he accidentally stumbled on a camp he believed was Tornow's. The fugitive wasn't there, but the rancher pleaded for assistance from Payette.

The sheriff agreed he would make one last venture into the woods to search for the outlaw — as long as the commissioners would pop a few bucks to pay for a posse one last time.

"If that is Tornow's camp, I should be back here with the fugitive in about three days," he told the commissioners. "I want this guy before I leave office." His plea, including evidence that the rancher had submitted, swayed the commissioners, one of which was unseated in the election.

"Hello, Dan. Want to go for a ride? I'm going to get Tornow," Payette said, giving the *World's* reporter Dan Cloud a call.

"Sure. What's up?"

"We got word a rancher lost a cow, and while searching for the animal, stumbled on a camp he believes is Tornow's. He wasn't there, but coals in the fire were warm, so Tornow is somewhere close. I'm leaving at 7:30. Want to tag along?"

"You bet. I don't want to miss any of the action. I'll try to get up there tonight and stay at the Montesano. I'll check with my editor. He should be here in about a half-hour. I'll call you back to confirm."

"And Dan, you better dress warm. We might be gone about three days, if he is there. They had a pretty good early snow a few days ago. The action is not too far from the homestead. It's in the low country, so the snow shouldn't be that bad."

"Right, sheriff. I really want to be there."

Cloud got the approval from his editor to take the trip. He dashed home, picked up a heavy wool coat, some snow boots and two flannel shirts, jammed them into a duffel, and gave a quick call to Lindy, his girlfriend.

"Hi, sweetie. How ya doin'?"

"Hi, Danny. I'm a little under the weather today."

"So sorry to hear that. I'm headed up country to get Tornow with the sheriff. Just wanted to give you a quick call before I took off."

"You gonna get him? Sure, I've heard that before."

"That's what the sheriff says. He's got a tip where he might be. I'll be gone, maybe three days."

"Just be careful he doesn't get you."

"I doubt the sheriff will let me accompany the posse all the way. We'll probably set up a supply base near the camp."

"That's good. I don't want you anywhere near that maniac."

"Well, I better run. Dad's taking me to Montesano tonight, because we leave at 7:30 in the morning."

"OK. Have fun. Just be careful."

Cloud was already in the coffee house when Payette arrived. He was sitting with other posse members, A. L. Fitzgerald, George Stormes and Charles Lathrop. Within minutes, Frank Getty and J. H. Cole arrived. All those present had been on previous posses, were excellent woodsmen and knew the territory like a book.

The entourage took the sheriff's auto to the Schaletzke ranch, about 20 miles north and east of Montesano, where the farmer and his two sons, had arranged for horses. Schaletzke explained that the camp he found was a short distance from the Tornow homestead.

"The cache is in the interior of an immense hollow cedar stump, which had been carefully covered over and snug with sleeping quarters fixed up inside," Schaletzke told the sheriff when the posse arrived. "We found the missing cow, nicely cut into beef outside the hut, cleverly concealed in the bushes. There was a storage of beef partially dried as well as a quantity of potatoes, apples, some blankets, old clothing and a Winchester rifle."

Much to Cloud's surprise, Payette let him accompany the posse into the camp. The young man was not a horseman, but handled himself well, keeping up with the group.

Two days later, there still was no sighting of Tornow; Cloud and three of the posse returned to Montesano.

Following is a portion of his article that appeared in the *The Aberdeen Daily World* on November 12:

Discovery of Tornow's camp was made accidentally by Ed Schaletzke, a rancher of the Upper Satsop district, and his two sons, Walter and Ewald, he reported to Sheriff Ed Payette on Sunday. A cow belonging to the family was missing last Thursday. The men started out to hunt for it. Beating through the woods, they came upon a hollow cedar stump in which Tornow had made a camp and where a quantity of meat, taken from the cow's carcass was found. Walter found the carcass nearby.

The Schaletzkes watched the place for some time; then the father and sons came to Montesano Sunday and reported the facts to Sheriff Payette, who got a posse together and left early Monday morning. Well before noon, they were at Tornow's camp and the posse kept watch at the site in hopes that the fugitive might return.

Proof that it is Tornow for whom the posse is watching is found in the fact that a shell from a Luger pistol, such as Colin McKenzie carried and which was taken from the body of the deputy by Tornow when McKenzie was killed last March near the Oxbow. The pistol shell was found near the cow's carcass. The pistol is not much in use and there is little possibility of the shot having been fired by someone other than Tornow, the sheriff said.

"When we got to the camp we found it just as Schaletzke had described it," said Payette. "The hollow cedar stump was admirable for Tornow's purpose. The Schaletzkes reported to us that when they stumbled onto this lair, Tornow's blankets and a rifle were leaning against a log. When we got there, the rifle and blankets were gone. Evidently Tornow, hearing the Schaletzkes approaching, calling to each other as they beat through the brush, had taken warning and hid in the brush nearby, watching them go through his camp."

The sheriff said Tornow wouldn't have likely shot at the men if he saw them and recognized them as they were neighbors and John had been at their home many times. It also appeared that he only had a pistol in his possession and he didn't wish to take chances with a pistol, no matter who was pursuing him.

"In the camp, we found a quantity of apples and potatoes. Also there was much meat taken from the cow. Some of this had been smoked for about two days

and will keep for some time," the sheriff reported. "Tornow had taken some of the meat with him. Much of the meat was uncured and neatly cut. What Tornow had intended to preserve, he had hidden so cunningly that it was hard work to find it. He had cut brush and stacked it around so that it was practically impossible to tell that the apparently natural growth had covered his supply. He had been curing some salmon as well as a large quantity of fish tails that was found, as well as a vine maple spear.

"While we were laying low and waiting for Tornow to return, we heard shots on a hill about three-quarters of a mile distant. We were not able at the time to locate the precise direction. When I get back, we will attempt to cover this hill thoroughly. I am satisfied that the shots were fired by Tornow," the sheriff continued.

The posse ran into severe rain storms that impeded trying to follow a trail and rendered a dog useless. The sheriff said unless the weather improved, chances of continuing the pursuit through the swampy land were unlikely. Tornow had protected his camp from the rain by construction of a crude roof over the huge cedar stump. What few tracks were found were obliterated by the downpours.

"I believe that Tornow saw us last Thursday," Schaletzke said. "The boys were beating through the brush in search of the cow and shouting to each other so as not to wander too far apart. They were talking in German; Tornow understands some German. They were talking about the cow, and undoubtedly the outlaw thought it part of wisdom to keep out of sight. I'm thankful for that, but I believe, if he was the 'Wildman' that everybody talks about, he could easily have taken us all out. He knows me, he knows my boys. We always called him the 'Gentle Giant' because he was so much bigger than the boys, bigger than any of us. I don't believe those stories."

The sheriff concurred with the rancher's report that the outlaw might have seen the family. "That they must have been very near him when he left camp and that he thought there was a possibility of them passing by without discovering his hiding place, is evidenced by his hurried departure. Perhaps he thought they might not investigate the stump; he left his rifle there, meaning to come back later and get it."

Payette said more evidence that the camp was Tornow's rests in the clothing that was found at the camp.

"In foraging around, we found a piece of cloth that I am sure came from part of the clothing taken from McKenzie's body by Tornow after the deputies were killed last fall. It is of a dark brown color and matches clothes that McKenzie was wearing at the time of his murder and which was taken from his dead body."

Payette said the next three days will tell the tale. In that time, Tornow should either return for his provisions or have decided that it is too great a risk to attempt to recover them. "I have hopes of capturing him this time," the sheriff said by telephone from the Schaletzke ranch this morning.

The sheriff reported that heavy rains continued and they found the Satsop "very, very high and fording was very difficult."

One week later, after the sheriff and all posse members returned to Montesano, Schaletzke approached the board of county commissioners, pleading for more help. It was a sudden departure from how he was feeling a week ago.

"It appears Tornow left the valley only so long as the sheriff posse was out, and immediately returned to his old haunts in hope of securing meat for the winter from straying cattle belonging to local ranchers," he told the panel.

"Last week I missed another cow — the third one this month — and, when I went to search for the animal, I finally discovered her across the river from Tornow's old house. She seemed very wild, but I succeeded in driving her home. As I was chasing her around the pasture, I noticed the tracks where she had been running. I also discovered tracks made by a man, a man with a very large shoe. The tracks showed the man stole up close to her, then she went wild.

"When I reached home and tied up the cow, I noticed that she had been savagely beaten over the head and almost killed. My theory is that Tornow had seen the cow in the remote pasture and being too close to the house, and not wanting to risk a shot being heard, had tried to kill the animal with a club. His first blow failed to kill the animal and she had run wildly around the triangular flat to escape death."

Schaletzke went on to say that he had been friends with the Tornow family, including John, but if he is the one doing these deeds, then he needs to be stopped at all costs. "He has become a menace to the Upper Satsop country and the people of that region are entitled to protection of their lives and property. There is not a problem confronting a sheriff's office anywhere in the country that equals this one."

The board took no action, except to tell Schaletze and Sheriff Payette that there is no more money in the budget to pay for a posse and the county has done all that can be done toward taking the outlaw. "There is already a reward of $3,000 offered for his capture, and if it can be proven that he is the murderer, an additional $2,000 would go to his captors," Commissioner Wilson noted.

"Schaletzke thanked the commissioners for listening to his plea, but said he hoped they would reconsider. "The case is a hard one to solve and it seems almost an impossibility that the man will be either captured or killed. He is probably the best woodsman in the county, a dead shot, keenly alive to his peril and is taking no chances of capture."

The commissioners responded that they were aware of all that, but their decision would stand.

———

Christmas came and went as Payette's days as sheriff quickly came near an end. His frustration mounted with no resolve in his numerous hunts with the posses to capture Tornow. It's now only one week until he relinquishes his post. When he took up the hunt in mid-November, he figured it would be the final one as the snow continued to mount in the Upper Satsop and Wynooche country.

But, when the phone rang on January 5 and it was Sheriff Lou Sanderson of Mason County, the juices began to flow.

"Ed, there's a chance we might be able to get your man," said Sanderson.

"How so, Lou?"

"A couple of hunters stumbled onto him yesterday when Tornow emerged from a makeshift cabin in the west part of my county near a Simpson logging camp.

"How do they know it was Tornow?"

"They both knew him and recognized him."

"You know, if it was Tornow and these guys are still alive, they are the first ones to see him and survive since this thing began. We've had lots of reports of sightings, but I don't believe any of them were the Wildman."

"These guys are positive. I know them and they are to be trusted," said Sanderson.

"So, what's their story?" Payette asked, still a bit skeptical.

"The hunters were out with their dogs, and when the animals began to bay, they turned to see what they had treed. They found the dogs baying before the door of a rough-hewn cabin. They said Tornow then emerged. That was enough, they said after recognizing him, and they took off running, trusting that their dogs would follow. They made it back to civilization and called me from the logging camp."

"Lou, do you have any men out there?"

"No, I have no money for a posse and besides that, the snow is too deep before you reach the logging camp. The guys said it's not too deep between Tornow's camp and the logging camp."

"You probably know that I only have a week to serve until I'm done, but I sure would like to get this guy before I hang up my badge. I'm going to make some calls and see if I can scramble some guys together and I'll get back to you. Are you at the office?"

"Yes, I am. If you get something going, please let me know and I'll try to join you. I know the area they are in. I'll also try to get those hunters to show us, if we can get up there to reach them."

"Great, I'll get back with you."

While Payette had no money to pay his contingent, several men still jumped on board. By 7 a.m., Payette, A. L. Fitzgerald, George Stormes and a new man, C. W. Jensen, were on their way north, where they expected to team with Sanderson at Frisken's Y, a railroad turnaround area west of Matlock.

The group headed north from there through Beeville, stopped briefly at the Hall ranch and continued up into the Lower Olympics until thwarted by deep snow. While there, Payette said, there was a report from a trapper, who informed the sheriff he was told Tornow had been shot in the back as he left his cabin. Sanderson said he doubted that as the man who told the tale, "is a known liar."

The men left the next morning and managed to get through the deep snow to the logging camp; a few hours later, they came upon the shack where the hunters said they saw Tornow. Deputy Sheriff Fitzgerald said the shack was bark-and brush-covered, and was a likely a temporary haunt of the hermit. He said the fugitive had "cut out a number of portholes in the cabin, and was prepared to give a warm reception to any visitors. Everything about the place was very crude and showed the murderer is reduced to the last extremity."

The deputies reported they surrounded the cabin and cautiously approached with cocked rifles; no one was inside. "Footsteps in the snow led away from the shack and were followed by men and dogs for three or four miles, until a ridge was reached where the timber was heavy and the snow light. Here, we lost the trail and the dogs were unable to pick it up again."

He said he was sure the footprints were Tornow's because of their huge size, and the fact that in the fresh snow, "you could see the track of a big toe on the left foot."

He said the men returned to the cabin to meet up with the sheriff and searched the exterior of the cabin; they found evidence of Tornow, uncovering a well-concealed cache that held two gun rods, one for cleaning a .25-20 rifle, the caliber carried by slain game warden, A. V. Elmer, and one for a .30-30 Winchester, the caliber owned by Tornow and also the Bauer boys, he is suspected of killing on September 3, 1911, the day this deadly manhunt began.

Two days later, Payette was back in Montesano, frustrated once more by weather and the elusive fugitive, who was now on the lam for just over 16 months.

"The snow on the ridge was at least 2 feet deep and growing deeper when we left," Payette told the *World* reporter after his return. "It began to snow again as we headed out. On the level stretches, we found at least 18 inches. Every track we found was covered in no time and we saw no traces of smoke."

Payette said there was little-to-no chance there will be any more reports before he relinquishes his duties as sheriff on January 13, just three days away.

"That will remain for my successor to locate and capture him, if possible," the sheriff concluded.

———

It didn't take long for Cloud to realize he would have to work hard to earn the same respect he had with the former sheriff when Schelle Mathews took over. As open as Payette's regime was, Mathews operated in a covert, perhaps even clandestine approach — as far as the search for Tornow was concerned.

When his usual questions about the hunt for the outlaw were met with "I'm not going to say anything about that" or even "no comment," Cloud knew he would have to find a mole, who would freely open up.

Since he was well known and well liked by everybody in the office, this was not a problem. His mole didn't appreciate the sheriff's secrecy surrounding the information. He would have to be discreet, however, as his job was at stake.

An example of what he was dealing with in comparison to the ease with which he developed stories under Payette's regime, is exemplified in his first article on the search under Mathews' rule that appeared on January 18, 1913. Even the headlines underlined the problem:

SHERIFF'S MEN
REPORTED TO BE
AFTER FUGITIVE

Secrecy is Maintained

Rumor Denied at Montesano
Office but Indications Point
To Possession of Hot Clue

That the hunt for John Tornow, alleged murderer of four, has been renewed and that a posse headed by Chief Deputy Ed Hoover, and including Ed Tribbetts and Con Elliott, formerly of the Aberdeen Police force, is now camped some distance up the Satsop River, waiting for tracks of the outlaw, is brought to Aberdeen today.

That report, denied by Harry Pennell, office deputy under Sheriff Schelle Mathews at Montesano, is generally accepted here as true.

Considerable secrecy surrounds the undertaking. It is stated that four dogs were purchased by the county in Spokane and shipped to Chehalis County by way of Tacoma. These dogs were not brought to Montesano, but unloaded at some point east of the county seat and taken to the woods to await the posse's pleasure, it is said.

It is also stated that several of the men more prominent with the posse, were leaving to hunt in Oregon, a trip they had planned before Sheriff Ed Payette left office.

Whether the posse has a clue as to Tornow's whereabouts is by no means certain. It is argued, however, that these men would hardly go out on a hunt when the snow depth is a matter of feet instead of inches, unless they have some definite information on which to base operations.

It is rumored within the past few days that fear of Tornow felt by inhabitants of the Upper Satsop region has enabled the fugitive to commit many outrages of which the public has heard nothing.

It is rumored that Tornow came to the door of a farmhouse and demanded milk from Mrs. Wright at her ranch, east of Matlock. She gave it to him and the heavily armed man left. Another story says that Tornow, on several occasions, had robbed a road crew working in Mason County, and that these thefts were not reported, even though they knew who had taken the food and other supplies. People, who live in the region which Tornow now roams, are said to be most unwilling to report his presence for fear of death.

Rumor that Sheriff Mathews may have some definite information concerning Tornow's present haunts, finds strength in statements made prior to the election by close friends, who declared on different occasions that Mathews would capture Tornow within a month after he had taken office.

The day Mathews was sworn in, he was confronted on the courthouse steps by longtime supporter George Spalding, a rancher, who lives on the Satsop.

"Well, Schelle, you tink you get Johnnie?" the elderly German asked as the World reporter witnessed the meeting.

"I don't know George, but I'm going to get him or he will get me."

"I don't tink you get him. Johnnie awfully smart in the woods."

"You may be right, George, but I'm going to do my best. He's ravaged these woods long enough."

"That's not Johnnie, not the Johnnie I know. Good luck, you'll need it."

Mathews is not in Montesano today, and it cannot be learned whether he has joined the posse in the woods. A few days ago, a number of men gathered in the sheriff's office discussing some plan, but the object of the conference was not made public.

It is said that Chris Jensen, who has been a member of a Tornow posse before, was asked to go out this time. It is declared that the men now out are well provisioned. Tornow has been seen but once in the last 16 months, and that recently when he surprised two Mason County hunters by emerging from a hut high in the hills.

Snow in the Upper Satsop country is said to be at least 3 feet deep. The last hunt for Tornow, which terminated a few days before Sheriff Ed Payette left office, was blocked because of deep snow.

At that time, Payette said he found snow more than 2 feet deep, and it is possible with all the snow which has fallen since, that it is more than 3 feet. The Payette posse, however, was close on Tornow's heels. They found two of his camps and took everything they found there, thus rendering it difficult for Tornow to elude escape much longer.

———

One of the goals Sheriff Payette wanted to accomplish before leaving office was to have a formal resolution from the state honoring the slain sheriff deputies Colin McKenzie and A. V. Elmer. Last fall, he attended the state sheriff's convention in Wenatchee at which time, a special committee was formed to draft that resolution.

A framed copy of the resolution arrived at Payette's home on January 22. The resolutions are beautifully embossed on parchment and a copy had also been sent to a member of the McKenzie and Elmer families.

The resolution, drafted by the committee to honor the memory of the deputies, slain March 9, 1912, while in performance of their duties, reads in part:

"Whereas, by the dastardly act of the assassin, the county of Chehalis and the state of Washington were deprived of the services of two brave men and fearless officers who were ever ready to respond to the call of duty; therefore be it:

"Resolved, that we denounce the deed as a cowardly act and trust that the murderer may yet be brought to justice; be it further:

"Resolved that these resolutions be spread upon the minutes of this association and copies be sent to Sheriff Payette and to the families of the deceased officers."

The former sheriff told the *World* that he "will preserve the resolutions and I greatly appreciate the gift as I was deeply attached to both officers, who lost their lives while in the performance of their sworn duty."

———

In early February, two youths told the Portland *Oregonian* they would be leaving immediately to hunt down Tornow. The young men, Charles Smith and Buck Nagel, said they were taking seven bloodhounds with them and will come back with Tornow and the $5,000 in reward money.

The *Oregonian* reported the youths say they have been training their hounds for months and they will "find his trail and not give up until we catch sign of him and shoot him on sight. We want no assistance from any other source. We'll get him ourselves."

Sheriff Schelle Mathews, at Montesano, acknowledged he had a call from the sheriff's office there, but had no other knowledge of the report.

———

As the snow began melting in the high country, reports of Tornow sightings began to escalate. Throughout the next several weeks, he was reported in Kitsap County, the county northeast of Mason, in the Seattle area and even in Port Angeles, where a few days after that report, he was said to be kidnapped and living a life of luxury in the Clallam County wilderness.

All of these reports proved fruitless in locating the fugitive or they were completely ignored.

On January 18, a report in the *The Aberdeen Daily World* said authorities in King County, going on descriptions furnished them, said they believed Tornow was not far from Elliott Bay, west of downtown. He was not sighted, nor was an investigation made.

On the same day, he is said to have been at the Thomas ranch in Olalla, east of Bremerton and a few miles from Port Orchard in Kitsap County. The report said he begged breakfast from the rancher, who fed him and was about to offer him work, but when he returned from the house to tell the man what to do, he discovered the man had fled the scene.

Shortly after that, a bundle of clothing was reported missing from a deserted house on the roadside, not far from Olalla. Later that day, Tornow is suspected of approaching another rancher asking if he could work. Late in the evening, the outlaw was recognized at Colby, on the extreme southern tip of Yukon Harbor, several miles north of Olalla.

At the last sighting, a sheriff's deputy was dispatched to the scene, but the reputed outlaw had once again disappeared.

A week later, the *Grays Harbor Washingtonian* reported that the fugitive was shot in the right leg and is hold up in the Upper Satsop. The story was told to a reporter by a barber in Hoquiam as told to him by Billie Charlie, an Indian living in the Humptulips Valley.

Following is a portion of the report in the "Washie" on February 26:

Indian says Tornow suffering from wound

"I had been out for a day's hunting and was on my way home when I struck the railroad track and called to my dogs. I noticed a man on the track some distance

behind me and I waited for him. The stranger was an Indian. He said he was going to Hoquiam, and I told him he could travel with me. After going a short distance, I slipped my pack off and gave him a sandwich. He was hungry and seemed grateful for the food.

"Before reaching Hoquiam, he told me a friend of his was visited by Tornow only a few days ago. The outlaw, he said, was on the Upper Satsop River. He had a long beard, his clothes were in rags and he wore burlap sacks on his feet. One leg was wounded, evidently by a rifle ball. The Indian said Tornow came to his camp and asked for matches and some lard. He also told the Indian he had shot a cow, but was afraid to take it.

"He said Tornow told his friend that he had found several freshly killed cows, but he didn't touch them, fearing poisoning. I did learn from the man, where his friend met Tornow. He said it was somewhere on the Upper Satsop."

When the sheriff's office was contacted to respond to this report, the deputy said the sheriff was out and the deputy had no comment, other than to say "We get reports like this all the time."

The next day, Cloud found out why he had been getting "he's out of the office" for so long when he repeatedly made calls to Montesano. Mathews had been in the lower Olympics for almost two weeks on his first venture out of the office and on the search for Tornow.

When he returned to Montesano, the sheriff's report was the same as it always was. Following is part of Cloud's story on February 27 in the *World*:

Sheriff Schelle Mathews returned yesterday from about two weeks searching the lower Olympics for John Tornow, and it is reported he is leaving again for the woods tonight or tomorrow.

The sheriff declines to give out any information.

"I have absolutely nothing to say," was his answer to every question that touched on the hunt for Tornow.

There are many rumors and stories afloat here about the search that is now going on. It is said there is a big posse of men in the woods in the upper part of the county, and in Southwestern Mason County. Not many of them are county men, however, that is certain. Most of the men are attracted by the reward of $5,000 for the capture of Tornow.

Old friends and acquaintances of the fugitive say that the story printed that Tornow is wounded in one leg is borne out by previous reports. Some of the sheriff's officers early in the year found tracks that were believed to be Tornow's showing him wearing only one shoe, and the other foot covered with some sort of bandage.

Commissioner C. N. "Bud" Wilson, who hunted deer with Tornow many times in early years, says "while there were several who could beat Tornow shooting at a mark, he was the quickest and most reasonably sure shot I have ever known and there is no question in my mind that he is insane."

Another Montesano man, who has hunted with Tornow, says John is the quickest shot he has ever known. "He would frequently shoot from the hip with unerring aim. I have known him to shoot twice at a deer before other hunters could get one shot off."

While there are many who predict that Tornow will never be captured, those who know the man and who know something of the territory in which he is said to still be living, say he will be taken, and that will be soon. They do not believe that the man will long stay away from the neighborhood of his old home, and they believe it is only a question of weeks until he will be taken.

As the search for the fugitive outlaw stretched into its 18th month, county commissioners reported the cost was rising rapidly. Nobody in the sheriff's office, with knowledge of expenditures, was able to say exactly what had been spent since funding was first requested in October 1911. A reasonable guess was it was well over what was offered for the reward, $5,000.

What was available was the sum since the first of the year when the winter search was mostly curtailed. The total was $2,500, this going to pay posse members and obtain provisions. The last search conducted by former Sheriff Payette was not originally funded, but the county decided to raid the supplemental budget for about $500 to pay the members of that posse.

Besides the sum disbursed by the county, a number of individuals paid from their own pockets for provisions and supplies while seeking the reward money.

A few days later, Sam Scott, a man living near Matlock, received a letter that indicates Tornow is now in the neighborhood of Port Angeles and has been there for a couple of weeks.

The letter is from Molly Bailey, who is living at the J. Sanders home in Tacoma. She says that she saw Tornow in the road near Port Angeles on the northern tip of the Olympic Peninsula, but that he refused to recognize her.

Miss Bailey knows Tornow well, the letter said. She says, in her letter, that she was in the neighborhood looking at some land. While driving along the road, she recognized Tornow and stopped to speak to him, but he refused to recognize her.

She said his hair was long and that his face was covered with whiskers. She didn't mention how he was dressed. It was about two weeks ago she saw the man.

One of the strangest accounts of the Tornow saga occurred three days later when Cloud received a letter from a William Kennedy of Seattle. Following is his report of the letter published in the *The Aberdeen Daily World* on March 15, albeit not on the front page:

POOR OLD JOHN TORNOW HELD IN CLALLAM WILDS

Gunmen Have Outlaw, Writes Seattle man Kennedy

According to a letter received on the Harbor yesterday from Seattle man, William Kennedy, John Tornow is living a life of luxurious ease in a cabin far up in the mountain vastnesses of Clallam County. John's life since his alleged "playfulness with a gun on separate occasions during the past two months, has been most romantic," if this document is to be believed.

He is said to have "collected sufficient thrilling experiences to write a book, which would put Bald Jack Rose's story of the New York underworld, now appearing in the Sunday papers, to shame."

Mr. Tornow was kidnapped from his headquarters on the Hoh River by Clallam County gunmen over a year ago, states the missive. "These men have succored the outlaw, feeding him on choice Porterhouse steak and blancmange (a sweet cake-like dessert, flavored with Irish moussé and almonds) ever since in a cabin especially built and equipped for his comfort."

The life of the gunmen has been fraught with care and worry, though, because one Henry Mack, who is the original Old Spicer, Daniel Boone and Lewis and Clark, all rolled into one composite mountain detective, watches him day and night, states the letter.

Kennedy goes on to write that the gunmen have secured the cooperation of some rich German wagon manufacturers, who are trying to smuggle John over into

Canada. Just what the reason, is not made clear, but it is presumed that John is to learn the wagon trade.

Kennedy, signing himself as residing at 410 Eleventh Ave., Seattle, is the author of the letter. He further deposes that a Chicago physician who happened to be in Seattle, attended to Tornow in the mountain some time ago when John was wounded. The doctor said Tornow was "about starved out and couldn't possibly have existed more than a month or so longer without food."

Kennedy says he talked with Tornow last summer and also with the gunmen and the Chicago doctor. Going on Mack, the sleuth's assertion, Kennedy says Tornow can be captured, and asks that help be sent from the Harbor to accomplish the desired result.

When the sheriff's office was apprised of this letter, which Cloud provided for them, the sheriff, of course, wasn't available. "Which part of this letter would you have me believe?" asked Deputy Sheriff Hoover.

"I don't know if any of it is true," the reporter said, "but you won't know unless you ask the sheriff in Port Angeles or someone to investigate, would you?"

"It's all poppycock. I don't believe he was anywhere near Port Angeles, and besides that, it's just a year ago that he killed the deputies. March 9th wasn't it? Sure it was. How could he have been kidnapped a year ago and also kill the deputies at the Oxbow? Like I said, pure rubbish, garbage. That's what we have to deal with. This guy has produced more tall tales than Aesop."

It became clear to Cloud that getting on the sheriff's good side was going to take some extra special work on his part. His networking with Payette was so comfortable. The sheriff would call him with invites to accompany the posse or even give him a phone call with office news, such as the appointment of Stormes as game warden, and this new guy …

"Things have got to change. I've got to corner that sheriff and tell him how I feel. If I don't do that, I'll never get anywhere with Mathews," Cloud said in frustration to his editor.

"Would you like me to go with you?" the editor asked.

"Thanks, but no thanks. This is something I've got to do myself. I don't like it, but it's got to be done."

Following the commission meeting on April 7, Cloud walked up to Schelle Mathews, who was back from the hunt for a short while. It

was his first face-to-face meeting with the sheriff since he took office
January 13, almost three months ago.

"Sheriff, I need a few minutes of your time. It's very important," Cloud said.

"Sure, kid. I got a little time. What's on your mind?"

"Well, not here. Can we go to the conference room or even to your office?"

"Let's go to the office. I'll be there in about 20 minutes."

"Thanks, that works for me."

Cloud walked down the steps and the short distance to the sheriff's office behind the courthouse. He was as nervous as he had ever been, even more so than before his first big assignment covering the Stapp trial for the *World*. He kept telling himself "Be smart, but be tough."

"C'mon in, Cloud," the sheriff said as the reporter prepared to knock on the window of the open door.

"Thank you, sheriff. This is very important to me. I want to talk about Tornow," he said, noticing the sheriff was silent at the mention of the fugitive, but had a smirk on his face.

"I'll come right to the point. Your silence is making it difficult for me to do my job. I've been covering this story from the very beginning. I feel like you don't trust me to do the job I am paid to do. In short, I can't get any information out of you."

"Well, kid. Thanks for your candor. I appreciate that. It has nothing to do with me trusting you. I've followed your stories for several years and I enjoyed them, but my approach to this is a lot different than Ed Payette's. Remember, I said during my campaign I wouldn't waste the taxpayers' money and also I said, I wouldn't be giving out much information."

"Yes, I recall that. And, I can say that you have been true to your word. I appreciate that you are sticking to your guns, but I just need to get a little bit more from your office. Can you and your deputies try to be a bit more helpful?"

"I'll see what I can do, but frankly I don't want everybody — and that includes John Tornow — knowing my every move. Lou, the Mason County sheriff, feels the same way. He's not giving his paper any info. If Tornow is in his county, he could make it to a store and pick up a paper, or

Schelle Mathews

steal one from a resident. This guy is hard to corral as it is. He doesn't need our help to be elusive."

"All I'm really asking is to be a little more responsive. You don't have to give out trade secrets, but frankly speaking, when you give no comment or say you aren't giving me any information and I'm going to print that, it doesn't put you in a favorable position with my readers, and my readers are your constituents."

"I see your point, kid. I'll say this Cloud, you got brass ones to sit here and unload on me. I like that. I think we'll get along better now."

"So, can you tell me what you've been doing out there the past few weeks, now that it's in the past?"

"Sure. We've been busy. I'll start at the beginning. The night after I took office, I had a posse of six men and we left on the search. They are all still with me."

"Can you tell me who they are?"

"They are all good woodsmen and good shots. Experienced in hunting quarry, though not necessarily the human kind. Bob Crinklaw, Louis Restloff, George Stormes, Con Elliott, Giles Quimby and myself."

The sheriff went on to explain they set up camp on the Tornow branch (Middle Fork) of the Satsop and crisscrossed all the country between the three forks of the river. They found old cabins that the "Wildman" had long deserted. Most contained dried meat and old rags; it appeared Tornow had made a hasty exit at one time or another. "As we found these cabins, we burned them to the ground, so if he returned, there would be nothing there."

Mathews explained that the process went on for a couple of weeks. "Then we got a definite break from a rancher that he was seen hanging out at the cabin close to a ranch, the night before. We hurried to the spot, but we didn't find any trace of the man at the cabin. Another wild goose chase we thought.

"Then one of the posse happened to notice a loose board along the foundation at the back of the cabin. Someone had stayed many times under the cabin, not in it. Such was the man we were hunting, a beast of the woods, who preferred to sleep as close to the ground as he could get. A cunning, crafty thing who probably peered at us as we passed by — just as he likely watched the posse remove the bodies of McKenzie and Elmer. It began to get on our nerves — his unseen presence. Carefully and cautiously we moved never far apart.

"I'm really impressed with Stormes. The sheriff made a good choice to name him game warden. He's a giant of a man. You could see him at any time, and as we paused to look around in the forest, there he was standing erect, his head sideways to catch the slightest noise, his gun ready. Always cool and collected, he had nothing to say, but I knew if the time ever came, that man would be handy and dependable."

Mathews said they found many places Tornow had been, but never a sight of him.

"I've heard grumblings around the courthouse that this is a waste of money — the search, I mean. You've been able to get some funding from the county, but what do you hear?" the scribe queried.

"I've heard that and they threatened to cut off the money. I told them, 'Do it, and I'll take the office force and keep after him.' The main business of this department until it is finished is to get the killer of these four men, and I'm going to stay with it until I finish that business."

Cloud realized once the sheriff got going, there was no stopping him. As belied his demeanor, the sheriff definitely had a passion for the work set before him.

"Thanks, sheriff. I feel better and if we can cooperate, I can do my job a whole lot easier than it has been. One more thing. Sheriff Payette was good about letting me tag along on searches. Is that something you will allow?"

"I'm not comfortable doing that. But, I'll say this. If we know Tornow is dead, you can count on me to tell you immediately and you can make the trip in to get the body."

"That's all I can ask," the reporter said with a smile.

"I'll tell you this. I said I would get Tornow within a month after taking office. That was pretty brash because the weather has been horrible. But, I'll say this now, and you can print this in your next story. I will have that outlaw either in cuffs or on a slab within a month. He's gotta come out of the upper country, and when he does, we'll be ready for him."

31. THE BIG BREAK, A TIP

April 1913

L

ast spring, veteran *Tacoma Times* reporter Fred Boalt journeyed into the Upper Satsop and Wynooche Valley to present a four-article series on the search for the "Beast-Man," John Tornow. That series included the reporter's trek to the Oxbow to recover the bodies of slain deputies, McKenzie and Elmer. Boalt's editor, with prompting from the reporter, knew it was time for an update. He sent Boalt back to the Olympics' hunting grounds with instructions to bring the readers up to date and provide new information as it is available. He would take the train from Tacoma to Montesano to begin his adventure.

The result was a guided tour through Tornow country and a four-part series of articles, the first two which brought Tacoma readers up to date, including the killing of the Bauer twins, the search through the winter of 1911, the killing of the deputies, McKenzie and Elmer in March 1912, and the hunt from that point to the present. His lively, descriptive and forceful writing is depicted in all four articles. Only snippets are included here:

Following is a portion of Boalt's lead-off article on April 14, 1913:

TORNOW STILL LIVES IN THE OLYMPICS
WINTER DROVE HIM TO CIVILIZATION
OUTLAW, MADMAN HAUNTS WILDERNESS

John Tornow lives!

They do not say so in Montesano. They will tell you there that the beast-man is dead. They will tell you that the wild did what organized society has failed to do — that it has killed John Tornow.

In Montesano, belief is the servant of hope. They wish John Tornow dead. The deputies have failed to "get" the outlaw, they have persuaded themselves that the wild has "got" him — as some day it must. Beasts or beast-men — the wild "get" them all in the end.

But Tornow is not dead.

I have been in his country — "the last west." I have found one of his many lairs. He had been there not more than 24 hours before. I saw his tracks in the soft earth. Walter Schaletzke and another were with me. They saw all I saw, and Schaletzke saw more. And the hound went mad.

It was bitter cold in the Olympics last winter, and the snow was deep.

"The winter killed Tornow," they say in Montesano. "The cold 'got' him."

But it is not true.

Tornow, however, is dead to the world he used to know.

There is a line which divides all life. The cougar is as firmly entrenched on his side of the line as we are on ours. Tornow hovered above the line.

Later in the first article, Boalt introduced the reader to the John Tornow he was becoming familiar with, "an elusive hermit, who preferred the woods to life in the community, a human creature, who found solace in the silence of the wilderness, a 33-year-old, who became resilient to the natural elements and who thrived in the most desperate of circumstances. For 19 months, he evaded several posses, deputies and bounty hunters. Somehow, he has survived two horrific winters and emerged strong in the spring to continue his treacherous existence."

This was not the "Beast-Man" or the "Wildman of the Wynooche" that many had described more recently, certainly after the killing of the Bauer boys. This was the Tornow that Boalt came to know more intimately by chatting with neighbors along the Satsop River, a man the community knew was a much different individual from the one authorities and bounty hunters were pursuing.

Here is the Tornow the Tacoma readers were introduced to through Boalt's writing:

Forces unseen and terrible, drew him across the line — forces which we, living snug in our houses, cannot know. They drew him when, a boy of 12, he shirked the farm chores, and, for months at a time, buried himself in the forest whose beauty filled him with wonder, whose silence filled him with peace.

At such times, he hated his own kind. The close atmosphere of a room stifled him. The idle talk, the boisterous rustic wit, the senseless laughter grated on him. He compared them with the whispering silence of the woods.

Yet he could understand the comforts that are so necessary to us on our side of the line. It is pleasant, when one is tired, to sleep in a bed, between sheets. It is pleasant to sit at a table, with one's kin about, and eat well-cooked food with knife, fork and spoon.

He could appreciate, too, a rifle made in a factory by men working certain hours, for certain wages paid in legal tender. A rifle gave him an advantage over his four-footed neighbors in the forest, just as his woodslore gives him an advantage over his two-footed enemies from our side of the line.

And so he hovered on the line.

Women especially, he disliked. "They talk too much," he once told Ed Schaletzke. He would not hunt or fish with talkative men. They "made him tired."

His matter-of-fact brothers could not understand him. Neighbors, who didn't know him, called him "queer." The brothers said he was lazy. They did not know.

I think he must have been conscious of the struggle that was going on within himself between civilization and savagery ...

For three solid years, he has lived in his wilderness. During that time, no man — save one, perhaps — can swear he has seen his face. During that time, he has become more and more the beast-man. It is impossible to believe that he will ever return to our side of the line.

Remember, he is not lonely. You and I, sociable and gregarious animals, would go mad for lack of human companionship. But Tornow is already mad; and he does not lack companionship. The wild is peopled with the spirits of his madness. He was a mystic before he became a beast. The ghost of the dead hound follows always at his heels.

For three years, he has not slept in a bed, or eaten food at a table, or washed his body with soap. His rags hang, tattered and sodden to his lean, giant frame. His hair and beard are long and matted. His fingernails are thick and pointed, like a cougar's claws.

He has caches everywhere. You could no more find them than you could find Tornow himself. You might pass close by them, but though he would be watching you, you would not see him. He has watched the posses a score of times.

Tornow is not dead. The wild died. But here is a curious case. The winter almost "got" him. To escape it and organized society, Tornow is compelled to turn to organized society for help.

I mean that on our side of the line, there is at least one man who is still his friend, who has aided him secretly. The forces on our side of the line are strong, too. The human side of Tornow is not quite dead."

Boalt's second installment recounted the early December search in which the Schaletzkes guided the posse to the hollow cedar, where their cow carcass was found, but the rifle, ammunition and some provisions the men had discovered earlier, were now gone. A crude vine maple and dog salmon heads were found at the site.

The article segued into the mystery man, who was aiding and abetting the fugitive, and later — could stolen newspapers tip off the outlaw?

... They found the shack empty. But there were clues aplenty, which cried aloud the story of Tornow's dire extremity.

First, a fish spear, crudely fashioned. The heads of dog salmon littered the rotted floor. Didn't it argue that Tornow's ammunition was gone, if he had taken to spearing fish? And why would he be content with the despised dog salmon when the streams were aswarm with trout?

And the posse followed Tornow's tracks many miles in the snow until fresh snow fell, obliterating the prints. And these prints showed that Tornow had but one shoe, and that so worn that the big toe protruded. The other foot was bare.

Hungry, sick, bare-footed, his ammunition gone, fleeing before deputies, the servants of organized society, Tornow died miserably and alone. Beasts ate his body.

That is Montesano's case, and it is strong.

But, the prints in the snow told of one fact which accounts for Montesano's secret disquiet. The trail led the posse to two logs exactly 10 feet apart.

The sick and starving beast-man, standing on the first log, leapt lightly to the second, a standing jump. The prints proved it. The light, feathery snow between the logs was untouched.

We come now to Tornow's one human friend.

"We know who he is," Deputy Fitzgerald told me, "but we can't prove anything against him. A hundred times at least, we have gone up into the Satsop and Wynooche country on Tornow clues, some false, some true. Trappers and ranchers meet him or run across the fresh tracks, or, as in the case of the four hunters, whose hound bayed at the shack, got him in circumstances which would have made his capture certain, if a posse had been there.

"But Tornow is always just gone when we arrive. Why? Who tips him off that the posse is starting? We know the man, as queer and crotchety as Tornow himself.

"Here is another curious circumstance. There are roads which, leading northward from Montesano and Elma, wind through the Wynooche and Satsop valleys, to dwindle to trails, and to lose themselves imperceptibly in the tangled forest.

"I have been up and down these roads, and I have talked with the ranchers. They complain that newspapers left in the rural free delivery boxes have been stolen.

I took the dates of which these papers were stolen, and, by referring to the files in the two newspaper offices at Montesano, the Chehalis County Vidette and Chehalis County Call, I made this discovery:

"Every stolen paper contained the news that a posse was starting on another hunt for the beast-man, or that some trapper or rancher had sent the sheriff word of his whereabouts."

It is pleasant in the foothills now. The bears, refreshed by their winter-long naps, are coming down from the mountains.

Tornow, too, has survived the winter, though it nearly "got" him. He is very much alive. Probably he has plenty of ammunition cached. He stripped the bodies of his victims of arms and ammunition, and he is sparing of cartridges.

He has a new pair of shoes, thanks, probably to the "friend on the outside." How do I know?

For proof you must wait until tomorrow.

Boalt's third installment recounts the beginning of his bold journey into the wild to locate the tree in which Ed Schaletzke and his boys felt certain the "Wildman" used as his camp since coming out of the high country in the Wynooche district earlier in the spring. It is Ed's oldest boy, Walter, who, although reluctant, agrees to guide Boalt. This rugged trek is described by Boalt in harrowing, mysterious and even chilling detail, befitting the 96-point headline, more than one-inch deep, screaming across the top of the front page of the *Tacoma Times*:

TORNOW STILL HAUNTS WILD

Here is the proof that Tornow lives:

It is, for several miles, a good road that leads north from Montesano up the Satsop Valley. Farther on it is a road. Then it becomes an indifferent road, and still farther on, a rotten road. And, finally, it isn't a road at all, but a trail that meanders through legions of spruce and hemlock and pines.

As you follow this trail northward, it is borne in upon you that Tornow can afford to laugh at the puny arm of the law. For the trail is to Tornow's kingdom as a single thread in ten thousand Navajo blankets.

From Grays Harbor country on the south to the straits on the north, from the Pacific coast on the west to Puget Sound on the east, is unbroken timber.

This is Tornow's kingdom.

The trail leads into the heart of it.

I found a guide at Montesano and we set out for the Schaletzke ranch, for in the Wynooche Valley, I found no trace of Tornow. I was beginning to think, that after all, Montesano was right and the beast-man was dead.

We passed the Tornow ranch, the Bauer homestead, and came at length to a branch trail to the left so narrow and obscure that we would have passed it by unnoticed, but for the mailbox on a post at the entrance marked "Ed Schaletzke."

Schaletzke went into the wilderness with a pack on his back 20 years ago, and cut the trail to the road.

The Schaletzke clearing lies five miles back from the main trail. We found Walter Schaletzke a phlegmatic, stalwart young man of 25 at the ranch house.

"Take us to Tornow's tree," I said, but Schaletzke shook his head.

"We have come this far, and we cannot find the tree alone," I pleaded.

"We would have to wade the river," Schaletzke objected.

I pointed out that the river was not deep. Then he told me the truth. He was afraid and ashamed of being afraid.

"I will go with you," he said. "But I will take the rifle and the dog. If Tornow is there, the hound will bay him."

We went by paths I could not see, over networks of fallen logs, around windfalls, through deep, silent groves where the forest floor was carpeted with moss, the tree trunks tapestried with moss. We plunged through underbrush so dense that we could not see 10 feet ahead. The parted branches whipped back and lashed our faces. And finally the river, swift-running and cold.

We waded it waist-deep, and once more were in the primeval forest. We gained a burnt-out clearing, and Schaletzke advanced warily, the hound, a young and beautiful bitch, straining at the leash and whimpering.

And when we reached the tree, the hound went mad.

The hair on her back stood erect.

"This is the tree," said Schaletzke, as he loosed the hound. She raced away into the underbrush.

"It is not the same as it was," said Schaletzke. Tornow has been here."

Together we went to the door of the lair.

"How do you know?" I asked, and as I spoke my nostrils were assailed by a stench coming from the lair so sickening that I turned my head away.

"When we first came here," Schaletzke explained, his eyes roving restlessly, "the smell was here. We came in January. The smell was gone. Now the smell is here again."

"A bear?" I suggested.

"Where are the tracks? A bear would scrape off hair against the bark. A bear's den is as filthy as a pigpen."

I know that smell. And so do you if you have ever visited a zoo or a circus menagerie. It is the beast smell, and it is not pleasant to human nostrils. It is the Tornow smell.

Do you doubt it? Wait.

"It rained night before last," said Schaletzke, "— hard. But the bitch has caught a scent. If she bays, run! And see!"

Directly in front of the door to the lair was a sharp imprint of a shoe in soft earth free from leaves and grass. The wearer of the shoe was going away from the tree. The shoe that made the print was a new shoe; at least the heel was not "run down."

Yet, they will tell you in Montesano that Tornow has but one shoe and that so worn that it has no heel at all and scarcely any sole, Boalt said.

Has the mysterious "friend on the outside" supplied the outlaw with new shoes?

Schaletzke was making further discoveries. Thirty feet away from the tree was the skeleton of the cow that Tornow shot last December. There was a loophole that Tornow cut in the trunk opposite the door, through which he fired the shot that killed the cow.

"But that shoulder has been moved," said Schaletzke.

"A bear might have moved it, or a cougar?"

"True," he replied, and entered the chamber, "and I followed."

Boalt went on to describe what they found at the lean-to. "There is a roof three feet from the ground and inside the trunk. It is made of bark. The chamber is circular and about five feet in diameter. Within were two pails — one a lard pail and the other a large tobacco can — filled with drinking water."

Schaletzke tasted the water. "It is fresh," he said. "And the pails were not on this side of the room. Do you say a bear moved them? And look here," he said, digging with his fingers into the weeds and grass with which the floor was bedded. They were comparatively fresh, though crushed down and bruised by a heavy body.

"Tornow's bed," said Schaletzke.

Beneath the layer was another, also of weeds and grass, but old and yellow and sodden with damp.

All the while Schaletzke was listening for the hound. Once, far away, she yelped sharply, but did not bay. Finally, she returned, panting.

"He has gone," said Schaletzke, and grinning for the first time. "But, he was here 24 hours ago, and he will come again. I'm going back."

I detained him long enough to get him in a picture of the tree.

Then we returned to the ranch-house, and my guide and I were as thankful as Schaletzke to get away from Tornow's tree.

———

Meantime, as Boalt and Schaletzke continued their search through Tornow country, little did the reporter know of the new development that had surfaced while the sheriff, ironically, was on his way to Boalt's hometown of Tacoma. That tip would set the sheriff's office all abuzz.

Would this new clue uncover fresh ground, or would it — like all those previous — lead to another dead end?

Sheriff Mathews was subpoenaed to appear in federal court in Tacoma, a date he could not avoid. On the way there, while on the train, Mathews got one of those breaks which must come in almost every case before it can be brought to a successful conclusion.

"I can't believe I am calling you," the sheriff said as Cloud answered the phone at his desk.

"Sheriff Mathews. Have you got Tornow?"

"No, not yet, but we're getting close."

"What's happening?"

"Before I tell you anything, you've got to promise you won't print a word of this until we've got him. What I am going to tell you is proprietary, but I feel sure we are going to get him. I'm telling you this now, so you can be prepared when the time comes in the next few days."

"I'm all ears. I am curious. Tell me what's going on."

"And you promise not to print it?"

"That's up to my editor, but I know we are not going to divulge any secrets that would compromise your position. I'll promise you that."

"I am now in Tacoma, summoned by the federal court, but we got our big break when I was on the train coming over here. A Harbor man, J. B. Lucas, was on the train, bound for Oregon. He's a real estate dealer and during the summer of 1912, he said he spent some time with cruisers and surveyors in the Oxbow area. He said he knows that territory frontwards and backwards."

The sheriff said the man knew him and recognized him, moving forward in the train to take a seat next to Mathews, asking him immediately if the deputies were still searching for the "Wildman."

"I know where John Tornow is — at least where he was last summer — and I wouldn't be afraid to bet he is there right now," he told me.

"I asked him how he knew it was Tornow."

"Well, I don't know that, for sure, of course, but I know where this 'Wildman of the Wynooche' has been hiding while you have been searching for him."

"For God's sake, man," I said to him. "If you know that, tell me, and tell me quick."

The sheriff said Lucas drew a little book from his pocket and scribbled a diagram as he talked.

"He asked me if I knew where the Pellishek homestead was on the West Fork of the Satsop. I told him I did."

"All right, good," he continued. "And he gave me these directions: You go to the Pellishek, and take the trail which runs from the Pellishek to the Benner cabin on the Wynooche — that's about four or five miles. About half-way between the Pellishek and Benner's you will find a brushed out section line, which the new logging surveyors cut out last year. Turn south on this section line and go a mile and a half to the section corner. Turn due west and then walk in a semi-circle to the shores of a little lake — about half a mile."

"Good gracious, sheriff it sounds like he was giving directions for a pirate treasure hunt," the scribe interrupted. "Sheriff, before you hang up, could you give me those directions again. I was writing them down, but I want to be sure they are correct."

"Sure, no problem. The sheriff said Lucas continued talking, most incessantly, without taking a breath. "Walk along the shores of the lake until you find a foot log. Cross the log and you will see a trail to the right, which leads to the rear of the cabin, a sort of a shake down. You will now be about four miles from the Pellishek."

"'I can find it,' I told him. "I knew exactly where it was."

"Tornow spent the summer there last year. I think that was after Sheriff Payette pulled the posse in mid-June. I stumbled onto the place quite by accident, rambling around one day. Lucky thing for me, I guess, that no one was home."

The sheriff said Lucas continued to describe the appearance of the cabin. "He didn't stay there long," he said. "It fitted exactly with the conditions of places he had stopped."

"I thanked him and as soon as I got to Tacoma, I put in a call to Deputy Quimby. I told him to hire Charles Lathrop, Louis Blair, Stormes and Elliott and to wait for further instructions."

"I've got a feeling, sheriff. My stomach is churning with excitement," the reporter admitted. "I've never felt this way. I've never had this assurance in my gut, but this could be, could be what you have worked so hard for, what I've labored so intensely on the last year and a half. Don't you feel it too? Don't you feel like this might be the end?"

"I try not to get on that kind of a high. I try to keep an even keel, but just between you and me, I sure hope so. I just hope my guys don't do something careless and he gets away again."

32. THE FINIS

April 16, 1913

S heriff Mathews arrived back in Montesano on the afternoon of Wednesday, April 16, three days after he had called Dan Cloud from Tacoma and shared his conversation with the reporter about the encounter with J. B. Lucas on the train.

He immediately put in a call to Simpson's Camp 5 to check on the progress of his new posse, but the director there explained the men gathered provisions and packed into the Pellishek, where they were awaiting George Stormes and Con Elliott to meet them.

The director said Deputy Quimby came by auto from Montesano to Frisken's Y, where he picked up Lathrop and Blair, who were arriving from Shelton. From there, they took the Simpson Logging railroad to Camp 5 and would travel the rest of the way, about five miles, on foot or on horseback.

"I assume they are all at the Pellishek, but there is no way to reach them," the camp super told the sheriff. "I can get someone out there in a day or so, but not before then."

"That's OK. I'll probably be up there in the next day or two."

Mathews hung up the phone and went over the plan with Deputy Fitzgerald, the sheriff emphasizing his explicit orders that the deputies were not to make any advances until he arrived.

"I told them all," said the deputy. "They said they understood and would await your instructions or arrival."

Mathews left the office about 6 and headed home. The exhausted sheriff retired about 8 and fell fast asleep.

At 10 p.m., his brief slumber ended when the phone rang.

It was Deputy Giles Quimby, the sheriff's brother-in-law, whom he had left in charge of the posse at the Pellishek. He was calling from Simpson's Camp 5.

His voice sounded nervous and panicky.

"Schelle, we found him! Lathrop and Blair are dead."

"Shocked beyond the power of words to tell, Mathews felt his knees wobble and he quickly grabbed a chair and sat down, then queried his deputy.

"What about Tornow?"

"I believe he might be dead."

"You don't know?"

"Not for sure. I got the hell out of there and wanted to report on the deaths of my two friends. I fired about seven times and I think I hit him. I saw his head fall and there was no gunfire after that. But, Schelle, I don't mind saying, I was shaking so bad, I couldn't load my last bullet. I waited 5 or 6 minutes. I was nervous as hell and I turned and ran. I figured if he was dead, he'd still be there tomorrow, and if not, well I was pretty sure he was hit, so he wouldn't go far."

The sheriff thanked Quimby for his report and said he would leave immediately by auto and be at Camp 5 in a few hours.

He was careful not to upbraid the deputy before signing off. He would save that for later.

"Damn guys," he shouted, slamming the phone against the wall box. This brought his wife, Amanda, out of a deep sleep.

"What's wrong honey?" she asked.

"Damn guys. They disobeyed me and now two of them are dead. Oh, not Giles," he said quickly realizing she might have thought he meant her brother.

"What happened?"

"I told Giles and the guys to wait for me to get there and not go after Tornow. I don't know what happened yet, but I will get to the bottom of it."

"So, who's dead?" she continued to probe.

"Giles said Lathrop and Blair are dead, but I got to get out of here and up there as fast as I can. If they are dead, and Tornow is too, it will likely be several days before I get back. I'll keep you posted, of course, by phone as I get a chance. The closest call box is at Camp 5."

"OK, dear. You be careful, especially if Tornow is only wounded. You know a wounded bear is twice as dangerous as one who isn't."

"I will, Mandy. See you as soon as I can."

It was about 2 a.m. when the sheriff arrived at Camp 5. His brother-in-law finally got a few winks, but woke when Mathews arrived.

"Just go back to sleep and we'll talk in the morning at breakfast," the sheriff told Giles.

"I'm so sorry, Schelle, so terribly sorry."

"I'm just glad you are all right. I want to hear all about it, but let's get some sleep."

The men awoke before daybreak and enjoyed a loggers' breakfast of sausage, bacon, eggs, toast and cottage-fried potatoes before settling down to talk about the circumstances of the previous afternoon.

"Was he at the cabin at the lake?"

"Yes, exactly where Lucas told you," he replied, "and I know what you are going to say. I tried to stop them, but they wouldn't wait. They said they knew where he was and they had a plan to take him out. I couldn't hold them back, so I figured I'd lay back a bit while they came in on the flanks of the cabin."

"You don't know if you got Tornow or not?"

"I didn't stick around to see. I think I did. I fired seven shots — the last one from my knees. I was too nervous and shaking. I drew a bead at his head as he fired from behind a small hemlock."

"Are you sure it was Tornow?"

"I don't know that for sure. Whoever it was, he looked more like a beast than a human."

"Where are Elliott and Stormes," the sheriff queried.

"I told them to wait at the Pellishek for you and they did, except when I came by there yesterday, they had gone down to the river."

"So, they don't know?"

"No. Nobody does, but you and Grisdale," Quimby informed, referring to the Camp 5 superintendant George Grisdale.

"I'm going to call Cloud and give him an update and see how quickly he can get up here. I told Fitzgerald to round up a half-dozen men and get up here as fast as possible. Why don't you see if 'Gris' can corral some of his loggers. I'd like to have at least 20 to go in there. Those bodies won't be easy to pack out, and if Tornow is one of the dead ones, he's going to be a handful as big as he is."

"Right, chief. I'll get right on it."

Mathews made a call to the *World* office and reached Cloud, who had arrived early at his desk.

"Hi, sheriff. What's up?" he asked the officer.

"I think we got him and I want you to hook up with Joe Searles. He's going to be deputized, but he's in Aberdeen and I told him to contact you to hitch a ride with him."

"I can do that. Do you have his number? I want to see if I have time to dash home and grab a bunk roll. No telling how long I might be gone. But, can you give me a few details so I can get something in today's paper?"

"I don't know a lot of specifics yet, but I'll give you what I can. Should be enough to get the word out. I'd forget about getting a sleep roll, Searles will be by your place soon."

After the conversation with the sheriff, Cloud sat down at his desk and pounded out the few details of the shooting that were available that morning.

**Louis Blair and
Charles Lathrop
Slain by Outlaw**

Trappers Hunting Tornow Killed in
Woods; Deputy Quimby Escapes
After Firing Perhaps Fatal
Shot at Fugitive; Posse
Now at Battle Scene

Louis Blair and Charles Lathrop, trappers, are dead, and John Tornow, outlaw and murderer, is believed dead, as the result of an encounter in the woods about 27 miles north of Montesano and eight miles from Camp 5 of the Simpson Logging Company at 5 o'clock last night. The shootout was between Tornow on one side and Lathrop, Blair and Deputy Sheriff Giles Quimby on the other.

Quimby, who escaped, is the slayer of Tornow, if the outlaw is dead.

The scene of the tragedy is near a wickiup Tornow had built close to the shores of a small lake between Sections 30 and 19, Township 21, Range 7, West, and only one mile from the Oxbow, where Deputy Sheriffs Colin McKenzie and A. V. Elmer were killed in March 1912.

Quimby is sure Lathrop and Blair are dead, but is not certain of Tornow's death, though he thinks the seventh shot, the last in his rifle that he fired at the outlaw, found its mark, according to Sheriff Schelle Mathews this morning.

Quimby remained at the scene of the tragedy 10 or 15 minutes after the last shots had been fired by himself and Tornow, and then detecting no signs of life, beat a hasty retreat to summon help. As he passed out of sight, he heard Lathrop's and Blair's dogs howling dismally by the bodies of their masters.

The sheriff said Quimby believed Lathrop and Blair were shot with an automatic revolver, probably the Luger, which Tornow took from the body of Deputy Sheriff McKenzie, killed by Tornow, along with Deputy Sheriff Elmer in March of last year. Blair and Lathrop were within eight feet of Tornow yesterday when he opened fire from behind a hemlock tree.

They had no chance. Neither was able to bring his gun into action. Blair fell at the first shot, Lathrop at the second. From behind his sheltering tree, Tornow poured shot after shot into the prostrate figures before him, while Quimby was directing fire at the outlaw from another direction. Tornow paid no attention, however, to Quimby, who fired every time Tornow thrust his head from behind the tree to take aim at the bodies.

At his last and seventh shot, Quimby said this morning that he saw Tornow's head drop to one side and that no more shots came from behind the tree.

This, and the fact that the dogs were left to bay undisturbed over the dead, lead to the hope that Tornow is at last dead.

Tornow's death is so uncertain that Sheriff Schelle Mathews, and a posse of six men are now at the scene of the tragedy prepared to prosecute to the end the search for the fugitive, should he have escaped Quimby's rifle. Mathews declared before leaving Camp 5 at 7 o'clock this morning that he would not rest until Tornow was captured or he himself was killed.

Two other posses have gone to the scene to bring back the bodies of Blair and Lathrop as well as that of Tornow, in the event of the latter's death.

Quimby is the only lawman in more than a year and half who has seen Tornow and lived to tell of it.

The notches of the outlaw's gun now total six, including the murder of his twin nephews, Will and John Bauer, on September 3, 1911, and that of deputies McKenzie and Elmer.

Quimby brought out the news of the battle last night, reaching Camp 5 about 8 and calling the sheriff in Montesano. Mathews immediately began collecting the posse and was on the road by 11 p.m. by auto, then on foot to Simpson's Camp 5.

Included in the posse are deputies, Quimby, A. L. Fitzgerald, George Stormes, Con Elliott, Frank Cole and Fred Robinson, a Hoquiam policeman. Joining them are Joe Searles and World reporter Dan Cloud.

Coroner R. F. Hunter, W. R. Whiteside, undertaker, and Gene McGillicuddy were on the road by 2 this morning to lead the group bringing out the bodies. Where the bodies will be taken is uncertain; it may be Aberdeen, but it is more likely, the bodies of Lathrop and Blair will be taken to Shelton. A brother of Louis Blair is expected to arrive today to take charge of the remains.

This was the information distributed to the newspapers, and while it was scarce of details, it also contained several snippets of information that were later proved to be untrue.

Ironically, the two most prolific reporters, who had followed the Tornow saga, were missing in action at the final shootout.

Fred Boalt, the energetic *Tacoma Times* reporter, was on a trail somewhere near the Oxbow with Walter Schaletzke, searching for the "Wildman's" latest hideout.

Dan Cloud, *The Aberdeen Daily World's* star reporter, who often served as correspondent for the *Chehalis County Vidette* and the *Grays Harbor Washingtonian*, suffered an ignominious setback as evidenced by this April 18 article in the *World*, some of which would later be proven false information:

World Reporter
Is Taken Ill On
Tornow's Trail

Dan Cloud, World reporter and correspondent for local papers, who accompanied Sheriff Schelle Mathews and his posse into the woods following the report of Wednesday's battle with Outlaw John Tornow, has fallen sick along the trail, and probably won't return to civilization until Sunday when the body of Tornow is brought out.

Cloud stood the trip in very well, but was seized by illness while on the return trail from the Simpson's Logging Company's Camp 5 to the hut, where the bodies of Tornow, Charles Lathrop and Louis Blair lay. He was forced to wait along the trail until evening when he was helped to a hut.

Telephone communication received by Mrs. Cloud today from Sheriff Mathews gives assurance that Cloud has been housed in a shack along the route, that plenty of provisions have been sent in and that men are in care of him.

Thus, news reports on the shootout over the next two days, were fragmented and contained numerous errors.

Prior to the confirmation of Tornow's death, the *Washingtonian* published an editorial in its April 18 edition. It was almost a pro-Tornow angle.

The ways of human nature are past finding out, and still more puzzling is the angle from which people see things. When a man takes to the woods and kills an average of three men a year for two years, thus having six notches on the stock of his gun, one would think that the execution of the murderer would be universal.

Yet, there are not found wanting men to say, "Why don't they let Tornow alone? He sought the wilderness with the evident intention of living his clouded life in solitude and far from his fellow man. But, no matter how far he went, he was followed, and in his maddened state, he has sacrificed six lives. If they had let him alone in the first place, six good men would now be alive."

One would think the man, who went forth into the wilds and "potted" Tornow, should have a medal and a place in the hall of fame. Yet, we have heard a perfectly good lawyer say: "If a man goes out and kills Tornow when the latter is not fighting, he will be guilty of murder. No crime has been proven against the outlaw. Nobody knows he killed all those men, and while it is perfectly proper for him to be arrested and brought in for trial, no man may kill him except in self-defense. As Tornow shoots fast and straight, there is small chance of getting him, unless he be taken unawares."

And there you are. But the vast majority of the people want this madman prevented from doing any further damage. It is true that up to this time, he has only killed those men who were hunting him, but he has rendered the forests adjacent to this Harbor, decidedly unhealthful and there is no means of telling how soon some innocent woodsman or prospector may fall victim to the deadly rifle of this insane outlaw.

The *World* was the first newspaper to confirm the death of Tornow in its non-bylined story of April 18, two days after the killing. The majority of the report came from Coroner R. F. Hunter, who, along with undertaker W. R. Whiteside, had returned to Aberdeen the day before.

Here is a portion of the story that appeared on Friday, April 18:

Tornow Dead Within Eight
Feet of Last Two Victims

John Tornow, outlaw and murderer is dead; slain most undoubtedly by Deputy Sheriff Giles Quimby in the battle late Wednesday afternoon in the woods about 5 miles from Camp No. 5 of the Simpson Logging Company.

Fifty men are working today to make a crude road over which the bodies of Tornow and his last two victims, Louis Blair and Charles Lathrop, trappers, may be brought out to civilization. It is not expected that this can be accomplished before Sunday. The bodies of Blair and Lathrop will be taken to Shelton, the home of both men, while that of Tornow will be brought to Montesano. Crews worked on the road until late last night and began again this morning as early as possible.

Coroner R. F. Hunter, Undertaker W. R. Whiteside and Eugene McGillicuddy, returned from the scene of the tragedy this afternoon, bringing with them details of the battle as mutely told by the dead bodies, supplemented by such facts as Quimby supplied.

Tornow met death within 8 feet of his two victims, and only about 2 miles distant from the Oxbow where a little more than a year ago, he ambuscaded and killed Deputy Sheriffs Colin McKenzie and A. V. Elmer.

Tornow was shot twice, once in the chest and once in the head, both wounds coming from the front and almost without question from Quimby's gun. The fatal shot badly shattered the outlaw's head, and he presented an awful sight to the posse that found the bodies yesterday about noon.

Lathrop and Blair were each shot once, both wounds being in the head. It is then supposed that Tornow turned his Luger automatic pistol, which he had taken from the body of McKenzie last year, on Quimby.

Blair fell first. He never had a chance to touch his gun.

Lathrop swung his rifle into position at the first shot from Tornow and fired three times, the empty shells being found nearby. He was evidently reloading his gun when he was killed.

Quimby fired a total of seven shots. The marks of six bullets were found on the hemlock tree behind which Tornow was secreted. These and the two bullets fired in Tornow's body account for 8 of the 10 shots fired at the outlaw. Lathrop, taken by surprise, probably fired wildly.

... Blair and Lathrop walked straight into Tornow's trap. They had small chance for their lives. The outlaw waited until they were nearly upon him before opening fire. Then he couldn't miss, his mark was too fair and the surprise of his victims too complete.

Tornow made his mistake in supposing that the party of his hunters consisted only of two men. It was his first fight on anything like his own terms, and it proved to be his last.

Tornow looks more like a gorilla than a human being. His hair and beard are long, black, unkempt and matted with dirt. His face is so tanned by exposure to the elements as to be almost black.

McGillicuddy, an experienced woodsman, said the trip to retrieve the bodies was by far the worst they had ever undertaken, grinning at the pun he had used with the editor. He said the walk in from Simpson Camp 5 to where the bodies of Tornow and his victims lay, was, what seemed like, between 17 and 18 miles through difficult terrain. "There is scarcely any trail; the way lies over windfalls and logs, under brush, wading through creeks, over hills and valleys. We had to cross the Schafer Creek three times. In the valleys, there was from 2 to 4 feet of snow," he said.

He said the journey from Montesano, which began about 1 a.m. Thursday, took 14 hours before they reached the shootout site. They had nothing to eat other than salmon berries from the time they left Camp 5 at 7 in the morning. Absence of a trail meant they had to hack and saw their way through brush.

The men approached the cabin with great caution, for at this point, they did not know for sure if the outlaw had been killed. The baying of the hounds might have meant Tornow was still alive. They spread out in all directions and Sheriff Mathews approached the shootout site first. He was the first to discover that Tornow was indeed dead and let out a whoop that signaled the hunt was over.

"It was like a Fourth of July celebration in there," McGillicuddy said. "The posse found the bodies lying, mostly in the same direction. Blair lay on his face. Tornow was slightly on his side, not standing upright with head drooped as Quimby had described earlier, but he was behind a tree that he had used as a shelter. Lathrop's body rested on its side with one hand grasping the pump lever of his rifle. A shell had jammed in the barrel and told of the desperate attempt he had made to defend his life. Three empty shells nearby indicated he may have fired as many shots before death overtook him. Some of the posse, who examined the barrel, believed his rifle had not been fired at all.

"The marks of seven bullets showed on the hemlock tree behind which Tornow stood. One of the seven had plunged into the bark, and this, we believed is the ball that entered Tornow's head and ended his career."

When the *Washingtonian* received notice of Cloud's setback, the paper immediately dispatched C. H. Packard, who hooked up with the posse and was the only local reporter on the scene, though it was not until April 22, six days after the killing, that the story was printed. The newspaper seized on this situation to highlight its exclusive report in the day's headline. Packard also was the only photographer on the scene. Following is Packard's article for the Hoquiam paper.

Finis of Tornow Story

Some new details of tragedy
told by only reporter
who visited the scene

Though the story of the murder of the two deputies, Louis Blair and Charles Lathrop, by John Tornow, and the killing of the outlaw has been told and retold by Giles Quimby, there are many details of the tragedy in the wilds not yet recounted.

The general impression that the camp where Tornow was found was one of several built by him after he became an outlaw is erroneous. It is an old camp built by hunters — possibly by Tornow and his father several years before the latter became an outlaw — and had not been occupied during the past winter.

The camp was an "A" shaped structure, the ground dimensions being 16 x 20 feet and the peak about 9 feet high. It was built of shakes split from a cedar tree which had stood about 400 feet to the west and which had been chopped down. Some of these shakes were a foot wide. They were placed around a rough framework of poles, with the lower ends sunk into the ground. Only a few were fastened with nails. The structure was divided by a partition through the center, a rough bunk occupying the south side of the west room and an open fireplace on the opposite side, over which a chimney of shakes had been erected. Frames for drying meat were built across the chimney. The east room appeared to have been used for a store-all and the south side for a fireplace, although there was no chimney or hole for exit of smoke. The door at the west end had fallen from its leather hinges, and for at least one season, had served as a walk leading across a low, wet spot to the doorway. This last fact was demonstrated by the accumulation of leaves and debris upon the upturned surface of the door. The east end of the cabin facing the slough or pond, on the edge of which Tornow had scooped out a small hole which he used for a corral for his supply of live frogs, was open and apparently had never been closed. These facts alone are sufficient to prove Tornow did not occupy the camp during the winter — that it was only one of several he visited occasionally.

The reporter said the only woodcutting tools found there were a small hand axe and a clasp knife, it is difficult for experienced woodsmen to accept the theory that Tornow built the camp after he became an outlaw. In fact, the moss-grown stumps and moss-covered trees are silent proof the cabin was at least four or five years old.

The camp was devoid of bedding, the only article of that description found being a small piece of an old blanket. The only cooking utensils were a 10-pound lard bucket filled with tea made from salal bush leaves, a smaller lard bucket containing a number of frogs' legs and a coffee can without handle or cover. If "several hundred pounds of elk meat was found at the camp" as reported in Seattle and Tacoma papers by long-range observers, no member of the party saw it, or heard of it until after he returned to the logging camp. Deputy Giles Quimby did state, however, that he and his companions had found the carcass of an elk the day before, Tuesday, killed by Tornow about three-fourths of a mile from the camp and a short distance from the route traveled by the posse which returned with him. One hind quarter had been removed. The only food found at the camp was the frogs.

Tornow had scooped out a small hole at the edge of the pond about 15 feet from the east end of his camp, where he kept his supply of frogs. More than 100 of these were strung on a piece of thread and were anchored for future reference.

This camp is in the southwest quadrant of Section 19, Township 21. It is not "located on an island with only one way to approach it and that across a foot log which he could have held against a small army," as one long-range reporter described it; but it is on the west shore of a small beaver pond, and near a lake that covers an area of perhaps 60 to 100 acres. The lake cannot be seen from the camp.

Courtesy of Polson Museum

Dogs guard the bodies of slain deputies, Charles Lathrop and Louis Blair. Photo was by C. H. Packard of the *Grays Harbor Washingtonian*, the first reporter to the shootout scene.

Deputies and others had searched in vain for this lake and camp for more than a year. Deputies Quimby, Lathrop and Blair reached it with the aid of a map and description furnished by members of the Simpson Logging Company. One of the company's surveying parties recently met Tornow in this vicinity, and he took luncheon with them, but, as he knew they were not looking for him, he did not molest them.

Supt. George Grisdale stated that ever since the murder of McKenzie and Elmer it had been almost impossible to get men to do the necessary cruising and surveying in that part of the country. "It is a great relief to us to know that the terror of the Wynooche is dead," said Grisdale.

The superintendent said other Tornow camps were found while cruising in the quarter-section post of Sections 16 and 17, Township 20, Range 7, but had not been occupied for several months. They contained a supply of dried elk and bear meat. The general impression prevails among cruisers and surveyors that the camp where Tornow spent last winter, and which was really his headquarters, is not far from the spot where Deputies Quimby, Lathrop and Blair found the remains of the elk.

Packard provided a detailed description of the shooting scene:

Six bullets were embedded in the tree from behind which Tornow shot — four of them within a radius of five inches and near the center, about the height of Tornow's head; one was on the south side; about eight inches higher, and the sixth was on the north side, 10 inches below the group. Two more had peeled the bark and cut into the wood on the north side for a distance of four inches before glancing off, and the ninth, had just grazed the tree where Tornow's head appeared when he took aim.

Tornow's left eye was closed as in sighting his rifle and the other was wide open. His last cartridge was in the chamber and the rifle was at full cock when Sheriff Mathews first reached the body. The left eye was opened later."

The distance from the spot where Tornow stood behind the tree to where Lathrop and Blair were when they fell, was between 16 and 18 feet; Quimby was about 75 feet to the rear of his companions.

The stock of Lathrop's gun had been splintered by one of Tornow's bullets.

Three of the four dogs which accompanied Quimby, Lathrop and Blair were guarding the bodies of their dead masters when the posse arrived Thursday afternoon. The animals began barking when the party was about a quarter of a mile from the camp, and continued until the arrival of deputies with whom they were acquainted. The dogs would not permit strangers to approach the bodies and photos were taken, showing the deputies and the dogs grouped about the bodies of Lathrop and Blair.

Courtesy of Polson Museum

Photo taken by C. H. Packard of the *Grays Harbor Washingtonian*, shows the posse outside of Tornow's shack. Giles Quimby is in the center.

The Simpson Logging Company rendered indispensable aid in recovering the bodies — in fact, they would not have been brought out for several days had not the loggers assisted. Manager Mark Reed held a train in readiness to bring the bodies down from the end of the track and he invited the authorities to call for as many of the men as needed. The second squad of 25 loggers, which went out after the bodies Friday, was headed by Foreman Joe Stertz, who kept his men moving in a systematic manner, following the squad of axmen which preceded them on a new and more direct route cruised out by Deputy Quimby. This latter squad included two brothers of Louis Blair. This party numbered about 40 persons. A few minutes after the start for the Pellishek camp with the bodies was made, a moving picture operator, a photographer and a reporter from Tacoma arrived. The "movie" man secured several views along the route, besides one of the demolished camp. The structure was partly torn down in order to obtain poles with which to make litters for carrying the body and also to ascertain if it contained any hidden caches.

"Tornow's jet black beard was neatly trimmed in Vandyke style, but his hair was long and unkempt," the reporter wrote.

The day after the official examination by Coroner R. F. Hunter and the sheriff, a watch and other articles identified as belonging to deputies McKenzie and Elmer were found; another more careful search of the several layers of clothing covering Tornow's body was made.

The reporter said "Tornow was wearing three pairs of pants made of ducking and they were worn according to age, the oldest worn on top, so as to be discarded easily. His shirt was in rags, but his shoes were relatively new and caulked.

Washington State Archives
Elmer's watch taken off the body of John Tornow.

"Among the articles found were a small open-face watch, a pocket knife which had been bought for McKenzie by Ed Payette when the latter was sheriff, Al Elmer's match safe with a bushel of matches, packed very peculiarly, some wrapped individually in pieces of newspaper. There was no reading matter and two .25 caliber cartridges had been reloaded. The name of W. Thurman was engraved on the inside of the case of the first watch found and supposed to have belonged to McKenzie. It was a Hamilton and the case number 2360057.

"Lathrop's watch, struck by one of the bullets, stopped at 15 minutes to 5 o'clock, verifying the statement of Mr. Quimby as to the time of the shooting and his departure for the logging camp."

The distance he traveled in about three and a half hours is at least 14 miles — four through the wilderness, about eight over a windfall-blockaded trail, and the remainder along the railway. Several miles of the trail were covered after dark, the entire trip being made in the fastest time ever recorded in this part of the world under anywhere near similar conditions of trail and light.

Lathrop and Tornow had been hunting buddies before the latter became a "jungle beast." They had hunted together several seasons over the same wilderness in which Tornow sought refuge, and Lathrop was confident Tornow would not shoot him if they met in the woods. That confidence, accompanied by a rifle, led the deputy to his death. Tornow is not known to have molested anyone he saw in the woods who did not carry a gun.

THE MAN THAT CONQUERED TORNOW
Washington State Archives
Giles Quimby

While Cloud was laid up with an illness, the *World's* other reporters and city editor Bill Irvine scrambled to cover the news. They wrote no less than five other stories to accompany the one about Tornow being found dead within 8 feet of his victims and the report on Cloud taking ill.

Six of the stories appeared on the front page, occupying all but a small portion of the paper's entire lead page.

• Quimby is unlikely to receive the $5,000 reward money because he was a deputy sheriff and couldn't collect for his deed, unless the county made a special exception in this case.

The story said the deputy would likely collect $1,000 of the reward money, which the state offered. The reward offered by the county included $2,000 for the arrest and conviction of the slayers of the Bauer twins, and $2,000 for the person, dead or alive.

The same story said Quimby will likely be a big draw as a vaudeville star and might be able to be induced to appear on stage and recite the story of the killing of the outlaw. It was learned today that those offers will be made to Quimby.

• Slain trappers Blair and Lathrop were known as the best woodsmen and were seeking Tornow for the $3,000 reward hanging on his head. Blair was better known in the county, having participated with nearly every posse, which had searched for Tornow since the killing of the twins. He was killed one day after his 31st birthday.

Lathrop was 41 and had arrived at Matlock from Bristol, Vt., about 14 years previous. He had worked at Dayton, east of Matlock, and for a time, was employed as a railroad man. The two men had most recently been employed by the Simpson Logging Co., and had resided in Shelton. They were regarded as the best of trappers in the region and Lathrop had hunted and trapped with Tornow about five years ago. Lathrop had also been on a few of the posses for at least a year.

• Aberdeen councilman Dan Pearsall, a posse member, who had hunted the Oxbow and Satsop regions for years and had run into countless hunters who had pursued Tornow, says "I have never thought that Tornow left the immediate scene of his murders. During the past winter, ranchers have now and then lost a cow, the remains of which were found, and chicken houses have been raided everywhere in the vicinity of Tornow's old home on the Satsop district."

He reported to the *World* that "One rancher told me that during the heavy snow that he heard a terrible noise in his chicken houses and the dogs kept barking continuously. The next morning he noticed tracks leading away from his chicken house.

"That Tornow remained around his shack after killing McKenzie and Elmer was evident to me when a part of us found pieces of elk meat that had been buried, the shoes worn by Tornow and the holster and handcuffs owned by McKenzie. It took time to bury all these things as we found them buried in different places and some distances apart."

• Tornow might have been responsible for a seventh victim. When he was killed he was wearing a pair of caulked loggers' boots and comparatively new. Where he got them is not known, but it is relatively certain he didn't buy them at any local establishment.

Connected with this detail, is the alleged disappearance of a logger in the employ of the Blakely Mill company from its camp near Kamilche, about five miles southeast of Shelton. The man, whose name cannot be learned today, has been missing two or three weeks, according to Superintendent Lee at the camp.

Posse members said the boots Tornow had when killed had not been worn long and were of a high grade and very expensive.

• Interestingly, a story on former sheriff Ed Payette's reaction appeared on Page 2.

Payette said he was most pleased with the outcome, saying to the *World* reporter: "Tornow's death puts an end to the feeling of unrest and uncertainty."

He gave credit in great measure to Blair and Lathrop. "They had been in my employ for many months," said the sheriff. "They were always on the job and tracked Tornow from place to place. They always kept me posted on any new evidence of Tornow, and the day on which they finally came face to face with him was the closing chapter in a long series of adventures in which they had always proved brave and true."

Payette said Quimby's shooting of Tornow was fortunate and at the same time lucky, a luck that might have come to any officer. He said Tornow was likely confused because a third party was involved in the shooting, something that hadn't occurred in previous encounters. The sheriff said, for the good work that Lathrop had done for him earlier, he had rewarded him with a bloodhound of which Lathrop was particularly fond, and which was doubtless with him on his fatal trip.

Cloud recovered from his "illness" quickly, hiking to Camp 5, then making it back out to Frisken's Y, before traveling by auto to Montesano and by rail to Aberdeen. He was at his desk by late Friday, just two days after the shooting, and submitted his story as told by Giles Quimby for Saturday's paper.

When he arrived back at the *World* on Friday, he called his parents, his gal, Lindy Fleming, and his editor. He decided to write a complete report of his travails for the editor, originally not for publication, but to let his boss know what happened.

But, the editor found the dissertation so interesting, compelling and informative that he decided to publish it, dispelling rumors that the reporter had taken ill or that he had died as some Seattle-area papers

BILL LINDSTROM

had printed. Those reports prompted a flood of telegrams to the *World* office early Saturday.

Following is the report in Dan Cloud's own words.

No, I am not dead, as I am told at 12 this morning that the Seattle Times reported, nor sick as the World had it last night, and not even a coward, at least of the sort that I understand was reported at Montesano. I simply gave out — utterly exhausted — after having reached nearly the end of the trip, spent a night in the woods alone, without arms, fire or food — even without water, except such as I got from sucking snow, and then after tasting food yesterday morning at 9 o'clock for the first time in better than 24 hours, walked back to Camp 5 and autoed into Montesano.

At that, I am the first newspaper man out from anywhere near the scene of the shooting. But let me tell you my own experiences. If I was anyone but a newspaper man, they would be worth a story in themselves.

I was preparing for bed when I got the telephone message of the shooting. I hustled out and got all that anyone could get on it from the sheriff and telephoned my story. Sheriff Mathews had ordered an auto to go out to the scene. Without any preparation I jumped into the rig and went with him. It was 1:30 in the morning when we reached Frisken's Y on the Simpson logging road — as far as autos could go.

We thought Camp 5 was down the track and started down that way, but luckily stumbled onto Benson's and Lathrop's (the latter one of the men killed) cabin. Benson and "Dutch" who had heard the news were laying awake awed by the

Washington State Archives
Quimby's badge

awfulness of the tragedy, for they knew more than we — that both of the deputies were surely killed. "Dutch" volunteered to get up and lead us to Camp 5 — which is five miles up the track from the "Y."

We reached there at 5 a.m. and went at once to bed, without even talking to Giles Quimby who was also in the foreman's house.

At 6, we were up and, while we washed for breakfast, Quimby told us his story. I saw the story wasn't there. The news interest of it after getting Quimby's story, was to know if Tornow was dead, wounded or still free in the woods. I believed my place was with the posse going to the scene, and from what they said, I reckoned I could go on out with them, learn the facts and get back, if not that night, at least early the next day. Now, understand that wasn't folly. They all figured they would get the deputies' bodies out, if not that day, then early the next.

I got a chance to send a verbal story of Quimby's interview out by Commissioner Bud Wilson, who I dare say phoned you, Mr. Rupp, as soon as he could. I couldn't get the wire there and join the posse which left at 7.

We ate a hasty breakfast and started — the sheriff's posse and a big bunch of men loaned by Camp 5 — to bring out the bodies of the dead. Shortly after 9, we were at the Pellishek cabin on the Wynooche. After a brief halt and a bite or two of raisins, we started on again. In spite of the broken rest, I was keeping up well in about the middle of the bunch until we left, what they were pleased to call, a trail and took up a mountain side, blazing a trail on our own.

That hill reaches an elevation of 3,500 feet — or at least I found antler moss up there and botanists have told me it doesn't grow at a lower elevation — and it was very steep, with the trail leading over and under logs and through brush. I was beginning to lag, but was not the last man by any means until, all of a sudden, my strength left me.

At the urging of those who had gone ahead I tried again and finally reached the top of the hill, but I was too exhausted to go further, and at my request they went off and left me, promising to return that way and pick me up as they brought out the bodies. They said the camp was two miles farther.

That was 11 o'clock. I dropped off to sleep. I awoke at 3 to find Trapper Benson standing over me. He asked me what was the matter and I told him. He said he was glad I happened to be there. He was bringing in two of Blair's brothers and they were just behind. One of them was lame and he thought they better wait there with me. He would go on and help carry the bodies out. When the men came up, after some objections, they decided to stay there, and Benson went on. We sat round for an hour or two. There was no sign of the party coming back. We hadn't heard a sound. Both of these two men were used to the woods and knew well how to follow blazes. They got to imagining there was something wrong and suggested if I was able, they would go on to the Tornow shack. I was rested then, and perfectly willing.

It was more than two miles from there to the shack. We went more than two miles and couldn't even see it. One of the men wanted to turn back. I was getting very tired and knew I couldn't make it back to the Pellishek, so I urged that we go on to the cabin or until we met the men carrying out the bodies, and the older brother also favored that. Then I thought I would stay all night with the posse, which expected to camp there.

Just at that time, we heard a hunter's horn. We yelled and got an answering shout. It proved to be "Dutch" and Benson, who were cutting across lots to find a

*shorter trail to the Pellishek. They told us that the bodies couldn't be brought out
'til morning, that Tornow was dead and that the guard left behind with the body
had scanty provisions as it was.*

*I feared I couldn't make it back — I suppose I knew it, but tried, for there was
now a big incentive. Here were the actual details of the big story. As we walked,
they told them to us. But it was only a few moments until all interest in the story
even left me. We were again climbing a mountain. Near the top I gave up and urged
the boys to go on, and when they come back in the morning to bring me some food.
Blair's brother was quite a ways ahead and was carrying a revolver that Mathews
had insisted I should have — though I know more about the use of flying machines
than of revolvers.*

Washington State Archives

**Posse members bring out the body of John Tornow. The body is wrapped in
canvas on the horse on the left.**

*I don't think he thought of the revolver and I didn't. I thought of matches, but
I supposed I had plenty. They didn't leave me without my urging them to do so, and
before they had gone 300 feet, I was sound asleep. In an hour or about sundown,
I awoke. I gathered some dry wood and found I had ten toothpicks and just three
matches. It took all three matches to light my fire. Pleased beyond compare that
I had managed to get a fire even with the last match, I sat down to watch it and
munch a bite of snow.*

*How it happened, I didn't know, but I dropped off to sleep again. When I
awoke, it was 10 o'clock, as near as I could make out by the moonlight. My fire was*

black, out, and I was cold and stiff and sore, for I had no coat — no man carried a coat on that trail. Those who started with them, hung them on bushes. I was a little frightened then, but I got up and moved around until a little of the stiffness was gone, and then I commenced pulling cedar boughs from fallen trees and piling them under a log for a bed. An hour or more of work warmed me up a bit, for it was a beautiful night, and fairly warm, even up there.

I burrowed in among the boughs and once again went to sleep. Except once when some wild animal, possibly an elk or deer — for elk signs are very plentiful there — walked through the brush not far away stopping occasionally to browse — except that once, for a minute or two, I slept until daylight at 5, when I was so cold I hustled out to slap and stomp some circulation into my body.

At about 9, the bunch of men coming back after the bodies reached me. They had a bottle of coffee that was still warm and a pancake sandwich with fat bacon for meat — but honestly, it was a swell breakfast. Also, they had brought one man, who expected to have to help me back to the cabin, but all the help he had to give me was to putter along slowly and let me rest frequently.

We reached the Pellishek shortly after 10, cooked some more breakfast for ourselves and a bunch of men on their way out, and then hiked it back to Camp 5 in a little better than two hours and 30 minutes. From there, you know rest of the story. I got in here shortly after 11 o'clock.

The only newspaper man who got out to the scene of the shooting was the Washingtonian's man, who got some pictures and who will probably be back today. It is possible the (Tacoma) Tribune and the Sun (Bremerton) men got in there today — they were headed right, but had the biggest part of their journey ahead of them when I passed them about 10 o'clock. If they got in, there isn't one chance in a dozen that they could get back before sometime today. This is a case of where those who lagged behind got the best of the story.

Washington State Archives

Posse members take a breather outside the Pellishek ranch.

The P-I man (Seattle) luckily got lost when starting and had to make it back to camp, where he got the story that really belonged to you. The men who had been to the scene of the shooting had agreed on the way out that the World was really entitled to the story and should have it first. But when they got to Camp 5, they found correspondents there with letters of introduction to the foreman from Mark Reed of the Simpson Logging Co., and they told the story.

I am dead tired, but I have sat up to write you a personal narrative after writing my story, which I hope will save me the blue envelope for this time.

Despite Cloud's immediate setback, he was still able to produce the first story of the shootout, straight from Giles Quimby's mouth, the only survivor of the killings and the only man, who knew the truth of what happened in the Wynooche woods on April 16, 1913.

Quimby gave this report from the trail in to the shootout site to Cloud in graphic detail with an almost unheard of four decks of headlines for the April 19 edition of the *World*:

THIRTEEN NOTCHES
ON TORNOW'S RIFLE;
EACH MAY BE LIFE?

This is Belief of Woodsmen Who Found
Outlaw's Gun in Cabin Where He Made
His Last Stand Which Ended Life

QUIMBY'S OWN GRAPHIC STORY
OF BATTLE TOLD BY DEPUTY

Mathews Had First Tip on Cabin By The Lake; Murderer
Stored Matches Carefully: Sight-seers and Camera Men
Now Flock to Scene of Tragedy

John Tornow's own rifle — his Winchester .30, that he used exclusively at the beginning of his criminal career, and which was found in Tornow's cabin in the woods, by Sheriff Mathews Thursday afternoon — has eight notches cut in one side of the barrel stock, and five in the other. None of them was cut very recently.

If, as many of the woodsmen who knew the wretch believe, those marks each stand for a murder Tornow committed, his total cost in lives has been 15. Anyway, whether the number is six, as positive records show, or 15, as the gun seems to indicate, the man had degenerated into little better than a brute, about on the level of a coyote, a beast that preys on offal and fights fiercely when forced to it.

The picture he made as he stood behind that tree last Wednesday afternoon, only occasionally showing his head, was, according to Giles Quimby, the most ferocious and most terrifying that one can imagine.

Trampling over the trail the morning after the shooting, and before he knew positively that Tornow was dead, Quimby told me the story of the fight. He was hollow-eyed from lack of sleep, his face was white and his eyes still showed the horror he had been through, but he must lead the crowd back to the scene of the tragedy, and probably wouldn't have been elsewhere if he could have. For Giles Quimby is a brave man, though a man of few words and those few say little of himself.

Washington State Archives

The hemlock tree where Tornow was secreted and subsequently fell.

"We had orders not to investigate the shack until Sheriff Schelle Mathews rejoined us," said Quimby. "He told us to locate it but not to go in until he was along. He had a tip and he insisted it was his right to lead the party in there, for he believed Tornow was there.

"The sheriff was delayed in rejoining us, and we had located the shack by the lake. We knew it was the place that had been described to us, though it didn't look quite as we expected it to. Wednesday morning the boys proposed we go take another look in the shack. I objected and reminded them of Schelle's orders, but they pooh-poohed and argued that three men were better than four, or at least as good, in a hunt of that sort.

"I didn't say more because to have done so, would have looked as if I was afraid to go with them, and I want to tell you they were two of the best men I ever worked with.

"We went over practically the same route we will go today. As we neared the little lake — it is only a beaver pond of five or six acres — we went very carefully. We could see the shack from places along the trail that we approached but there was no sign of anyone being about. It looked deserted.

"When we reached the banks of the lake, the boys walked out on a log in the lake to get a sight from another angle at the shack. I think now that Tornow must have seen them then, but that he probably didn't know there were three of us until later.

"*The place was as still as a grave, except for the croaking of frogs. The boys could see from there that there were no portholes in the cabin and suggested we go to the shack from the back. I was walking behind them. I motioned that we ought to get a more distant view of the front before approaching, but they paid no attention to my signals and while I walked at an angle through the brush to a tree that stood about 60 feet from the south side of the cabin, the other two walked up behind the cabin, and then along the south side where just about the front of the shack two big logs were laying in a V-shape, with the point to the corner of the cabin. Out of the log on the south side of the V, there grew a good-sized tree. As the boys stepped opposite, or nearly opposite, this tree as if to get a peek over or around the wide end of the V, I heard a shot.*

"*I saw Blair falling and instantly there was another shot and Lathrop fell. I think they were both killed instantly. At least when I looked at them again, they were both dead. I am certain.*

"*In just a fraction of the time it takes to tell it, it all happened. I saw that fearful head bob from that tree and shoot, I think with an automatic revolver, and I shot at it. I thought then at first he was shooting at me when there were repeated shots, but I now think maybe he never saw me and was shooting at the boys — that he thought it was one of them, instead of a third person that was shooting at him.*

"*We fired seven or eight shots, I think each, but he wasn't much of a mark. I thought once when he leaned further out than usual that I got him in the chest, but he dodged back and there was soon another shot from him. My last shot at him, I noticed one thing peculiar. The head didn't seem to dodge behind the tree, but rather to droop down. I am almost certain I hit him, but we can't be certain until we get there. I would rather you didn't repeat it, but I believe we will find him dead.*

"*God, but he was an awful sight! I couldn't see much, you can imagine in a fight like that as to detail, but he appeared black and fierce and wild-looking. I can see that face every minute since the fight.*

"*After he stopped shooting, I waited for him to show his head again. I guess I waited there five or six minutes, watching for him. Then I began to get a sort of buck fever, I guess. I was nervous and shaking all over. My two companions were dead. Suddenly I realized that in that condition, I couldn't hit the side of a barn, and I began to dread that I would see that head dodge up again. Then I knew it was time for me to get out of there. I backed out through the brush until I could get some trees between me and where Tornow had been shooting. I didn't know what to do at first. It was 5 o'clock. I knew if I was going to get the word out of the death of the boys that night, I would have to go. So I lit out for Camp 5. I was there shortly after 8:30.*"

The Aberdeen Daily World headline of April 19, 1913.

Understand, this interview was given in answer to questions, in a disconnected manner while on the trail in to get the bodies and see if Tornow was dead, but the facts as related by Quimby are borne out except in two or three particulars by what the posse found when they reached the cabin late Thursday afternoon. Tornow did know that Quimby was shooting at him, for he fired some shots at Quimby as is proven by two or three bullets imbedded in the tree behind where Quimby had stood. It was the short-barreled Marlin Model 94 that Tornow took from Deputy McKenzie's body last year, he used in his last battle, instead of an automatic revolver as Quimby believed. And Lathrop shot at least three times after he went down, and tried to shoot a fourth time, but one of Tornow's shots split his stock. Probably the average man in a like position as Quimby would have known less than he of the true happenings.

... It is wonderful how the interests of the nation seem centered in that little logging camp right now. Dozens of autos were standing along the tracks for five miles yesterday and all manner of people came in at Camp 5. They came to the camp by train, auto, horseback, wagon and on foot. All of them are crazy for some small souvenir of the battle and the outlaw.

Moving picture cameras sent in yesterday, have photographed today every bit of the journey on the way out from the scene of the tragedy. Pictures have been taken, also of the cabin in the woods, the battle ground and the bodies of the three men. Eagerness to see Tornow is uppermost and there have been numerous demands that the body be placed on exhibition, even if an admission fee should be charged. This will not be done, however.

Fred Tornow, one of John Tornow's older brothers, arrived today from Portland, where he has a logging business. He shook hands with the sheriff and said he cherished "no hard feelings" as the result of his brother's death, merely remarking the sheriff and his force had "done their duty." Then he proceeded to make arrangements for the outlaw's funeral.

The bodies were brought out early Saturday after more than 40 men, mostly from Simpson Camp 5, labored through the day and night Friday to prepare a crude road, a project that was completed much quicker than expected. From the shootout site, the bodies were carried on make-shift stretchers by a number of men through the dense underbrush a distance of about six miles to the Pellishek ranch, where they were met by horsemen.

John Tornow's body is propped up and tied to a tree. Deputies George Stormes, left, and Con Elliott pose with him.

The posse is shown around the body of the slain outlaw, John Tornow.

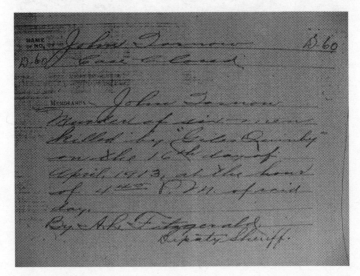

Coroner's report on the death of John Tornow, signed by Deputy Sheriff A. L. Fitzgerald.

Tornow's body is propped against a bench. Postcards were made from many of the photos taken in the woods and sold for 25 cents.

Charles Lathrop

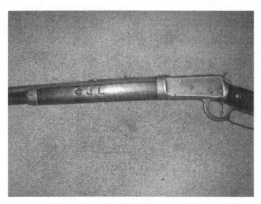

This is the .94 carbine that belonged to Charles Lathrop. Note his initials. Lathrop left this gun with his roommate. It was later shipped to Noah Lathrop, father of Charles.

Watch worn by Lathrop was struck by a Tornow bullet. It is stopped at 4:45.

Courtesy of Lathrop family

Four great-grandsons of Charles Lathrop are shown at the slain deputy's tombstone in Bristol, Vt., in 2013. From left are, Duane, Donald, Dave and Doug. All but Donald attended the victims' memorial dedication in April, 2013.

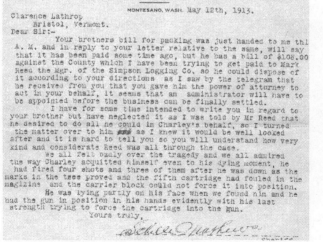

Sheriff's Office

OF CHEHALIS COUNTY

MONTESANO, WASH. May 12th, 1913.

Clarence Lathrop,
    Bristol, Vermont.
Dear Sir:-

Your brothers bill for packing was just handed to me thi A. M. and in reply to your letter relative to the same, will say that it has been paid some time ago, but he has a bill of $108.00 against the County which I have been trying to get paid to Mark Reed the Mgr. of the Simpson Logging Co. so he could dispose of it according to your directions as I saw by the telegram that he received from you that you gave him the power of attorney to act in your behalf, it seems that an administrator will have to be appointed before the business can be finally settled.

I have for some time intended to write you in regard to your brother but have neglected it as I was told by Mr Reed that he desired to do all he could in Charley's behalf, so I turned the matter over to him as I knew it would be well looked after and it is hard to tell you so you will understand how very kind and considerate Reed was all through the case.

We all felt badly over the tragedy and we all admired the way Charley acquitted himself even to his dying moment, he had fired four shots and three of them after he was down as the marks in the tree proved and the fifth cartridge had fouled in the magizine and the carrier block could not force it into position.

He was lying partly on his face when we found him and he had the gun in position in his hands evidently with his last strength trying to force the cartridge into the gun.

Yours truly,

Courtesy of Lathrop family

This letter was sent on May 12, 1913, by Sheriff Schelle Mathews to Clarence Lathrop, brother of Charles.

From the Pellishek to Camp 5 was another six miles. The posse then transported the bodies on horseback another five miles to Frisken's Y, where Tornow's body was taken by Sheriff Schelle Mathews' auto to Montesano. The bodies of Lathrop and Blair were transported by rail to Shelton; Blair's body was taken to Centralia for funeral and burial at the Washington Lawn Cemetery. Lathrop's body was transported to Bristol, Vt., for funeral and burial.

Viewing of Tornow's body was virtually a circus sideshow from the moment the outlaw was discovered dead until he was interred at the Grove Cemetery near Matlock. Before the body was wrapped for removal to the Pellishek, many photos were taken, showing the rugged corpse upright, tied against a tree with a couple of the posse on either side of him, or prone on a bench or wooden slab.

Several photographers, most prominently William Hawkes of Montesano and J.P. Ladley of Aberdeen were in that party before the bodies were brought out. They produced postcards of the outlaw's body in various stages. It was believed as many as 20 different postcards were made. These were developed in Montesano and sold for 25 cents each. They were gobbled up as fast as they could be produced.

In addition, cameraman and moviemaker, D. P. Lea of Aberdeen, produced a series of slides from the scene, on the trail carrying the bodies out and at the Montesano funeral home. These slides were shown for several months at movie theaters in Aberdeen, then throughout the Tacoma and Seattle areas. Throngs gathered to see these snapshots of the end of the longest manhunt in state history to that date.

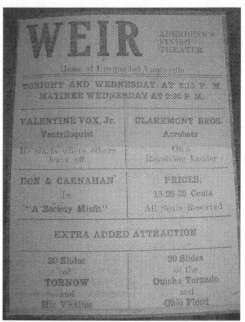

Flier for the Weir Theater in Aberdeen features 20 slides of Tornow and his victims.

There were about 20 slides, not motion pictures, depicting the scene of the last stand, the posse escorting the bodies out of the woods, the cabin, which was Tornow's last hideout. The slides were very clear and offered a glimpse into the terrible conditions the deputies endured at the shootout.

In Aberdeen, manager Ed Dolan, secured an exclusive showing at the Weir Theater for Saturday and Sunday showings. He said it was necessary to give four shows to take care of the immense crowds; the theater was packed to capacity for all showings. An extra day was added on Monday, showing the slides prior to a double-billed movie.

At Montesano, where Tornow's body was taken, more than 1,500 viewed the corpse, which was cleaned up, his beard shorn and hair clipped. The body was stripped of its many outfits and rags. His feet were bare, but wrapped in bandages because of serious blisters.

The *Chehalis County Vidette* wrote: "Never in the history of Montesano has so much excitement run riot in the county seat as it did Saturday night when the body of John Tornow, outlawed hermit of the Satsop forests, was brought to the city morgue and laid out for close examination by the coroner and authorities."

When the body first arrived at the G. L. Storey morgue on Pioneer Street on Saturday night, officials announced that the crowd, which had already gathered in large numbers would not witness the body. The people would not leave and officers had to force their way past the crowds to get into the building. The outside noise was such a clamor that officials decided to relent and let the crowd get a glimpse of the county's famous criminal.

In less than 30 minutes, about 750 people passed through the door and got a brief view of the gruesome sight, prone on the undertaker's slab. A *Vidette* article noted that about one-fourth of the visitors were women and children. "Some of the children cast one hasty glance at the slab and hurried by."

When the first half of the onlookers had passed through, the doors were closed and the autopsy commenced. Coroner R. F. Hunter, undertaker W. R. Whiteside and about a half-dozen other forensics folk, participated. The body was identified by Ora Wilson, a longtime friend of Tornow, Commissioner C. N. "Bud" Wilson, who had known the fugitive long before he was a criminal, and a neighbor, E. A. Bacon, who had hunted with the man in earlier years.

They said Tornow looked much like he did when they last saw him about three years ago. His hair had grown long, but a mirror and pair of scissors found in his cabin, proved that he kept himself as tidy as possible, though not in recent months.

The autopsy revealed there were two serious wounds, both made from the soft-nosed bullets that were fired by Quimby. Lathrop, who it was thought by some might have hit Tornow, had used the steel-jacketed bullets. The examination also proved conclusively that no shots had been fired into the body after Tornow was dead. All wounds were determined to be from Quimby's gun. This dispelled the rumor that had surfaced about a member of the posse firing into Tornow's head when his body was discovered behind the hemlock.

The first wound, which would not necessarily have been fatal, entered the neck at the left side and went under the shoulder blade and was lodged just under the skin below the right shoulder blade — in line with the direction from which Quimby was shooting.

The second bullet entered just in front of the left ear and likely glanced in and exited above the ear. There was a wound on the right side of the head which cut away some of the outlaw's black hair and fractured the skull. The bullet that proved fatal struck just under the left ear and came out at the top of his head. This bullet was soft-nosed and completely fractured his skull.

Following the autopsy, the gathering crowd was once again allowed to view the body, which was dressed for the funeral.

33. GONE, BUT NOT FORGOTTEN

April 21, 1913

The final curtain dropped on the most unusual chapter in Northwest criminal history on Sunday, April 20, 1913, when John Tornow was buried in a little cemetery about four miles from the Tornow homestead on the Upper Satsop.

He was buried alongside his parents, Daniel Frederick and Louisa Tornow, who passed away in 1909 and 1910, respectively. In this cemetery also are the first two of his alleged victims, his twin nephews, John and William Bauer, and his niece, Mary Bauer, who died following a botched abortion.

Three Tornow brothers — Fred from Portland, Edward and William from Shoalwater Bay — many old neighbors and acquaintances, who remembered John the boy, not the beast-man criminal he became, a few newspapermen and a handful of curious strangers, were on hand. Minnie Bauer, sister of the slain outlaw, had moved to California. For some reason, John's other brother, Albert, did not attend.

The brothers wept openly, but said nothing when it came time to eulogize their sibling.

The Rev. R. L. Shelly of the First Christian Church of Montesano offered a few words of prayer after the simple, wooden coffin arrived along with a 15-auto caravan from the county seat. Following the prayer, friends and neighbors draped the coffin with flowers, then provided a floral covering on the grave after the dirt had been shoveled onto the coffin. This was not a mawkish sentiment for the man, who had been the terror of the Northwest for 19 months, but an act of love and respect for a family who had suffered, and for the families of the victims, who had been aggrieved even more.

The minister offered no sermon, only uttering a final prayer as the body was consigned to the grave; moving picture cameras rolled, recording the last of the outlaw.

As the dirt began to fly into the grave, farmers and neighbors shared stories of the John Tornow they had known.

They remembered the boy many had grown up with the 10 year old, who had cheated death when he narrowly survived a bout of the German measles; they remembered the youngster, who before he was a teenager, had acquired a love of the woods, spending as many as two weeks at a time in his "holy place" — his natural resource habitat; they talked of the young man, who was the tireless worker, even at a young age; the son, who helped his father the most, clearing the property and planting or harvesting crops; they also remembered the man, who developed a keen sense of marksmanship and was a dead shot from the hip.

Some also recalled the Elizabeth School Christmas program in which John participated in on at least two occasions — as a 16-year-old and again two years later. He was part of that program, along with a couple of his brothers, the Bauer twins, their sisters and many of his neighbors.

Tombstone of John Tornow, which was dedicated in front of more than 300 people in 1987 at the Grove Cemetery. Prior to that, a broken stone and coffee can marked his grave.

Some remembered the long hours he spent with his dear twin nephews, teaching them all he knew about fishing, hunting and surviving in the wilderness. They spoke of his great fondness for his sister, Minnie Bauer, mother of the twins.

Those who came to pay their respects knew an entirely different human being from the one that was being buried.

They spoke nothing of dementia, nor of insanity or madness, the adjectives used to describe the recluse once the manhunt began.

They knew the man, who pined for his woods, and would have likely been comfortable there the rest of his natural life — if he were only left alone.

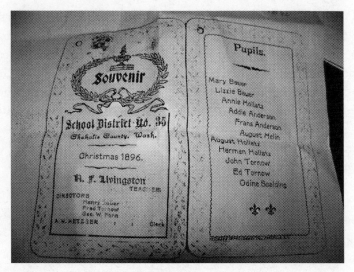

Photo courtesy of Velma Hollatz

Elizabeth School's Christmas program in 1896 shows John performing with his brother Ed, Mary and Lizzie Bauer. Henry Bauer and Fred Tornow are among the directors.

That wasn't the case. Instead, they were laying to an eternal rest, a man made crazy by man, or as one writer called it a man, who was "Guilty by Circumstance."

"John, you are peaceful now in death. You are gone, but you will never be forgotten," his friends seemed to echo.

Meantime, Blair's body was shipped to Centralia, where he had lived until the last two years when he moved to Shelton. The body was accompanied by Blair's longtime friend, W. A. Ida. He was the son of Joseph C. Blair, a contractor, and stepson of Mrs. Blair, proprietress of the Kentucky rooming house in Centralia. The 31-year-old trapper and hunter was unmarried and is survived by two brothers at Shelton, Will and Boyd, a brother, Eli at Olympia, a brother, Al, and sister, Mrs. Whittaker in British Columbia. He also has a half-brother, Harry Blair of Centralia, a stepsister Mrs. Bernice Mackey and a stepbrother, Ernest Prather of Centralia.

A most lavish funeral was held on Wednesday, April 23, a week after the killings and the chapel of the Sticklin undertaking parlor was jammed to capacity. Sheriff Schelle Mathews of Chehalis County and Deputy Sheriff Giles Quimby, hero of the shootout, were in attendance.

"With eyes that seemed to pierce everything before him, Quimby, the only witness to the fierce, but short, battle in the woods, occupied a front seat," noted an article on the funeral in the April 24 edition of the *Centralia Chronicle*. The reporter said Quimby's "countenance scarcely changed during the entire service, but it was plain to see he was still feeling the effects of the awful strain he has been laboring under the past week."

The Rev. H. W. Thompson, mayor of Centralia, conducted the service and delivered a 10-minute message, nearly breaking down several times. He read scriptures from Psalms 90 and 139. In his message, he stressed, "We cannot tell ourselves when we may be taken out of this life, nor in what manner death may come. The lesson I want to bring to you, who are gathered here today is that you should always be on duty. Make your everyday life such that you will be prepared for the final summons at any time."

The mayor went on to say that Blair and his companion died like "heroes on the battlefield. They died while in performance of their duty ... not only the community where he lived, but the entire state is thankful to him for having put out of the way the half-insane outlaw who has been a menace to the surrounding country."

His final soliloquy was stirring with not a dry eye to be found.

"The law must be served. We can have no liberty without law. Law is a barrier between anarchists and desperadoes on one hand and peaceable citizens on the other. Life is more terrible than death. Death should have no terror for those prepared for it. It is the beginning of all things; death is the end."

Pallbearers included Mathews, Quimby and George Stormes, a sheriff's deputy and game warden. Flowers cascaded around the coffin, which was taken to Washington Lawn Cemetery in the city and followed by a large crowd, where the concluding simple service consisted mainly of a prayer, offered by Thompson.

Blair had never met Tornow, but was fully aware of him, having served on posses soon after the bodies of the Bauer twins were discovered. He was a trapper of a renowned reputation. At one point, he and his brother, Will, brought in a winter's catch of bounty scalps, which included 67 wildcats and two cougars, for which he was paid $177.50 in 1908. The cat bounty then was $2.50 and $5 for cougars, far less than the $20 in 1913.

The body of Charles Lathrop, was shipped by the Simpson Logging Co. to his hometown of Bristol, Vt., then taken to the home of his sister, Mrs. Arthur (Cora) F. Gove, in South Bristol, Vt., where a family funeral service was held. Costs for shipping the body, including preparation by undertaker F. C. Willey, totaled $307.90. The county compensated Lathrop at $4 a day for his work with the posse, totaling $108, which was subtracted from the bill. Sheriff Schelle Mathews tried unsuccessfully to get reimbursement from the county to pay the $199 balance on the shipping bill.

Lathrop, 41, was divorced, but he and his ex-wife Louina (Hall) had a son, Thad Lathrop, 20, who attended the service. Lathrop's father, Noah, a well-to-do contractor and timber man, also attended; his mother, Rachel, is deceased. In addition to his sister, Cora, 38, Lathrop has two younger brothers, Clarence, 39, and William, 35.

Lathrop came to the Northwest from Vermont in about 1898, settling in Matlock, where he was a logger. About 1908, he became employed with the Peninsular Railroad and lived in a rooming house in Dayton, just west of Shelton. He took to the woods to earn additional funds through trapping and even trapped with his assailant for a time. In 1909, he collected his last bounty for a cougar, bringing the skin with him when he came in for provisions while he was hunting Tornow. He was paid $20 for that bounty.

The Rev. E. J. Klock of the Congregational Church officiated. Pallbearers included his brothers, Clarence and William, Craig Shedrick and Cullen O'Bryan. Burial was at Greenwood Cemetery in Bristol and an attractive memorial stone was erected.

————

Quimby was hailed as a hero by the sheriff and had been besieged by vaudeville directors to tell his story on stage. One such invitation was $5,000 for a 20-week engagement in which he would tell his story and pictures of the episode would be shown. This was from Universal filming studio in Portland, Oregon. He declined all requests, humbly saying it wasn't the proper thing to hunt down a criminal in his line of duty and then accept money for telling how it was accomplished. This was in keeping with the modesty that Quimby exemplified throughout his role in the search for Tornow.

Mathews praised his lieutenant, despite being unable to restrain Blair and Lathrop from advancing on Tornow ahead of the sheriff.

"Giles motioned the boys to wait for the dogs to go ahead and even spoke softly telling them to wait and send in the dogs first," the sheriff said, "but, they did not know fear and their whispered reply was 'To hell with the dogs.'"

While others lauded the sheriff in ridding the hills of Tornow as was his election platform, Mathews shunned the accolades. "I want no credit in this. Give it where it belongs — to Giles Quimby, whose caution placed him where he could fight and who stood up and fought in the most trying position that a man could be placed, doing remarkable execution."

Meanwhile, Quimby indicated he might ask the county to try him for first-degree murder in the death of John Tornow in order to "clear himself from criminal or civil suit that might be brought by friends or relatives of Tornow." The deputy told Deputy Prosecuting Attorney A. E. Cross that he was considering such an action and solicited the counselor's view on the matter.

"There is absolutely no question that he will be cleared, the evidence being found in the woods, sufficient to show that he believed he was defending his life, even if Tornow had not been an outlaw with a price on his head," Cross said. "Quimby will not be brought to trial unless he demands a hearing. I understand Quimby's line of reasoning and how he feels about the affair. It is impossible to see what might come up in later years."

Cross said, if Quimby were cleared then, under no circumstances, would he ever be held liable for his act.

Quimby told Cross that he asked for a hearing in the woods from Sheriff Mathews, wanting to be cleared at that time of any wrongdoing. The sheriff declined, saying no action would be necessary.

In the ensuing days, the sheriff and his deputies made close examination of items found in Tornow's possession, and made one critical clarification.

The rifle with 13 notches discovered at the scene, was not Tornow's; it belonged to Charles Lathrop. The notches did not pertain to human lives lost, but to deer that Lathrop had shot. Still, this was not Lathrop's primary weapon. He had a .94 carbine with his initials CJL etched on it, but he left that weapon at the cabin of his roommate James Benson. This eventually was sent to Lathrop's father, Noah, in Vermont. Lathrop took with him the much lighter .30 Winchester, the same weapon that Tornow shot. It was this rifle that he had with him in the firefight.

Lathrop also had a watch in his possession. When deputies found it, they were aghast. The timepiece had a bullet in it and the watch stopped at 4:45, pinpointing the exact time of the shootout.

The watch that was taken off Tornow's body was definitely identified as the one given to Colin McKenzie by Mrs. Hill before the deputy headed into his last search. It was made certain by Robert Shane, who had been associated with McKenzie in his photography studio in Aberdeen.

The timepiece has a Hamilton movement in old-fashioned James Boss gold case with the engraving "W. Thurman" inside. The watch is 17-jeweled and has been repaired at least twice. At the time of McKenzie's death, his brother, R. F. McKenzie, said his mother had inquired about the watch and would like to obtain it, in the event it was found upon Tornow's death. The brother was in town to claim the watch; Mrs. Hill agreed Mrs. McKenzie could have the watch.

TORNOW AND THE PRESS

Newspaper editors lost little time in sharing their opinions of the 19-month saga of John Tornow, some lamented the situation that seven men had died in this long pursuit, others were almost apologetic, but aside from the local papers — *The Aberdeen Daily World*, the *Chehalis County Vidette* and the *Grays Harbor Washingtonian* — only the *Seattle Post-Intelligencer* and the *Tacoma Times* knew what they were talking about.

From the *Morning Olympian* in the capital city this incredulously bizarre editorial was published:

"While there is no question but that the killing of John Tornow is a good thing for all concerned, there is just a touch of the pathetic in his violent taking away. In one respect he died in a right fashion, because he perished quickly by a bullet, but he sold his life dearly. In checking up on his wild and mad career, it is plain how the person sets himself up against the majority, who becomes a law unto himself and who is of no use, is naturally forced out of the world.

"He is useless and there is no place for him. Tornow killed his two nephews out of revenge and to right, as he imagined, a wrong. Then he became the hunted outlaw. He was in a worse situation than a bandit. He started in to play a lone hand against the entire world and civilization, and the result was inevitable. He sought the mountain fastness and the wilds of the unfrequented woods, but he was found, hunted out and killed. The condition of the desperado's body showed him to be not of the kind that can surmount obstacles. He allowed himself to degenerate into a primal savage. He neglected his personal habits, and the fact that this may have been the result of his unsettled mental condition is the pitiful side of the case.

"He couldn't get above his surroundings. An unkempt person, matted hair, filthy clothing made of gunny sacks, a diet of frogs and traps made of tin cans do not mark a first-class bandit about whom a romance can be woven. Tornow's death is a good thing for all concerned, but he belonged in a mad house, and not behind bars, had he been captured."

On April 21, *The Aberdeen Daily World* published a gruesome picture of the decidedly dead John Tornow lying on a slab prior to being wrapped and prepared for being taken out of the woods. He cradled a gun in his arms. Apparently there were many phone calls and comments objecting to such sights in a family newspaper. It appears on Page 439 in this book.

Editor/publisher Werner Rupp wrote his comments for the April 22 edition, justifying why the photo was printed when the newspaper had a policy not to publish photos of bodies:

WHERE BLAME LIES

"We want it distinctly understood that publication yesterday of a photograph of Outlaw John Tornow as he appeared in death was not done on the initiative of this paper, but in response to a very large and insistent demand. In other words, The World yesterday gave its readers what they asked for, and what they wanted.

A paper cannot do otherwise and live. Hundreds of these pictures were sold at Montesano for 25 cents each and hundreds here for a lesser price. Photographers could not keep up with the demand. The newspaper can't be blamed for that. Thousands of people crowded around the little morgue at Montesano Saturday, where Tornow's body lay. Many made the trip from here solely for the purpose of seeing the body. The authorities were compelled to let the people in to view the body. Had they resisted, a riot might have occurred. The newspaper can't be blamed for that.

The newspaper has no more interest in printing accounts of crimes than readers have in reading them. We submit this whole Tornow incident for the study of these critics of the press who tell us how to run a paper, declare what should and should not be printed. We reiterate what we said a few days ago — namely that the press will be what the people want it to be. The paper that does not serve its readers, cannot exist. We confess we think it no genuine service to print such pictures as that of Tornow or such stories as those of his crimes, but it is a service the people demand. This is a practical world where law will do nothing that public opinion does not first support and approve."

One of the more ludicrous opinion pieces came from the *Saturday Review*, a weekly edited by Col. Frank Goss, a member of the state Legislature from King County, and author of the anti-hanging act, which was on the statutes at the time. This editorial was so preposterous *The Aberdeen Daily World* took the editor to task in a scathing rebuttal the following day.

First a few nuggets from the *Review* of what the *World* editor Werner Rupp called "maudlin rot."

ANTI-HANGING REASONING

"John Tornow, made mad by the oppression of neighbors and former friends, the man-beast of shrieking newspaper frenzy, has paid the penalty for his crimes — assuming for the sake of argument that he was guilty of crimes — when he snuffed out the lives of several men who fell victim to his gun. Tornow was clearly a victim of circumstances over which he had no control.

"He wanted to be left alone, but his neighbors and relatives would not respect his wishes, and a quarrel over a dog, probably a cur animal at that, led to the warfare that resulted in the death of eight men before he himself proved a good target for the bullet of a man-hunter shooting with his eyes closed.

"Tornow, it should be remembered, never shot save in self-defense. The first murders committed by him might have been committed in self-defense; certainly they were not deliberate and premeditated. Two men went to his cabin following a quarrel and when the three men met, two of them died.

"Yet Tornow was the kind of man that some men and women and newspapers would hang by the neck until dead as the penalty for — what? Was Tornow guilty of deliberate murder, or did he strike in defense of his home and those things that he considered his rights? Who shall tell, Tornow's hunters and other enemies being dead and Tornow himself no more? But under the old law of the state, Tornow, if captured alive, might have been executed for defending his own life, although he had been a quiet, peace-loving citizen until strangers intruded on his privacy and interfered with his liberty. It was for the protection of just such men as Tornow that the bill abolishing capital punishment in Washington was passed by the last Legislature."

On Rupp's Opinion Page on April 24, the newspaper published the entire *Saturday Review* editorial and followed it with his discerning rebuttal.

"For the sake of clarity, we will assume that he (Frank Goss) knows nothing of the Tornow case. For the same reason he should have not attempted a discussion of it, for in maudlin rot — mind you, this is not personal, for we like Frank — absurd sentimentality and downright ignorance, the foregoing comment exceeds anything bearing on the case we have yet seen and goes the lurid press worse than 'one better.'"

He then went on to dispute nine of the claims from Goss listed above:

• Tornow was never "made mad by the oppression of neighbors and former friends." Nobody before hinted as much, and no one acquainted with the facts ever thought it;

• Tornow was a "victim of circumstances over which he had no control." No. He made his own circumstances and was his own victim;

• His wish to be "left alone" was gratified for two years before his first crime — the shooting of his twin nephews. Nobody molested him or tried to. He was living his life as he wanted to live it and even found various jobs in the woods to his liking.

• The "quarrel over a dog, a cur animal at that, led to the warfare that resulted in the death of eight men." This was the imagination of a lurid reporter and a lurid paper. It led to no "warfare" and even the man who invented it, said that. A cur? No, Tornow's dog was old to be sure, but still a comfortable companion. There were six deaths, not eight, although the *Review* and other metros maintained that Tornow was responsible for the deaths of two trappers in 1910. It was never proven and their bodies never discovered. Save for a warrant for insanity, Tornow was never pursued for the death of the trappers or anyone else until the deaths of the nephews.

• Tornow's first crime was "wanton and deliberate" so far as anyone knows. Two men did not go to his cabin following a quarrel. He allegedly killed his twin nephews at a point two miles from their own home and no one knows definitely to this day why he did it. There was no quarrel so far as anyone knows. On the contrary, Tornow was very fond of these same two nephews.

• Tornow never struck "in defense of his home." He ambuscaded, waylaid and wantonly killed. He abandoned his home, deliberately discarding it; Tornow's own life never needed defense until he committed a crime.

• Tornow was not a "madman made mad by men." He was mentally deficient from boyhood and rendered abortive all efforts to cure his deficiencies;

• "Strangers never intruded on his privacy or interfered with his liberty." His relatives tried to help him. The right of a mentally defective man to liberty does not exist.

• It was for "the protection of just such men as Tornow that the bill abolishing capital punishment in Washington was passed by the last Legislature." God help us. Who else can protect us? Where else can we turn? We cannot protect ourselves. Tornow killed two strapping boys, nineteen years old. Why? They hadn't harmed him, hadn't molested him in any way. They were his sister's boys. She deserves sympathy in her sorrow. Perhaps Goss will allow, as we understand his article, the boys deserved to die by Tornow's hands and Tornow must be considered first.

• Then men went in search of Tornow. All wrong is the logic of Goss's argument. Tornow had a right to his liberty; any attempt to shut him up, to put him where he could kill no one, must be viewed as an outrage. According to the Goss reasoning, McKenzie deserved to die, so did Elmer and Lathrop and Blair, and Quimby, we suppose, is not a man, but a thing unthinkable.

What arrant rot! What utter nonsense!"

The *World's* editorial staff didn't stop there. The next day, a lengthy opinion piece took to task, the *Tacoma Tribune*, lambasting "the paper that printed trash," saying its report "was concocted out of the low imagination of some half-intelligent cub reporter."

Not only is the article salacious, but it had Tornow climbing a "pine tree, from where he shot at the men. Quimby heard two shots and ran toward his companions. He was in time to see the desperado jump down from the tree. Quimby emptied his rifle at the outlaw and fled. Tornow, evidently surprised at the appearance of the third man, fled also."

The paper then had the audacity to claim it was the "only newspaper in Tacoma and Seattle, which had an authentic account of the shooting of the two trappers by the outlaw from first-hand information obtained at Camp 5, 10 miles from the shooting."

Rupp goes on to say the story was meant to be "dramatic, we suppose. It was not. It was inexcusable because Camp 5 was in possession on Thursday (April 17 and published on the 18th), of Deputy Quimby's really descriptive story — a thousand times more dramatic than the *Tribune's* strained hodge-podge — and because the news editor of the *Tribune*, the copy editor, the proof reader, the linotype operator, even the office boy and the janitor ought to know that there isn't probably a pine tree within 200 miles of the scene of the tragedy."

The editorial said the story was a "rotten fake." Every Associated Press paper had Deputy Quimby's story Thursday afternoon that was sent out by the *World*, whose story "still stands as the most nearly correct, concise account of the whole awful business of any that has been printed. It squared with the facts as the posse found them upon reaching the scene of the shooting."

Even Fred Boalt fell victim to the "pine tree" description in his *Tacoma Times* article.

The opinion piece later praised the *Seattle Post-Intelligencer* for being "first rank for its sane, well-written, extremely sensitive and accurate account," noting the *P-I* was the only metro paper not to fall victim to misspelling Tornow's name at the outset. Some papers called him "Turno, Turnow and even Tunro."

The *P-I* also posted an entirely different look at the Tornow incident, comparing the fugitive's situation to that of world-renowned conservationist John Muir in an editorial on April 23:

THE DIFFERENT TWIST

John Muir, explorer, naturalist, author, kindly gentleman is 75 years old today, April 23, 1913. He was born in Scotland, but known most of his life as an American. After graduating from the State University of Wisconsin at Madison, he embarked on a career that was to bring him fame as a geologist, explorer and naturalist. He has traveled extensively on six continents and now lives in Martinez, Calif., engaged in writing and publishing his memoirs of his own life, emphasizing his life in the woods north of San Francisco, now named Muir Woods.

"In his love of the woods, John Muir is at one with John Tornow, the outlaw and murderer, carried yesterday to an obscure grave, while the whole community sighed with relief at the end of a worse than worthless life.

Now, what is it that makes one man who loves the woods, the trees, the flowers, the singing brook, life in the open and the great heart of wild beautiful nature, a great naturalist and the other a notorious outlaw whose very name is one to frighten babies?

Perhaps different treatment and a more thorough understanding of his youthful mind might have made Tornow a great naturalist, too. Who knows? We are giving some attention to babes and the young nowadays and despite all pessimistic beliefs to the contrary, the world is better and more intelligent than it was in the days of our fathers. It is just possible that a little more intelligence will reduce crimes."

The late Alvin Spalding of Elma stands on the Tornow log at the final shootout site at Tornow Lake in 1987. He had been taken to the site 30 years earlier by Albert Kuhnle, who was with the posse in 1913.

This bullet casing, left, was unearthed by Dana Anderson at the shootout site. At right is the camera used by J. P. Ladley to photograph the shootout scene and during the bringing out of the bodies. Both items are in the museum in Matlock.

Dana Anderson of Matlock holds the charred rock that he unearthed at the shootout site in 1987. Anderson used a metal detector to find this rock and others, along with square nails, a half of a file and a 1910 dime, among other artifacts that are in the museum at Matlock.

EPILOGUE

April 1913 to April 2013

Those who thought the story was over when Tornow was buried, will be sorely mistaken. For the next year, there were arguments between county commissioners, Quimby and Attorney W. H. Abel, representing the families of the dead deputies, Louis Blair and Charles Lathrop, over payment of the reward money.

It started innocently on April 22, less than a week after the killings, when the commissioners made the statement, though took no action, that Quimby would receive the full $4,000 reward for killing Tornow. Quimby also stated: "If I receive the full reward, I will see that the families of Blair and Lathrop are given equal shares."

It was just a month after that when the State Attorney General W. V. Tanner announced that the state would pay nothing of the $1,000 state reward to Quimby or the families of the dead deputies because "they were all deputized and not entitled to any of the money."

Two weeks later, the county took action to set aside $4,000 to be paid equally to Quimby and the families of Blair and Lathrop "for services rendered" since they are not entitled to the reward money, as both the state attorney general and the county Attorney General Stewart ruled.

Sounds like the issue is settled, right?

Wrong.

Over the next five months, there was still no payment made and Abel filed suit on behalf of his clients, which included Joseph Blair, father of Louis, and Thad Lathrop, son of Charles. Abel said, in his suit, that he could produce "about 20 witnesses to say that most of the wounds on Tornow were produced 20 hours after he was killed."

Sheriff Mathews duly noted that the autopsy showed all of the wounds on Tornow were made before death. The sheriff said that should dispel any ugly rumors, but "if anyone has any evidence to the contrary, I will be glad to have it." None was produced.

Thad Lathrop (or his father Noah since Thad was 20 and still considered a minor) wasn't satisfied with one-third of the reward. His suit, filed August 14, 1913, asked for $5,000 from the county for "damages sustained by the wrongful and malicious killing by John Tornow of Charles Lathrop. Superior Court Judge Ben Sheeks disallowed the claim, and it was dismissed on March 4, 1914.

Meantime, members of the Aberdeen City Council made an appearance on July 24 to present Quimby with a gold sheriff's star badge. Councilman Warren Egerer made some brief comments on Quimby's valor before presenting the badge. "I wish to present this gift to you on behalf of the city of Aberdeen for risking your life under the most nerve-trying circumstances in a rifle duel in which you were compelled to take the life of John Tornow. You are honored for suppressing the pall that had hung over the community and I assure you that you have endeared yourself to all that know you."

Quimby tearfully accepted the star, saying "this means more to me than all the gold in the world. Please thank all those responsible for surprising me with this. It is most appreciated."

The star was solid gold and worth $60.

It appeared that the lingering issue of payment would finally be settled when the county commissioners, after setting aside $3,000, assigned the decision to Judge Sheeks, who gave his decision on November 3, 1913.

The judge ruled that the county was within its right to make the payment, noting that "the important part of the arrangement was not as a deputy, but he was given the authority for the undertaking of the search for John Tornow — an obligation that does not rest merely on seeking to earn a reward offered. The fact that it might have been thought advisable and that he was clothed with the authority of a deputy sheriff should not mitigate against him when considering compensation for such services."

After Sheeks' ruling, Abel filed a demurrer, objecting to the decision and further tying up the issue in the legal system. Then attorneys Campbell and Stewart, representing the county and Quimby, filed their own demurrer, challenging Abel and sending the issue back to the court.

On December 26, Sheeks overruled the demurrer by Campbell and Stewart.

No payments were made and the issue was quiet until March 16, 1914, when Abel sent a scorching letter to the county commissioners, which said his life was threatened because of the suit against Quimby over the payment of the reward. The commissioners said "it should have been written on asbestos and distributed with fire extinguishers" it was so scathing.

Abel claimed on March 14 that Quimby came to his office and "informed me that I would not live until the trial of the case brought by myself to prevent the payment to him of the Tornow reward of $4,000.

"In view of the fact that C. N. Wilson, chairman of the Board of county commissioners, is a relative of Quimby, and Schelle Mathews, sheriff of this county, is a brother-in-law of Quimby, and Giles is a deputy sheriff under the law authorized to go armed, I have decided to address this letter to you informing you what I intend to do and my reason for it.

"I have decided to drop the suit because of the threat to my life, and I owe a greater debt to my family than to Chehalis County. Second, in order to prevent the reward of $4,000 to Quimby or one-third of it, would rely on testimony from the board and the sheriff to prove that it was not a salary, but a reward ... I don't think you would deal with it fairly. Third, it may be said that my life was not actually in danger and that the law would protect me, but when a deputy sheriff threatens my life publicly, and I understand he has threatened others, to whom am I going to go to for protection?"

The county was left agog over the letter, which according to the *Chehalis County Vidette's* article on March 17, "Nothing has stirred greater interest here in a long time than the letter sent yesterday to county commissioners by Attorney W. H. Abel of Montesano in which the commissioners are sharply attacked and Deputy Giles Quimby is accused of threatening Abel's life."

In this article, Quimby sharply denies a threat and the story goes on to talk about Quimby's modest behavior throughout the issue. "No one here believes Quimby threatened Abel's life. They don't think Quimby is that sort of a man, and they argue he would never go to Abel's office as the attorney said, without an invitation. It's a political mistake by Abel," said Commissioner Wilson.

Quimby didn't answer questions about his relatives, except to say "I never asked for a position for any relative, and there is no man can say I have."

With the suit dropped, the county finally, on June 14, 1914, paid Quimby one-third of the $4,000 or $1,333.33 for services rendered. No other payments were made, leaving the relatives of Blair and Lathrop without any remuneration.

JOHN TORNOW'S PROPERTY

While the probate for the Tornow family property took several years to reach conclusion, such was not the case with the property left by the outlaw, John Tornow. By April 22, six days after his death, an administrator was appointed. Commissioner C. N. "Bud" Wilson, who had acted in the same capacity in the family probate, was named to represent the deceased man.

The petition showed Tornow was worth $3,164 (worth $73,246 today) of which $1,664.91 was in certificates at the Montesano State Bank. The remainder comprised the two Aberdeen properties, Lot 4, Block 3 of the Stewart's Park Addition, plus one-fifth interest in the Northwest quarter of the Northeast quarter; Northwest quarter; and northern half of the Southwest quarter of Section 18, Township 19 North Range 6 West.

The petition for the estate shows that W. M. Tornow, Albert Tornow, Fred Tornow, E. W. Tornow and Minnie Bauer are the sole heirs of the estate. It also shows that Ed Tornow conveyed his interest in all land in Section 18 to his other brothers and sister.

A hearing was set for July and the issue was settled as described later that month.

The Aberdeen property, however, went back to the original owner, Jean Stewart, who sold it to R.W. Wallace in 1914. Interestingly, Minnie Bauer, John's sister, became owner of one of the lots in 1915 for two years. In 1948, the property was sold to the City of Aberdeen, which built the first Robert Gray Elementary School on part of the original Tornow lots.

The Tornow property in Section 18, Township 19 North Range 6 West, was eventually sold and today is part of the massive Schafer Bros. holdings.

WHERE DID THEY GO?

• Henry and Minnie Bauer moved to San Diego in 1911 and farmed there. Henry died at age 78, in 1935, but Minnie lived until age 98, dying in 1965. Both are buried in San Diego, in the Cypress Lawn Mausoleum and Crematory. Their surviving daughter, Elizabeth, married Harold Kurtz of San Diego. He died in 1945, but she, like her mother, lived to age 89, dying in 1977.

• Ed Tornow and his wife, Sadie, moved from Porter to South Bend (Shoalwater Bay) prior to his brother John's death. He lived there for a number of years, working in a logging camp and also running a movie house, according to his daughter, the late Norma (Tornow) Mathiesen. They also lived at Raymond, Willapa, Enumclaw and Tenino in Washington state, and in Springfield, Oregon. He later divorced and married his second wife, Maggie in Longview, where he lived the rest of his life. He died in 1954 and is buried in Longview.

In 1987, the author interviewed Norma Mathiesen and her husband, Jim. She said then she didn't believe John killed anybody. She also said, until she was interviewed, "the family never talked about the story. I was 15 when I first heard the story." Norma also revealed "Dad said John never killed the boys, and I will swear to it until I die. He said the boys' dad (Henry) wanted him killed. She told about her dad's stories growing up. "He and dad slept in the same bed. Dad said he went to bed and when he'd wake up, John wouldn't be there. He'd wake up in the morning and John would be there, "crept in like a deer," she said. Norma agreed to come to the tombstone dedication of John Tornow in 1987 and unveiled the memorial as more than 300 people watched at the Grove Cemetery in Matlock.

Ed had two daughters, Norma and Ruby (Schultz) and a son, August, who was a Prisoner of War, held by Japan in a camp in Germany. S/Sgt. Tornow had ditched his B-17 in the Bay of Biscay and was captured in March 1943. The wounded Airman was released in December 1943. His daughter, Mary, who lived in Mossyrock in 1987, also attended the tombstone unveiling, just a few weeks shy of passing away from cancer. She told the author lots of stories, but emphasized "John wasn't retarded. He was sharp as a tack," my dad used to say.

The other Tornow boys were pretty well scattered through their adult life. Fred stayed in the Oregon area, where he owned a logging operation. He married Elinor Trouty in 1908; he later moved to Clallam Bay, Washington, and is buried there; William (Bill) and his wife, Susie, lived in South Bend (Shoalwater Bay) for a while, then moved to Longview and Centralia. He died after lingering with Alzheimer's disease in a Centralia nursing home. Albert lived for a time in Elma and Montesano, then moved to Garibaldi, Oregon, where he lived until his death.

• Giles Quimby continued to work as a Deputy Sheriff, and that may have been his only job as his death announcement lists that as his only occupation. After he had eaten dinner at the Beehive Restaurant on December 4, 1947, he was crossing the street to the Montesano Hotel, where he lived, and was struck by an auto. He died on January 3, 1948, and is buried at the Wynooche Cemetery in Montesano.

Interestingly, Quimby nearly didn't make it to participate in the Tornow saga. As a 22-year-old in 1893, he and sister, Stella, along with friends Laura Moak and Thomas Birdwell, were taking a row boat ride along the Chehalis. For some reason, Quimby stood and the boat overturned, spilling all four into the water. They knew how to swim, but their heavy clothing weighted them down. All four had to be rescued, and while one of the girls was unconscious when rescued, all four survived.

• Dan Cloud and Lindy Fleming. What happened to them is unknown. Lindy is one of those characters established for Dan's convenience. She did not really exist. Dan, however, is very much real and the apple didn't fall far from the tree in his family. His father, Daniel was married to Cora. Elder Dan was born in Iowa in 1871 and started a distinguished career in journalism by founding the *Ashton Leader* in Iowa (now defunct). In 1900, he went to the University of Washington, where he graduated, then had positions with the *Tacoma Daily News* and the *Tacoma Ledger*. Then in 1909, he purchased the *Lynden Tribune* in Lynden, Wash., which he owned until he purchased the *Chehalis County Vidette* in 1916. He owned and edited the paper until retiring in late 1922, due to poor health. He moved to his farm at La Pine, Oregon. His farewell column said he was "not going there to die, but to get well and I will be back." Three months later, he passed away on January 24, 1923. Later, the University of Washington established a scholarship in his honor for editorial writing. The Elder Cloud had a family of journalists: a brother Carl, editor and publisher of the Riddle, Oregon, *Enterprise*; a half-brother, Nathaniel, editor of the *Bellingham Herald*; his son, Ray, editor of the Everett *Herald* and former publisher of the *Ferndale Record*; and, of course, young Dan. He graduated from the University of Washington' then started his career at Bellingham, presumably while dad was publisher at Lynden. He moved to the Grays

Harbor area in 1910 and began his career on the Harbor at the *Vidette* as an intern. By 1911, he was full-time with *The Aberdeen Daily World*, where he worked for a number of years.

• W. H. Abel was born in England in 1870, but was raised and educated in Kansas and moved to Montesano in 1892. He was briefly a teacher and newspaper editor before being admitted to practice law in 1894. He became one of the state's leading attorneys, working many important trials, including the prosecution of the IWW (International Workers of the World) after the 1919 Armistice Day killings in Centralia. He held numerous statewide board positions in his industry and also in education. He has donated hundreds of volumes to libraries at Washington State and Gonzaga Universities as well as the Montesano Library, which bears his name. The W. H. and Ella Abel Memorial Scholarship has been established in his honor. His home, the Abel House, is in Montesano, where it is privately owned after being a bed-and-breakfast for a number of years.

• John Tornow is buried in the Grove Cemetery, south of Matlock; his gravesite has been visited by thousands throughout the years. Or has it? If folks pay tribute in front of the tombstone, they might not be doing it right. According to Rex Valentine, an internationally acclaimed poet and Realtor from Montesano, they might have it all wrong. Valentine, who is also a professional dowser in which he uses an L-shaped or Y-shaped divining rod to point at the grave and get earth's radiation or energy from it, John is not buried in front of the tombstone as are others. "I pointed my rod in front of the graves of his parents, and also the Bauer boys, and felt the motion of the rod from their graves. I pointed it at John's grave and got nothing." So, Valentine went behind the grave, "and the stick started moving," displaying the energy. So, was John's wooden coffin dug up after the service and buried later at the back of the grave to discourage grave-robbers.? It makes sense, if you believe in dowsing.

TARZAN AND TORNOW

What do Edgar Rice Burroughs' mythical jungle man and the "Wildman of the Wynooche" have in common?

Maybe nothing. Maybe everything.

It's interesting to note that Burroughs loved to hunt in the Olympic Mountains and frequented his favorite haunts while the search for Tornow was going on. Did he have contact with the Wildman? Probably not, but he likely was aware of what was going on.

According to a biography of the adventure writer, "Edgar Rice Burroughs: The man Who Created Tarzan," by Irwin Porges, (1975) Burroughs had developed his protagonist, John Carter, for his first novel "Under the Moon of Mars," then completely revamped his Carter makeup. This coincided with a visit to the Northwest. Here is Burroughs' description of the new Carter, which became his first novel in September 1911. Porges says Carter was a romantic hero in the most glorious tradition. He was an adventurer, whose only means of livelihood had been fighting." The writer is more explicit:

"A splendid specimen of manhood, standing two inches over six feet, broad of shoulder, narrow of the hip, with the carriage of the trained fighting man. His features were regular and clear cut, his hair black and closely cropped, while his eyes were of steel gray, reflecting a strong and loyal character, filled with fire and initiative."

Burroughs, of course, fictionalized Carter, the tall Virginian, as one who is transported to Mars.

No connection to Tornow there.

But, how about Tarzan?

When he wrote the first Tarzan book, it was initially called "Outlaw of Torn." He switched that to "Tarzan of the Apes," published in 1912, immediately after "Mars." But, he turned "Outlaw of Torn" into a five-part serial in *New Story Magazine,* from July to September, 1914. His protagonist was Norman of Torn, who by the age of 18 was the best swordsman in all of England and who had a huge bounty on his head. "He could be caught by no one," Burroughs wrote. This became a book in 1927.

Burroughs was obsessed with the name "John" and named his protagonist John Clayton in "Lord Greystoke." He told his brother he wished he had been named John, and for a time, thought of changing his name officially, but never did.

Some magazine stories in later years, describe Tornow as a "Wildman, swinging through the trees like some Tarzan figure." Historians debunk this description of Tornow.

Remember, the hunt for Tornow didn't begin until after the boys were killed in September 1911, but Tornow is already legend, having begun his solitary woods life nearly two years prior.

Is this mere coincidence or did Burroughs actually become influenced in his writing by the escapades of Tornow, the "Wildman of the Wynooche?"

1986-1987

These two years were important in keeping the Pacific Northwest's famous legend alive. Many events transpired during these two years, starting with a forum at Matlock, Washington, that drew 298 people into a bandbox gym at Mary Knight School. The event was initiated by then-school superintendent Rand Iversen, who along with Bill Lindstrom, moderated this forum and a couple more. Iversen also started the Tornow room at the school's Matlock Museum, which houses posters, photos, clippings, videos, DVDs and items dug up by metal detectors at the shootout site.

Iversen, Dana Anderson, Ron Fowler, Lindstrom and others also began their search to discover the actual shootout site. Fowler had been shown the site many years prior by Albert Kuhnle, who had been with the final posse to bring out the bodies. Fowler found it again and also located the fallen log near where the deputies were slain. Lindstrom

Norma Mathiesen, daughter of Ed Tornow, unveils the new Tornow tombstone in 1987. The stone was constructed by Marty Schmid of Aberdeen and is made of grey Ashland, Oregon, granite and depicts the Bauer boys on a bear hunt.

had been shown the site in 1987 by the late Alvin Spalding of Elma. Using a metal detector, Anderson uncovered a charred rock that signified the possible campsite. When his detector picked up a 1910 dime, they knew they were in the right area. In rapid fashion, Anderson's crew found square nails, a half a file, a knife, bullet casings and many other bits of metal and glass fragments, now on display at the Matlock Museum.

In June, 1987, more than 300 turned out on a scorching hot day to witness the unveiling of the Tornow tombstone at the Grove Cemetery. "When I first started doing research, nothing but a small rock and coffee can marked the grave," Lindstrom recalls. "That wasn't right. I didn't want to glorify a suspected murderer, but he still deserved a proper grave. I met Tom Roberson of Elma, who had started researching the subject and wanted to erect a new stone. I contacted the Grays Harbor County Commissioners, who were convinced of our plan and approved funding."

Meantime, a memorialist, Marty Schmid in Aberdeen, heard of the project and insisted on making and paying for the stone. "It's something I wanted to do for a long time," he admitted. "I know the story and I want to donate that stone." With design by his assistant, Marsha Peterson, and materials from Grays Harbor Marble and Monument, he fashioned a 3-foot granite stone with an engraving by Peterson showing two boys hunting for a bear. Roberson also played guitar and sang the song he had written: "Ballad of John Tornow."

A few days before the gravestone dedication, television station KOMO (Channel 4) in Seattle came to the area and filmed for four hours. The film crew was taken to the old homestead, the cemetery, the Bauers' old home and the museum. The four-hour filming merged into a 2:45 minute segment on the evening news, a huge time in those days. Many dignitaries attended and shared their stories of growing up with the Tornow story, including state representative Max Vekich, County Commissioner Mike Murphy, PUD Commissioner Tom Casey and Superior Court Judge Gordon Godfrey, who at the time had been researching the story for 15 years. Norma Mathiesen, daughter of Ed Tornow, unveiled the tombstone.

The inscription on the granite stone is simple: "From Loner, to Outcast, to Fugitive: John Tornow, Sept. 4, 1880-April 16, 1913"

That year also, Roberson and I attempted to get the tiny area that locals call "Tornow Lake" officially recognized as such by petitioning the U.S. Bureau of Geographical Names." We had the late Bill Spiedel, a board member, and founder of the Seattle Underground Tour, on our side, but in

Dora Hearing, 93, attended the tombstone unveiling and talked about her family leaving goods for Tornow. She also was interviewed and spoke at a forum in 1987.

the end, it was denied by a 4-2 vote. The decision wasn't because we "glorified a murderer" as a member of the Grays Harbor Sheriff's Department claimed, but "because it didn't have water year round, thus not fitting the requirement to be called a lake," the board said.

Joe Mooney, writer for the *Seattle Post-Intelligencer*, was on our side and lamented the decision, saying the board got "stuffy."

Mooney continued his diatribe against the board: "They had a chance (and blew it) to name a state lake officially after a man who was gunned down near its shores 74 years ago."

Spiedel said the board was trying to "neaten everything up. We are not honoring (Tornow), but the best story to come out of Grays Harbor in years."

As Mooney stated, "It doesn't matter that the lake has an official name or not. The people in Elma and Matlock and all parts are going to continue to call it Tornow Lake."

Perhaps, eventually there will be a motion to call it "Tornow Marsh" or "Tornow Swamp."

Later in 1987, John Tornow was included in a set of trading cards, "Legendary Badmen of the West." His card in the box, along with Billy the Kid, John Dillinger, Butch Cassidy and the Sundance Kid, Bonnie and Clyde, Cole Younger, Pancho Villa, John Wesley Hardin, Frank and Jesse James, Calamity Jane, Pretty Boy Floyd and Harry Tracy.

The front of the Tornow card includes a photo of the dead man lying on a stump with

John Tornow was included in this trading card set "Legendary Badmen of the West," along with villains like Billy the Kid, John Dillinger, Bonnie and Clyde and 49 others.

the headline from *The Aberdeen Daily World* "Outlaw Tornow and Victims' Bodies Are Brought Out," a reproduction from April 1913. The back of the card, entitled "The Wild Man," is a short, but accurate account of the Tornow manhunt from the shooting of the Bauer boys to his ultimate death.

The company, which also specialized in pornographic trading cards, is no longer in business.

2013 — A CENTURY LATER

Starting in February, 2011, a grassroots committee was formed with the vision of establishing a memorial to honor the six victims of the John Tornow saga on the 100th anniversary of the shootout, ending in Tornow's death on April 16, 1913. Bob Dick was the group's first president, others included Dana and Faaea Anderson, Ralph and Susan Larson, Justin Madanifard, Wally Metzger, Doug Rice and Bill Lindstrom.

From left, Nathan Morris and Rudy Mackiewiez, Shelton High School juniors, assist Dana Anderson in building the memorial to the six victims alleged to have been killed by John Tornow 2013.

Bob Dick photo

The author, left, is pictured with Justin Madanifard and Dana Anderson at the dedication of the Tornow Victims' Memorial on April 20, 2013.

Dana Anderson, left, playing Giles Quimby, and Justin Madanifard, playing Tornow, pose for a serious photo prior to the videoing of the final shootout re-enactment in March 2013. At right, Madanifard warms his hands over a campfire, during the re-enactment, shot by Mark Woytowich.

Actors depicting the posse, talk prior to the re-enactment of the final shooting of John Tornow in 2013. From left, Bryce Mode (Charles Lathrop), Shawn Beebe (a deputy), Joe Rothrock (Louis Blair) and Dave Boos (a deputy).

Bryce Mode, left, as Charles Lathrop, and Joe Rothrock, as Louis Blair, stalk their prey, the Outlaw John Tornow.

John Tornow fires at the fallen deputies, Blair and Lathrop, with a revolver. He had taken a Luger off Deputy Colin McKenzie the year before.

Minnie Bauer is portrayed by Tracy Travers and flanked by Jayden Colby, left, who played William Bauer, and his brother, Kyler, who played John Bauer, in a re-enactment of the shooting of the twins, filmed by Mark Woytowich in July 2014.

Gerad Low, Dave Boos and Dana Anderson carry the body of one of the Bauer twins into the homestead. The boys were shot 1 ½ miles from the homestead and their bodies carried by the posse back to the home for an autopsy and a funeral the next day.

Doug Rice photo

The author jumped into the seat of the original buggy that belonged to the Tornow family. It is now owned by Doug Rice of Montesano and may be viewed at his Running Anvil Ranch on Black Creek Road.

This is the charred rifle Bill Hyde of Aberdeen, Wash., and his dad found in 1944 in a burned-out cedar stump near the final shootout.

This Tornow Dr. sign intersects off the West Boundary Road in the Upper Satsop near the Bauer homestead.

The gravestone of Giles Quimby in the Wynooche Cemetery in Montesano. Quimby was killed when hit by a car after he left the Beehive Restaurant and was crossing the street to the Montesano Hotel, where he lived. He died January 3, 1948.

Rich Travers, right, of Montesano plays "John Tornow," a song he wrote, on radio station KIX in Aberdeen. Stations interviewed committee members during the week of the memorial dedication in 2013.

Dana Anderson and Mark Woytowich are shown in the committee's booth at the Old Timers Fair in Matlock. Visitors saw Tornow memorabilia and purchased books, DVDs, hats, coffee mugs, among other items.

They worked feverishly, meeting nearly monthly to meet their goal. Later, Madanifard was named president, and others joined, namely Tracy Travers, Rudy Mackiewicz and Rex Valentine. On March 8, 2013, a forum was held at the Matlock Grange. Mark Woytowich of Hoodsport, Wash., filmed the event and a re-enactment of the final shootout was filmed the following weekend. Madanifard, a tall, bearded, quiet man, perfectly displayed Tornow mannerisms as the outlaw. Anderson donned hunter's apparel to play the part of Quimby; Joe Rothrock was Blair and Bryce Mode was Lathrop. A DVD was made and is sold today.

A new website was established that month by Travers and has been updated since by Lindstrom. The site is www.johntornowoutlaw.com Through the first year, it had more than 20,000 hits.

The memorial was rapidly taking shape behind Anderson's direction. It became the Eagle Scout project of Rudy Mackiewicz and the Senior project of Nathan Morris, both Shelton High students. Together, with Anderson and a crew of family members, they not only fashioned the memorial, but crafted a nearly wheelchair-accessible path in the wilderness about 100 yards from the spur road to the memorial site. More than 150 people attended the dedication on a chilly, cloudy April 20, 2013, including three great-grandsons of Charles Lathrop — Duane and David Lathrop from Bristol, Vt., and Doug Lathrop from Houston, Texas. Several individuals shared their stories, including Mike Fredson, author of "Beast-Man," a book about Tornow, published in 2004. In addition, Rich Travers and James Dunne sang and played guitar to Tornow songs they have written. All DVDs are available through the website.

Until 2013, the only recognition for the victims was a small plaque in the Grays Harbor County Courthouse that honored the memory of slain deputies, Colin McKenzie and A. V. Elmer. It says:

"While attempting the capture of John Tornow met death at his hands in the Oxbow country, March 9, 1912.

To honor the memory of these heroes, friends have erected this tablet. They died without hope of reward."

In 2014, Woytowich began video work on a DVD, depicting the shooting of the Bauer twins; This took place in the woods on the Bauer property, in the home and at the cemetery. Jayden and Kyler Colby played the twins and Tracy Travers was Minnie, their mother.

IF YOU GO

TORNOW HOMESTEAD: From Highway 8/12, go north on the Brady-Matlock Road (Middle Satsop) just past the seven mile marker. Homestead site is on the left, but the only original building is the shed behind the house. It is a private residence. From Matlock, it's 13 miles south on right.

GROVE CEMETERY: Continue north another six miles. Cemetery is on the left. From Matlock, seven miles on right.

MATLOCK MUSEUM: Continue north another six miles. Museum is at Mary M. Knight School on the right in front of the school. From Matlock, three miles on left.

MATLOCK: Continue north another three miles to stop sign.

FINAL SHOOTOUT, VICTIMS' MEMORIAL: Located 26.9 miles north on the Wynooche Valley Road, accessed from Highway 8/12 at the Devonshire Exit. Look for a "T" on a cedar post on the right side. Park on spur on right or off the road; walk around barrier and downed tree across path; walk about 50 yards and the improved trail is on the right; walk up the path about 100 yards to memorial. From Matlock, stop at the grocery store and asked directions to Wynooche Valley Road, then turn right to just short of MP 27 on right.

ANDERSON'S POEMS

In 2013, Dana Anderson of Matlock wrote two poems that describes the saga of John Tornow. Whether it's fact or fiction, the story continues to be an interesting one and commands a great deal of opinion from many in the Northwest.

FRIEND OR FOE
© Dana Anderson 2013

Friend or foe, we'll never know
Nothing but skills to lend
With a gun and bow, love's hard to show
John's world for ours wouldn't bend

Friend or foe, we'll never know.
His life to defend,
Just leave me alone, with a cry and a moan
The forest his only friend

Friend or foe, we'll never know
Putting him down was the trend.
Seek not to judge, then look within
My message sure to send

Friend or foe, we'll never know
Trial by fire, thoughts ascend
Things not sure, what is the cure,
Peace and justice would never blend

Friend or foe, we'll never know
The fire to attend,
Time passes slow. Winter doth blow,
Wishing time would slowly mend

Friend of foe, we'll never know
Speaks the owl, as the sun descends
Where rivers flow and the tall trees grow
Judgments set, there's nothing to amend

Friend or foe, we may never know
I can hear it in the wind,
Lessons learned that we may grow
Might triumph in the end.

THE HIDEOUT
© Dana Anderson 2013

I see the wind in the trees, and the wet from the rain.
Oh hear my joy, and feel my pain.

I sit like an Eagle, up high in the tree.
From hunter to hunted, they're after me

The truth of the forest, like the black of the night,
My loss is my gain, I'm free and will fight.

I've been and done and seen and had,
Some not so good, some not so bad

Sparks dancing atop the lonely fire
The early years, a fond desire

Friends long ago, the logging chokers
Now the deer and the bear and the small-legged croakers

The forest of trees, so straight and tall,
So many of them, I know them all

They're brothers of mine, so straight and true,
The wind and the rain and the Eagle flew

THE SATSOP SHOOTIST
© Gerald D. Schaefer 2013

John Tornow grew up on a small farm,
Away from the city and possible harm.
John soon learned to live off the land,
Hunting and building shelters by hand.

He turned into a crack shot by age ten,
Spent days in the forest at every den.
No one knew how to deal with him,
A boy all alone who looked so thin.

As a teenager, John became a recluse,
Stayed away from family and the abuse.
His parents placed him in an institution,
He escaped to the forest as a solution.

A warning was sent for all to hear,
"Keep out of my forest and stay clear!"
For over a year, John was never seen,
But logging camp surplus he would glean.

His twin nephews entered the forest to hunt,
As two rifle shots sounded so blunt.
When the twins did not return that night,
A small posse was sent out at first light.

The twins were found lying side by side,
Each shot came from where John would hide,
All knew John must have committed the act,
The arrest warrant listed each needed fact.

A deputy and game warden entered the woods,
Looking for crude shelter or John's goods.
All of a sudden, several shots rang out,
Both men fell dead without time to shout.

For over a year, area searches were made,
All hopes to find John began to fade.
Reports were made to each town and county,
Guides and loggers were after the bounty.

Then a sighting was reported near the Oxbow,
A shelter found near a quiet stream flow.
Deputy Quimby and two trappers slowly moved in,
Using large trees as cover, again and again.

Suddenly shots came from behind a fir tree,
Both trappers fell dead during the shooting spree.
Quimby fired at the tree, then ducked down,
After an hour, he quickly left for town.

A large nervous posse returned to the site,
Each man well-armed and ready to fight.
They split up and surrounded the fir tree,
Found John dead, so they smiled with glee.

John was taken to town for all to see,
The dirty and haggard man was finally free.
No one would ever invade his world again,
Sadly, six men dead was his final sin.

BIBLIOGRAPHY

Research for this book included the following newspapers from 1910-1914:

The Aberdeen Daily World, Chehalis County (Montesano) Vidette, Grays Harbor Washingtonian (Hoquiam), Mason County Journal (Shelton), The Olympian (Daily Olympian, Olympia), Tacoma Times, Tacoma Tribune, Tacoma Ledger, Tacoma News, Centralia Chronicle, Portland Oregonian, Lynden Tribune, Bellingham Herald, Peninsula News (Port Angeles).

The following books or magazines were researched:

Anderson, Harley, "Six Notches on Tornow's Gun," Pioneer West, March 1968.

Bristow, Allen P., "Phantom of the Forest," True West, 1999 46-49

Carlisle, Norman, "Stalk for a Wildman Killer," True, 1950

The Everett Herald, "The Legend of John Turno," 1968, 6-9

Fowler, Ron, "Guilty by Circumstance," 1997

Fredson, Michael, "Beast-Man," 2002

Fultz, Hollis, "The Saga of the Satsop," Famous Northwest Manhunts and Murder Mysteries, 1-24

Goss, Fred, "End of the Wildman," Saturday Review of Literature, April 1913

Hillier, Alfred J., "John Tornow, the Outlawed Hermit," Pacific Northwest Quarterly, 1944, 223-232

Holbrook, Stewart H., "Half Century in Timber, a study of the Schafer Brothers Logging," 1945

Holbrook Stewart H., "Tarzan of the Timber," Coronet 1952 141-144

Holbrook, Stewart H., "Wildest Man of the West," American Mercury 1943, 216-224

Holcomb, Lew, "Kill-Crazy Hermit of the Oxbow," Authentic Detective Cases 1953, V6, No. 1 1953 36-37, 68-75

Jameson, Earle C. "Stalking the Oxbow Forest Killer," Official Detective Stories 1938 8-11, 42-44

Morgan, Murray, "The Last Wilderness," 203-207

Lind, C.J., "Oxbow Manhunt," True Frontier, January, 1974 33, 45-46

Lindstrom, Bill, "Wildman of the Wynooche," Peninsula Magazine, 1988, 72-74

Lindstrom, Bill, "Wildman of the Wynooche," On The Harbor 2001 44-61

Lucia, Ellis, "Timber's Comstock Lode: The Lusty Saga of Grays Harbor" Northwest Magazine, April 2, 1967

Porges, Irwin, "Edgar Rice Burroughs: The Man Who Created Tarzan," 1975, 128-132, 153

Reed, Caroline, "Wild Man of the Oxbow," Evergreen Magazine, March 1947 13-14, 25

VanSyckle, Edwin, "The River Pioneers," 1982, 332-336

Washington State Archives: Grays Harbor County Government, Sheriff, John Tornow Documentation, 1911-1998, Washington State Archives, Southwest Regional Branch, Olympia, WA. Jan. 2014.

Zawislak, Ed "Wishkah Pioneers," 1981.